# MORE THAN A FEELING

A CARDINAL
Springs
NOVEL
more than
a feeling
LAUREN MORRILL

# MORE THAN A FEELING

## CARDINAL SPRINGS

LAUREN MORRILL

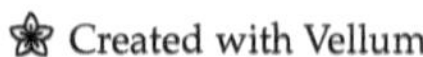 Created with Vellum

*For Tiffany Schmidt, my wingwoman*

# AUTHOR'S NOTE

The heroine in this book, Grace, lost her mother in childbirth. This occurs off-page, but this book does tackle her and her family's grief. If that's going to be difficult for you, please feel free to set this book aside. If and when you feel ready, it'll always be here for you.

# CHAPTER 1

## DECKER

WELCOME TO CARDINAL SPRINGS, HOME OF NHL STAR DECKER BROOKS!

Even though my entire life has gone to shit, I can't help but grin as the metal road sign comes into view. I press the pedal to the floor, and the engine of my 1977 Bronco roars as I speed past the evidence that at least *someone* in my hometown is proud of me. Unfortunately, I'm spending my summer in a place where the single most exciting thing ever to happen is me.

Not that I have anyone but myself to blame for that. Brielle's face when she delivered the verdict is burned clearly into my memory. And here I thought most of what our head of publicity did was arrange charity events and make TikToks.

"No boozing, no women, and for god's sake, no press," she told me as I sat slouched in Coach's office, my long legs splayed out in front of me. I was still nursing a tweaked hip flexor from the last game of the season. Brielle stood beside the big man, who sat behind his enormous glass desk, beefy arms crossed over his chest, glowering at me.

I should have heeded the warning in that glower, but I've never been very good at keeping my mouth shut.

"Perrault is a fucking asshole—*he* should be the one abstaining from women for the summer, not me!" I cried.

Our normally unflappable publicist let out a sigh so deep I was surprised it didn't blow my hair back. She shook her head slowly, as if to say, *Not even* I *can help your ass out of this one, Brooks.*

That was when Coach sat up in his chair, his elbow planted on the desktop as he pointed a finger directly at me.

"You keep your head down and your ass out of trouble, or so help me god, the only place you'll play hockey is down at the local Y, you hear me?" His voice was a growl; he fucking *meant* it. And that time, I snapped my mouth shut. Coach had often threatened to make me run drills till I dropped or even bench me, but he'd never once threatened to end my career. That was when I knew I was in deep shit.

So my trip to Vegas with the boys to drink and gamble and unwind after an epically shitty season?

Not happening.

My cabana in Tulum?

Canceled.

The cabin in Big Bear for the Fourth of July?

Well, that's still reserved for the guys who didn't get themselves thrown out of Game 7 of the Stanley Cup Finals. My name's on the rental, but my ass will be at home.

Well, not at *home*. Fuck, even holing up in my condo in Chicago is off the table. The paparazzi camp out there more often than not these days. That's what happens when you show up on red carpets and at club openings with international pop superstars. And Oscar-nominated actresses. And supermodels.

Fuck, the *supermodels*.

That's where it all went wrong. Because I'm not the only one in the league who's interested in supermodels. I'm just the one who wound up in a VIP section of a Chicago club with a smoky-eyed, willowy brunette in my lap, not realizing she was someone *else's* smoky-eyed, willowy brunette.

Coach can tolerate a lot, but once you start getting ejected from games because your off-ice antics translate into game-time brawls…well, then you're fucked.

That's when you wind up sentenced to a summer in your sleepy hometown forty miles east of nowhere, the only place on planet Earth so quiet and boring that not even *I* can get into trouble.

As I make my way down the two-lane rural highway, cornfields flying past me, my too-long hair escaping from its rubber band thanks to the wind whipping through the open top of my car, I glance at my watch. I have plans to meet up with my childhood best friend, Archer McBride, but I've got a good hour before then. So as I approach Hominy Lane, the last country road before I hit town, I slam on the brakes and hang a hard right. The squeal of the tires sends a chill up my back, and I lean into the turn, loving that centrifugal force.

Fuck, is this going to be my last thrill of the summer?

The little yellow house appears on the horizon, rising out of the cornfields. I could drive here in my sleep, though it's been years since I was last here for the funeral.

Ms. Suzanne was Coach's wife—my high school hockey coach—and though she works at the local library, she was always around at the school, quick with a cold Gatorade or a sympathetic ear. Most of us called her Mrs. Coach, and while she took care of all us hockey boys, it was a little different for me.

The road is flat as anything, nothing but cornfields in all directions save for the house with its white columns and green front porch. I turn off the main road and onto the gravel drive, slower this time, because I know Ms. Suzanne will have words if I come screeching up to her garage.

My feet have barely touched the gravel before I hear the slap of the screen door.

"Decker Brooks, I thought I felt trouble in the air." She's standing on the porch, arms crossed over a worn Cardinal Springs Hockey T-shirt, her curly gray hair beneath a red bandana. But unlike every other person who's been disappointed in me lately, Ms. Suzanne is smiling.

I take the four steps up the porch in one long-legged leap and let her wrap me in a hug that's way too big for such a small woman.

"Good to see you, hon," she says, pulling away to give me a once-over. "Can I make you a sandwich?"

Right away, I feel the knots of tension in my shoulders loosen just a little bit.

"That depends. You got the good peanut butter?" I ask.

Stepping inside the house, I let out a slow breath to keep the emotions at bay. The last time I was here, way too many six-foot-something men were crowded into this tiny house in black suits, pretended we weren't on the verge of crying our eyes out. It didn't seem fair that a man as strong and good as Coach Haskell could be taken so soon, but pancreatic cancer is a real bitch. He stood no chance. He was gone before I could make it down to say goodbye.

I swallow past the itch in my throat and follow Ms. Suzanne through the sunny house full of books and hockey memorabilia and into the kitchen, which hasn't changed since the first time I wandered in here as a high school freshman. I take a seat at the chipped Formica table and watch as she slaps together the single greatest peanut butter and jelly sandwich I've ever had, then or now. She has barely dropped the plate in front of me before I'm lifting it for a bite.

She slides into the chair next to me. "Just like you remember?" she asks.

"You know, I still make these before every single game—same peanut butter, same Smucker's grape jelly, same grocery store wheat bread, and they never taste the same as yours."

"Should I start FedExing them to you? Seems like you could use a boost after this season." She arches an eyebrow at me.

I groan. "Tell me you weren't watching."

"Of course I was watching. I never miss your games," she

says, and the tenderness in her voice damn near breaks my heart. Because even though she saw me play like shit and end the season in a gloves-off fight that sent me to the locker room, Ms. Suzanne is still here, welcoming me into this kitchen, making me a peanut butter sandwich with a smile. "So, what's this visit about? You lying low?"

"Head down all summer," I confirm.

She nods. "I think it'll be good for you. This fresh Midwestern air, blue skies, old friends. You'll go back next season ready to kick some ass and hoist a cup."

At the mention of Lord Stanley's cup, I knock on the table three times, a nervous tic I've had since I joined the league. I hope more than anything that I'll get to hoist the cup a third time before my career ends, a milestone that, at thirty-three years old, seems to approach faster the harder I try to skate away from it.

I glance at my watch.

"You've got somewhere to be? Don't let me keep you," she says.

I shake my head. "I can stay."

"No, no, sounds like I'm going to be seeing an awful lot of you this summer, so go on and hit the road. I bet Archer is waiting for you."

I take the plate to the sink and rinse it before setting it gently on the porcelain. Then I follow Ms. Suzanne back to the porch. I'm about to step down onto the little gravel path when she calls my name. I turn and see her leaning against one of the columns.

"You were always a good kid, Decker. You didn't have enough people telling you that," she says, causing my heart to squeeze. I have to clear my throat to keep the emotions at bay. "And even though you try your level best to hide it, I know you're a good man. You just need to trust that if you show people the real you, they'll love you for it."

I want to say something, to thank her, but that feels too small for all she's done for me. And anyway, I don't know if I can get words past the lump in my throat. Best I can do is raise a hand in response, give her a tight smile, and drive away, hoping I can live up to her belief in me.

———

Downtown Cardinal Springs hasn't changed much. It's still incredibly generous to refer to the small courthouse square and the few blocks extending in either direction as "downtown."

I pull into an empty spot in front of the limestone courthouse and am shocked to find a meter. There was no paid parking in Cardinal Springs last time I was here, but at least they put in the new meters that take credit cards. I can't remember the last time I carried quarters. Probably not since college, when I used them for laundry, and…well, let's just say I didn't do a whole lot of that back then.

I'm feeding my debit card into the machine when my phone buzzes with a text.

ARCHER

Practice running a bit over. Meet me at the arena in twenty?

I sigh just as the meter charges me a dollar fifty. Guess I'll be playing tourist while I wait for Archer to finish up. He's been coaching the Cardinal Springs High School hockey team and teaching history ever since Coach Haskell died. Which at least means that as soon as school lets out next week, he'll be free to hang out with me for the next three months while I try to amuse myself in the world's most boring place.

"Mom, it's him!"

A little voice comes from the Tahoe parked next to me, where a mom is about to load a toddler into the car. Standing next to her is a small boy, maybe nine or ten. I don't spend enough time around kids to know how old they are by sight.

"Hi," I say, giving him a little wave, and he stares up at me with wide, unblinking eyes. I smile at his mother, who adjusts the toddler on her hip and gives me a tight-lipped smile in return.

"Are you really Decker Brooks?" the little boy asks, lisping at the end of my name.

"Sure am. You a Grinders fan?" I flash him my best media smile, the one I use when we do outreach in schools or at children's hospitals. The one my teammate and captain, Gavin Stackhouse, calls "the all-American grin."

"I have a Grinders jersey at home! It's a Buchko jersey, but you're my second-favorite player for sure. My dad took me to a Grinders game for my birthday last year, but you guys lost to the Panthers. But you scored the only goal."

"I remember that game. A real heartbreaker. But we'll get 'em next time," I say, feeling the dimple in my left cheek deepen as the all-American grin widens. Still, the mother keeps her jaw set.

"Well, it helps when you don't fall down," the kid says. I have to hide my wince. I'm never going to live down that Game 7. "I play. Just peewee, but I'm a pretty good winger."

"Well, keep at it, little dude, and soon you'll be in the pros."

The kid swallows hard, then practically whispers, "I want to be just like you when I grow up."

At this, his mom huffs out a laugh, then rolls her eyes a little. "Well, not *just* like you, right?" she says to me with what I think is supposed to be a knowing smile, but fuck, it just makes me feel like a derelict.

Still, I brighten that all-American grin and turn back to the kid.

"Practice hard and listen to your mom, and you'll be fine." I ruffle his hair and give his mom one last winning smile, because that's what I do. You can look me dead in the eye and say I'm a shit role model for children, and I'll just take it like the joke that I am. I don't get ruffled. Unless it's the last few seconds of regulation in Game 7 of the Stanley Cup Finals, that is.

Fuck.

Now I'm in a bad mood.

I walk down the sidewalk, leaving the mom to wrestle the kids into the car. It's a beautiful day with one of those endless, blue, early-summer Indiana skies, the sun warm but the breeze cool. I figure I might as well take a little stroll through downtown while I wait for Archer to finish. I can see what all has changed around here, get the lay of the land and try to imagine spending my summer in one dull square mile.

The square is surrounded on three sides by two-story brick-and-limestone businesses, all topped with offices or apartments. But the north side of the square features a small park with a white gazebo in the center, some well-kept flower beds, and a few hulking old oak trees. Two teenagers huddle over an iPhone underneath one of the trees while an elderly man sits on the steps of the gazebo with his aging Yorkie. When I was fourteen, I carved my initials into one of the oak trees in the corner of the park, and I head over to check in on my artwork.

I'm halfway around the bandstand when I notice a pair of shapely legs sticking out of an enormous urn-shaped concrete planter. The thing sits on a stone platform and is at least seven feet tall. The legs are kicking wildly, like the owner is scrambling for purchase. I glance around, looking for the person filming this for TikTok or some shit, but the teenagers are still solidly absorbed in their phone, and the man with the dog is now walking slowly out of the park. I turn back just in time to see the legs slide farther into the planter, a terrified squeal accompanying their wild kicking.

I dart over and reach up, grasping the hips of the woman who's found herself ass up in a public park. Her body goes rigid under my hands.

"I've got you," I say in what I hope is my most trustworthy not-a-creep-copping-a-feel voice. "I can let you go if you don't need my help."

"Um...well..." I can tell she's doing some kind of calculation down there. She must decide I'm her only option, because she finally says, "Okay. Yeah. Thanks."

She starts to wriggle again, and I force my eyes away from that tight little ass. Otherwise, I will quickly go from Good Samaritan to fucking predator.

"Just hold still," I say, my fingers digging into her waist. I'm a strong guy, but she's above my head and thrashing like a fish on a hook. She's seriously testing my conditioning here. "Let me—"

At that moment, a stiff breeze rolls through the park. The hem of her dress flies up, giving me a eyeful of white cotton dotted with little red cherries. Goose bumps rise on the backs of her thighs, and she stills.

"Is my whole ass out?" she screeches, then reaches back for the hem of her dress, which is currently flapping around my hands at her waist. Unfortunately, that pulls her completely off balance, and she starts to tip back into the urn headfirst.

"Hold still," I grit out, my fingers digging into her hips. "I'll get you—"

"There's no way you can just lift—" she starts. But she doesn't get a chance to finish that sentence, because with one breath in to stabilize my core and a flex of my biceps on the exhale, I have her out of the urn, her ass sliding down the front of my body. The breeze picks up again, and her raven hair tickles my jaw as I slowly lower her to the ground.

As soon as her feet are safely on the sidewalk, I release her and take a step back. My mind is still stuck on those red cherries when she finally turns, her cheeks flushed. Whether that's from my hands on her or the fact that she was very recently upside down, I can't tell.

And I guess I'll never know, because as soon as her baby-blue eyes meet mine, they narrow, her soft pink lips drawing down into a deep scowl.

"It's *you*," she says, her voice full of nails.

It takes me a minute to put the pieces together: those piercing blue eyes, the thick dark hair, that exasperated look. But now I realize I know her, even if I haven't seen her in a long time.

"Baby Gracie?"

# CHAPTER 2

## GRACE

*aby Gracie.* The nickname has my knee twitching, eager to connect with his testicles.

"Don't call me that," I snap, then huff out a sigh at my childhood nickname, the result of being the only girl with four overprotective big brothers. I've finally managed to break my brothers of it by handing out nut shots with every utterance, but Decker hasn't been around much these last few years (thank god), so he must not have gotten the memo.

Decker's eyes go wide, his mouth dropping open before he doubles over with a hearty laugh so deep and loud that it scares a flock of birds out of a nearby tree.

"Holy shit, it *is* you!" His eyes travel up and down my body—a body he was all too close to just a minute ago. Dammit, and to think I enjoyed that slow ride down the front of a muscular stranger. But of course the universe could never be that good to me. It just had to be Decker fucking Brooks. "Dang, girl, you certainly grew up."

That sets off an involuntary spark in my pants places, but I ignore it. "*You* certainly didn't."

Of course he blows right past the dig. "What's it been? Like, five years?"

"I'm surprised you even remember that." It was at Archer's wedding, and Decker brought some dour supermodel as his plus-one. She frowned in every photo and did coke off the cake table. He got so drunk that he passed out in our backyard after the reception.

He gives me a wicked grin. "You're still mad at me about the dress thing, huh?" When I tried to haul his ass inside so he didn't die from alcohol poisoning in the grass or get carried off by raccoons, he barfed down the front of my bridesmaid dress. Clearly he thinks this is a hilarious memory.

"Decker, your list of sins is longer than a CVS receipt," I tell him. "What are you even doing here?"

"Speaking of sins," he says, shoving his hands in his jeans pockets. I hate the way my eyes snag on his muscular thighs straining against the fabric. He must get his pants specially made to fit those absolute tree trunks. But when I move my gaze upward, I just find myself staring at a broad expanse of muscled chest covered in a too-tight navy Henley. "I'm under strict orders to lay low this summer, so I figured, what better place to do that than sleepy, boring old Cardinal Springs? How much trouble can a person get in around here?"

I arch an eyebrow at him. "I'm sure you're going to find out."

"You know, I said I was sorry. About the dress thing." He's making an appropriately apologetic face, but when it comes to Decker Brooks, I trust *nothing*.

"You didn't, actually. You said, 'The pink goes really well with your eyes.'"

Decker groans. "I haven't been able to drink sangria since."

I roll my eyes. "What a tragedy. I'll add you to my prayer list."

"You McBrides always did have those beautiful baby blues," he says with a wink.

And that's Decker Brooks in a nutshell: roll right past your transgressions and seal it with a smile. The man could flirt with the dead and get a number. Unfortunately, I've known him my whole goddamn life, so the shine has long worn off that particular penny. He is very pretty, and very famous, and very, *very* toxic. All my most irritating childhood memories star Decker Brooks, who —for some reason, despite growing up in one of the newly built lakefront McMansions out on the county line—was always at our cramped and chaotic little ranch house on Gardenia Street. Given the nonsense I saw him get up to back then, it's completely unsurprising that he grew up to be the NHL's most notorious bad boy. The tabloids, who usually ignore hockey, constantly print photos of him with his flavor of the week, coupled with shots of whatever monster fight he started or ended at his most recent game.

"What the hell were you doing in that urn?" Decker asks.

I glance up at the giant concrete planter, then at the egg in my hand, which I had just managed to snag before I tipped.

"I let the teen board hide the eggs for the library Easter egg hunt, and some of them got a little overzealous, so there were a few left behind." I hold up the egg that was probably once a lovely shade of red but now looks a whole lot more gray. A week of baking in the sun will do that. "I'm retrieving them before they start to stink."

"Wasn't Easter more than a month ago?" he asks.

"It rained for the entire month of March and most of April, so we did our big egg hunt a couple of weeks late," I say. I hold the egg up to the light. "The kids made their own natural dye. This one was made with beets. It used to be cherry red."

"Speaking of cherries…" he says, waggling his eyebrows and glancing down at my hips. "Nice panties."

My entire being recoils. I don't know if it's the smarmy smirk on his pretty face or the fact that he just used the word *panties*, which always makes my skin crawl. Something about this moment causes my brain to short-circuit, and I reach out and slap him on his big broad chest.

With the hand holding the week-old egg.

And when the shell cracks and the hard-boiled guts squelch across his pecs, it emits a smell that could clear the park.

"Best of luck on your summer of celibacy, Decker," I say, smiling, and then march off through the grass.

---

By the time I pull open the door to McBride Hardware, the cowbell tied to the door jangling hard, I have not calmed down. I stomp across the scuffed linoleum of my father's store and make my way behind the counter, where Dad is sorting a box of tiny screws.

He glances up with a smile. "Just in time. Corianne's exp—*Christ*, what is that smell?" Dad takes a full step back, knocking the box off the edge of the counter, sending tiny screws pinging across the floor.

In my fury, I've managed to block out the rotten-egg smell emanating from my right hand. It was probably fairly dispersed by the spring breeze (and my angry gait) as I stomped across the square to the store. But now that I'm inside, where the stench is mixing with the smells of WD-40 and wood chips, it's absolutely nauseating.

And yet I can't help but smile, imagining Decker Brooks spending his first moments back home scrubbing rotten Easter egg out of that infuriatingly fitted Henley. It's just too good.

"Sorry, just retrieving the last of the Easter eggs," I half explain. I turn to the old farmer's sink mounted behind the register—a hazard of clerking at a hardware store is that your hands are constantly covered in grease or potting soil or the slobber of a dog who knows to jump up on the counter for one of the milk bones we keep in a box back here.

"I'm just gonna go change for my session," Dad says, his hand over his nose and mouth, trying to ward off the smell that's being pretty stubborn in the face of this lemon hand soap. Still, I don't miss the slight blush that creeps into his cheeks at the mention of his weekly training session with Corianne Hathaway.

My dad is fifty-five but still looks strong and vital, his hair thick and black with only a hint of distinguished gray at his temples. He's tall and looks like he's spent his whole life working with his hands, so hale that you might miss the slight wince when he stands after sitting for too long or the way he rubs his back when rain is coming. In the spring of my senior year of high school, Dad was delivering a truck full of mulch when he was hit out on Highway 41 by a drifting dump truck. He had to be cut out of his pickup like a sardine. He fractured his back but was unbelievably lucky to recover, thanks to a good surgeon and several months of in-patient rehab, followed by a few years of out-patient rehab and physical therapy.

At the time, my oldest brother, Archer, was in his third season in the NHL. Dan was getting his MBA at Harvard, Owen was in medical school at IU, and Felix was almost done with his master's program in engineering at Purdue. With all of them in the midst of pursuing lifelong dreams, it fell to me to stay home and help dad, to take over the store. My only plans at the time were to graduate from Cardinal Springs High and head to Indiana University. I wanted to major in English because I loved to read, but I had no idea what I was going to do with it. Was I really going to ask my brothers to put their educations and careers on hold for *that*? They had big plans, and all I had was a love of books and a boyfriend committed to playing basketball for IU.

This is the part where I lament my lost dreams, right? Except I actually think everything worked out exactly the way it was supposed to. I'm twenty-three, I have no student debt, I spend my days running the youth services department at the local library, and I can still help my dad out at the store when he needs it. Of course, Dad doesn't need my help so much anymore, and while I love running story time and recommending books, cleaning trash out of the book return for minimum wage is less than ideal.

And Dad's doing great, aided by the weekly personal training sessions that keep his back in tip-top shape. Corianne Hathaway is forty-nine, has a riot of curly silver hair, teaches yoga twice a week, and could probably bench press me. The exercise has been great for Dad, but lately I've noticed that their training sessions are growing more frequent, even though he's been stable a long time. I guess it's good that he has a friend.

I kneel and start picking up the screws. I have to chase down one that has rolled beneath the counter, and I curse myself for throwing on this damn sundress this morning. It has now screwed me over twice. As my knees grind into the linoleum, I can't stop thinking about my bare ass flapping in the breeze in the town square. I don't want Decker Brooks knowing anything about my underwear. Most of his underwear experience, if the press is to be believed, is with taking it off or discovering that whatever it girl he's taken to dinner isn't wearing any. My cherry-print cotton undies with a full seat must have been quite a shock to his system. Not that I'm embarrassed by them. I'd rather eat my own hand than wear a thong. I have enough irritation in my life without adding my underwear to the list.

I pop open the register and set about organizing the cash drawer, turning all the bills in the same direction and rolling change. When I pull open the drawer beneath the counter to look for fresh penny rolls, I discover a glossy brochure for Indiana University's School of Library and Information Science.

I'm flipping through it when Dad walks out in his gym shorts and an old Cardinal Springs High Hockey T-shirt. I hold up the thick booklet. "Dad, what's this?"

"Oh, I got that in the mail. Figured you're doing so great at the library, maybe it's time for you to take it to the next level." He gives me a nervous smile. "I appreciate all your help, honey—you know I do—but I don't want to hold you back."

We've been having some version of this conversation for several months now. I've tried to explain that I'm perfectly happy, but Dad either isn't listening or doesn't get it. And I'm too tired today to take another swing at it. So instead, I swallow my sigh. "Thanks, Dad," I say with a smile.

"You'll think about it?" His face is full of hope and fatherly concern.

I nod. The truth is, I've done nothing *but* think about it. It's the talking-about-it part that's hard, the *doing* that is fucking terrifying. Breaking out of my box, taking a risk, putting it all on the line and trying something new scares the ever-living shit out of me. Because the truth is, I don't want to go to college. And I don't want to spend the rest of my life working at the library, either, though I do love parts it.

For the last couple of years, I've had this tiny little kernel of dream that I tend to like it's a baby bird. I've done research and attended webinars, and I have a whole notebook full of the start of a business plan. I even took a few business courses online through the community college, but I kept that to myself. I've done everything but the doing, as my grandmother used to say.

But now it's time to let this baby bird of an idea fly, and that's where I'm stuck.

I want to open a bookstore. Here in Cardinal Springs, where right now you can only buy a slim selection of paperbacks from the Walmart out near the highway unless you want to drive nearly an hour to a store in Bloomington. Most everyone here just orders from Amazon, which is a real shame, because for being one of the biggest, most technologically advanced businesses in the world, their recommendation algorithm really sucks eggs.

Obviously we at the library fill some of that gap, but we're just a small branch, part of a larger underfunded library system. We can barely keep up with ordering the newest releases. We've got plenty of voracious readers who've run out of books in their preferred genres, and it's hard to meet their needs.

So I want to open a little spot near downtown where people can find their next favorite books. Where they can meet other book nerds and talk about the latest things they've read. Where kids can discover a love of stories and adults can rediscover the wonder they once experienced.

But starting a business takes money. It takes time. It's a risk, and my family has never been very good at letting me take those. I'm the baby, after all, the only girl raised by a grief-stricken father and four rowdy older brothers, all of whom channeled their own grief into taking care of me.

I haven't mentioned my dream to any of them, partly because I'm scared they'll try to talk me out of it and partly because I'm scared they'll do what they always do: try to help me. My dad and my brothers love paving the way for me, and it's all too easy for it to turn into that overprotective "let me do it for you" thing that I hate. I know it's ridiculous, but they all have their dreams, and I finally have mine. I don't want to lose it to a flurry of well-meaning men who will "help" it right out of my hands.

That's why I've done everything in secret. But now I've reached the point where if I take the next step, I'm not going to be able to hide it from them anymore.

When I finish with the register, I notice that Dad forgot to put out the chalkboard sign we use to advertise our latest specials, so I grab it and carry it out to the sidewalk. I set it up so everyone knows that bags of mulch are buy one, get one, then turn to face north. Three blocks up, my eyes land on the low brick building that used to be Quinn Cameras. Brady Quinn sold and repaired cameras and developed film there for forty years, and his father did the same for forty years before him. Brady retired and closed the shop last fall, and it would be the perfect spot for my bookstore. Original wood floors—a dark, rich wood, shiny and full of knots—under the old carpet. Lofted ceilings with exposed beams, and a big front window perfect for displaying the latest releases. It's large enough that I could have a full children's section with a story time space, and there's a loft area where I could host author events or kids' parties.

The only problem is the FOR SALE sign in the window. Brady isn't interested in renting out the building; he wants to sell the place and use the profits for an epic retirement trip where he can finally take his own photos. I could scrape together enough money to open and pay the rent with a small business loan, but I definitely don't have the capital to buy a building, nor do I have the credit.

And so for now, my dream is just that.

# CHAPTER 3

## DECKER

The Frank Northern Ice Arena smells exactly the same as it did fifteen years ago: a noxious mix of cold rubber and teenage BO.

I love it.

Out on the ice, about a dozen boys in red practice jerseys are running passing drills, the *skish, skish* of their skates sending a comforting chill up my spine. Over the tinny speakers, the *Jurassic Park* theme plays.

Archer McBride, my best friend and college roommate, is standing center ice, surveying the boys. A former NHL player, he's tall and still has the lean muscle of a professional athlete even though he hasn't played in five years. He's got that thick, dark McBride hair that he wears longish, and unlike in his hockey days, he now sports a full beard. With his arms crossed over his chest, he looks every inch the hard-ass coach.

"Carrying on Coach Haskell's legacy, eh?" I nod up at one of the black speakers mounted behind the goal.

Archer makes his way over to me. "Hey, he was right—they all take it more seriously when there's orchestral music playing," Archer says with a laugh. He reaches out for a handshake that becomes a backslapping hug. "You should've seen 'em when I tried putting on something modern and peppy. Their little hormone-addled, barely developed brains had them skidding all over the ice like puppies hopped up on Pixy Stix."

"Well, whatever you're doing is clearly working." I nod at the shiny new banner hanging over the press box, declaring Cardinal Springs the Indiana State High School Hockey Association champions. "Congrats on the season."

"I'd say the same to you, but it seems you and your guys forgot how to skate this year," Archer says, his eyes trained on the ice. "Or maybe you just forgot that the puck is supposed to go *in* the goal, not a few feet wide of it?"

I watch a gangly kid take a nice slap shot, but the goalie gloves it. "You teaching your boys to talk trash like that?"

"You know it," Archer says, finally turning, his mouth curving into his trademark smirk. It earns him a solid punch in the arm.

"There's always next year," I say.

He cocks an eyebrow at me. "Is there?"

"To be determined," I mutter. Archer knows my situation. Hell, there's very little about me that he doesn't know, which I can't say about pretty much anyone else. "Let's see how good a babysitter you are this summer."

Archer scoffs. "You fucking kidding me? That responsibility better come with hazard pay."

"Can it really be that much worse than a roster of high school boys?"

Archer cuts his eyes to me. "Yes, Decker. It can be so *very* much worse."

He blows his whistle, and the boys hustle over to the bench, skidding to a halt in a spray of ice.

"Nice work, boys. I know it's the offseason, but I'll be hosting optional weekly practices through the summer, plus a July skills camp, for anyone who's interested. If you're hoping to play next season, I highly recommend you get interested. If you've got a conflict, talk to me. Remember, this only works if you talk to me. Any questions before we break?"

A skinny kid who looks like he grew six inches overnight and is still trying to figure out what the fuck happened to his legs raises his hand. Archer tips his chin at the boy. "Bergstrom?"

Bergstrom shifts on his skates. "Yeah, Coach, uh…I just, uh…is that…I mean, well—"

"Spit it out, Bergstrom," Archer says, his deep voice channeling both his father and Coach Haskell. It's the same voice he used with me in college when he was trying to get me to put the beer bong down the night before a game. It only worked on me about half the time, but this Bergstrom kid swallows hard and stands up a little straighter. Then he looks at me.

"Are you Decker Brooks?"

It takes work not to wince at the way his voice cracks on my last name. Poor kid.

I give Bergstrom a two-fingered salute. "That's me."

The rest of the boys stare at me open-mouthed, way too many sets of braces flashing my way.

"Are you gonna coach us?" I think the comment comes from the goalie, who's absolutely drowning in his gear, but he's still wearing his mask, so I can't see if his mouth is moving.

I bark out a laugh. "Nah, I'm just a player," I say, glancing over at Archer. He shakes his head, probably imagining what damage I'd inflict on a bunch of impressionable teenagers. Hell, their parents would probably revolt if they heard I was in charge of their precious spawn.

With a few more encouraging words and a stern warning not to be "idiot assholes" this summer, Archer blows his whistle, and the boys waddle off to the locker room. Archer drags a bucket of pucks toward the boards, and we take a seat on the bench. Then Archer sniffs.

"You know, I wasn't going to say anything because I figured it had to be one of the boys, but they're gone, so now I've gotta ask…what the fuck is that smell?"

God, I've actually gotten used to the noxious odor of rotten egg that lingers on my shirt despite a hearty attempt to scrub it in the arena bathroom. But now that Archer mentions it, my nose wrinkles, and I can feel Grace's hand smashing into my chest. And then I picture those cherry panties clinging to that luscious ass, and shit, now I've gotta shift in my jeans so her goddamn brother doesn't knock me into the ice like old times.

"Funny story—I actually ran into Grace," I say.

"Oh, right, the Easter eggs," Archer says with a nod. I forgot how much everyone knows about everything in a small town. "Damn, she got you good, huh?"

I chuckle. "Yeah. I didn't recognize her at first, actually. She certainly grew up."

Archer's brows knit together, his jaw clenching. "Stay the fuck away from my sister, dude." His tone is half mocking, but the other half? Well, it's just another reminder that I can't escape my reputation, not even with my best friend.

"Obviously," I reply. And I mean it. The last thing I want to do is to fuck around with my best friend's little sister. I just need to get that message to my dick, because he clearly has his own agenda. "Anyway, I'm off women."

Archer raises that eyebrow again, and it makes me want to slap the look right off his face. Mercifully, he lets that one lie for now. "We on for dinner?" he asks.

"Yeah, I just need to meet with the real estate lady. She's going to show me a few places that are available for the summer. Still cool if I crash with you until I find something?"

"Long as you don't mind that the guest bed is wedged between a treadmill and a squat rack."

When Archer left the NHL after his injury, he took his education degree back to Cardinal Springs and became the high school's history teacher and hockey coach. His wife, Cassie, lasted in the middle of Indiana for exactly one year before she hightailed it back to Boston, leaving only divorce papers behind. I wasn't exactly surprised. Cassie was a textbook WAG, and she thought she had married well. Archer was a rising star in Boston; her worst-case scenario was that she'd have to follow him to

Winnipeg or some other freezing northern city, but at least he'd be a star with the paycheck that came along with it. But a high school history teacher in small-town Indiana? Yeah, she was never going to stick around for that. I wondered at the time why Archer never tried to get a job with the league or become an announcer. Cassie might've been willing to put up with that.

Probably not.

"I'll be at the Half Pint around five thirty. Felix will be there, and Owen if his appointments don't go late," Archer says. He passes me a key to his place. "Do us all a favor and shower first? You smell like death farts."

"Yeah," I say, the egg smell sending my brain glitching right back to the littlest McBride. Surely it's just a symptom of the fact that I'm staring down the barrel of a summer of celibacy. My brain (and my dick) will catch up soon enough. "I'll see you guys there."

# CHAPTER 4

## GRACE

t's Friday, and the Half Pint will get rowdy later tonight, but at five o'clock, it's only at a comfortable simmer.

Wyatt, one of my best friends and the Half Pint's best bartender, pulls half a dozen pints for the construction crew in the corner, piling them on a tray that she hoists expertly onto her shoulder. Her hips sway in that way I can never replicate; when I try, I end up looking like a drunk doing a field sobriety test. She stops at the table and cocks a hip to balance the weight, then reaches for the first glass.

"Here, lemme help you, honey," Dwight Jackson says, reaching for the glass nearest him, but Wyatt deftly intercepts his wrist.

"No disturbances in the Force, Dwight," she says, releasing him with a sharp glare. "Unless you want to upset my delicate balance and wind up wearing each and every one of these drinks." And because the men who drink at the Half Pint know Wyatt isn't one for empty threats, he sits back and lets her work.

Back behind the bar, she pulls a pint of my favorite dry cider and slides it in front of me. Beside me, my childhood best friend, Carson, is lazily stirring her Diet Coke.

"Are you sure you don't want any rum in that to celebrate the end of the school year?" Wyatt asks her.

"You know I'm a lightweight, and I have to go in and pack up my classroom tomorrow. I do not want to be hungover while I attempt to sort through eleven thousand broken crayons," Carson replies. She's just finished up her first year teaching kindergarten at Cardinal Springs Elementary. She spins on her stool to face me. "Besides, I want to be stone-cold sober when I ask you what you were doing in Decker Brooks's arms."

"Please tell me it hasn't hit the phone tree," I groan, barely resisting thunking my forehead onto the bar.

"No, but I ran into Mrs. Eberle at Kroger, and she asked me if you two were dating, which was weird, because I thought he lived in Chicago," Carson says. "So what's he doing in Cardinal Springs, dragging you out of a decorative planter?"

"Wait, Decker Brooks the hockey star?" Wyatt leans her elbows on the bar. "The naked one from the magazine?"

My mind flashes directly to the *ESPN* Body Issue where Decker posed in nothing but his skates with his hockey stick covering his...uh, hockey stick. I take a long sip of my cider, hoping it will wash away the image of Decker's abs glistening like an ice rink.

"I know him more as Archer's best friend and my lifelong nemesis, but yeah, that's the guy," I grumble. I always forget that Wyatt didn't grow up here, so she doesn't have the same memories of Decker Brooks that I do. She moved here ten years ago to raise her fourteen-year-old sister after their mother went to prison for check fraud. By the time she got here, Decker had already graduated and left.

"Is he as pretty in real life as he is in those slo-mo gifs of him walking into arenas in suits?" Wyatt asks.

"I didn't know you were a hockey fan," I say.

"I'm not. I'm a hot men in suits fan," she replies.

"Can we please get back to the thing about you being in Decker Brooks's arms in the middle of Henry Park?" Carson asks.

I give them a quick rundown of what happened with the urn and the Easter egg, leaving out the part where my ass was on display and Decker got an eyeful of my panties.

"Well, that's way less exciting than I was hoping," Carson says, turning back to her Diet Coke.

"Come on, you know I would never willingly let Decker put a hand on me. He's the *worst*."

"Is he, though?" Wyatt asks.

"He's perpetually thirteen years old," I say. "He's also a lout and a lothario and a lush—"

"Okay, there, little librarian—we get it, you know the big words," Wyatt laughs. Then her eyes flick to the entrance to the Half Pint. "Looks like it's gonna be a McBride family takeover tonight."

I glance over my shoulder to watch three of my four brothers amble through the front door. Owen, Cardinal Springs's only pediatrician, is still in scrubs, and Felix, who has a thick coating of dirt on the knees of his jeans, must have come straight from a job site. He started his own construction company after college and can most often be found manning a power tool or climbing a ladder. A half second behind them comes Archer. All three of them are tall with the same thick dark hair and blue eyes.

Which means…

"Goddammit," I mutter, spinning away from the door.

"Oh, I've got a few L words for *him*," Carson whispers as Decker Brooks strolls in behind Archer. His thick, wavy blond hair is loose around his jaw, and he's changed his shirt. Now he's wearing a gray CSHS Hockey T-shirt, the logo stretched across his sculpted chest, the sleeves straining around his biceps.

"Holy fuck. He looks Photoshopped," Wyatt mutters.

"Yep, looks just like he does on the internet. And those are all his real teeth, too," Carson says.

"Since when are *you* such a Decker Brooks fan?" I ask.

"Hey, I like hockey. *And* the pregame arrivals in the suits," Carson replies.

Wyatt leans across the bar to me. "If you're not gonna, can I?"

I roll my eyes. "Wyatt, trust me, you don't want to. Spend about six seconds on Google, and you'll realize he's an absolute dog. A bad boy, and not in the fun way."

"It would probably be a *little* fun." Carson blushes from the tips of her ears down to the neckline of her delicate floral blouse. It's the kind of fun Carson has only read about in books, and thanks to her ultraconservative parents, those books had to be hidden deep in the back of her closet and read by flashlight late at night. Since she still lives with them at twenty-four, I finally got her a Kindle for her birthday so she could read her favorite smut out in the open without steam coming from her parents' ears.

"Pass. I don't do bad boys," Wyatt says.

I blink at my friend, who is standing behind a bar in a vintage Guns N' Roses T-shirt she's cropped short and a pair of painted-on bell-bottoms. Her curly brown hair, which she wears in a shoulder-skimming bob, is usually highlighted with at least one or two Crayola colors. Today she's sporting vibrant lavender highlights with a few royal-purple lowlights for dimension. She has an impressive collection of tattoos and several visible piercings (and, as I know from one night the three of us spent spilling secrets by the lake with a bottle of tequila, a few not-so-visible piercings). Wyatt is the kind of person who can wear a leather jacket and not look like she's cosplaying The Fonz. She's absolutely the coolest, most badass person I know, and I've always figured her taste in men matched her taste in clothes: worn and dirty and rough. Not that I'd know, because she never dates in town. *Avoiding the gossip*, she always says, and having grown up in Cardinal Springs, I get it.

"Not that I'm encouraging you—*either* of you—to spend a single solitary second on Decker Brooks, but you do realize that's a tad ironic, no?" I say.

Wyatt shrugs. "Bad girls? They're fun. But bad boys are never worth the effort. They're so busy trying to prove they're tough that they don't actually give a shit about you. Gimme a good boy who approaches bringing a woman to orgasm with the same tenacity he brought to, like, making the dean's list or acing the SATs." She nods at the construction workers, who are trying to get her attention, and starts filling more pint glasses. Then she winks at us. "*Those* are orgasms worth having."

At the mention of orgasms (and definitely not at the sight of Decker Brooks splayed out on a wooden chair in the corner of the Half Pint, wearing that shirt that is at least two sizes too small—what an asshole), my thighs clench. It has been entirely too long since I've had an orgasm that didn't come from my own hand.

A wedge of daylight creeps into the bar, signaling another arrival. I look up just in time to see Cannon Brentwood stroll in with a couple of guys.

*Fuck.* If my tenth-grade chemistry teacher can get his ass in here, then this bar will be packed with all my least favorite men.

Cannon is the reason I haven't had an orgasm with another person in quite some time. Partly because we broke up two months ago, but mostly because he stopped coming through on that front long before then. I wish I could say the lukewarm sex was the reason our relationship—which began back in junior year of high school and continued long distance during his four years playing basketball at IU—ended, but that was honestly the least of our problems.

"Want me to tell him to beat it?" Wyatt asks, eyeing the guys, who are all wearing expensive chinos and polo shirts.

"I can't dump a guy and then evict him from the only bar in town," I sigh, though I'd really like to say yes. Watching Wyatt throw guys out of the Half Pint is honestly one of my favorite pastimes. "Besides, I'm trying to move on. It's a small town, and I don't need the drama."

"Well, tell your brothers that, because Felix is throwing Cannon a look so dirty, this bar is going to need a hazmat team to clean it up," Wyatt says. She wiggles her purple nails at me. "I just got these done this morning, I'd really like to avoid any shenanigans that might put them in jeopardy this evening, *mm-kay?*"

# CHAPTER 5

## DECKER

"Fuck that guy," Felix spits. Archer's little brother's calloused hand closes tightly around the neck of his beer as he lifts the bottle for a swig.

"What guy?" I glance toward the door, where a convention of preppy dudes in polos are sliding into a booth.

"Brentwood," Felix says. "The one with the floppy hair and daddy's money."

Other than looking like he probably has a tattoo of his fraternity letters, he seems like any other random boring dude in khakis. "What's his deal?"

"He and Grace dated for, like, forever," Owen says. He rolls his neck, obviously tired from a full day of examining snotty, coughing children. If this were the season, I'd make sure he stayed at least a dozen feet from me in case he still had grubby little-kid germs on him. I cannot afford so much as a cold during the season, not this late in my career. "They got together in high school."

"She's never said, but the rumor is that he cheated," Archer says. "She cut him loose."

"And thank god, because I was starting to worry she was going to marry him and I'd have to look at that smug face at every

Christmas and Thanksgiving for the rest of my life." Felix drains his beer and sets it down on the table with a loud thud.

"He played basketball for IU all four years. Big star on campus, forgettable player on the national stage. He tried for the NBA but got left with his dick in his hands when the draft was over," Archer adds with a little laugh.

"Now he works at his father's car dealership and struts around like he invented money," Felix says.

"Grace dated *him*?" I can't picture her with a guy like that, a smug fucker in boat shoes in the middle of southern Indiana. I mean, it's been a while since I've spent any time around her, and our few minutes in the park this afternoon hardly count as a meaningful reunion, but she's always struck me as a nice girl who doesn't put up with shit. Her brothers instilled that in her early on. It surprises me that she'd spend the better part of a decade with a guy her brothers don't want to share a bar with.

"Yeah, until, like, a couple months ago," Owen says.

"Guess she finally noticed he's a douchebag," Felix bites out.

Something about the way these guys are so openly hostile about that smug little shit pulls at my gut. There's no one more overprotective than a McBride brother, but still. "Did he…hurt her?" I ask.

Archer shakes his head. "He seemed…fine? Just too bland and boring to act as slick as he does."

"I tried to ask her about it at family dinner once," Owen says. "She told me there was no need to discuss it because it was over and that was all I needed to know."

"If he'd done anything, we'd have been the first to pound him into the ground. Trust me when I say I'd kill for the opportunity to knock the smirk off that guy's face," Felix says. "But I think he was just your garden-variety asshole boyfriend, and—thank god —she finally got sick of it."

A slender bartender with Axl Rose's face across her chest slides up to the table with a tray full of beers. "These are courtesy of your little sister, who kindly requests that you not make a scene with Cannon Brentwood," she says with a smile, though her eyes say, *Try it and feel my wrath.*

"Don't worry, Wyatt, we're not going to start any shit," Owen says.

"Yeah, I'm actually more concerned about this guy," she says as she slides a beer in front of Felix, who is still glowering in the direction of Cannon's booth. She takes the last beer off her tray, which she tucks under her arm as she holds the glass out to Owen. But when he reaches for it, she pulls it back. "You sure I can trust you not to throw down in the name of brotherly love?"

Owen blinks at her. "You honestly think that of this crew, *I'm* the one you have to worry about?"

"It's always the quiet ones," she says with a wink, then sets the beer down in front of him.

———

A few hours and several beers later, the Half Pint is buzzing like a beehive in spring. A lot of familiar faces have turned up, most of them happy to see me, a lot of them equally happy to tell me what's wrong with my game. I may have driven four hours south of Chicago, but without an NHL team of their own, Indiana is still Grinders territory. And they're pissed about my performance. I've had just enough beers to hang on to my easy smile and laugh like I'm in on the joke, but my patience is wearing thin. Do these people honestly think I haven't been kicking my own ass about that disastrous breakaway or the fight that got me ejected? I knew Perrault was baiting me. I'd known he'd try it before the game even started, and I still took a swing. Did I lose the game for my team? Rarely does it come down to a single player, a single moment, but I sure did my level best to tip the scales.

Fuck, I need another drink.

"Anybody want anything?" I ask the McBride boys as I stand and turn toward the bar. They all wave me off, deep in conversation about the Colts' prospects for the fall, so I make my way to the now-crowded bar. I spot an opening and don't realize until I wedge my hip in, leaning an elbow on the bar, that I'm pressed up against the littlest McBride.

Grace is still wearing that flimsy floral sundress, and when the silky fabric brushes my arm, it sends my brain cartwheeling back to the park and the feeling of her ass coasting down the front of my body.

I shake my head to try and evict the thought, try to call up a younger Grace instead. Grace with braces and glasses, whining because she wanted a turn with the Xbox. Grace threatening to tell on us for shooting off bottle rockets out of our hands or sneaking Halloween candy before trick or treat. Grace pitching a fit because her dad wouldn't let her watch horror movies with us or tag along to the mall.

But try as I might, I can't call up a single image of Grace McBride that doesn't involve her long toned legs or tight round ass. To say nothing of the smattering of freckles on her nose that wiggled when she glared at me, just like she's doing right now.

"Decker," she says, my name somehow sounding like a curse.

"Cherry," I reply, the nickname tumbling out of my mouth before I can run it through my filter. And thank god, because the fury it elicits makes those fucking freckles dance. Turns out teasing Grace McBride is still really fun.

"Have you been hit in the head with a puck so many times that you can't remember my name?" she snaps.

"It's just hard to call you Grace after I saw you dangling out of a planter. Hardly living up to your name."

"Well, if we're playing by those rules, should I call you Trip?" She smirks, and my stomach tumbles.

I feel an odd cocktail of emotions when I hear the nickname. The first is, *fuck that,* I'm not going to be defined by her or anyone else by one of the worst moments of my career. But also…she watched me play? Why does that make my insides ignite like a gas burner?

Something on my face must betray at least part of my reaction, because her expression softens just a hair, and she waves the bartender over.

"What'll it be, pretty boy?" the purple-haired bartender asks, and Grace huffs out a laugh.

"There's a nickname I can get behind," I say, letting the wink-and-laugh Decker slide back into place. But I could use a little something to help him stay. "I'll take a tequila shot. Top shelf."

"Anything for you?" Wyatt asks Grace.

"My treat, Cherry," I say with a wink.

She rolls her eyes. "Ugh, that nickname's gonna stick, isn't it?"

I'm about to lob a comment back at her, enjoying this banter, when I glance over my shoulder and catch sight of Archer. He's watching me, his beer hovering near his lips, his brows furrowed like he's trying to solve the Sunday crossword puzzle. And that's all the reminder I need that this particular woman, despite her cute underwear and her long legs and her quick wit, is not for me.

I turn back and notice the half-empty pint glass on the bar in front Grace, no longer sweating, the bubbles long gone. It's a dark golden color—cider, maybe. Grace, for whatever reason, is taking it slow tonight.

"I'm good," she says.

I nod. "Fair enough. Barkeep?"

Wyatt produces the shot, along with a lime wedge and a salt-shaker. "Figure a pretty boy like you plays by spring break rules," she says with a smirk.

And even though just a second ago I told myself I'd walk away, I turn to Grace, saltshaker in hand. "You game?" I ask, cocking an eyebrow.

What the fuck am I doing? Her brothers are sitting at a table not fifteen feet away. My best and oldest friend would pound me into the ground if he saw my tongue get anywhere near his baby sister. Frankly, I should probably kick my own ass just for asking.

Luckily, she rolls her eyes. "I'd sooner carve my eyeballs out with soup spoons."

I decide not to tell her that there are women who would probably pay good money for the privilege of my tongue on their neck. But I'm on hiatus from that scene, and besides, I don't think it would help my case with Grace McBride.

Not that I need to be making *any* case with Grace McBride.

"I'm sure your bartender friend can provide you with the necessary supplies," I reply before swapping the saltshaker for the shot glass and tossing down the burning tequila in one fast swallow. I set the empty glass down on the bar with a loud clink, and then glance back at Grace, whose eyes are on my mouth. So I shoot my tongue out and swipe the last of the burning liquor from my lower lip, grinning at her. A rosy flush blooms in her cheeks, and she spins away from me on her barstool.

God, she's fun to play with.

"Wyatt, I need to use the ladies'," Grace says to the bartender, sliding off her stool and pretending I'm not here.

As soon as she's gone, I reach for her pint glass and take a swig. Warm cider, sickly sweet. I grimace. Yup, she's been working on that for a while.

"Put that on my tab," I say to Wyatt, nodding at the warm cider and slapping my card down. It's probably about time to call it a night before this shot kicks in and I start thinking about Grace McBride's cherry panties and wind up doing something truly stupid. The kind of thing I promised Brielle and Coach I'd avoid.

I settle up my bill, tipping 100 percent, because you can say a lot of things about me, but *stingy millionaire* is never going to be one of them. I turn to head back to Archer and the guys, but a swaying figure catches my eye.

Cannon Brentwood is heading for the back hallway where the bathrooms are. The same hallway Grace just went down. Just before he disappears, he trips over fucking nothing.

Cannon has not stopped at one shot, apparently.

I head after him without thinking, which is my specialty. Just before turning the corner into the hallway, I hear the two of them talking. I lean against the ancient, graffitied pay phone, attempting to listen around the corner.

"You can't possibly be thinking about trying to move on with *Decker Brooks*." From the slurring, I assume it's Cannon. "He's basically a one-man pussy posse."

*Thanks, dickbag.*

"Cannon, walk it off," Grace says, but her voice is gentle, like she's talking to an overtired toddler.

"I'm *fine*." He drags the word out for a few extra seconds in a way that says he is decidedly not. "What the hell do you think you're doing?"

"The beauty of not dating you anymore is that I don't have to explain a damn thing to you," she says, annoyance creeping into her voice. *Atta girl.*

Cannon lets out this noise that is probably supposed to be a scoff, but thanks to the alcohol in his bloodstream, it leans more toward a snort.

"There's no way a guy like *that* is gonna go for someone like *you*," he says, and though I can't see him, I can practically hear his sneer.

Every muscle in my body tenses. This little motherfucker can talk shit about me all day and all night. I can take it. But what the fuck is he doing, trying to tear Grace down like that? Suddenly all I can think about is what else he must have said to Grace over the course of their relationship and when she finally cut his ass loose. It doesn't sound like this is the first time he's let shit like this fly, and when I peek around the corner and see the way Grace is standing there, steady as a statue, her expression one of practiced impassivity, it doesn't look like the first time she's heard it, either.

Without thinking, I swing around the corner, planting myself behind Cannon, face-to-face with Grace. Her eyes lock with mine, and I notice that despite her placid facade, her eyes have a watery look. Her jaw is set, like she's trying hard to keep her chin from quivering.

That asshole has her on the verge of tears.

He leans into her, thinking he's being all suave and whispering in her ear when in fact he's speaking at full volume. So he doesn't see that I've stepped up behind him.

"Decker Brooks has had fucking supermodels, Grace. *Supermodels.* You think you stand a chance in hell of pleasing him?" He lets out another theatrical scoff that's forceful enough that he stumbles forward a step. Grace jumps back. "Been there, can say with certainty, *fuck no.*"

Grace sucks in the shallowest of breaths, and with it comes this soft little sound, like a whimper. She *whimpers*, and in that instant my vision goes black. My arm shoots out, my hand landing firmly on Cannon's shoulder, and with a quick yank, I spin him around. He sways slightly in his loafers, then has the audacity to grin at me.

The twist of his lips is enough to turn my stomach.

My fingers clench at my side, my elbow pulls back, and in a move that feels as familiar as gliding across the ice, I let my fist fly.

# CHAPTER 6
## GRACE

"And I heard that Grace and Cannon were kissing, and Decker Brooks pulled them apart before he punched Cannon."

I sigh. I've been overhearing versions of this conversation since I stepped out my door this morning. Hell, I could practically feel the spiritual force of the Cardinal Springs gossip mill grinding its gears as I fell asleep last night.

So far, no one has landed on the truth. Probably because I'm still not entirely sure what the truth *is*. Cannon said those hideous things to me, and then Decker appeared out of nowhere and knocked him out. I didn't stay to sort out the hows or the whys, because as soon as Cannon groaned and I knew he wasn't dead, I turned and marched right out of the Half Pint, not stopping until I got home. I didn't meet Decker's eyes. I didn't say a word to him. I just focused on getting out of there before my brothers or my friends or the rest of the town could get involved in…whatever *that* was.

But *whatever that was* was determined to find me, as is evidenced by the very loud conversation happening in front of me in the line at Crimson 'n' Cream this morning.

"See, now, I heard it was *Decker* doing the kissing." Susan

Eberle, who's been teaching junior English at the high school since before we McBride kids were even an idea, is an unrepentant gossip. And when paired with Lizzy Booth, who cuts hair down at 'Do, it's a wonder their conversation doesn't cause enough friction to actually catch fire. The two of them are pressed shoulder to shoulder as they eye the muffins in the case.

"That boy always was trouble," Lizzy says. "What's somebody like Grace McBride doing with him, anyway?"

"Her brothers are usually much better about taking care of her," Mrs. Eberle says, then clucks her tongue like a mother hen. "Archer must be blinded by his friendship. It's keeping him from stepping in like he should."

Okay, I don't know why, but that's the line, and these two biddies have just sprinted past it.

I sigh again, this time louder and more theatrically, which Mrs. Eberle should recognize. She also taught drama, and I learned to project from *her*.

Their heads whip around in unison, and when they see me, a momentary look of panic ignites in their eyes. At least Lizzy has the good grace to include a twinge of guilt in hers, too.

But Mrs. Eberle recovers quickly. What a pro.

"Oh, Grace, honey, how are you after all that mess last night?" Her voice drips with pity, but her eyes say she smells blood in the water. She wants the story.

I know that whatever I say right now will be repeated as soon as I walk out of the bakery. And probably not accurately, either. Which takes a little bit of pressure off, I guess.

"I'm fine," I say, and suppress an eye roll at Mrs. Eberle's faux-sympathetic nod. "Those boys and their drunken foolishness... who knows what goes through their heads?"

Well, at least that's the truth. I have no idea what got into Cannon, and I can't even pretend to understand what Decker thought he was doing.

"Oh, so you weren't..." Mrs. Eberle waggles her fingers, as if that's the international symbol for fooling around.

"Susan," Lizzy says, swatting at her friend. "Mind your business."

*She's too busy minding everyone else's,* I manage not to say out loud.

"Not a bit." I flash her my very best Grace McBride smile. I look Mrs. Eberle dead in the eye. "Gosh, I just have no idea how that kind of gossip gets started."

Lizzy bites her lip to suppress a giggle, and then Daphne calls for the next customer in line, ending this inquisition. And hopefully halting the gossip mill for now, though in Cardinal Springs, I know that's wishful thinking.

———

There's plenty of speculation about the end of my relationship with Cannon, but no one really knows the truth. I let everyone think he and I simply grew apart, that the breakup was mutual. Some people even assumed he'd dumped me—he's the rich, shiny golden boy of Indiana basketball, after all. I let them believe that, because I have to coexist in this town with Cannon Brentwood for the rest of our lives. As the heir to his father's car dealership, he's certainly never leaving Cardinal Springs. I love my life here, too— my friends, my family—and if my plan to open the bookstore pans out, I'll be putting down roots for real. It's just easier to smooth things over and move on.

That doesn't mean Cannon isn't a grade-A dirtbag with a nasty habit of getting, well, nasty when he has a few too many drinks. Which started happening a little too often after the draft didn't work out and his life as an NBA player dissolved before his eyes.

But nobody knows that, because I keep Cannon's secrets in an effort to keep the peace. That's the deal. He walks away, and I don't talk. His reputation matters to him more than anything, and I don't particularly want to be on the wrong side of the Brentwood family.

But last night, Cannon broke the treaty. And now the whole

town is chattering about why Decker Brooks laid him out in the back of the Half Pint while he was talking to me.

If I want all of this to simmer down so we can return to our previous detente, I'm going to have to talk to the asshole. A task that, after last night, I am loath to do.

Cannon lives in what he calls a cabin down on the shore of Lake Callaghan, but "cabin" is a gross understatement. That makes it sounds cozy and dark, with heavy log walls and dense trees and a wood-burning fireplace or two. In reality, Cannon's house is a modernist glass box with an immaculately cut green lawn rolling down to a man-made stretch of sandy beach. The back, which faces the water, features a multilevel deck nearly as big as the house itself, with an outdoor kitchen and a TV the size of a Fiat. There's a stone pool and a hot tub and a firepit, all of which you can enjoy while the dark blue waters of the lake glitter before you.

It was all paid for by Cannon's father, of course. Just because his son's NBA dreams failed to materialize didn't mean he had to give up the NBA lifestyle.

The plan was for me to move in there with Cannon. But the closer I got to doing that, the more I started to see what my life would really be like there, with him. And I didn't like what I saw. The way he'd begun to unwind after work with several glasses of bourbon. The way he complained about everything, then turned those complaints on me. The way he expected me to fill in all the gaps in his new life and blamed me for everything that was missing when I didn't.

That alone was enough to make me want to end things.

And then, when I went over one day to measure the exterior shed that Cannon said I could turn into my reading nook, I found the cell phone. His cell phone, but not the one he talked to me on. This one was filled with numbers of women whose names I didn't recognize and text threads that would make even the most prolific romance author blush. I saw more tits in the thirty seconds I spent scrolling than I would've seen at the Diamond Lounge out by the highway.

And that was when I realized all the late nights, all the business trips, all the guys' weekends…they were lies.

My heart pounds hard as I climb the steps to his front door. My hand shakes as I reach for the doorbell. Cannon really only gets mean when he's drunk, and by now he's surely sober enough that I can talk to him. Still, I steady myself as I stare directly into the tiny eye of the camera on the doorbell, my jaw set. I will not let him have the satisfaction of knowing that he rattled me last night.

*You think you stand a chance of pleasing him?*

My stomach turns at the memory of those words, how it felt to hear them out loud.

When the door swings open, I can't suppress a gasp. There's a large bruise the color of summer hydrangeas blooming on the apple of his left cheek and wrapping around the side of his eye. Decker punched him like it was Game 7 of the Stanley Cup Finals, only Cannon wasn't wearing a helmet.

The rest of Cannon looks like death warmed over as well. His eyes are bloodshot, his skin pale and mottled. His dark hair sticks up in wild tufts. As if I need more evidence that he was drunk out of his ever-loving mind last night.

"What are you doing here?" he grumbles, then turns and shuffles away, leaving the door open.

That's a good question. I should be more than done with him. I *was*. But thanks to his mouth and Decker's fist, I'm back in it, and if I want out again, we need to talk.

I take his grumbling as the best invitation I'm going to get and step inside, shutting the door with just enough force to make him wince.

"I came to bring you muffins, find out how you're doing, and ask you what the hell happened last night."

Cannon pauses, then pivots, silently padding back to take the muffin bag and coffee cup out of my hands. He mutters, "Thanks," before he turns and heads to the kitchen. *Asshole.*

I follow him as he drops the muffin bag on the gleaming marble of his kitchen island, then leans back against the counter to take a long swig of coffee. "I stood in line for those muffins and had to listen to all kinds of theories about what went down last night," I say. "Funny thing is, I was there, and I haven't a clue."

"Yeah," he says, as if that's an explanation. He scrubs his palm over his face, hissing when he forgets and presses on his fresh bruise. Then he sighs. "I was really fucking drunk."

"No kidding," I snap. "Do you remember any of it?"

"I remember seeing you in the Half Pint talking to Decker Brooks, and then I remember Decker Brooks punching me in the face," he says. "I'm pretty sure there were some things in the middle that were…not great."

"That's an understatement," I say.

Cannon has the gall to roll his eyes. "Do you want to tell me what I said that made your new boyfriend knock me out?"

I slam my hands on the countertop loud enough to make him wince. "Decker is not my boyfriend, new or otherwise. And if he were, that would be absolutely none of your business. He just happened to be standing nearby when you started spewing a particularly foul brand of invective, and he reacted. I wish he hadn't punched you, but I won't lie—you deserved it."

He doesn't ask what he said, which is fine, because I don't want to repeat it. I hope never again to hear even an echo of those words that confirmed my worst fears about my relationship with Cannon—that I wasn't good enough, that I disappointed him, that the problem was me. I found a good therapist and a half-decent meditation practice and am on the way to convincing myself those are lies, but hearing him say it out loud? It set me back.

That's why I just stood there last night, tears welling in my eyes, until Decker stepped up.

It's why I start blinking quickly now at the memory.

"Fuck," Cannon mutters. He sighs, his shoulders rolling in as he stares at his bare feet. At least he seems to know he fucked up. I'm mostly here because I'm afraid last night was the start of a new normal. I need to know he isn't going to do that again.

I hope to god he won't.

"Yeah," I say. "Anyway, I just wanted to make sure your brain isn't oozing out your ears and that you don't plan on doing anything stupid like pressing charges."

"Pretty sure that ship has sailed," he says. "He sucker punched me in a bar full of people, including the sheriff. I'm pretty sure my dad already got involved."

I sigh. "Cannon…"

"What?" He sounds like a child being scolded.

I level him with a look. "Your drinking is a problem."

His eyes cloud over, and I tense up. I didn't mean to go there. He isn't my responsibility anymore. But I loved him once. Maybe some part of me always will. And I can't just sit back and watch him slowly destroy himself.

Then suddenly, the Cannon Brentwood I remember from high school reappears, as if the man in front of me has time traveled. He smiles that golden-boy grin, and were it not for the sickly pallor and the shiner, he'd look for all the world like he just won the Big Ten tournament.

"It was a Friday night, Grace. I acted like a fool, and I'm sorry. Won't happen again," he says. Then he reaches into the bag and pulls out a plump raspberry white chocolate muffin, the top glittering with the thick sugar crystals Daphne sprinkles on before baking. He takes a bite and grins. "Thanks for the muffins. I don't deserve them, but I appreciate the delivery."

His eyes close, and he focuses on chewing and swallowing, then sips his coffee with a relaxed smile.

"Fine," I sigh. As much as I want to push him, to make him see what he's trying so hard to look away from, I also just want to get out of here. A determined Cannon Brentwood can be a dangerous thing, and it seems he's set his mind to pretending everything is fine, just fine. "But I need to know that whatever happened last night in that hallway was a one-time show. We have to coexist in this town, and you cannot be a dickbag to me. So keep your mouth shut, or I'll start blabbing. Mutually assured destruction."

And then I turn and walk out of Cannon's house, not for the first time, but hopefully for the last. And as I go, I let myself revel in the feeling of him behind me, of the door slamming on this conversation, on him, on my past.

# CHAPTER 7

## DECKER

"Living up to your name there, huh, Deck?"

I glance up from behind the bars.

Of my *cell*.

The problem with knocking out a golden boy in the one bar in a tiny town is that it's pretty likely that the sheriff will be drinking nearby. Like, on the third barstool from the door. And Sheriff Woods, though he's a nice old guy, was more than happy to slap his cuffs on me after all the havoc I wreaked on Cardinal Springs when I was a teenager. I have a feeling this arrest has less to do with knocking Cannon Brentwood out cold on the chipped linoleum of the Half Pint and more to do with the *multiple* times I egged Woods's police cruiser growing up.

Upon bringing me in around ten p.m., Sheriff Woods informed me that he would *not* be waking up a judge to handle this and that I would be spending my first night back in my hometown in the dank embrace of the Cardinal Springs Jail.

It was among the worst nights of sleep of my life. Partially because I kept replaying the vile shit Cannon said to Grace and the wounded look on her face when he said it. And partially because as soon as a judge woke up in the morning, I knew I was likely going to find myself in exactly the kind of shit I had been warned to stay out of.

I lasted less than twenty-four hours.

What a fucking achiever I am.

"Tell me that prick isn't pressing charges," I say, pressing my palms to my eyeballs.

Sheriff Woods raises his eyebrows, as if to say, *Are you fucking kidding me?* "Mr. Brentwood was knocked unconscious. And though I dare say that may have had something to do with drinking damn near a whole bottle of bourbon, your fist certainly didn't help. Luckily, he doesn't appear to have any broken bones or other injuries beyond his pride. Unfortunately for you, the Brentwoods take their pride pretty seriously."

*God. Fucking. Damn it.*

I let out a long groan and flop back onto the paper-thin mattress that covers the metal cot in the cell. My back screams at me for my dramatics, but my back can get in line. There's going to be an awful lot of screaming aimed my way when the front office gets wind of this. Being charged means calls to my lawyer and my agent and the Grinders press office to tell Brielle that I set a land speed record for fucking up.

"Now, it's not as bad as all that," Sheriff Woods says, leaning back onto his desk. He shines an apple on his uniform shirt and takes a large bite. "I talked to Judge Patel first thing, and you didn't hear this from me, but after the way that Brentwood boy tortured her son all through school, she's more than happy to offer you a sweet deal."

Small towns—maybe not as bad as I thought.

"What's the deal?" I ask.

Sheriff Woods grins. "You perform a hundred and fifty hours of community service for Cardinal Springs, and upon completion, your record will be expunged," he says. "Well, I should say your *new* record. That time you boosted Ralph's cruiser when you were a senior and drove to Sonic for cherry limeades will remain."

"I brought back drinks for everyone, if you'll remember," I grumble.

"Which is why you only got a misdemeanor, you little shit," he says with a laugh.

I sigh. One hundred and fifty hours of community service? I try to do some mental math, but I'm too sleep deprived to even begin doing division. But I have the whole summer, and I'll gladly do twice that if it means the Grinders never have to hear about this. I know my lawyer would have me killed if she knew I was contemplating making a deal without her input, but just the thought of alerting anyone in Chicago to this incident makes my career flash before my eyes.

I'm not ready to be done with hockey yet.

"So, what, I'll be picking up trash on the side of the highway?" I say.

"Actually, I have an assignment for you."

Ms. Suzanne appears in the doorway, a grease-spotted brown paper bag and a to-go coffee cup in her hands. I bolt upright on the cot, feet on the floor, posture ramrod straight.

"Decker, I'm disappointed in you," she says, and my heart immediately sinks to my feet. But despite her best effort to level me with a stern look, I don't miss the way the corner of her mouth is twitching with a barely repressed smile. "If you were going to get arrested, you could at least have broken that kid's nose."

Sheriff Woods pulls the keys from his belt and ambles over—taking his sweet time, I notice—to unlock the cell. As soon as the door swings open with a horrible screech, I'm up and out. Ms. Suzanne hands me the coffee and the bag.

"One of Daphne's muffins. She did raspberry white chocolate this morning. One of the perks of being woken in jail is that the muffins are still warm from the oven," she says.

I open the bag and take a long inhale of the buttery, sugary goodness. During the season, I stick pretty closely to a training diet that involves a metric ton of lean protein and vegetables, prepped by a humorless personal chef who works for half a dozen members of the team, and a shit ton of good carbs right before games, but during the summer I'm able to relax more. And I forgot about Daphne Holland's muffins, made fresh every morning at her bakery, Crimson 'n' Cream.

I pinch a chunk off the crispy muffin top and pop it into my mouth, not even bothering to suppress a groan from the warm burst of flavor.

"So, what's the assignment?" I ask.

"Don't talk with your mouth full," Ms. Suzanne replies. She smiles at Sheriff Woods and turns toward the door. She pulls it open, then calls over her shoulder, "Just meet me at the library Monday morning. Nine a.m."

# CHAPTER 8

GRACE

"Grace. Hey, Grace!"

I'm two blocks from my apartment when I hear Decker call my name. My shoulders slump, and I feel the beginning of a tension headache at the base of my skull. I half hoped that after the disaster in the bar, he went slinking back to Chicago, but no. There's no shame on his face as he jogs toward me in the same clothes he wore last night.

How does he do that? I had to do an hour of yoga and a twenty-minute meditation to be able to walk out of my apartment after the embarrassment of last night. The fact that he heard what Cannon said about me makes me want to melt directly into the ground.

I think about making a run for it. My apartment is close—I could disappear behind the door and ignore him completely. I've already dealt with one boneheaded asshole this morning. Surely that's enough.

"Grace, wait up."

I pause on the sidewalk. Literally running away from him would only add to my humiliation, so I guess it's time to face the music.

"Fresh from jail?" I ask him when he stops in front of me, his tall frame blocking out the morning sun. At five foot ten, I was always the tallest girl in my class; half the boys had to look up to make eye contact with me. I hate that I like the way Decker makes me feel small, almost dainty. I also hate that in an effort not to look him in the eyes, I wind up staring directly at his chest, a view that definitely does not suck. That too-tight T-shirt hugs his pecs like it was sewn directly onto his body.

"I wouldn't say fresh," he says with a wry grin. "That cell must not get used much. The mattress smelled like something out of my grandma's attic."

"Sheriff Woods only keeps that cell for when you roll through town, Decker. It's either that or lock you up in his backyard kennel."

"He still have that pair of Bernese Mountain Dogs?" he asks with a grin. "Mother and Fucker?"

"Max and Fletcher," I snap. The wider he grins, the more my teeth grind. "Different pair now, but yes."

"Hell, I'd love to snuggle with those guys for a night. Much warmer than the steel cot."

I roll my eyes. "Yes, well, forgive the sheriff for not considering your comfort during your stay in *jail*."

At that, he has the good sense to look sheepish. "Yeah. I wanted to talk to you about that. Are you—"

I hold up my hand to silence him, and like the good boy he definitely isn't, he snaps his mouth shut.

"I don't want to talk about it, Decker. I just want your assurance that it'll never happen again."

"But—"

I narrow my eyes at him. "*No*, Decker. You already stuck your nose—or your fist, rather—where it doesn't belong. Please just leave it."

I can tell he doesn't want to drop it. I can tell he has questions, opinions, advice, all of which I'm already getting via texts from my brothers. I do not need it from him, too.

"I talked to Cannon this morning, and he's not going to make trouble," I continue before he can say anything else. "It was just a drunken mistake."

Decker's brow furrows. "You went to see him? Grace, after last night, that seems really stu—"

"Hey! The only one who resorted to violence last night was *you*, buddy, but you don't see me getting skittish with you."

His eyes grow wide. "I was defending you!"

"I have four overprotective older brothers, Decker. I don't need a fifth. I can handle my own shit."

He looks skeptical. "Can you? Because that asshole seemed entirely too comfortable talking to you like that. Like he's done it before. And I'm damn sure your brothers don't know about that, because if they did, he'd be six feet under by now." He cocks an eyebrow at me, and I look away. Still, I'm pretty sure he can read the truth on my face. His expression softens. "Damn, Grace. You don't deserve that."

Oh god, pity is worse than advice. Now I'm well and truly done. "I know that, Decker. That's why he's not my boyfriend anymore. I handled it." I snap my fingers in his face. "Keep up."

"It didn't seem handled." He reaches out like he's going to lay a hand on my shoulder, but I shrug him off.

"Back off, Decker. I'm telling you I don't need help, especially from some overgrown teenager who can't keep his dick in his pants or his hands to himself."

He blinks at me, jerking back slightly, like I've slapped him.

"Anyway, I went to see Cannon to make sure he wasn't going to press charges, but he said that ship had sailed."

"Yeah. Well, that's handled," he says. He shifts nervously, clearly uncomfortable.

Of course he probably made the whole thing go away with one phone call to his team. Professional athletes have high-powered lawyers and the might of global sports franchises behind them. I guess it was pretty ridiculous to think I needed to stick my nose in to help him. He can get himself out of trouble now, just like he always has.

"Which did you use to save you ass this time?" I scoff. "Your dick or your money?" He looks genuinely wounded, but I decide I don't care. "Whatever, let's just forget all of it, okay? I'll stay out of your business, and you stay out of mine, and everything will be hunky-dory."

He snorts, whatever discomfort he felt about his arrest melting away. "Hunky-dory, eh?"

I shake my head. God, how does he always manage to bounce back so quickly? To pivot directly to joking, to teasing, to that smooth, smug smirk? I know he's a disaster, so how does Decker Brooks always seem to have his shit together?

Or maybe he just doesn't actually care about anything. That would certainly make it easy to let everything roll off your back.

"Whatever, this conversation is over. I'm going home before too many more people spot us talking and the rumor mill starts spewing flames."

Without waiting for another word from him, I pivot and start walking. I can immediately tell he's right behind me. His heavy footfalls on the pavement rumble through my belly in a way that I do not appreciate.

I shoot him a stern look over my shoulder. "Why are you following me? Stop following me."

He rolls his eyes. "I'm not following you. We're just walking the same direction."

"Where are *you* going?" As far as I know, his parents still live in the Gothic stone mansion on Burrow Road, out by the lake. Unless he's staying with Archer, who lives six blocks in the opposite direction on Nokomis Avenue, at the far edge of downtown.

"There." He points at the pink door between Daphne's bakery and the engraving shop that does all the Little League trophies. The door that leads up to my apartment.

I whirl around to face him. "Excuse me?"

"I'm here for the whole summer, so I decided not to burden Archer and got my own place. I rented an apartment above Crimson 'n' Cream."

My stomach does some very intricate choreography as the reality of his words sink in. Because *my* apartment is through that pink door and up the narrow steps. And so is another apartment directly across the hall. Mine is above the engraving shop, and the other apartment—empty, as far as I know—is above Crimson 'n' Cream.

Which means Decker Brooks is my new neighbor.

# CHAPTER 9

## DECKER

On Sunday morning, I wake up feeling like I've been thrown from a rooftop and hit every awning on the way down, probably due to the air mattress I borrowed from Archer. And the night I spent in a fucking cell.

"Dude, you can just sleep here until you get a bed," Archer had said as he'd handed the box to me on Saturday. Thanks to my time in the Cardinal Springs Jail, I hadn't actually spent a single night with him.

"Yeah, I know. But I just want to get settled in my own space," I'd said. But that impulsive decision—like most of my impulsive decisions—bit me squarely in the ass when it turned out the air mattress was about four inches too short for my six-foot-two frame and had a slow leak to boot.

Waking up with my ass on the cold floor means I spend Sunday hunting down necessities for my completely empty apartment and trying to work the crick out of my neck. God, I miss my massage therapist. The Grinders team trainers would kick my ass if they knew how I was treating my body. A night on an air mattress was fine when I was in my twenties, but at the ripe old age of thirty-three (and with every joint feeling rickety thanks to over twenty-five years of hockey), turns out that shit can ruin me.

It takes some heavily greased palms and an hour-long drive to Bloomington to hit the Target, but by Sunday night, my apartment has a California king mattress and box spring (flat on the floor, but bed frames are overrated), bedding, two sets of towels, some plates, cups, and silverware, and one pot with a lid. I figure that'll keep me going for a bit, or at least keep me from waking up with my spine in knots.

And the whole time, I can't stop thinking about the fact that just across the hall, Grace McBride is doing lord knows what in her cherry panties.

The only thing that distracts me is my least favorite activity—googling myself. But it's a necessary evil. Anybody with an iPhone and a TikTok account could rat me out to the world. So I scroll through social media and gossip sites, just to be sure my bar fight is still a secret. But all I find is evidence of what an absolute fuckup I am.

*…brain-dead penalty…*

*…dirty hits mask lazy play…*

*…vicious fights are just symptoms of hockey's toxic masculinity…*

*…time for the Grinders to dump Decker…*

Every once in a while, the image of Grace McBride's cherry panties muscles through the muck, and I click to distract myself, the whole miserable cycle starting again. This summer of keeping my head down and my dick in my pants is already getting to me. That's the only explanation for my wandering thoughts.

On Monday morning, I stand on the stoop of the stone Tudor mansion I grew up in, set back from the road and surrounded by a copse of trees. I'm sure most people would just throw open the doors to their childhood homes, walk in, and call out greetings. A good number of those people could probably expect enthusiastic replies.

As for me, I reach out and press the brass button, listening as the symphonic doorbell chimes throughout the house.

Of all the people I've disappointed in my life, my parents are at the very tippy-top of the list.

My mom answers the door in a pressed gray pantsuit, her head cocked to the side as if wondering if this is a prank. I guess a surprise visit at my age is a bit of a joke. She gives me a prim smile.

"Decker, welcome," she says, opening the door so I can step inside. "Here for a visit?"

"Yeah, for the summer, actually," I say. I probably should have called to tell them my plans, but I'd settled for a quick text this morning to see if they were available for breakfast. I received a simple yes. That was it—no questions, no excitement, not even any punctuation or instructions for when I should drop by. My parents eat breakfast promptly at seven thirty every morning before they head off to work. Even on the weekend, it's seven thirty, then off to the golf course or to church.

It's possible there was a mistake at the hospital and their law-abiding, academically gifted child is two counties over, wondering why his sports nut parents won't stop yelling at the television.

My mom just nods, asking no follow-up questions, and gestures for me to come with her. The house is exactly as I remember it, dark and cold and quiet. My parents are hushed-voices people; I don't think I've ever heard them yell. My earliest childhood memories are of them imploring me to use my "indoor voice."

I still don't have one.

I follow my mom through the living room, down the hall past the kitchen, and onto the glass sun porch they call the solarium, where my father is already at the breakfast table with dry wheat toast and a poached egg, his coffee black and steaming in the Princeton mug he uses every morning.

"Decker, good to see you," he says with all the warmth of a practice rink.

My parents have never understood hockey, but they tolerated it. They signed me up on the advice of a child psychologist who told them some physical activity might help with all my excess energy. I kept my grades up solely because it meant I got ice time, and that was good enough for them. And when I went off to college, they could pretend it was because I had a bright academic future and not because I was really fucking good at checking bodies into the boards.

But when I left Minnesota after my freshman year to enter the draft, my parents were horrified. The thought of their son being a college dropout, even if it was to join a top-tier NHL team where I'd see playing time in my first season, was enough to shut them down for good. I stopped coming home to listen to them ask me when I was going to finish my degree.

We aren't estranged by any means. Our relationship is just… strange. My parents usually make it up to one home game per season. I always put them up in a box, away from the circus of the crowd, and they still meet me after every game looking seven shades of horrified. The brutality, the intensity, the fans—they don't understand any of it, and by extension, they don't understand me.

I do make an effort to try and understand them. My mother is the chair of the economics department at Indiana University, and my father is the dean of the law school. My mother went to Harvard and Princeton, my dad went to Yale and Princeton. They're academics through and through. The fact that their son turned out to be a jock with ADHD who got accepted to a state school only because of an athletic scholarship is deeply confusing to them.

"Hi, Dad," I say, taking the empty seat. I don't bother trying to quiet my booming voice, which bounces off the glass. They'll be annoyed with me either way, and after so long, their judgment feels like a family tradition. "How's shakes?"

My father, with his perfectly combed and gelled hair, already in his suit for Monday meetings, blinks at me over his coffee mug.

"Things are good," he finally says. "I'm teaching patent law again this semester, which is always a fun one." His tone betrays absolutely none of that fun. And I'm not 100 percent certain I know what a patent *is*, so I don't have any follow-up questions.

"That sounds great," I reply. I take a bite of dry toast and swallow hard, smiling as my mother pours me a cup of black coffee. I wait, even though I know no questions about *my* job are coming.

"Decker says he's here for the whole summer," she says.

"Oh? Do you not have…practice?" Dad asks, his eyebrows lifted.

"Summer's the offseason. Training camp starts in September," I remind them. I've been playing professional hockey for a decade, but they still don't know when the official season is. This is how it always goes. I'm too loud; they make ham-fisted attempts to talk about hockey; I get annoyed and ratchet up the snark; they grow terse. The vicious cycle spins on.

"Given any thought to what you're going to do next?" Dad asks.

I tense, my hip flexor and bum shoulder yelling at me. This chair is uncomfortable as fuck, as is this conversation.

"Indiana has an excellent kinesiology program," Mom says.

It takes actual effort to relax my jaw.

"Good money in that," Dad says. "I remember how much we paid that conditioning coach when you were in high school."

"Not as much as the NHL pays me," I reply, staring angrily down at my toast.

"You're putting money aside, right?" my mom asks. "Conservative investments for retirement and medical care? You're in a high-risk profession; I imagine you'll be paying for it in doctor visits for the rest of your life. You know, Dr. Sebastian in my department is doing some really interesting research right now on the financial outlook for professional athletes. I believe he's focusing on football players, but really, how different can it be? It's truly shocking how fast that money disappears."

She's ostensibly talking to me, but the only people interested in this conversation are her and Dad.

"Make sure you have your lawyer keep tabs on your accountant and financial planner," Dad adds. "Some of those folks can get predatory when that kind of money is on the line. They start skimming, moving money around, making risky investments or skipping tax payments."

I drop my toast on my plate and lean back in this accursed chair. "I put most of my money in Bitcoin, but I do set aside fifteen percent for lottery scratchers, so I'm feeling good about my retirement," I say, holding up my crossed fingers.

Across the table, my parents freeze, their brows furrowed. It takes them a minute to realize I haven't actually dumped all my millions into cryptocurrency and lottery tickets. That's genuinely what they think of me.

"It's all fun and games until you're broke and in court, Decker," Dad says.

"I'm good, Dad," I tell him, though I think he only barely believes me.

Silence descends upon the table, save for the clinking of silver on the good china. I want to fold in on myself until I no longer exist at this table, having the exact same conversation I've been having for more than ten years. Every single time I see them, it comes back to this. I've tried to explain that talking about the end of my hockey career is bad luck and that it makes me deeply uncomfortable. But my ever-practical parents cannot fathom this. They want to know what's going to happen when hockey is over, if I'm going to go back to school, how I'm going to support myself.

I have one year left in an eight-year thirty-five-million-dollar contract, and assuming I don't fuck up too bad over the next year, I could be looking at a decent (though much shorter) extension. Knowing that the average professional hockey career ends around age thirty, I've tried to be smart with my money, which meant hiring someone much smarter than me to manage it. Whenever hockey ends for me—and I hope that won't be soon—I'll be more than okay financially.

Emotionally? That's another story.

What will I do with all the pent-up energy I've been able to let out over a dozen years of professional play, to say nothing of the ten additional years in peewee, high school, and my brief stint in college? What will I do without the structure of training and practice and games that's held up my entire adult life? What will I do without the roar of the crowd, the thrill of victory? Without those long, hard games that go into multiple overtimes, my body stretched to its limit, nerves jangling like a can full of pennies? Hockey is my whole fucking life, even though the press likes to act as if it's the off-ice shit that matters. The ice, my skates, my stick on a puck, a body flying into the boards—that's who I am in my bones, and I have the cracks and scars to prove it.

It would be great to talk this out with my dad, to have my mom reassure me. I'd be happy to have *those* conversations with my parents, but they're not interested. To them, hockey is just a game. What I do is no different from joining a pickup basketball league and quitting when you tweak your knee. They'll be thrilled when hockey ends, because it'll mean I might take one of the acceptable paths they imagine for me.

So here I am, stuck at this overly formal dining table, picking at a poached egg I don't even want while my parents act like my multimillion-dollar professional hockey career is akin to ditching college to follow Phish around in a van.

And I do what I always do; I make a joke. I make *myself* the joke.

But no one at this table is laughing.

# CHAPTER 10

## GRACE

wo weeks ago, Suzanne gave me a stack of printed pages with a sticky note on top that read in her slanted cursive, "Look what those bastards have done now."

It was a copy of the newest state budget, and right there in black and white was the reality that our already meager library funding from the state was about to be cut in half. That will definitely mean fewer hours, probably none at all on the weekends. There will be fewer new books, no programming, and a major staff culling. It means I'll lose my job for sure, and while that sucks on a personal level, it also means that Cardinal Springs will have no one dedicated to youth services anymore. No one running story times or teen board meetings, no one keeping track of new picture book releases or YA series. Suzanne will do her best with the remaining part-time staff, but she'll basically have an entire library to run on her own, and although the woman is superhuman, even *she* can only do so much. So the children's department will become a dusty ghost town, and that will really hurt Cardinal Springs.

Suzanne, of course, knew I wasn't going to look at those pages and lose hope. She's the one who trained me, after all, when I was wasting away behind the counter of Dad's hardware store, sorting nails and doing inventory and wondering when my life would begin. She's the one who offered me a part-time job at the circulation desk, which grew until I was in charge of the entire children's department, including collections and programming. I still have to empty the book return and pick weird objects out of books—tissues, napkins, slices of cheese, and once, a thong. But the less savory parts of my job are balanced out by baby story hour, craft time, and helping kids find their new favorite books. I just wish I weren't doing all that for minimum wage.

Which is why Suzanne keeps slipping brochures for the American Booksellers Association into my mailbox.

I do want to leave the Cardinal Springs Library eventually, but I don't want it burning behind me when I go. So am I going to let it get decimated by something as little as a state budget cut?

Absolutely the fuck not.

After Suzanne left me that packet, I spent a week marching around angrily, and then I spent a week brainstorming and researching. And today, even though my surprise new neighbor did his best to derail me this weekend, I have a plan.

I glance around the table at the people I've gathered to help me. Suzanne is here, of course, her eyes twinkling with the excitement of having a secret—I've already filled her in. Carson, now on summer break, is seated next to me, because there's nothing I don't tell her about, and she couldn't wait to jump in and help. She knows how much the free programs we offer help her students and their parents.

The rest of the people here are local folks, members of our community board, like Daphne Holland from the bakery and Carlos Alvarez, who manages the credit union. I've also invited Abby Snick, mother of *two* sets of twins, who's been bringing her kiddos to story time since they were born. Having four big-headed babies use her belly as a studio apartment has basically given her superpowers.

"Welcome, everyone. I'm so glad you could join us for what I think is going to be a very exciting project," I say with a smile and a swell of confidence. "Yes, Abby?"

The blond mother in stretchy athleisure lowers her hand. "Sorry, Grace, I just wanted to let you know that I'm going to have to duck out after an hour. Ben has an allergist appointment."

"Not a problem," I say. "We're going to get right to it. So, as I mentioned in my email, we need to figure out a way to keep all our children's programming running even with the state budget cuts."

Carlos mutters something in Spanish that I'm going to have to ask him to repeat after the meeting, because it sounds like a phrase that could come in handy. Daphne lights up, but I charge on before she can say anything.

"This is bigger than a bake sale, unfortunately. I already spoke with Mayor Linden, and while the city can increase our budget a tiny bit, it's not nearly enough to cover the losses." I reach for the stack of papers I brought with me and hand them to Carson, who starts passing them around the table. "My plan is to bring back the Cardinal Springs Book Festival."

"Oh, I used to love that! Such a fun weekend," LaTosha Reynolds says. She owns a spa downtown that Wyatt swears will take five years off your face. "Why did it go away?"

"COVID," several folks mutter in unison.

"That's right. We paused the festival in 2020, and unfortunately it just never made it back onto the calendar. But I think we can resurrect it in an expanded format that will help us raise some good money. We've done it in the past, so there's no need to reinvent the wheel, and because it's an annual event, it can help us cover the shortfall every year."

"I think it's a spectacular idea," Suzanne says.

"Thank you," I reply, warming to the praise. It revs me up, which is good, because this will be a *huge* task. "Now, this year it's going to be a quick turnaround if we want to put it on the week before school starts, as we've done in the past. This year, that would mean the last weekend in July. Normally we'd spend a full year planning something like this, but we're looking at two months. So we'll need as much help as everyone can offer."

"Once the kids start camp, I'll have lots of free time," Abby says.

"I just hired a second aesthetician, so that should free me up a bit," LaTosha adds.

"You have my full support," Carlos says, knocking on the table.

I begin running my volunteers through the plan. I've already reached out to some Midwestern authors to see if anyone is free on such short notice, and fortunately I've gotten good responses. We can start building the festival around the folks who have already said yes and lock down some more as we go along.

I'm just about to dive into the calendar when the conference room door opens with a loud creak and Decker pokes his head in, his hair slipping from behind his ears.

My eyes narrow as he looks around the table, his eyes landing on Suzanne before he asks, "Am I in the right place?" I think he's attempting to lower his voice for the library, but it still booms through the tiny conference room.

I open my mouth to tell him this is a private meeting and that he needs to stop stumbling into my life at every turn when Suzanne flashes a smile and waves him in. He enters, his large frame taking up entirely too much space in the cramped conference room.

"What are you doing here?" I ask, feeling my enthusiasm and professionalism start to flag.

Decker glances at Suzanne again, his eyebrows raised. "Is this where the, uh—community service—"

"*What?*" I bark.

Abby's eyes widen, and I can tell she's psyched to absorb some Cardinal Springs gossip. Luckily, I know the only people she'll tell are her eight- and ten-year-old twins, and they're not very good listeners. Carlos quickly pulls out his phone and snaps a photo, probably for his wife, Inez, a massive Grinders fan, and

Carson looks like she's just turned on the latest episode of *Real Housewives.*

"Yes, dear, you're in the right place." Suzanne smiles again, gesturing to an empty chair at the end of the table—the one opposite mine, meaning his brown eyes are pointed directly at me.

"Suzanne, what's going on?" I ask, trying to keep my voice low. As if that matters when we are all crammed into a tiny windowless conference room. Everyone can hear every word.

Which is why Suzanne addresses the entire room when she replies. "Mr. Brooks will be joining us as part of a community service agreement stemming from..." She pauses, searching for words.

"Because I laid out Cannon Brentwood for shooting his mouth off. This is how I'm going to repay my debt to the fine citizens of Cardinal Springs," Decker says with a slightly sheepish grin. I notice that he leaves me out of his explanation, and I'd be appreciative if I wasn't so irritated.

Abby and LaTosha trade giggles, while Carlos snorts. None of them seems surprised, which sucks, because it means that news of the scene at the Half Pint has spread all over town.

"Frankly, we all owe *you* one for that," Carson says. I kick her under the table.

"Seriously?" My voice is definitely no longer a library-appropriate whisper. I stare daggers at Suzanne, hoping for answers.

"We'll chat after the meeting," she says, then waves her fingers in a *go on* motion. Next to her, Abby checks her phone and mouths the word *allergist.* If I don't get control of this meeting, I'm going to lose them. Literally. My plan leaves very little room for error. And while Decker Brooks sitting across from me at this suddenly-too-small conference table feels like a major error, it's one I definitely don't have time to deal with now.

I have a library to save.

———

When the meeting is over, I wait until the last of my committee members is gone before I let the smile drop from my face. *One* person still hasn't left; he's currently struggling to unfold himself from the narrow chair he's been shifting in for the last hour.

I don't want to say another word to Decker. Fortunately, it looks like it's going to take him ten minutes to extract his large frame from that chair. I stomp out of the room and begin making my way across the information commons. I have books to shelve and story time in half an hour.

But Decker is quicker than I expected.

"Hey, Grace, can I—"

I spin on my heel. "No, you cannot," I snap. "You've only been here for seventy-two hours and I've already had more than enough of you."

He shoves his hands deep in the pockets of his jeans, his shoulders rising like, *Aw, shucks, ma'am, I don't mean no trouble.* I'm not buying it. Decker Brooks *is* trouble. He doesn't even have to try. "But I—"

"Can't you pick up cigarette butts in Henry Park or scrub pots at the synagogue's soup kitchen? What could you *possibly* contribute to a *library*?"

Suzanne appears beside us, her voice a stern whisper. "Why don't we take this to my office, boys and girls?"

Miracle of miracles, Decker snaps his mouth shut and follows Suzanne back behind the circulation desk. Her office is small and mostly taken up by a hulking old tanker desk, the green paint chipped. There's only room for one wooden chair across from her it. Decker steps aside, gesturing for me to sit, but I just glare at him and stand.

"Now, the two of you are going to be working together for the next couple of months, and it would be extremely helpful if you didn't disrupt the library's peace daily." She folds her hands on the desk, her eyes moving between us. "So let's talk this out."

My brain feels like the margarita machine at the Half Pint,

frozen and swirling with thoughts. Things like *I can't work with him* and *He'll ruin everything* and *Can he even read?*

But I know Suzanne well enough to keep those thoughts to myself. Instead, I cross my arms and say, "One hundred and fifty hours? Seriously? There's no way."

"It's totally doable in eight weeks. And as much as you like to pretend you can run every show all by yourself, you're going to need help, Grace," Suzanne says.

I sigh. "Okay, fine, but from *him*?"

"I'm standing right here," he says. The low scrape of his voice sends a chill up my spine that drives me insane. I hate the way my grown-up body reacts to Decker Brooks. It was never like this when he was a loudmouth teenager and I was a gangly kid. There was *nothing* about Decker I found attractive back then, but suddenly my body is acting like it doesn't remember any of that. Not the way he'd muscle me away from the Xbox or sneak Halloween candy from my bucket or convince my brothers that shooting off bottle rockets was a good idea, calling me a tattletale when I worried they'd blow their fingers off. Instead, my body's all like, *Look at that shaggy hair falling over his deep brown eyes* and *Look at those biceps—he could probably bench press you* and *Might feel nice to dig your heels into that round, muscular ass.* God, he looks like a composite of every filthy romance hero I've ever read, and it makes me mad.

My body is a fucking traitor.

I force my eyes skyward, eager to get control of my irritation with Decker. "Yes, Lurch, we can all see you. The office isn't that big, but *you* certainly are."

"I'm choosing to take that as a compliment."

I refuse to look at him, but I can practically hear his grin.

"It's not one," I snap. I hate the way he brings out my inner thirteen-year-old.

Decker throws up his hands, and I have to duck to avoid getting whapped by one of his enormous mitts. "Look, I know this isn't what you planned, but I promise I'm not going to be any trouble. I'm trying my best to stay *out* of trouble this summer."

"Yes, and that's worked out so well for you thus far," I mutter.

"But now I'm occupied," he says, like he's proud of himself for getting assigned court-mandated community service. "Before, it was idle hands and all that."

Now I do look over at him. I can't believe this man is a professional athlete and a millionaire. "What are you, a toddler?"

"Boys and girls!" Suzanne says with that imperious voice she reserves for…well, actual toddlers. It can usually make a small herd of three-year-olds snap to, and it also makes Decker and me both shut our mouths immediately.

Suzanne turns to me. "Grace, I understand that this wasn't part of your plan and that Decker may not be your first choice for a teammate." I scoff, but one arched eyebrow from her has me standing up straighter. "But you need to suck it up, cupcake. Decker is here to help, and he will, *won't he*?" And with that, she turns her stern eye on Decker, who takes the warning like it's being delivered by his coach or his lawyer. He nods and mutters a quiet, "Yes, ma'am."

Pleased, Suzanne gives us a quick nod. "Now, my suggestion, Grace, is to use Decker as your manual labor to do all the grunt work for the festival. He can run errands and make copies, and as we get closer, he'll be quite useful when it comes to setup and teardown." I feel a minor victory when I don't take the opportunity to glance at his biceps. "But in order to fulfill his community service requirement, he'll also need to do things around the library—shelving, maybe some minor maintenance. So keep that in mind. He'll report his hours to you, and you'll sign off on them as his supervisor. I'd like you to give him an honest chance, here. If it doesn't work out, it doesn't work out, and I'm sure the sheriff can find something else for him to do. But I really think this is a good idea and will work well for everyone."

*His supervisor?* God, now I'm basically his babysitter, but I manage to keep my complaints to myself. I can tell from the set of

Suzanne's shoulders that she's done with back talk. And seeing as how she's *my* supervisor, I'm not inclined to give her much lip.

Suzanne glances back and forth between the two of us. "Are we good? Do we have an understanding?"

"Yes, ma'am," Decker says.

"Heard," I add.

"Good," she says, glancing down at her watch. "Now, if you'll excuse me, I need to go. Mrs. Waters is coming to meet with me so that I can reassure her that the books her daughter is checking out are, in fact, 'appropriate.'" She gives the tiniest eye roll, and then she disappears, leaving me alone with Decker.

He opens his mouth, but I'm not in the mood, so I cut him off. "I don't trust you, but I trust Suzanne. So be here tomorrow morning at eight. I'll put you to work."

And then I march out to find a fountain soda the size of my head to alleviate the stress headache that always seems to come along with Decker Brooks.

# CHAPTER 11
## DECKER

The McBride family home is a low brick rancher that, while old, is also neat as a pin. The grass is always perfectly cut with geometric lawnmower lines—Archer, Dan, Owen, and Felix used to trade off doing it. There's a row of bright pansies atop fresh, earthy mulch in the front garden bed. The mailbox has been newly painted a glossy black to match the front door, which has a shiny brass knocker. You could probably fit four or five of this house in the one I grew up in, but it has always contained far more love and excitement than mine ever did.

I lift the knocker and bang it once, twice, eliciting a cacophony of barking from behind the door. When it flies open, Grace is standing there, holding the collar of a black dog who is desperately running in place, trying to escape her grasp. When she looks up and sees me standing on the stoop, her eyes go wide, then narrow, and she lets go of the collar. The dog leaps up on me, bouncing on his hind legs as he attempts to lick the scruff off my face.

"Who's this?" I ask, grabbing him around the middle and tugging him up into my arms. I fucking love dogs, and the only benefit of eventually retiring from hockey will be that I'll finally be able to get one. My parents always refused, saying a dog would make the house smell and ruin the original wood floors, and now that I play more than forty road games a season, there's no way I could have one. But someday, I look forward to letting a giant fuzzy mutt sleep at the foot of my bed.

"That's Puck," Grace says.

I set him down, and he starts licking my sneakers. "I think he likes me."

"He's a terrible judge of character," she says, mouthing *traitor* at the pup. "Sic 'em, killer."

Puck drops onto his haunches, his tongue lolling out while his tail pounds a happy rhythm on the wood floor.

"Well trained, too," I say. I reach down and rub the scruff behind his ears. "Puck, huh? You a hockey fan?"

"Puck as in Shakespeare," she says. "*A Midsummer Night's Dream?*"

I shrug even though I get the reference, because I like how the dumb jock thing exasperates her. I shouldn't enjoy teasing her so much, but I revel in the enormous eye roll she gives me. "What are you doing here?" she asks.

"I'm here for dinner. Archer invited me."

She only barely manages to swallow her annoyed growl. "I didn't know you were coming. Not sure I made enough."

I raise an eyebrow. "You cook?"

"There'll be plenty, Gracie," Archer says, appearing at her side. He hip checks her, making her let out another exasperated growl, then pulls the door open to welcome me in. "You're in luck. Grace made meatloaf. You're just in time."

The house is exactly how I remember it: modest and cramped and as welcoming as a warm hug. It does smell markedly less like body odor than it did when I hung out here regularly, now that all four McBride boys have moved out. Felix, Owen, and Archer are all here in Cardinal Springs, of course, but last I heard, Dan was in New York doing something with investment banking. Whatever it is, it takes up a lot of time and makes him a lot of money. He rarely makes it back to Indiana.

We pass through the living room, where the walls are covered with framed photos, nearly all of them candid snaps of kids making wild faces or darting half out of the frame. My parents only ever hung the annual posed family portraits my mother scheduled with professional photographers, usually on our Christmas vacations to either somewhere with snow or some-where with a beach (or the year we went to the Cape, both).

Pictures of Mrs. McBride, who died when Archer was in third grade, are everywhere. Her in her off-the-shoulder wedding dress in the late eighties, then holding baby Archer, then holding baby Dan a year later, then baby Owen and baby Felix a year after that. My heart squeezes at the photo of baby Grace, snug in just her father's arms, the four little McBride boys squeezed in, peering down at their new sister. Grace is the only one who never got a picture with her mother.

I remember going to the funeral with my parents. Mr. McBride looked ashen and rumpled, the four boys sitting beside him in their suits and ties. Gracie, just days old, was still in the hospital and would be for several months as she fought to grow big enough and strong enough to come home to her family. She'd arrived too many weeks early, and there'd been complications that had taken Mrs. McBride less than an hour after Grace had been born. I remember wanting to go sit by Archer, to put my arm around him and shield him so he could cry without anyone seeing. I didn't really understand death, but I understood how badly my best friend was hurting. But my mother had tugged on my collar and told me that wasn't "appropriate." So I remained sandwiched between my parents, my eyes itching with tears I tried so hard to hold back.

I clear my throat to remove the lump brought on by those memories and follow Archer and the delicious smells of food through the small living room and into the dining room, which barely fits the McBride family dinner table. Sliding glass doors at one end open onto the deck, and I remember times when there were so many guests here that they had to throw open the doors and put two card tables at the end of the dining table, one inside and one just over the threshold.

But today it's just Felix and Owen sitting at the table with Mr. McBride. Archer takes the seat he's been sitting in since childhood, leaving me the empty one beside Grace. She stiffens when I sit.

"Decker! Great to have you back," Mr. McBride says. He reaches for the bowl of mashed potatoes and passes it to me. I can feel Grace's eyes on me, judging how much I'm taking, even though there's so much food on this table I'm surprised it doesn't creak under the weight. "Congrats on the season."

"You mean the part where he biffed it on a breakaway and then got ejected for taking a cheap shot at Perrault?" Felix asks as he shovels roasted carrots onto his plate.

"Well, maybe not so much that last bit, but on the whole, you had a strong season. Thirty goals and eighty-three assists. One hundred and thirteen points is pretty good for an old guy." He winks as he says it, but I'm still stuck on the fact that he knows my stats, can rattle them off like that. I'm not entirely sure my dad knows what an assist even is, but Mr. Bride has always been this way. He was on the sidelines of every peewee and high school game, carting us to tournaments and cheering louder than anyone else in the stands, even when we were little and he had to strap Grace to his chest in a carrier, changing diapers at intermissions and giving her bottles in the stands. It almost made up for the fact that my parents could never be bothered to show up to my games.

"How's the shoulder holding up?" Archer asks.

I give it a roll almost as a reflex, sending Grace ducking out of the way of my elbow. "Holding up. Had that one dislocation in the preseason, but I've been on top of PT for it, so it hasn't really been a problem." Not entirely true. By the end of the playoffs, it felt like someone was trying to rip my arm off and beat me with it.

But if you're not limping to the final buzzer, you didn't play hard enough.

Of course, it all hurts a lot less when you hoist the cup, so yeah, my shoulder is feeling pretty shitty right now. I give it a gentle rub before reaching for my fork again.

"This meatloaf is really good," I say.

"Thanks," Grace says begrudgingly.

"Is this one of your book club recipes?" Owen asks, looking up from his phone. He's spent half the meal tapping out texts.

"Owen, put the phone down, please?" Mr. McBride asks.

"Sorry, Dad, I've got a patient with a fever. The mom needs some reassurance," he says, never looking up from his phone. Mr. McBride harrumphs, but Owen just shrugs. "Small-town practice. I'm always on call."

I can tell Mr. McBride is going to poke his son a little more, so I try to redirect.

"Book club?" I look over at Grace, who opens her mouth to answer, but Felix jumps in.

"Yeah, Grace is in this book club where every month they pick a cookbook and everyone makes a recipe." Felix forks an enormous bite of meatloaf into his mouth.

"Big fan of the prep for those meetings," Owen says.

"It's over in Bloomington," Archer adds.

"Really wish you could do your meetings here," Mr. McBride grumbles. "I worry about you doing that drive in the dark."

I can't help but notice that I've gotten information about Grace's book club from everyone but Grace.

"The bookstore sponsors the club, and the bookstore is in Bloomington," she says with a smile. "There's not a bookstore in Cardinal Springs."

"You should start a club through the library. It'll keep you off the roads late at night," Mr. McBride says.

Grace lets out the smallest sigh, so quiet that no one else seems to notice. I probably only catch it because I'm sitting right beside her. But instead of protesting, she picks up the basket of rolls and passes it to Felix, who has just popped the last bite of his into his mouth. He takes one with a smile.

"Speaking of driving, Gracie, when can you bring your car over so I can change your battery?" her dad asks.

Her smile grows thinner. "Dad, we've talked about this. I take it to the dealership."

He points at her with his fork. "They rip you off at the dealership."

"They do all the maintenance, and that keeps the car under warranty."

"Warranties are a scam," Felix says, which causes Grace's jaw to tighten, but her smile doesn't drop. "Hey, also, last time I was over, your toilet wouldn't stop running. I can pick up the parts and fix it for you after work tomorrow. You free?"

"Another day, maybe? Tomorrow I have to drop off all the food pantry donations we collected at the library," she says, and her smile brightens again. "We collected six barrels of canned goods, which is great!"

"I can do that for you," Archer says. "You shouldn't be lifting all those boxes. I'm out for the summer, so I've got free time."

Grace lets another minuscule sigh escape. "Sure, Arch. Come by anytime tomorrow, and I'll show you where they are. Just park your truck by the back door so we can load everything in."

The rest of the meal passes in a blur of teasing and sports talk while Grace quietly passes dishes before anyone can ask for them. I haven't done a dinner like this in years. I've mostly stopped going home for holidays, since my parents always just talk over me or around me, addressing me directly only to express their disappointment that I haven't yet "grown out of hockey." (That particular comment came the Christmas after I won the Stanley Cup for the first time, an achievement my parents saw as the obvious end of my career.) I forgot how good it feels to be surrounded by boisterous conversation and people who understand me. It makes me want to come back to Indiana for Thanksgiving just to sit at *this* table.

The conversation turns to conditioning, and Felix asks me about my lifting and cardio regimen during the offseason.

"I need to join a gym around here, if you've got any recommendations. I don't think my apartment is big enough for a full set of weights," I say, taking a second slice of meatloaf. "And then I can use a bike for cardio. I'm less of a runner these days, with these old knees. A sponsor asked if I wanted to run the Chicago Marathon for charity last year, and as much as I wanted to say yes, there was no way my body could take it."

"The library is actually putting together a team to run the Indianapolis marathon for the children's hospital," Grace says. "We're going to do group runs and bring in some folks to do informational sessions on training and nutrition. Should be a good series of programs. I'm thinking I might sign up to run the half, actually."

Archer's fork pauses at his lips. "A half marathon? Seriously?"

"No. Absolutely not," Mr. McBride says, shaking his head in case anyone missed the vehemence of his words. "That's not a good idea, Gracie."

This time she skips the sigh. "Why not?" she asks, her voice even, but I don't miss the way her grip tightens on her butter knife.

"Have you talked to Dr. Pitrushkin?" her father asks.

"Dr. Pincushion says my heart is fine," she replies, and I snort at the name. No one else laughs, though. And then the sigh comes. "Exercise is good for me."

"But endurance running? That kind of stuff hurts even the healthiest people, right, Owen?" Mr. McBride turns to his son, who pauses, his fork hovering in front of his open mouth.

"Uh, I mean…" Owen's eyes dart over to Gracie, then back to his father. "Just make sure you talk to Dr. Pincu— Dr. Pitrushkin before you start training. He may advise you to wear a heart monitor. He can tell you what to look for, and I'm happy to help."

"You're a pediatrician," Grace mutters under her breath.

"Corianne does Zumba down at the rec center. That might be better for you," Mr. McBride says.

"Yeah, okay. I'll check it out, Dad," Grace says. She pushes her chair back, her shoulder knocking into my arm as she stands and picks up her plate. "I should probably head out. I've got a beast of a day tomorrow training this community service case. He's a real pain in my ass." She glares down at me.

"That's not what you said when I kept you from falling on that ass in the middle of the square," I say, then point my thumb over my shoulder at her as I turn back to the table. "I caught this one upside down in one of those giant stone urns in Henry Park. Would have gone tumbling right onto the pavement if I hadn't been there to catch her. Flashed her ass to the whole park."

The table explodes with the familiar laughter of a family dinner, a camaraderie I never had as an only child. It feels good.

"My Grace never could live up to her name," Mr. McBride says, wheezing.

"Remember that tap recital where her feet went out from under her and her skirt wound up over her head?" Felix says.

"Who could forget when Graceless took the stage?" Archer says with a snort.

"I was *five*," Grace says, that muscle in her jaw working overtime. She turns to me, eyes narrowed. "Thanks, Decker. I *so* appreciate you sharing that little anecdote with the table. Don't be late tomorrow, okay?"

I clear my throat and try to look contrite, but from her narrowed eyes, I can see she's not interested. "I would never, boss," I reply, but she's already halfway to the door before I can finish the sentence.

Fuck. I was just trying to make conversation. I thought gentle teasing was the McBride family love language. Then again, I'm not part of the McBride family, no matter how much I hang around.

# CHAPTER 12



arrive at the library at 7:55, because Coach Haskell always used to say, "Early is on time, on time is late, and late is benched." And while I'm sure Grace would take great pleasure in benching me, I'm not about to give her that satisfaction. It's a quiet morning, the air still cool. As the day goes on, it'll start to feel more like summer, but at the moment it's perfect weather for waiting outside the library, sipping the coffee I picked up from Crimson 'n' Cream on my way here.

Grace strolls up a minute later in a light-blue dress that brings out her eyes, her hair braided over one shoulder. I assume she'll be putting me to work shelving books or performing manual labor, so I'm wearing black joggers and a T-shirt.

"I hope I'm not underdressed," I say, forcing my eyes away from the smooth skin of her bare legs and the leather sandal straps winding around her delicate ankles.

She looks me over, her expression impassive. "Not at all," she replies. "Follow me."

Grace leads me through the library, pointing out the circulation desk, the information commons, the fiction and nonfiction sections. Then she leads me through an arched entryway, and suddenly everything is much, much smaller and much more brightly colored.

"This is the children's section," she says. "And your first task is right back here."

I follow her to the back corner, where a group of parents waits on a set of wooden risers covered in brightly colored carpet squares. They're all holding babies who look like they're too young to chew food. So it's deeply weird when Grace hands me a book called *Doggie Counting* and points to a chair in front of the crowd.

"I'm going to need a few more instructions here," I say, opening the cardboard book.

"Read it. And this one, too," she says, handing me another one called *The Bellybutton Book*. "Out loud. The babies really respond to Sandra Boynton."

I glance at my audience members, half of whom are asleep. The other half are drooling or bucking to escape their parents' arms, and at least two look dangerously near tears.

"I have a hard time believing that," I say.

"Make sure to do voices," she says. "The babies *love* voices. And when you're done with these, you'll lead them in song."

My eyebrows shoot up. "In *what* now?"

"I assume you know 'Wheels on the Bus'? 'Baby Shark'? Don't worry, I printed out the lyrics for you. They're under your chair."

The chair, by the way, is roughly the size of large cereal box and probably meant for someone who is still learning their colors.

I look back at Grace, arching an eyebrow. "This is hazing. You're hazing me."

She grins. "Hey, if you don't think you're up to the task of library community service, I'm sure Sheriff Woods can find you something else," she says.

And then everything clicks. I see exactly what's happening here. Unfortunately for Grace, she's made a gross miscalculation. Because I, Decker Brooks, am a competitive asshole. I *never* back down from a challenge, and I never play a game I don't intend to win. She wants to play with me? I'm in. And I'll give as good as I get.

So I give her my best trademark all-American grin and tuck both books under my arm. With a two-fingered salute. Her smug grin wavers just a bit, just enough to know that already I'm foiling her plan. Then I turn and stroll towards that tiny chair.

———

"Excuse me, dear, can I ask you a question?"

It takes every bit of control I have to suppress a sigh and keep from glancing at my watch to see how many minutes are left in senior hour. It feels like I entered some kind of portal when I walked into the library and now every minute lasts at least forty-five. It's like a Vegas casino—once inside, you completely lose track of space and time. Except here, instead of losing money, you just lose your mind.

After baby story time, during which half my audience screamed like they were being murdered, came toddler story time. Despite what I thought was a very rousing reading of *Chicka Chicka Boom Boom*, most of my audience members spent the whole time sprinting away and being dragged back by their parents.

After that, to my surprise, Grace led me into the computer lab and pointed at the information desk at the front of the space. "Senior hour starts in five minutes. You'll be in here answering technology questions," she said.

"But I don't know anything about computers," I said. "Nothing specialized, anyway."

"Oh, you don't have to worry. The questions won't be particu-larly technical."

I should have known from the quirk of her lips that this wasn't going to be an easy assignment.

Oh, don't get me wrong—the questions haven't been hard. They've been shocking in their simplicity, in fact. During the eter-nity I've been sitting here, I have helped two older ladies download photos of their grandchildren from their email and print them. I have helped a man in a VFW hat retrieve his Facebook password. I have helped a woman named Manuela make a call on her iPhone, a woman named Cheryl make the font bigger on her iPhone, and a man named Jeong turn the flashlight off on his iPhone. And I have helped eleven people save documents as PDFs.

It hasn't been hard, but it has been fucking exhausting.

I smile at the elderly Black woman standing before me, all five foot nothing of her birdlike frame clad in a heavy cardigan even though summer decided to make a surprise appearance in Indiana this morning. It's gotten blazing hot out, and the air conditioning in the old library can barely keep up. The woman's knobby knuckles grip the handle of a pink metallic cane with an enormous silk flower tied to the top. Her puffball of white hair glows against her dark skin

"Yes, ma'am, what can I help you with?" I say.

"Oh, none of that *ma'am* business. My name is Leona Tingle," she says, offering me her free hand. I take it gently in mine, her skin cool and papery.

"Nice to meet you. I'm Decker Brooks," I say.

"Ah, yes, the famous hockey player," she replies with a wide smile that makes me grin in return.

"That's me. What can I help you with?"

"Well, I was hoping to get a book recommendation." I open my mouth to tell her I don't know anything about that, but she charges on. "Grace usually helps me. She knows just what I like, but I can't find her."

"Oh, well, that's not really my area of expertise, but I could…" I glance down at the computer on the information desk. I know how to use Google, and Grace made it very clear that I needed to handle this on my own. And while this isn't *exactly* a game, I still want to win.

"Wonderful. I love a good romance, the spicier the better. I'm old, but I'm not dead, you know? I dabbled in paranormal, but that just didn't do it for me. I have too many questions about how cold those vampires must be, and the Omegaverse is just weird. So I tried motorcycle club romances, and those are just delightful. My husband, Omar, rest his soul, used to ride an old Harley, and those books bring back such good memories." She winks, then tosses her head back for a naughty cackle.

*Wow. Get it, Ms. Tingle.*

"Those led me to my current obsession," she says with a grin. "I'm currently in my why choose era."

I'm not totally sure what that is, but the breadcrumbs leading up to it already have me blushing. "I'm sorry?"

"Why choose. They used to call it reverse harem, but that term is so distasteful, so now we say why choose. It's where the heroine has more than one hero. Often many more, in fact. I recently read one where there were *eight*." She makes a face and shakes her head. "But eight is too many. I think three is probably my max. More than that, and it gets much too unwieldy."

"Sure," I say, trying to keep my mind from conjuring up images of what she might mean. This is definitely not what I expected from senior hour.

"For character development, of course," she says with a wink.

"Of course," I say, letting loose a low chuckle. "And Grace helps you with this? With finding these particular books?"

"Oh yes, she has wonderful recommendations. She's very well read, that girl. She never steers me wrong," she says. "She didn't give me the book with eight men, by the way. That was me going rogue. I should always listen to Grace when it comes to the smut!"

I bark out a laugh just as Grace appears in the doorway of the technology lab, her eyes wide.

"Ms. Tingle!" she says, her voice at the very loudest "library-appropriate" volume. She scurries across the carpet, careening around desktop computers and rolling chairs like she's in a very quiet version of *American Ninja Warrior*. When she skids to a halt between us, she flashes me a wide-eyed smile. "I can take this one!" she says, panting from her near sprint. Her freckles seem darker against her red cheeks, and she adjusts the hem of her dress.

"Oh, hello, Grace, dear. Mr. Brooks here was just about to help me find a new book to read. I was telling him about *Eight Is Never Enough*, but I tell you, it is *more* than enough. I hate to yuck anyone's yum, as the kids say, but no thank you," Ms. Tingle says.

"Ms. Tingle says you have quite a lot of suggestions for, uh, the *yum*," I say, trying not to think too hard about Grace reading so-called smutty books. The joggers I'm wearing are too fitted to let my mind wander in dirty directions.

Grace's cheeks burn a fiery crimson, which detracts from her attempt to look at me with narrow-eyed sternness. "Big kid story time is in five minutes," she says. "You can go ahead and get set up in the children's section."

"Will I be needing a poncho for this one, too?" I ask. A spot on my shirt over my left pec is still damp from where I washed spit-up off of it in the bathroom, and while that experience is one I hope not to repeat, I don't hate the way her eyes skim across my chest, then dart away, the flush spreading to her neck.

"The big kids tend to keep their bodily fluids on the inside," she says. "Just look out for Nimesh Joshi. When he gets going about Minecraft, he can be a bit of a spitter."

# CHAPTER 13

## GRACE

've just finished covering the newest Magic Treehouse book in protective plastic and applying the barcode when my watch dings to remind me it's the end of big kid story time. Well, it's ten minutes until the end of big kid story time; I want to arrive just in time to watch the whole thing go up in flames.

I know hazing Decker is wrong. And trust me, it wasn't easy to give up my favorite part of being a children's librarian—running a whole morning of kids' programs—to my mortal enemy. But I've been Nice Girl Grace for far too long. Nice Girl Grace stayed with Cannon for about two years longer than she should have. I shook myself free of one asshole, and I'm not about to let another walk all over me.

So far, the morning has gone better than I expected. Toddler story time was the best. Judson Carbondale, who just learned the word *poop*, screeched it loud enough to take paint off the walls, and his mother was too busy ogling Decker to try and quiet him down. To say nothing of Isabella Kinicki spitting up on him during baby story time—that was far more than I could have hoped for. I'm definitely going to have to write that little baby a college recommendation. Ms. Tingle threw us an interesting curve ball at the end of senior hour, and I fully expect a string of obnoxious barbs from Decker about reading smut, but I'm sure he can't come up with anything I haven't heard before. And anyway, all the gray-haired folks waving their iPhones at him before that did their job. From the way he walked away from senior hour, I figure he's mere moments from requesting a trash bag and an orange vest.

Or hell, maybe he'll even choose jail. That would be fine with me.

I place the Magic Treehouse book on the new releases table, where it's promptly whisked away by Eleanor Williams, who will have it read and returned by tomorrow, then tiptoe back to the story corner. A couple of years ago, I oversaw a complete renovation of the space. In addition to new paint and a good steam cleaning of the old industrial carpet, I convinced my brother Felix to build us a set of wooden risers covered in carpet squares to give the space the feel of a real theater. The kids love it, and it also gives the parents plenty of space to spread out. Do we sometimes have to stop the toddlers from launching themselves off the third level? Yes. Is it high enough for them to actually hurt themselves? No. Do I love every second I spend back there, capturing the imaginations of kids big and small? Absolutely.

And when someday I finally, hopefully, *maybe* open my own store, I look forward to recreating it all without the tangled web of library bureaucracy that sometimes holds me back. Am I happy to be running this book festival? Yes. Does it annoy me that I'm basically hosting a bake sale to cover my own minimum-wage salary? Also yes. But when I eventually leave, I want my job to be there for someone else who will help make the children's section the wonderland it should be.

The sight of the story corner always brings me a little shiver of excitement, reminding me of all the work I've done and all the big moments that have happened here. But now, just before I turn and behold the bright, bold, colorful space, I feel a cloud of something akin to doom. Because if we can't pull off the book festival in two months, this whole area is going to become a ghost town. Sure,

Suzanne can try to marshal a fleet of volunteers to do story times, but there won't be any continuity to the programs. There will be no one to follow these kids as they grow, to give their parents a rest, to spot areas of need and think of ways to support them before they start school. One of my greatest triumphs of the five years I've spent working at the Cardinal Springs Library was helping to identify Nora Coughlin's dyslexia when she was just four years old. Her mother was able to get her early intervention tutoring here at the library, and now, at seven, she's burning through Dog Man books faster than I can put them on the shelves.

A cheer explodes from around the last bank of shelves that causes me to jolt. When I arrive at the story corner, I see that Decker has dragged over one of the little study tables and has an open bin of Duplos on the floor next to him. He's got a collection of red and blue Legos scattered across the table, and the kids are all gathered around him with rapt attention.

"Okay, these big ones," he says, holding up one red Lego and one blue one, "are the defensive players. Their job is to protect the goal and the goalie." He points to a red rounded Duplo at the end of the table; the corresponding blue one is at the other end. "And how do they do that?"

"By knocking the center and wingers down!" Nimesh Joshi cries, pointing at the small square Duplos that I assume are meant to represent the offensive players. Even from here, I can see some saliva fly out of his mouth.

Decker doesn't flinch, just nods. "That's right. And what else?"

Nora Coughlin, her blond curls in pigtails, a Dog Man book tucked under her arm, raises her little hand. Decker gives her an encouraging nod, and she clears her throat like a tiny professor, sitting up straight in her pink metallic wheelchair that matches the bows in her hair. "Also by using their sticks to pass the puck away to their offense, or by putting themselves in the way of the puck and getting hit."

"That's right," Decker says, his smile wide.

"If you had told me that Decker Brooks, hockey's bad boy, was a child whisperer, I would not have believed you." Nimesh's mom, Aanya, slides up beside me, her eyes on the big man surrounded by tiny bouncing children. He keeps moving the Legos around the table and explaining hockey strategy, and they could not be more into it. "Nimesh has already asked me if I can get him some skates, which is a miracle, because I've never been able to find an activity that could lure that kid away from his laptop."

"Yeah, Decker is…" I don't know how to finish that sentence, because everything I would have said about him up until now certainly doesn't line up with the scene in front of me.

I watch as he gives Amelia Ephron a high five for pointing out which is the left wing and which is the right. Her cheeks flush a deep red, and then she slides one of the metric ton of elastic friendship bracelets off her wrist as passes it to him.

"For me?" he asks, taking the pink-and-blue beaded bracelet.

"I made it for when I went to see the Taylor Swift concert. The movie, I mean. We couldn't get tickets to the real one," she says, her shy voice wavering so he has to bend down and turn an ear to her. "That one's for 'Shake It Off,' which is what my dad yelled at the TV when he watched the Grinders in the playoffs."

Decker lets out a hearty chuckle and slips the bracelet onto his meaty wrist, the elastic straining. "Thanks, Amelia. This is awesome. I'll put it in my locker next season for good luck."

Amelia looks so happy I swear that child could achieve liftoff.

"Will you be back next week, Mr. Decker?" Nimesh asks, quivering with excitement.

And finally, Decker looks up to see me watching the whole scene. He lifts his hand and gives me a little two-fingered wave, shrugging as he cuts his eyes down at his little toy hockey rink.

"I hope you don't mind—I went a little rogue with the program," he says. He lifts a battered old picture book called *Lucy Tries Hockey*. "Nora here helped me find this one with the online card catalog."

The words *card catalog* coming out of Decker's mouth do

something weird and warm to my insides, my lips parting slightly as I exhale. He cocks an eyebrow at me, and I quickly pull myself together. Because this is big kid story time, not Magic Mike library fantasy.

"Please, Miss Grace? Can Decker come back?" Nimesh begs, fully jumping up and down now.

"Please? Please?" The rest of the kids join in the chorus.

"Uh, well, yes, if he's interested," I say, and then bite back a grimace, because as much as I want to haze him, I shouldn't put him on the spot in front of the kids.

"That would be great," Decker says, and he doesn't sound at all like he's trapped or trying to appease them. He seems genuinely enthused to be invited back by this tiny adoring audience. He reaches down and ruffles Nimesh's curly hair. "These little dudes are awesome. Maybe next week I can bring a stick and we can work on our slap shots with some balls."

I open my mouth to shut that plan down—one wall of the story corner is entirely windows looking out onto the meditation garden at the back of the library—but Decker quickly amends, "Foam balls, of course."

"Of course," I reply.

The children let out a cacophony of cheers that are definitely not library appropriate, but before I can make the quiet coyote symbol with my hand, Decker raises his, and the kids immediately hush. "Okay, then, I'll see you all back here same time next week. Hands in." He shoves his meaty mitt into the center of the table, and all the little hands slap down on top of it. "This is the library, so I want a whisper of *story corner* on three, okay?"

All the kids nod, lips zipped, and Decker counts them off. And to my shock, when he hits three, every one of them lets out an enthusiastic whisper of, "Story corner!" Not even Nimesh's voice cracks a decibel.

The kids scatter with their parents, leaving Decker to swipe the Legos back into the box. My eyes linger on the tiny friendship bracelet on his wrist, surrounded by light blond hair and the veins in his muscular forearms. My mouth goes dry, all the moisture in my body heading south. Shit, I cannot keep having this physical reaction to him. And this time it doesn't even come with a side of annoyance, because as much as I hate to admit it, he thoroughly killed it at big kid story time.

Perhaps sensing my eyes on him, Decker glances up at me, his eyebrows raised in question.

"That was…interesting," I say.

A little bit of pink tints his cheeks, and it's…*adorable.*

"Yeah, the book you left me was all about rocks, and I'm sorry, but that shi—*stuff*"—he darts a nervous gaze around to make sure no little ears heard his near swear—"puts me to sleep. I figured I might as well try something closer to my wheelhouse."

"That was a really good move," I say, the compliment tasting weird in my mouth. "The kids were certainly into it."

"I think they were," he replies. He snaps the lid back on the Lego bin, and I watch him press his lips together to try and suppress a grin. And not a smug grin, either. He looks…proud.

And goddammit, I'm a little proud of him, too. It's really freaking weird. I squint at him, but I can barely see a trace of the drunken mess I peeled off the lawn after my brother's wedding or the pesky teen who tortured me. All I see is a grown man riding high on the victory of having captured the attention of a bunch of kids. I know how good that can feel, eliciting enthusiasm from little people. It's my favorite part of the job, and he did it well. It makes me…like him?

No. Not that.

I shake off the feeling and glance at my watch. "Hey, so, it's noon, and you've had a busy morning. How about I sign your community service form and we call it a day, grab some lunch?"

Wait, am I offering Decker Brooks lunch? With *me*? Did he cast some kind of spell on me when he uttered the words *card catalog*?

"That sounds perfect. I'm starving," Decker says. In one swift movement, he hoists the heavy bin of Legos onto his shoulder.

"Let me just put this back in the storage room and hit the restroom. I'll meet you out front in five?"

I'm left nodding silently, watching his broad shoulders carry the bin of Legos that requires me to consciously lift with my knees. Sometimes I settle for just sliding it across the carpet.

———

"Four down, one hundred and forty-six to go," Decker says, then lifts a triple bacon cheeseburger that looks like it's testing the structural integrity of the bun. We're sitting in a booth at Pete's Diner downtown, a short walk from the library. "Probably shouldn't make a habit of doing half days if I'm going to get through all these hours before the season starts."

"How did you end up with community service, anyway?" I ask. I drag a French fry through a river of honey mustard and enjoy the salty-sweet crunch on my tongue.

Decker raises an eyebrow. "Uh, you were there."

I grimace as the memory of Cannon's words and Decker's punch floods my brain. "No, I know," I say, trying to wave off the images. "I just mean, how did your big fancy lawyers not take care of it?"

"I only have one lawyer, and while she's just five feet tall, she *is* fancy as shit, I'll give her that." Decker reaches over and steals a fry off my plate so fast I don't even have time to react. He ordered a side salad and muttered something about balance, but clearly stolen fries don't count. "Anyway, I'm trying to keep the lawyer from knowing about this one."

"Why?" He reaches for another fry, but I'm ready this time, and I slap his hand away. He laughs and pretends to look wounded.

"Because if my lawyer finds out, the team will find out," he says, then takes an enormous bite of burger.

"And?"

He sets the burger back down on his plate and pokes at his

salad with his fork, taking several silent seconds to chew and swallow. Finally, he sighs. "I've got a bit of a reputation," he says.

"Oh, I've heard," I say.

A spark flickers to life in his brown eyes. "Have you?"

"Not something I'd be overly excited about if I were you." I start ticking items off on my fingers. "There's the paparazzi, and the fights, of course, and supposedly two of Taylor Swift's songs are about you? Oh, and you did coke off a stripper's ass in Vegas."

Decker sighs and throws his hands up. "It was salt for a tequila shot, she consented, and I tipped her heartily," he says, swiping several of my crispiest fries. I narrow my eyes at him and tug my plate closer. I haven't had to be this vigilant at a meal since my brothers were teenagers. "Also, I've never met Taylor Swift—we just happened to be in the same place at the same time on three separate occasions, and her fans like to read tea leaves or whatever. But yes, you've got the gist. Anyway, the press office was already getting a little tired of my antics, and then when said antics spilled over into gameplay, Coach was none too pleased."

"You mean the Game Seven fight?" I ask.

His face clouds, and for a minute, I think he's going to shut down this conversation. Instead, he stares down at his plate and says, "There was this woman—"

"Imani Menendez," I supply, because let's not pretend that one of the world's biggest supermodels is just *some woman*. She's a six-foot-tall willowy goddess who spends her spare time and money advocating for domestic violence victims and lobbying Congress about gerrymandering. She recently enrolled in a master's program at Harvard to study public policy. She deserves some fucking respect on her name.

"Okay, People Magazine—yes, Imani Menendez. She likes hockey players, apparently, and unbeknownst to me, there may have been a smidge of overlap between Elias Perrault and me. He's had it out for me ever since I stripped the puck off him and scored in overtime two seasons ago." Decker laughs, relishing the memory. "He said some shit right from the jump, and I tried to ignore it, but he kept chirping, and next thing I knew, I was throwing off the gloves and he was playing possum. I got ejected."

"What did he say?"

Decker glances around the diner before leveling me with a thunderous glare. "Shit about her that I will never repeat," he says. "Just the fact that those words live in my brain makes me want to end his career."

The righteous anger in his voice makes me nudge my plate in his direction. The man defended the honor of Imani Menendez. He deserves a French fry, which he takes and chews as if he's wishing he were pulverizing Elias Perrault's bones instead.

"As for your original question, I'm under strict orders to be a good boy this summer if I want my hockey career to continue."

"And do you?"

He pauses, a fry at his lips. "What?"

"Want your hockey career to continue."

"Yes," he says, the vehemence practically blowing my hair back.

"Well, it's good that you punched a guy on your first night in town, then."

Decker raises an eyebrow. "The irony has not escaped me."

Our waitress swings by to refill our water glasses and drops another plate of fries on the table with a wink at me.

"Thanks, Delilah," I say, pushing the plate toward him. "Enjoy. It's the offseason."

"I usually try to eat better in the offseason because I'm not burning a metric ton of calories playing fifty million hours of hockey," he says, but he places one of his long, strong fingers on the rim of the plate and pulls it toward him. "Anyway, I promise not to be a pain in the ass this summer."

"Don't make promises you can't keep," I say. "But credit where credit's due—you did pretty great with big kid story time."

A touch of pink floods Decker's cheeks. "I did rock that one, didn't I? I can't say the rest of the morning went all that well, but at least I ended on a high note."

"You did," I say. He bites the corner of his full lower lip to suppress a smile, and I have to swallow hard to push past whatever weird feelings that causes inside my body. "You won't have to do all that shit normally. I was actually sort of, well…"

"You were hazing me," he says.

I nod.

"Hoping I'd quit and beg for highway cleanup?"

"Or jail," I say.

Decker laughs. "Fair enough. I probably deserved it. But I really will do whatever you need me to do, even if it's reading to a bunch of tiny humans who probably can't even see colors yet."

"Hey, I like baby story time! Although the babies don't usually have such a violent reaction to the sound of my voice." My eyes drop down to the stain on his T-shirt from where Isabella spit up with the force of a fire hose as soon as Decker started reading. Unfortunately, the stain only serves to highlight the sharp curve of his pecs. My god, the man looks like he's carved out of marble.

I quickly turn my gaze back to his and find that he's smirking, having caught me ogling. *Goddammit.* I'm barely okay with acknowledging to *myself* that I was ogling Decker; I certainly don't want *him* to know about it. "Don't worry, you don't have to do that again. I will, however, let you keep big kid story time if that's something you're interested in. We could count your prep as part of your community service hours, too."

"Really? Yeah, I think I'd like that," he says, smiling as he tucks back into his burger. "But senior technology hour is all you."

I smile into my grilled cheese. "Fair enough."

And then a piece of French fry bounces off my nose. Decker waggles his eyebrows at me. "Don't think I've forgotten about your smut recommendations, though," he says. "I'm going to need some of those."

"Please let us never speak of that again," I say, my cheeks warming.

"I do not agree. Ms. Tingle says you've got the good stuff, and I want in."

"Talk to me in fifty community service hours," I tell him, buying me time to dig up an absolutely unhinged dark Mafia romance that will traumatize him and end this conversation forever. Joke's on me, though, because the filthy traitor that is my brain starts dragging up scenes from the dozens of hockey romances I've read and subbing Decker in for the heroes. I clear my throat and give my head a little shake, pretending I'm trying to toss a rogue strand of hair out of my eyes. Anything to wipe away those images. "You're not ready for the hard stuff yet."

We finish our lunch, and Decker pays for both of us, leaving an absolutely eye-watering tip. I start back toward the library, and he falls into step beside me. I work to ignore the frizzle of delight I experience from having a man this tall next to me. It's not often that I get to feel small. Cannon was only an inch taller than me, but Decker towers over me enough to block the sun. But I remind myself that so does my brother, and that banishes whatever gooey feelings I had coming on. Even if my affection for Decker thaws slightly, it doesn't erase the fact that he's Archer's best friend. Hell, he's practically my fifth brother. I'm obviously in desperate need of a good lay, and my lady parts are misfiring thanks to the drought. Wyatt's been trying to get me to download a dating app and extend my radius to Bloomington "for some of that good college D," but so far I've been hesitant. Maybe that hesitation ends now.

"So, where you off to?" Decker asks.

"Hmmm?" I nearly trip over my own toes at the sound of his voice scraping up my spine. Please, god, don't let that warmth I feel be a blush creeping up my neck. "Uh, I've got to head back to the library. We got a new box from our distributor, so I need to get those scanned in and onto the new releases table."

"I could go with you. Help out," he says, and when I glance

up to meet his warm gaze, he shoves his hands deep in his pockets. "You know, for the hours."

I actually want to say yes. I think I might kind of *like* having him sit on the circulation desk counter and gently tease me while I cover books, but again, that is *surely* my hormones misfiring. And that's why I need some space right now.

"Nah, this is a one-person job." I need to redirect these dirty thoughts like they're a naughty toddler playing with matches. "Tomorrow I work at the hardware store in the morning, so you're free until Thursday morning at eight. We'll do a full day. Sound good?"

Decker gives me that little two-fingered salute that filled me with rage this morning but now just elicits a tiny eye roll.

"Guess I'll head home, nap off that burger, and then maybe head to the gym. My PT sent me some training plans for my hip. And my shoulder. And my perpetually angry knee," he says. He reaches his arms straight up over his head, his biceps flexing and his shirt rising to reveal what is probably usually an absurdly toned midsection but is currently too full of bacon and French fries. And somehow that is…sexier? Jesus fuck, I have *got* to find a man or a dual-action vibrator before I turn into one of those cartoon dogs whose panting tongue rolls out like a red carpet every time I see this man. Can he, like, fart or be a dick or something so I can realign my thoughts, please? Universe? Does anyone hear me out there?

"Well, look at you two. Don't you look cozy?"

I whirl around to see Mrs. Eberle sauntering up the sidewalk, a large bouquet of sunflowers wrapped in paper bundled in her arms. Her lips are curled into a Cheshire Cat smile that says, *As soon as I walk away, I'm going to blab to every single living soul I see and probably also some trees and a park bench or two.*

This is not what I had in mind, universe.

I'm about to try and defuse the situation, or maybe just take off at a dead sprint, when Decker puts his arm around me and pulls me into the warm little nook of his shoulder. My feet tangle, and I have to press my palm to his chest to catch myself, my fingers running over the sharp curve of his pecs.

"The coziest," he says, his tone dripping with hot honey. I glance up and see him flashing his most shit-eating grin at her. "We're thinking a spring wedding and six kids."

Mrs. Eberle's smile widens; she's now dangerously close to looking like a hyena baring its teeth. She catches my eye, and I can see the whole goddamn monologue forming in her brain.

She drags her eyes back up to Decker. "Still the jokester, I see," she says, then gives me one last look and a tiny shake of her head before brushing past us down the sidewalk.

"Still a nosy bitch, I see," Decker mutters, and I hope to god she's out of earshot.

Suddenly I snap back to reality. I shove him off so hard he collides with a parking meter.

"What the hell was that?" I look back just in time to see Mrs. Eberle disappear around the corner. At least she won't see the fisticuffs.

Decker rubs his elbow, which caught the edge of the meter. "Mrs. Eberle was my nightmare in high school. Her class almost kept me out of the state championships my senior year. One of the perks of being an adult is that I can finally mess with her."

I huff out a sigh and work not to stamp my foot. "Dammit, Decker," I grind out.

"What?"

I blink at him. How is he this fucking dense? "Now she's going to go around town telling everyone we're together. It hardly matters that she knows you were fucking with her. Just the fact that we were that close to each other is enough for her."

He shrugs. "Who cares?"

"I care," I snap.

Decker scoffs. "You shouldn't."

"Says the guy who gets to waltz out of town and never deal with the consequences of his actions. I have to live here, and you antagonizing Susan Eberle makes my life exponentially more difficult, as does having to put out that fast-burning fire of a rumor that you and I are fucking."

And then he's grinning, his brown eyes twinkling. "So wait, are we together, or are we just fucking?"

I feel a full-body record scratch when I hear Decker say those words. Unbidden, I imagine his strong arms pulling me in, his weight on me, that scruff on his jaw raking across my cheek, my neck, my…*oh god*.

I blink and drag my brain back to reality. To this sidewalk. To Decker's smirk—that fucking smirk he's always aiming at me and everyone else he needs to Jedi mind trick into forgetting he's a total pain in the ass. The smirk that always manages to get him out of whatever trouble *he* caused. That smirk paired with his brown eyes is practically lethal. Thankfully, I'm immune.

I *am*.

And to prove it, I'm going to download a dating app tonight.

# CHAPTER 14

## GRACE

"Okay, you're all set," Carson says, holding out my phone and reaching for a slice of pizza from the Red Bird box on my coffee table. I take a sip of pinot noir and reach for the phone, but Wyatt swipes it from Carson's hand. She taps at the screen, her brow furrowed. Then her lips quirk up and she finally passes it over.

"What did you do?" The screen glows in my hand, the yellow logo of the dating app taunting me.

"I swapped the photo of you dressed as Miss Frizzle from Halloween at the library for one of you dressed as a lifeguard from Halloween at the bar," she says with a devious grin.

Sure enough, the screen displays a picture of me grinning in a red bathing suit cut way too high in the thighs and holding one of those red floatie things from *Baywatch*. I open my mouth to protest, but Wyatt cuts me off.

"All your other photos are very sweet and prim. You need at least one where they can see that you're sex on legs," she says around a mouthful of sausage and cheese. She waggles her eyebrows, and Carson reaches up for a high five. "I mean, come on, there's zinc on your nose, and you're wearing a visor. You look hot, but not, like, *come and get it* hot."

I swipe through the rest of the photos. Carson and Wyatt immediately nixed all my initial picks, combing through their own phones to find the perfect shots for my brand-spanking-new profile. There's a smiling snap of me from Wyatt's birthday—I will admit I was having an excellent hair day, and my eyes are sparkling, nearly neon blue. There's one of me swinging a hammer from when my brothers and I built Dad's backyard fence, a tool belt slung around my hips. Wyatt claims it makes me look "strong yet sexy, a real guy's girl." And even though I'm pretty sure there's something antifeminist about that, I have to admit that the picture *is* pretty good.

As soon as I left lunch with Decker, I put up the Bat-Signal, and my best friends responded. Wyatt has been on the apps for years, regaling us with tales of dates both scorching hot and laughably bad. Carson only waded in this year; according to her, once she left college, her dating options dried up like her mother's cornbread. They wasted no time downloading what they claim is the perfect app for me, one that puts the women in control and promises the bare minimum of trolls and dick pics. ("Not *zero* dick pics, because that's a promise no one can make," Wyatt told me.) And I need all the help I can get. I have no idea how to navigate a dating app. I barely know anything about dating at all. My last boyfriend was also my prom date, and we broke up only a few months ago.

I blow out a deep breath and navigate to the home screen.

"Get swiping!" Carson says. She raises her glass in a toast. "To hot guys!"

"And good dick!" Wyatt adds.

I grimace. "Now?"

"Yes, *now*. It's after work on a weekday. This is when guys are swiping through the app. You might even have a date set up before you go to bed tonight."

I swallow hard. Until this afternoon, I had exactly zero plans to date anytime soon. Obviously, I'm completely over Cannon; the cheating gave me a head start, and his words at the bar last weekend sealed the deal. But now, with the book festival piling my plate high, dating was at the bottom of my priority list. My hormones, however, have clearly not gotten the memo, which is why I keep getting the hot-and-hornies for Decker. I can't even read a romance without subbing his face in. And after today's disaster in front of Mrs. Eberle, it's time to put an end to this once and for all. If I can find a nice guy and bring him home for some extracurriculars, maybe I can finally calm my libido, stop imagining Decker pressing me into a mattress, and focus on my job.

And yet I can't bring myself to swipe. Just the thought has my stomach dancing the samba. Cold beads of sweat prick the back of my neck, and I let out a shuddery breath like I've just gotten off a roller coaster and am trying to find my balance. I feel like the tension in my body might explode out of my fingertips and send my phone directly out the window of my apartment, so I thrust it out and cry, "Help!"

"On it," Wyatt says immediately, taking my phone. I collapse back onto the couch, bouncing with a little *oof* onto the center cushion. Wyatt drops down next to me, and Carson scoots in on the other side. "Okay, let's do this."

Wyatt starts swiping at a speed that frankly makes my head spin. I watch guys whiz by with their hoisted fish and their low-slung ball caps and their shiny sports cars.

"Hey, wait, he looked kind of cute," I say as a smiling guy with hair curling out from beneath an IU baseball cap disappears.

"His bio said, 'Looking for someone with no drama,'" Wyatt says. I stare blankly at her. "That means *he's* the drama."

Two more guys disappear before Wyatt pauses on another man with day-old scruff and a nice smile. She flips through his photos.

"Oh, skip that guy," Carson says. "He's clearly hatfishing."

"What the hell is that?" I ask.

"It's like catfishing for bald guys. If someone's wearing hats in all his photos, he's trying to hide the fact that his hairline is receding. Which is fine, but if he's trying to hide *that*, what else is he hiding? You want a guy who's secure with himself."

Over the next half hour, I learn that if all a guy's photos are selfies, it means he doesn't have any friends. If someone says he's "not into politics," he's almost certainly an idiot or an asshole (or both). Bathroom selfies are an automatic no, especially if the mirror is filthy. Any guy who uses his bio to neg other women—looking for someone "who can hold a conversation" or "isn't vain"—is a hard pass. If he's looking for "a woman with a good sense of humor," he wants someone who will laugh at *his* jokes.

"And it's almost guaranteed the jokes won't be funny," Wyatt says.

I feel like I'm back in AP English, trying to decipher the language of James Joyce. Only I understood Joyce a hell of a lot better than I understand twenty-something single dudes.

"Why am I doing this?" I groan as the eleventy-billionth photo of a trout whizzes past. "We've been at this for nearly an hour, and I don't think I'd let any of these guys change my tire, much less take me out on date."

"You could just meet a guy in real life," Wyatt says. "That's what bars are for."

"I'd rather date one of the fish," I say, taking my phone back. "Like, not one of the fish-holding guys—one of the actual dead fish."

"What about someone you already know?" Wyatt says, her grin widening, her eyebrows waggling. "Like…Decker Brooks?"

My belly clenches, and Carson snorts beside me.

"What? You're single. He's single," she says.

"He's single like the open seat on a carnival ride is single," I shoot back, and Wyatt laughs.

"I don't even know what that means. Listen, neither of you is looking for anything serious. Hell, he's leaving at the end of the summer. It's perfect!"

"It's disgusting. Having sex with Decker Brooks would be like licking a subway seat," I say, but my body positively lights up at the idea.

"No," Wyatt says. "It would be like enjoying a dessert baked by the best pastry chef in the world. You think women would keep coming for him if he wasn't talented? I mean, look at all the famous women he's dated. They could be in *any* man's bed, and they chose Decker's. That's got to mean something."

"She's got a point," Carson says.

I roll my eyes, shoving away thoughts of all the other women Decker has slept with. Another reason I can't get hung up on him. I'm definitely no Imani Menendez. "I think some women will fuck an empty potato sack if it's rich and famous."

"My god, Grace, you're practically pulling his ponytail on the playground and running away to hide under the slide," Carson says. "The lady doth protest too much and all that."

"All I'm saying is that I have no interest in Decker Brooks, and even if I did, he has no interest in me. He's been with Oscar winners. *Plural*, Carson. It's not happening."

"Grace, if you don't want to have a fling with Decker, that's fine. But don't think for one single second that it's because you can't get it," Wyatt says. "You're smart and funny and gorgeous, and I don't know what happened with Cannon, but I hope you can move past it and be open to finding what you really deserve."

I swallow the lump in my throat. I can't believe I'm lucky enough to have these amazing women in my life to pump me up, even if they are trying to throw me into bed with my teenage nemesis.

"Thanks, friend," I say.

"And by that, we mean a large and very talented penis," Carson says.

"Jesus Christ, Carson," I say, though I can't contain the bark of a laugh that explodes out of me. At least now I feel ready to dive back into the app.

I snatch my phone back from Wyatt and swipe right on the first guy who comes up. Unfortunately, then I notice that he's standing in front of a lifted pickup and wearing a Joe Rogan shirt. I groan. I should just delete this blasted app right now.

An hour later, the first bottle of wine is gone, Taylor Swift is on the Bluetooth speaker, Carson and Wyatt are singing into the empty bottle, and I've swiped right on three more guys.

There's a knock at the door.

"Coming!" I shuffle over, my phone in one hand, my wine glass in the other. I think I might have cracked the code on how to effectively use this app, and it involves pinot noir. I take a swig from my glass, slide my phone into my back pocket, and open the door.

Standing there in a plain white undershirt that's stretched across his muscled chest and a pair of gray joggers that leave me wondering about his undergarment situation, his feet bare and his hair wet, is Decker Brooks.

It's like someone 3D printed my dirtiest fantasies.

I swallow the wine before I accidentally spray it across his chest.

I need to find a date *quick*.

"Having a party?" Decker leans his forearm against the doorframe and looks over my shoulder, a thing he can do because he's *tall*. So tall that he has to duck to avoid hitting his head on the top of the doorway. Part of my gulp of wine takes a detour into my lungs, and I clap a hand over my mouth as I cough. He arches an eyebrow at me.

"Just my besties," I say, my voice gravelly. Behind me, they launch into the bridge of "Cruel Summer." They're deep enough into the second bottle of wine that if Decker steps into this apartment, I'm not entirely sure that they won't start blabbing to him about my new dating profile. And the very last thing I need is Decker Brooks knowing about that. He'd tease me mercilessly, then spill to Archer, and by the next family dinner, every single McBride would be weighing in on my dating life. No fucking thank you. I need him out of here. "Girls' night. Is the music too loud? I can turn it down. Sorry about that."

I start to shut the door, but Decker stiff-arms it. The move should not be as hot as it is.

"Actually, no, the music is fine," he says, and then he looks down at the floor, a lock of his wet blond hair flopping over his eyes. If I'm not mistaken, there's a slight flush to his cheeks. "I just wanted to come over and apologize."

Record scratch.

"Apologize?"

He shoves his hands deep into the pockets of his sweats, drawing my gaze down to the way they stretch across his—*nope*, no no no. Eyes up, missy.

"Yeah, for the thing with Mrs. Eberle," he says. "I shouldn't have instigated. I know she's a gossip, and I know that shit makes life harder for you. Which I promised I wasn't going to do. I still maintain that she sucks, but you didn't deserve that."

"Oh," I say, and it comes out breathy. Because watching a barefoot Decker, fresh from the shower, sincerely apologizing might just be my kink.

My phone dings in my pocket, and, still in shock that the biggest man-child I know just told me he's *sorry*, I mindlessly pull it out. The screen flashes to life with a notification from the dating app. It's a new message from one of the guys I swiped right on. I actually got a response.

Decker's eyes drop to my phone, and he definitely recognizes the notification. I brace for teasing, but he just presses his lips together in a firm line, his brows knitted together like he's working to solve an algebra equation.

"Uh, thank you," I say, shoving the phone back in my pocket. "For the apology. Accepted and forgotten. Thanks."

Decker watches me, and I know my cheeks are crimson. Whether it's from the wine or being caught with the app or the entirely too sexy man standing in my doorway, I can't tell. But if he has anything to say about the notification, he keeps it to himself. Instead he gives me a little nod.

"Okay, well, that's all. I'll let you get back to your girls' night."

"Thanks," I say. Again. Because suddenly, I don't know how to talk to Decker Brooks. Not when I'm drunk and trying to find a date to distract my hormones from how hot he is.

"See you Thursday morning. Good night, Grace," he says, his voice dropping down into an octave that makes my insides clench. And then he turns and pads back across the hall. I stand there until his apartment door closes behind him with a soft thud.

In my pocket, my phone dings again. Another message from a dating app guy.

This time I ignore it.

# CHAPTER 15

## DECKER

Thursday morning, I wake up feeling like I've been hit by a school bus full of toddlers, and not from my Wednesday workout with Archer. I'm exhausted from spending an entire sleepless night tossing and turning, my head aches from blowing my nose, and my body feels like it's been transformed into a simmering vat of snot.

So the knock on my door at seven thirty feels like a personal attack.

Sometime around five, I woke up drenched in sweat, so I'm down to my boxer briefs and have yet to summon the energy to remedy that. I can't bring myself to care, so I shuffle to the door like this and pull it open, letting out a low groan by way of a greeting.

Grace stands in the doorway in a pair of faded jeans and a pale blue T-shirt that says, SHE'S READING AGAIN, HOW NOVEL in swoopy script. Her long dark hair is gathered into a low ponytail pulled over her shoulder, and she's gripping the straps of an overstuffed canvas tote bag. Her eyes drift down my bare chest, pausing at the waistband of my black boxer briefs and widening. And I feel too shitty to even appreciate the ogling. Or tease her about it.

And teasing Grace is quickly becoming one of my very favorite things.

"What are you doing here?" I grunt.

"I came to see if you wanted to walk to work together," she says, her cheeks red, her eyes diligently staying above my neck. "What happened to you?"

I lean against the doorframe and sigh. "I'm going to guess it was that adorable little blond girl who sneezed directly into my eyeballs two days ago. Or maybe the small child who thrust his sticky fingers into my mouth? Or the kid who asked questions by leaning in so close I could smell his lunch." I let out a thunderous sneeze that causes Grace to leap back. "How are you not taken down by this? Those kids were crawling all over you, too."

She grins. "Well, I've been at this a lot longer than you have. My immune system is made of well-seasoned cast iron at this point."

I sniffle. "Mine is made of recycled toilet paper, apparently."

"Poor baby. But take heart," she says, hoisting her tote bag higher on her shoulder. "You will never be as sick as you are when you've contracted a virus from a toddler."

"How does that help me now?" I grumble.

She shrugs. "It doesn't. But it should give you hope for the future. This is the worst it'll ever be." She glances at her watch. "I've got some time before senior hour starts. Hang tight, I'll be back in ten."

I'm tired just watching her bound down the stairs. I can barely summon the energy to shut the door. All I can do is shuffle back to my bed and pitch forward. And then whatever was keeping me from sleeping all night finally releases me from its grip, and I barely have time to wonder what she's doing or if I remembered to leave the door unlocked for her before my eyes drift closed.

––––––––

My memories of the rest of the day are spotty. I know that at one point, Grace knelt beside my bed and poked me hard in the shoulder. When I finally sat up, she thrust a bottle of Gatorade and a handful of pills at me. She must have explained what they were, but I paid little attention, just tossed them down and collapsed back into bed.

When I finally sit up and fumble for my phone, I see that I've been asleep for nearly ten hours. It's almost six thirty p.m. now. My bedside table is stocked with a box of Kleenex, a glass of water, a fresh bottle of Gatorade, and a blister pack of pills. Come to think of it, that *table* definitely wasn't even here this morning. There's also a humidifier bubbling away beside me. My nose feels a little clearer, enough that I can smell something salty and delicious. And that's when I notice that I'm not alone.

Grace is standing in my little galley kitchen, her back to me as she stirs a pot of something that makes my stomach growl. I blame the medication she gave me for the way I let my gaze linger on her ass in those jeans. When she reaches up into my cabinet to get a bowl, her shirt rises, and I catch a sliver of aquamarine panties with…goldfish? I squint—yep, orange-and-white chubby-faced goldfish.

My body begins waking up, cock first. *Fuck.*

"Are you making soup?" I croak, my voice gravelly from disuse.

She glances over her shoulder. "The only thing in your cabinet was an old can of Raid, and the only thing in your fridge was beer. Are you a functioning adult?"

"I just moved in." I pluck my T-shirt off the floor and shrug it on, then my gym shorts. I shuffle into the bathroom and take care of some very necessary business after a ten-hour NyQuil nap. When I emerge, I find two steaming bowls sitting on the little breakfast bar, along with an open bag of oyster crackers. It's not until I settle onto one of the two barstools that I realize those weren't here this morning, either.

"Did you put these together?" I ask. I wiggle, and it's sturdy.

There's a stack of broken-down cardboard boxes by the door, an overflowing trash bag of Styrofoam packaging next to it. That's when the entertainment center catches my eye. And the coffee table. "Did you put *all* my furniture together?"

"Yes," she says, taking the barstool next to me. "Eat up. This is a Barefoot Contessa recipe that will revive you."

The soup is delicious, salty and hearty, with a tomato base and white beans and vegetables. A moan rolls right out of me as I swallow the first mouthful, letting it soothe my sore throat.

"I know everyone swears by chicken noodle, but I think minestrone is superior for sickness. Spinach and sweet potatoes and cannellini beans are much better for you. Plus the garlic bruschetta will help clear out your sinuses." She pushes a bread basket toward me that smells so strongly of garlic that my eyes water. "The recipe only called for one clove, but I'm sorry, that's not even worth the knife work. I measure garlic with my heart, and my heart said to burn your taste buds right off."

I chuckle and dip a crusty slice into the soup. It's *intensely* garlicky, which a) actually does clear my sinuses and b) tastes fucking delicious.

"Lucky for you, my heart measures garlic using a similar metric," I tell her. "Now, can we get back to my furniture?"

"Oh yeah." She glances around the room and shrugs. "When I came back with all your sick supplies—"

"I'm going to Venmo you for all that, by the way. Just let me know the total," I say, pointing at her with my spoon, but she waves me off.

"Your apartment just looked so…sad. It was so empty, and there was this tower of boxes that I figured had to be furniture. So yeah, sorry I opened your mail, but something had to be done. And anyway, putting together flat-pack furniture is maybe my love language? It feels like a 3D puzzle."

I snort. "You're a special kind of dork, you know that?"

I brace for an eye roll, the dancing freckles that signal her fury, but instead I get a grin. "In fact, I do."

I swallow another hearty spoonful of soup, and true to her word, it does feel like it's reviving me, enough that I begin to wonder what's caused this change in her attitude. Maybe it was the apology, which she definitely deserved. But that memory only serves to remind me of the notification on her phone, that familiar logo. It makes the soup go sour on my tongue. Not that I give a shit about her dating life. That's her business.

"You okay?" she asks, studying me as I begin to spiral.

"Yeah," I shake off that unpleasantness. "And thank you. For the medical care and the home renovations. It's actually starting to look like I live here."

"You're going to need more than one spoon if that's your goal," she says. I glance down and realize that the flatware I'm using isn't even mine. "I brought that over from my place. Who has only one bowl?"

"A single guy," I reply.

"Not planning to do any entertaining this summer?" She waggles her eyebrows.

"In fact, I was ordered not to."

Her smile drops, and I swear to god, a light inside me dims with it. "Oh, right," she says. "Sorry about that."

"You've got nothing to be sorry for," I remind her. "That order predated you."

"True, but then it was my honor you were defending," she says.

I raise an eyebrow at her. "Does this mean we're actually going to talk about what happened?"

She sighs. "He was drunk. He apologized and promised it would never happen again. The end."

I have so many more questions about that asshole and their relationship, but the finality in her *the end* tells me not to push. And besides, I'm eating a home-cooked meal she made off dishes she brought to my place, sitting on barstools she put together using an Allen wrench and instructions that may or may not have been in comprehensible English. So I'm not exactly in a place to argue with her.

"Oh, and also your sink wouldn't stop dripping, so I took care of that," she says around a mouthful of garlic bread.

My eyebrows shoot up. "Are you kidding me right now? I feel like you could barely stand my presence until Tuesday, and now you've spent all day playing home improvement fairy? For *me*?"

She shrugs. "Look, I'll never cop to the fact that I said this, but the truth is that you punched Cannon, and while that caused some problems for me, a small part of me found it intensely satisfying to watch. So consider us even."

I grin, but I bite my tongue and stop myself from taking a verbal victory lap. I'll just have to quietly enjoy this inside my own head. And I do, conjuring the image once again of Cannon and his smug, stupid face crumpling to the floor of the Half Pint. Then I glance up at Grace, who is folding a dish towel (also not mine) on my counter, her hair in a dark messy bun on top of her head. A few strands have fallen down into her blue eyes, and my fingers itch to tuck one of them behind her ear.

"Hey, how did you manage to do all this and go to work?" A coffee table, an entertainment center, two end tables, two barstools, and an entire gourmet meal from scratch? I'm shocked she managed to get that done in one day when she had other things going on.

"I called in. I have a ton of vacation days saved up, and Suzanne covered senior hour when she heard you were sick." She ladles another serving of soup into my bowl, then nods at a foil-wrapped loaf by the stove. "She brought banana bread over, by the way."

I cock my head. "So you've been in my apartment all day? While I slept?"

My apartment is a studio, large, long, and narrow with wood floors and exposed brick on one wall. My bed is by the front windows that face Main Street, then there's an open space that until recently contained only a sofa and a television, and then a galley kitchen with an island and breakfast bar. But it's still just one room. I can't believe I was comatose in my underwear while she Mary Poppinsed around this place all day.

"Yeah," she says, her cheeks flushing. "Luckily you sleep like the dead. And you snore, by the way."

I choke on a mouthful of soup. "I do not! That must have just been because I'm sick."

She grins. "Sure, yeah. Okay."

I narrow my eyes at her but can't suppress the quirk of my lips, salty from the soup. "Watch yourself, Graceless."

At that, Grace points the ladle at me. "If you ever call me that again, I'm going to sneak in here and remove the screws from one of these stools, and you'll never know until you sit down on it."

My mouth drops open. "That's devious."

She arches an eyebrow. "I'm a crafty bastard."

"And a handy one, too."

I take in my apartment, which until today barely looked inhabited. Suddenly it feels warm and homey. The rug I ordered has been rolled out beneath the coffee table. There's a floor lamp beside the couch, filling the space with a warm light. The television, which was sitting on the floor this morning, plugged into a neon-orange extension cord, now sits atop the wooden entertainment center, the cords gathered and tucked behind it. I can't believe she spent the day putting all this together. And cooking. And fixing my sink. This woman is Rosie the Riveter with a bonus chef's knife.

"Hey, why was your brother saying he was going to come fix your toilet if you have the skills to fix my sink?"

She shrugs. "They baby me. It's easier to just let it happen."

I think back to dinner the other night at the McBride house, when everyone talked *about* Grace or *at* her, but never *to* her. How her jaw ticked every time they butted in, ordered her around under the guise of helping. How have they not noticed that this beautiful grown woman has everything under control, always, at every moment? Either they are really stupid or she's really good at hiding it.

Watching her start on the dishes, moving deftly around my kitchen, I'm pretty sure it's the latter. Grace wasn't kidding—she really is a crafty bastard.

And it's sexy as hell.

I shift on my stool, letting the cold metal touch the backs of my thighs and trying to shock the blood from my lap back up into my brain.

"So, when's my next shift, boss?" I ask, rising from the stool to take my bowl and spoon to the sink.

She pivots, wipes her hands on her jeans, and then reaches up and rests a palm on my forehead. Her skin is cool and soft, and I have to stop myself from leaning into her touch. When her gaze catches mine, her sapphire eyes suddenly warm, her lips parting. The pads of her fingers brush my face.

Then she takes a step back and pulls her hand away, plunging it back beneath the faucet to wash the chef's knife that definitely didn't come from any of my drawers.

"No fever, and I don't think you had one this morning, either," she says.

"You checked?"

"You don't remember?"

"I was pretty out of it," I say, suddenly furious that she touched me and I have no memory of it. I want to tuck the high-light reel of her delicate hand on my forehead into a safe place to play back later.

"Well, I think you should probably take the rest of the week off, just to be safe. You can come back with a vengeance on Monday."

I freeze. "Same shift?"

"You mean am I going to make you run the story time gauntlet and man the senior hour desk?"

"Hey, at some point you and I are going to talk about Ms. Tingle's romance novels."

A blush blooms on her cheeks, red as a candy apple and just as delicious. I have the urge to rake my teeth across them. "I will let you shelve books with your earbuds in if you promise never *ever* to make me discuss that with you," she says, her eyes firmly on the dish she's scrubbing a little too frantically.

"No deal," I reply, because I want more of that blush. While Ms. Tingle's words were a shock, the thought of hearing them drip out of Grace's mouth does something very dangerous to my body. The feeling is new, and I want to explore it. "You need to explain the why choose universe to me."

"Decker, if I attempted to explain the depth and breadth of the romance genre to you, your head would explode."

I waggle my eyebrows. "Now you're just tempting me."

She places the clean bowl in a dish rack that also doesn't belong to me, wiping her hands on the borrowed dish towel before turning to me. "We'll at least save it for a day when you're not high on NyQuil. You need to be stone-cold sober to hear about tentacle romance."

All dirty thoughts of Grace flee my mind. "I'm sorry, *what?*"

"Google is free," she says with a smirk. "But I wouldn't, if I were you. I'm headed home now. I put the extra soup in a Tupperware in the fridge. You can microwave it, but it'll taste better if you warm it in a pot on the stove. The microwave makes everything taste like nuclear baby food. I left a little saucepan for you to use—it's in the big cabinet underneath the island. The garlic bread will probably come back to life if you put it under the broiler. And there's butter in the fridge to go with Suzanne's banana bread— the extra-salty European butter, *you're welcome.* Now, get some sleep. You're due for another dose of NyQuil, but don't take more than you're supposed to unless you want to lose days of your life."

My mind, still foggy from the meds and the ten-hour nap, whirs at her instructions, at how busy she's been. How busy she always seems to be. At how she's taking care of me and how much I like it. It's all a little too much for me, this feeling of being cared for. All I manage to say is, "Do I own Tupperware?"

She shakes her head with a wry grin. "You do not. I'll be expecting that back. Run it through the dishwasher on the top rack. Good night, Decker. Feel better."

And then my Mary Poppins, who definitely doesn't seem to hate me anymore, is gone.

# CHAPTER 16

## GRACE

t's Friday night, and Carson and I are whizzing down a two-lane highway in my blue MINI Cooper, the tiny car filled with delicious smells.

"What did you get?" Carson asks, tightening her grip on the foil-covered platter in her lap as I take a turn a smidge too fast. The drive to Bloomington, where our cookbook club meets, is an hour, and we got on the road about ten minutes too late today.

"Minestrone." I glance down at the Tupperware on the floor between Carson's feet to make sure it's safe. I'm still scarred from February's meeting, when the lid popped off the container of Bolognese I made and flooded the passenger seat. I had to get my beloved MINI detailed three times to get the smell of tomato and oregano out of the car. The garlic bread is wrapped loosely in a tea towel and nestled in a bread basket on top. "It's really good."

"I can't believe you always practice your recipe," Carson says.

"The one time I didn't, I drastically undercooked that lamb and no one could eat it," I reply. I started learning to cook when I was in high school and got sick of the rotation of burgers, fried chicken, macaroni and cheese, and spaghetti with jar sauce that my dad cycled through. He has never particularly liked cooking, but he had kids to feed, so he got about seven recipes down pat and stuck to them like a religion. Finding the cookbook club a couple of years ago, when Carson was in college at IU, has really helped expand my repertoire. "Anyway, this time it didn't go to waste. Decker came down with the toddler yuck, so I used him as a guinea pig."

I can't look over at her, because the road is dark and there are deer that sometimes kamikaze in front of your car, but I can practically hear Carson's eyebrows rise. "You cooked for Decker?"

"Well, I cooked for *me*, but I shared it with Decker," I say. And that's true. I had planned to share my recipe test with Dad until I saw Decker's sweaty, snotty state.

Again, Carson's facial expression is loud. "Decker was sick, so you made him soup. To make him feel better."

"Again, I was making the soup anyway, and he just looked so gross and pathetic. And you should have seen his apartment. It looked like he'd been robbed—just a mattress and a television on the floor and this mountain of boxes from Amazon. It was truly the saddest thing I've ever seen."

There's a long pause, so I reach over and turn up the volume on the nineties SiriusXM station pumping out of my speakers. My hope is that the Spice Girls will drown out whatever Carson's brain is doing, but no dice. She reaches over and slaps the button to turn the music off. The silence is very loud.

"So do we not hate Decker Brooks anymore?" she asks.

And that's the question, isn't it? I didn't tell the girls that Decker came to apologize on Tuesday, because at the time I could barely believe it myself. I told them he asked if we could turn Taylor Swift down, and they responded by cranking it louder and scream-singing the ten-minute version of "All Too Well." So, a win for everyone.

But later that night, I lay in bed, my head full of images of that high, tight hockey ass in gray sweatpants and the sound of his voice saying, "You didn't deserve that." I'd finally let my fingers creep down into my panties to relieve the tension so I could fall asleep.

Spoiler alert: it released no tension at all. Especially not when Decker opened his apartment door on Thursday morning. Was he feverish and snotty? Yes. Was he nearly naked and cut like a Greek god? Abso-fucking-lutely.

And something about a man that tall and strong laid low by toddler germs…well, I fully lost my head, called into work, and played Florence Nightingale for him like some pathetic little kid with a crush. And other than the one time he called me Graceless, there was no trace of the teenage Decker Brooks who used to taunt and torture me. There was no sign of the adult Decker Brooks who made bad decisions. There was just Decker, who was maybe becoming something like a friend?

Who I sometimes picture naked?

To say my feelings for Decker have become a weirdly seasoned stew of confusion is an understatement.

"I don't think we hate Decker, no," I finally concede. Carson makes a little *hmmm* sound but doesn't say anything else. Because she is my best friend and has been since I was born and her mom would babysit for me to help my dad out. Carson knows me better than anyone, and she can tell that no matter what questions she asks, I won't have answers. I flat-out do not know what my feelings for Decker are.

I flip the stereo back on, Matchbox Twenty filling the tiny car.

"What did you bring?" I ask.

"Chocolate-dipped brown sugar shortbread," she replies.

"How do you always manage to snag the desserts?"

"Deva always goes around the circle," she says. She reaches beneath the foil and pulls out a cookie, passing it to me. The shortbread is perfectly sweet, buttery, and crumbly on my tongue. Carson is the best baker I know. "Why do you think I always sit to her right?"

"Carson Webber, you're an evil genius," I say, popping the last bite into my mouth.

"More like I have anxiety that requires me to control every

second of my life and I've learned to use that to my advantage," she says.

I pull the car into a parking spot on the courthouse square and throw it in park. "As long as you're using your powers for good," I say.

Carson winks. "I made a double batch so you can take some home."

"You are my best friend in the whole wide world."

Red Books is in downtown Bloomington, across the street from the grand limestone courthouse and nestled in the middle of a block of historic brick buildings with businesses at street level and apartments upstairs. The shop adjoins a little locally owned kitchen supply store called Inner Chef, which boasts a demonstration kitchen in the back. Inner Chef is owned by Eloise Bailey-Mehta, the wife of Deva Bailey-Mehta, who owns Red Books. Which makes it the perfect spot to host our cookbook club.

Carson and I walk down the block toward the bookstore, food in hand, pausing at the front window of Red Books to check out the new releases. In one corner, there's a display of books for upcoming book clubs.

"Oh, they're reading the new Sarah MacLean for the romance book club in July!" Carson says, gazing at the feisty woman in the candy-colored ball gown on the cover.

"You should go," I say. I pull the door open for her and enjoy the burst of cool air that comes out. It's still early June, but it's already midsummer hot. "You're such a historical girlie."

She sighs. "I feel weird going alone."

Carson's always had a hard time doing things by herself, which is ironic, since she's an only child. But she was a late-in-life surprise for her parents, who'd been told it was unlikely they'd ever be able to have children. Her mother was nearly forty-five when Carson was born, her father almost fifty. They considered Carson to be their little miracle sent straight from God, and they protected her fiercely. Were it not for all the time she spent at my house growing up, dodging my rowdy older brothers as they swore and wrestled, she'd probably be a hell of a lot more sheltered than she is. She grew a lot when she went away to college at IU, but she joined a sorority right away, so she always had built-in buddies at the ready. When she graduated and accepted the job teaching kindergarten at Cardinal Springs Elementary, she moved back in with her parents to save money and also to help take care of them. (Her parents are now in their seventies, and Carson doesn't say it, but I can tell she gets nervous every time they have doctor's appointments). She swears it's just temporary, but that was a year ago, and there has been no movement on the apartment-hunting front.

"I'd go with you, but with the book festival, I just don't have room in my schedule for another night in Bloomington." I like the drive here—it's easy, and if Carson's with me, we spend the time gossiping or listening to a podcast or singing very loudly to Taylor Swift. But it's a commitment.

If I ever get to open my own store, we won't have far to travel at all.

"It's fine," she says, still staring dreamily at the book that I know will be coming home with her, even if she doesn't join the book club. "I mean, during the school year I don't really have time for two book clubs anyway. I'd only be able to do June and July, maybe August."

"You could always drop cookbook club. I know cooking isn't your favorite."

"But I like being with you! And like I said, I've engineered it so I always get dessert, and baking isn't terrible. At least the experiments are delicious."

Since we've arrived a few minutes late, we hurry through the cozy bookstore with high ceilings, the original wood floors creaking beneath our feet. The back of the store opens up into Inner Chef, and that's where we find the rest of our crew, dishes laid out on the counter and people moving down the line with paper plates. Every month, Deva picks a cookbook and everyone cooks one recipe from it. Except for Denise, who is retired and can never stop herself from making at least two more unclaimed recipes as well. This month we've done Ina Garten, and the food is absolutely fantastic.

"I love Ina, but I feel like there's just not enough of *her* in the cookbooks. It's all pretty straightforward. I like something with more narrative," says Regina, a studio art professor at IU who always chooses an ambitious recipe. This time she has brought a Tuscan turkey roulade that is so delicious I can't believe I didn't order it off a menu.

Amelia, a single mother who works for campus parking and—per her own admission—can't cook for shit, glances up from her plate. "You mean like the ten-thousand-word tomes before every internet recipe?"

Regina shakes her head. "Not necessarily. But a little more, I don't know, *oomph*. More meat on the bones."

Deva, her long gray curls braided and pinned up like a milk-maid, pops one of Carson's cookies into her mouth. "Well, maybe now would be a good time to tackle *Salt Fat Acid Heat*."

"I watched the show on Netflix, and it was incredible," Carson says.

Deva nods, pulling out her phone to make a note. "Let's do that for July, since a lot of folks are going on vacation—it has recipes, but it's more a book about food and cooking. Something you can read by the pool. I'll order catering for that one instead of everyone cooking."

Everybody nods, and with that, we've satisfied the talking-about-the-book portion of book club. The truth is that these nights are basically just glorified dinner parties. What makes this group fun is that the women are all ages and from all walks of life. Like Martha, who works in campus housing and always chooses one of the more ambitious recipes, then completely forgets to cook it and winds up bringing something she picked up from Kroger on her way. But she tells the most hilarious stories about the dorms, and so we forgive her.

Martha is partway through an animated tale about a roommate conflict over a goldfish that ended in fisticuffs when Deva sidles up to me. "MIBA just announced that their next conference will be in Indy this fall, if you're interested," she says.

Carson, who's digging into a piece of white chocolate toffee, leans in. "What's MIBA?"

"Midwest Independent Booksellers Association," Deva replies. She turns back to me. "I'd be happy to list you as a store employee so you can get a discounted pass. Even if you just come up for one day, it'll be a great opportunity to learn."

Deva knows all about my dream of opening a bookstore, and she's one of my biggest cheerleaders. She opened Red Books right after she graduated from IU with a degree in chemistry and no desire to see the inside of a lab ever again. One night at book club, I had a smidge too much wine and stayed late to barf out my entire business plan onto her. When I was tipsy and talking to Deva, it all felt close enough to reach out and grab. But the next morning, I remembered that my minimum-wage job at the library would make it nearly impossible to save up the money for startup costs.

So it remains a dream—one I haven't shared with anyone else, not even Carson. So I swallow down my mouthful of turkey and say, "Yeah, it'd be a good place to hear about new titles. For the library. I'll check it out and let you know."

Deva simply raises an eyebrow at me, not saying anything more. But later, when we're at the register paying for the stack of books we picked out (including a copy of *Salt Fat Acid Heat*), Deva slips a brochure inside the book and slides it across the counter toward me.

"There's never a good time," Deva says, leveling me with a look. "Which means it's always a good time. Make the leap, Grace. I know you can do it."

# CHAPTER 17

## DECKER

Toddlers are biological weapons. That's the only explanation I have for how a cold acquired from a person not yet large enough to say their own name could take a grown-ass man down for four days. And I'm supposedly an elite athlete. I was seriously questioning that designation on Thursday, but by Sunday morning, I feel like I've got my lungs back. My sinuses are clear, and my nose isn't running (much), which means it's time to get back to my summer training plan. I'm too old to be slacking like this, cold or no cold.

Archer and I have fallen into a good rhythm with lifting at the gym, but today I just need to decompress. I need quiet and blood pumping. So I lace up my sneakers and drive out to Meade's Quarry, the trail Archer and I found back in middle school. The old limestone mining trail weaves through the surrounding woods and has incredible views of the crystal-blue water of the quarry below.

I park my car in the gravel clearing, put in my earbuds, and fire up a playlist full of hard-driving electronic metal. I need a fast beat that I can settle into, one loud enough to keep too many thoughts from crowding my mind.

I take my time stretching, giving extra attention to my

tweaked hip flexor and my shoulder—at this stage in my career, I can't afford to skimp. I try to imagine that every minute I spend stretching adds a minute to my game-time, and that helps me stay in it. When I feel loose, I finally take off into the little clearing in the trees where the trail starts. It's a cool morning, and the shade swallows me up. I follow the dirt trail as it winds through the wilderness. I skip the first overlook, enjoying the sweat and the pounding of my heart, the impact of my feet on the earth as I run. Soon, though, the twinge in my knee reminds me of my age and that although the weather and scenery beg for more mileage, my body does not. This is why I don't usually run, opting instead for a bike or an elliptical. I just couldn't bring myself to be inside today, surrounded by people and staring at a television that may or may not replay some of my greatest failures.

I slow my pace a little, hoping that will calm my knee. As I settle into the new rhythm, my mind is free to wander. Just two weeks ago, my summer plans looked very different. It's hard to believe that I've managed to derail everything so quickly and so completely.

That's not to say that all hope is lost. I may be the library's bitch this summer, but big kid story hour didn't suck. While I was recovering the last few days, I even planned next week's session. I ordered some kid-size hockey sticks, foam balls, and a small net to set up in the library so I can teach the kids stick handling. I even found a book for kids about hockey history; if the library doesn't have it, I plan to donate it.

I should really go ahead and order a Peloton for my apartment so I don't have to rely on these nature runs. They're nice, but fuck, my knee does not like this. If I can do regular bike workouts and lift with Archer, I might just come back this fall stronger than I left. That's one perk of not spending the entire summer partying and drinking in various Caribbean locations. My thirty-three-year-old body certainly can't take it like my twenty-three-year-old body could.

As if to remind me of my age, my knee lets out a screech of pain that forces me to a walk.

I know the reality. Most hockey players retire in their early thirties. Some continue for longer, assuming injuries don't take them out. I've had plenty of those, but thus far I've been able to rehab everything—some better than others, as my knee is reminding me right now. But I'm held together with toothpicks and duct tape at this point. My skills and my hockey IQ are carrying me through, not my body. And new guys with fresh knees are coming into the league every day. Guys as big as me, as smart as me, who have long careers ahead of them.

Soon one of my rebuilt joints or raggedy muscles will launch a serious protest, and then I'll be left to evaluate my future. I've been with the Grinders my whole career, but if I stop performing, stop being able to put in the minutes, they'll either cut my pay or trade me for peanuts to some low-rent team with no hope of making the playoffs, much less winning the cup. Of course, I could get out before that happens, retire when I'm still on top, but that thought sours my stomach. I start running again, knee be damned, just to distract myself from it.

I know I can't ignore my future forever. I'm set financially, but what will I do with all that time once I'm not playing eighty-plus games a season, traveling and conditioning, doing camp and practice and press? I've never liked golf. I have no interest in playing the stock market or sitting on a board. I need to work. I need things to do, a place to be, people who need me. Unfortunately, I'm not good at anything besides hockey. I could coach or commentate, maybe, but neither of those actually excites me. The thought of sitting in a cold arena, listening to the roar of the crowd but never feeling the glide of the ice beneath my feet? Fuck that.

I pick up the pace to match the nu metal track screaming in my ears, stubbornly pushing through the pain in my knee, my feet pounding the Earth. I round a curve and pop out of the trees and into an open field of tall grass, the dirt trail widening.

And that's when I see her. Hot-pink shorts and a black stripey sports bra, her dark ponytail bobbing out the back of a baseball cap.

My mind immediately goes to the chorus of *nos* at the McBride family dinner table. Grace had said she was "thinking" about running a half marathon, but her gear, her gait, and her steady, quick pace say this is not her first run. Nowhere near it.

I slow and give myself five seconds to admire the flex of her calves, the curve of her ass, that sliver of tanned skin, glistening with sweat, at the small of her back. When I hit five, I'm overcome with the feeling of being a first-class creep. Even if I weren't her older brother's best friend and, until very recently, her sworn enemy, I'm still a guy running behind a single woman alone in the woods. Not good.

"Tighten it up," I mutter to myself.

She must have her own earbuds in, because she doesn't hear me approach. And I definitely don't want to sneak up and scare the shit out of her, so I loudly clear my throat. Finally she glances back, doing a double take I'm surprised doesn't give her whiplash. Then the toe of her sneaker catches on a root or a rock, and she pitches forward.

"Grace!" I call, my heart dropping into my sneakers as I watch her tumble. I break into a sprint, reaching out an arm like I can catch her, but I'm too far away. She goes down hard in the dirt, a gruff cry tearing from her throat.

I skid to a stop and drop into a squat next to her. She sits back on her butt and folds over. I place a hand on her shoulder, giving a little tug so I can see if there's any damage. "Fuck, Grace, are you okay?"

She lifts her head and glares at me, shaking my hand off like I shoved her to the ground myself. "Go ahead," she mutters like she's spitting a mouthful of gravel.

"What?"

"Call me Graceless, or whatever other smartass remark you've got ready." She leans back on her hands, her face tipped toward the sun as she lets out a long sigh, and now I can see the blood pooling on her knee and running down her shin.

"I wasn't— Jesus, Grace. You're bleeding."

"I'm aware," she says, her chest heaving, her eyes still aimed firmly at the sky. Her face is going white.

I reach for her but stop short of laying a hand on her. She seems anxious, and she already shook me off once. "Are you, uh—"

"I hate blood, okay? Especially my own." Her eyes flutter cautiously down to her knee, and she lets out a low moan that, were it not for the crimson river running down her leg, might do something to me.

"Okay, well, let's take care of that, then." I spot a metal bench near the edge of the quarry and scoop her into my arms.

"What the hell?" she protests as I nestle her against my chest, pressing her face into my shirt. She feels so good there I half want to skip the bench and carry her all the way back to my car.

"Keep your eyes closed." I try not to jostle her as I pick my way through the grass. I deposit her on the bench, then reach for the back of my shirt and tug it off. I start with the trail of blood running down her shin, wiping it up until there's no trace of red. Then I reach for her water bottle, still clutched in her fist. I pour cold water over her knee and feel for the least sweaty part of the shirt to press against the wound. When I pull it away, I see that the cut isn't particularly deep—just some good old-fashioned road rash. I brush away a few pieces of bark and gravel, causing her to hiss in a breath. I whisper an apology, and when the scrapes are as free of debris as I can get them out here in the middle of the woods, I press the shirt back to her knee to stop the bleeding. "Okay, you can open your eyes."

She squints one open, peering down at her knee like she doesn't trust me, like there's going to be a goddamn massacre waiting there for her, but all she sees is my wadded-up wet T-shirt pressed to her skin. And then her eyes follow the length of my arm up to my shoulder and sweep across my bare chest. Her breath hitches, her lips parting slightly, and fuck if I don't have to avert my eyes just to keep things PG.

"Why are you shirtless?" she asks.

I arch an eyebrow at her. "Do you run with a first aid kit?" I pull the shirt away to check her wound, and sure enough, it's done bleeding. Now it's just angry and red, and I'm sure it'll turn a fun fiesta of colors tonight when it starts to bruise.

"Shit," she mutters.

"Mess up your training plans?"

"I'll be fine," she says, pinching her lips together.

"Ice it when you get home, and elevate it. Make sure you rest it up good if it hurts. You don't want some dumb skinned knee to turn into a chronic injury because you didn't let it heal."

She glares at me. "Did you go to medical school when I wasn't paying attention?"

"Sorry." I hold up my hands in surrender. She seems determined to be offended by me at the moment.

She sighs. "No, I'm sorry. You're just trying to help."

"Seems like a lot of people are just trying to help you. I can see how that would get kind of annoying." I take a seat next to her on the bench. We both stare out at the quarry for a beat, taking in the clear blue Indiana summer sky and its reflection in the water.

"It's fine," she says finally. "It's a good problem to have."

"Can I ask you a question?"

"Sure."

I want to look over at her, but I keep my eyes on the quarry. She won't let me pry into her personal life if I'm staring at her like it's an interrogation. Grace keeps everything close to her chest.

"Why did you lie to your family?" I ask.

"What?" Her head swivels to face me, her ponytail whipping around. I take that as an invitation to meet her gaze. Her blue eyes nearly match the water and the sky.

"You said you were *thinking* about training for a half marathon, but it seems like you've already started. This trail is six miles, so you must be a fairly regular runner. You acted like you didn't even own sneakers at dinner the other night."

She turns back to the horizon, her shoulders rolling in. "I don't like to give them more reasons to worry about me. Sometimes it's easier to show them everything is fine after the fact instead of letting them imagine the worst."

"And why would they do that?"

She sighs, an ocean of unspoken emotions cresting into waves. "So, I was born with a ventricular septal defect, a usually-not-scary heart defect that heals on its own as you grow up. But because I was born early and had some lung issues, it kind of exacerbated everything else. I ended up having heart surgery when I was two to repair it. I've been fine ever since. But it scared the shit out of my dad, who passed that on to my brothers, so they all treat me like I'm made of candy glass."

I vaguely remember Grace's surgery. I was ten and mostly consumed with my own childhood drama. But I remember Archer being out of school for a week, going to stay with family while his dad was in Indianapolis at the hospital with Grace. I knew she was having surgery on her heart, but anything beyond that was meaningless to me at that age. Mostly what I knew was that Archer swore she'd be fine, and I always assumed she was.

But heart surgery at two years old? Yeah, that's pretty fucking scary. I'm not a parent, but thinking about Mr. McBride, a young widower with five kids, one of whom had to have her chest cracked open as a toddler? Shit, the idea steals my breath.

I must have been silent for too long, my brows knitted together in worry, because Grace pivots on the bench, her eyes narrowed.

"I'm not reckless," she says, her voice full of nails. "I talked to my doctor, so I know it's safe. In fact, he encouraged me to do it. But my dad can't look at me and see anything but a helpless little baby fighting for her life. And then there's what happened to my mom. So here we are."

I sneak a sidelong glance at her. "Have you talked to him about it?"

She barks out a laugh. "I can't believe I'm talking to *you* about it." Now her focus is back on the horizon, putting distance between us. "Please don't say anything."

"Of course." Archer is my best friend, but there's no harm in keeping this secret for her. "But if you don't want anyone to know, why are you out here? This is Archer's spot. He's the one who first found it."

"Archer doesn't run anymore. Because of his knee."

Of course. I'm all too familiar with Archer's knee injury. Not just because my own knee is staging a serious protest right now but because the injury that ended Archer's NHL career? It was from a hit I landed on him.

I glance over and see that she's clenching her jaw, probably thinking about the opening game of Archer's fifth season, when the Grinders went up against the Cutters. The Chicago/Boston rivalry was fierce, and the sold-out crowd in Chicago was loud. Three minutes into the first period, I laid a forecheck on Archer, right into the boards. It was a clean hit, perfectly legal, but he lost an edge as he was getting up to chase the puck, a freak accident. I can tell it's just one more item on the laundry list of reasons why Grace thinks I'm a massive shitheel.

I'm sitting there, stewing in my own misery, when my damp shirt smacks me in the chest.

"Sorry about the blood," she says. She stands, testing her knee. After a few bounces, she seems confident it'll hold up.

"Blood doesn't bother me," I say. "Hazard of playing in the NHL."

"Well, sorry about your shirt, then."

I shrug. "It's a Grinders shirt. I have roughly ten thousand of them. I have enough of these babies that I could soak up the quarry."

If it was just her blood on the shirt, I'd put it back on, but I poured ice-cold water on it to clean her cut. So instead, I tuck it into the waist-band of my shorts. And then I let myself enjoy the way she has to drag her blue eyes away from my pecs. But I don't smirk. I keep my mouth still, my expression passive, because if I've learned one thing in the two weeks I've been accidentally torturing Grace McBride, it's that flashing her a smirk is like waving a red flag in front of a bull.

I do flex, though, just a little, and watch her blush.

"You good?" I ask as she hops back and forth.

She nods. "Yeah, I don't think I actually hurt anything, other than the top couple layers of skin and my pride."

I wave her off. "Nobody saw it but me and the trees, and like I said, I won't tell."

She takes a sip of her water, then offers it to me. I didn't bring water, since a six-mile run is not major cardio for me. I've got a bottle back in my car, and that'll do me fine. But I take it anyway and lift it to my mouth. As soon as the metal touches my lips, I get the flavor of her lip gloss—strawberry, I think. And fuck, it's good. Sweet. It makes me want to taste more of her. As I hold out her water bottle, I swipe my tongue along my bottom lip, picking up the flavor there, savoring it.

And Grace watches me, her eyes on my lips, my tongue. Her focus on me causes a rush of adrenaline that makes me feel like I'm standing at the edge of the quarry, my toes hanging over. Like at any moment I might jump. Or fall. Or like maybe I'm already falling.

When she takes her water bottle back and her fingers brush mine, it feels like someone has touched a lit sparkler to my hand, the fizzy heat rushing up my arm, through my shoulder, and directly into the center of my chest. I nearly jerk away.

"Thank you," she says, and it yanks me back to the reality that I'm sitting here with my best friend's little sister. I just helped her with her bloody knee like when we were kids, that's all. I'm just getting used to this new life I'm living for the summer and the fact that I haven't touched a woman in months. *That's all.* It's a simple animal reaction, and I just need to spend a little extra time in the shower with my hand when I get home.

"No worries," I say, shaking off the electricity zinging through my body. "Besides, I haven't properly thanked you for taking care of my snotty ass the other day. Or for the barstools. Or the entertainment center or the coffee table or the end tables. Or the sink. You're pretty handy."

She blushes. "You don't grow up in a hardware store without picking up a few tricks."

Not that her family has noticed, but I keep that thought to myself.

"Well, I'd like to return the favor," I say.

At that, her blush blooms and spreads down her neck. I didn't intend the innuendo, but hot damn, I like the look of crimson in her cheeks. I like that her mind just went there. It makes my mind want to follow.

"Easy, trigger—I meant, like, dinner or something," I say with a laugh, hoping I'm hiding the fact that I was right there with her.

She swats at my arm. "Jesus Christ, Decker, not every woman on the planet wants to fuck you."

At this moment, I'm only wondering if one *particular* woman wants to fuck me, which is a line of thinking I need to shut off immediately, because a) Archer would put my balls on a spike and b) these running shorts are entirely too thin for those kinds of fantasies. I need to get this conversation back on the best-friend's-little-sister track ASAP.

But my mind is otherwise occupied, leaving my mouth to run with no guidance.

"How about skating lessons?" I say, then immediately cringe. *Skating lessons?* It sounds so dumb, like the most desperate, obvious pickup line. One I've definitely used before and that has definitely gotten me laid.

More than once.

And there I go, thinking about the youngest McBride in my bed again. This is obviously what happens when I attempt a summer of quiet celibacy. My horny brain starts misbehaving. I wind up punching a guy and lusting after my best friend's little sister.

"You want to give me skating lessons?" Her tone holds nothing but skepticism.

Well, shit, what am I supposed to say now? *Never mind, I didn't mean it, that's a move reserved for picking up women, and I really don't want to interrogate why I tried it on you?* All I can do now is try to ride this out.

"I am a professional," I remind her.

She rolls her eyes. "Brooks, your ego knows no bounds."

"Come on, McBride. What are you, scared?"

She tilts her head back and laughs. "Thanks, but I think I'll pass. Let's just call it even, okay?"

I nod, letting out a slow breath. Probably for the best. My mouth wrote a check my ass definitely shouldn't cash.

"Okay, well, I think I'm gonna..." She nods at the trail, her ponytail swinging.

"Yeah, of course."

"If you don't mind, could you go first? You're faster than me, and I don't want to feel you on my heels for the next two miles, nor do I want the humiliation of getting passed."

"How about you run that way and finish the loop, and I'll double back. I could use the extra miles." I couldn't, actually. I'm going to have to rig up an ice bath in my tub when I get home just to appease my knee. But my knee can shut the fuck up. Right now, I'm only interested in appeasing Grace.

And when she smiles? *Victory.*

"Thanks. See ya, Deck."

She trots away, and I give myself the gift of watching the muscular curve of her ass in those pink shorts as she goes. If we're keeping secrets out here in the woods, then I can just add this one to the list.

———

Later, when I'm back home and in the shower, the hot water sluicing over me, clearing the sweat and trail grit from my body, I let my hand drift down. I wrap my fingers around my shaft, hard from the moment I stepped under the water. Hell, I've been half hard since I watched Grace jog away from me. Now I let my eyes drift closed and think of her. The pink shorts, the sweat running down her soft belly, the movement of her ass, her full tits as she ran. And also the way her blue eyes roamed across my chest, the way her chest rose and fell with her heavy breaths. And then suddenly there she is, moving easily through my kitchen, ladling soup into a bowl for me and telling me when to take cold meds. Putting Tupperware in my fridge, assembling my barstools. I think of her furrowed brow when I tease her and the way the freckles on her nose dance when she gives it right back. Her laugh, big and rich, her head tossed back, and the flush on her cheeks when she catches me looking at her. *Really* looking at her.

Her smile.

And as the arousal builds, the tension spooling between my shoulder blades, racing down my spine, I throw my other hand out to brace myself against the shower wall. The pressure builds to a feverish release, and I bite back a shout, coming to thoughts of Grace McBride smiling at me.

# CHAPTER 18
## GRACE

<br>

*To: <gmcbride@cardinalsprings.gov>*
*From: <molly_black@brentwoodauto.com>*
*Subject: Friday meeting with Mr. Brentwood*

*Grace,*

*Mr. Brentwood regrets that he must move your meeting. He can see you at 4:45 p.m. in his office. Unfortunately, with his full schedule, he can only offer you fifteen minutes. Please arrive five minutes early to ensure that the meeting begins on time.*

*Sincerely,*

*Molly Black, Executive Assistant*
*Brentwood Auto—Ford Lincoln Nissan*

<br>

'm clenching my phone so tightly in my fist that I'm surprised the glass doesn't shatter. Fifteen minutes? *Fifteen minutes?* We've gone from an hour-long lunch meeting at the country club to fifteen minutes in the office of his dealership? At least, I hope it's in his office. From the sound of this email, I wouldn't be surprised if Cannon's dad makes me do my pitch underneath a used F-150 during an oil change.

I grit my teeth and try not to scream. But when I reread the email, I hear it in that prissy tone Molly Black likes to use, and a guttural sound climbs up my throat. Molly likes to pretend she's hot shit because she's Burch Brentwood's personal assistant, as if she's sitting at the right hand of Christian Grey and not central Indiana's largest automotive dealer. To say nothing of the fact that I remember when Little Miss Business Suit threw up Smirnoff Ice into her purse the morning of our high school graduation.

I should have seen this coming. I was a little bit shocked when Burch Brentwood, Cardinal Springs's wealthiest resident, agreed to meet with me in the first place. I've always suspected Mr. Brentwood isn't my biggest fan. The whole time Cannon and I were together, it seemed like he hoped his son would find himself someone who could do the whole Susie Homemaker thing, someone who wore prim dresses and had standing hair and nail appointments, someone who could host dinner parties and raise perfect children. That was never going to be me. But now that I'm no longer in line to be his daughter-in-law, maybe he's feeling more kindly toward me.

And I have to shoot my shot, because Brentwood Auto sponsors everything in Cardinal Springs. Without his support, there's no way I'll be able to get the book festival off the ground. I need his sponsorship dollars for the up-front costs associated with putting on an event of this scale.

But whatever goodwill I had with the Brentwood family seems to have crumbled overnight. If I had to guess, I'd say Cannon's bruised and battered face has something to do with this brush-off. Goddammit, Decker. That one punch is really screwing with my entire summer.

I wonder if Mr. Brentwood hopes this email will save him from having to refuse me the money, if it's a hint that I shouldn't bother showing up to the meeting at all. Well, joke's on him, because I'm not that easily deterred. I'll make my pitch while test-driving a broken down Nissan Sentra if I have to. I'm getting those sponsorship dollars.

And I know just how to do it, too.

I find Decker in the back room, sorting book returns onto metal rolling carts. He holds up a battered orange paperback. *"Triple-Duty Bodyguards,"* he reads, his eyebrows raised. "This is about an actress and all three of her bodyguards. At the same time! Do you think Ms. Tingle has read this one?"

"Twice," I say. "I need you."

He glances at the book, then back at me. "You, uh…do I need to call some teammates?"

I snatch the book from his hand, placing it on the fiction cart with more force than I usually use with library materials. "Not like that, you perv. I need help with something for the book festival. The reason you're ostensibly here?"

Now his eyebrows shoot up to his hairline, like that's more surprising than asking him to call his goalie to help double-team me. "Damn, and here I thought you'd never trust me to get near your special project."

"Desperate times," I mutter, clutching my phone.

"Put me in, Coach," he says with a grin.

———

I pull the MINI into an open spot in front of the dealership. This is the new one, built last year on the outskirts of town, a glass-and-concrete behemoth with a veritable ocean of cars stretching in every direction. It's one of six dealerships Mr. Brentwood owns across central Indiana and by far the largest.

When the car stops, Decker pries his knees from his chest and climbs out of the car, towering over the roof.

"Hey, how about while we're here, we look at getting you a big girl car?" he says, rolling his shoulders.

"It was half a mile. Toughen up, cupcake," I say.

"We should have walked," he retorts.

"Sounds like you know how you're getting home, then," I shoot back.

Decker looks up at the sign over the modern glass-and-metal dealership. "Brentwood...as in your ex-boyfriend?"

"Yes," I say, glancing around, but Cannon doesn't appear to be working. Or if he is, he's making himself scarce. And thank god for that, because I'm hoping Mr. Brentwood will forget—or at least ignore—what happened between Decker and his son.

But Decker, for once, is a step ahead of me. "So you want me to go in there and sit across from the man whose son I leveled and ask him to write us a big check?"

"No, first you're going to sincerely apologize, throwing yourself at the mercy of the car king of central Indiana. You will grovel and grin and do your charming Decker Brooks *thing*, and *then* you'll ask him to write us a big check."

He grimaces. "And you think that'll work?"

I sigh. It's a long shot, I know, but I'm desperate. According to my calculations, the festival will bring in more than enough to get the library through another year, but I can't make it happen without a hefty chunk of startup money we do not have. Cannon's dad has the deepest pockets in this town, and he sponsors everything. I swear, Mr. Brentwood must get off on seeing his logo on signs and merchandise. He has sponsored the new Jumbotron at the high school stadium, a new playground at the elementary school, two dog parks, a running trail, a bike service station, and every youth sports team in town. Would I prefer that he just write a check directly to the library to help offset our budget troubles? Yes. But I've learned that rich people don't like to actually *solve* problems; they like to help *you* solve problems. Teach a man to fish, or whatever paternalistic nonsense they tell themselves so they can sleep at night. And if Mr. Brentwood refuses to teach me to fish, I'm going to have to recklessly apply for a bunch of credit cards and charge the festival just to get it off the ground.

"Luckily for both of us, Mr. Brentwood thinks the sun shines out of the ass of every professional who wears a jersey, and I know for a fact that he's a Grinders fan. So while this could backfire, you're all I've got," I say.

Decker smirks. "You're whoring me out."

"I absolutely am," I say. "Will you do it?"

"I will," he says after a theatrical pause. "But you have to go skating with me tomorrow morning."

I roll my eyes so hard I feel the strain in my eye sockets. "You're blackmailing me?"

He shrugs. "I'm negotiating."

He's clearly taking my advice to *do the Decker Brooks thing*. His smile is easy, his hazel eyes warm in the summer sun. He's got one hand tucked in the pocket of his shorts, the other running through his shaggy blond hair. God, he's like a walking magic trick. If we weren't in this cavernous dealership that makes every sound echo like the Grand Canyon, I'd scream.

"Fine," I say through gritted teeth. "Let's go."

Brentwood Auto is simultaneously the coldest place on Earth and an oven, thanks to the sun beaming through the windows. Every wall features sports memorabilia, from signed Hoosiers gear to Pacers jerseys to a signed Peyton Manning headshot. There's even a framed checkered flag that once flew at the Indy 500.

"This place looks like the unholy love child of a TGI Friday's and a Dick's Sporting Goods," Decker says, and I shush him.

Above us, hanging from the rafters, are championship banners celebrating the last twenty years of achievements for every Midwest sports franchise, including the Grinders' two Stanley Cups. Decker glances up at them as we pass, then mutters, "Whoring me out."

"Shut *up*," I whisper in my most terrifying librarian tone.

I weave between shiny new sports cars and hulking pickups, Decker trailing behind me, until we reach the back corner of the dealership. Molly, her face perfectly contoured, hair in loose waves, lips overlined, is parked behind an expansive desk with two monitors. She taps away at the keyboard like she's writing the great American novel. I don't know if it's the speed of her fingers or the bloodred, half-inch talons attached to them, but I have serious doubts that she's typing any actual words.

"I'll be right with you," she says, a smile on her face but her eyes squarely on her computer.

"We're here to meet with Mr. Brentwood," I say.

"Yes, if you want to take a seat, I'll let him know you've arrived," she says. Her voice drips honey with heat shot through it.

"Molly, his office is made of glass. He's right there. We just made eye contact," I say, nodding at the wall of windows behind which I can see Mr. Brentwood leaning back in a futuristic office chair that probably cost more than my car. He's wearing a starched white Oxford shirt with a red Hoosier tie that looks remarkably similar to Molly's white blouse and red scarf. An uncharitable part of me wonders if Mr. Brentwood bends Molly over that stupid glass desk when he stays late at the dealership while Mrs. Brentwood plans her next dinner party back home. Like father, like son?

Molly finally looks up from her screen to glare at me, then picks up her phone and presses a button. "Grace McBride and *guest* are here to see you," she says. I can't help but roll my eyes. She definitely had a photo of Decker from his rookie season up in her locker senior year, and he was definitely not wearing a shirt in it. "You can go on in," she says after hanging up.

I huff out a sigh, but before I can stomp into Mr. Brentwood's fishbowl of an office wound tight as a spring, Decker places a hand on my lower back. The pressure is light, but the warmth causes me to suck in a breath. He ducks down until his lips are centimeters from the shell of my ear and whispers, "Relax, Cherry. Flies with honey and all that."

Muscle memory makes me want to snipe at him for the nickname, shake off his hand, roll my eyes. And I ready myself to do all of that, but then he leans in even closer, his lips just barely brushing my earlobe. "You got this," he whispers.

The vibration of his voice travels down my spine and settles low in my belly. A calm comes over me like a spell. I *do* got this.

Decker steps around me and opens the office door, holding it so I can go in front of him. And when I walk through that door, my shoulders are squared, my chin lifted.

"Grace, good to see you," Mr. Brentwood says, but he offers me only a brief nod. It's not until Decker is standing next to me that he stands and extends his hand. "Mr. Brooks, a pleasure to meet you."

*Is it? Because this is the man who coldcocked your idiot son* is a thing I don't say out loud but desperately want to. This reaction is why I brought Decker along, after all.

"Nice to meet you as well, sir," Decker says, and we sit when Mr. Brentwood gestures to the pair of chairs across from his desk. "You have an impressive dealership here."

"Can I interest you in a new truck? We just got the newest models, and they have some impressive tow power," he says.

"Well, I don't do much towing, to be honest, but perhaps you can talk me into something when we're done here," Decker says with an amiable chuckle. And holy shit, I don't know if I've ever seen Decker Brooks use his charm for good before. It really is a sight to behold. I want to turn and gape at him, but frankly it feels like it could be dangerous, like staring at the sun during an eclipse.

"Why don't we get down to business, and then maybe we can take a test drive," Mr. Brentwood says, his eyes never once leaving Decker's. I might as well be sitting in the lobby.

"Well, first of all, I'm afraid I need to apologize to you. The incident at the Half Pint was obviously regrettable." Decker offers a contrite half smile, tucking his chin for maximum effect.

Mr. Brentwood blinks, completely unprepared for this turn. His slick car salesman persona slips just for a moment, but then he tugs it back into place.

"Oh, well, yes, that was…unfortunate," he says.

Decker nods. "It was, sir. I let myself down, my coach down, my team down. The Grinders see me as a leader, and it's important to me to be that for them off the ice, too. I certainly didn't that night."

I have to bite my lip to suppress a grin, because from the look on Mr. Brentwood's face, he has completely missed the fact that although Decker just apologized for letting everyone down and besmirching his good reputation, he certainly didn't apologize for punching Cannon. There was a whole lot of passive voice in that apology. Decker fights a little dirty off the ice, too.

"Well, the Grinders certainly are lucky to have you," Mr. Brentwood says, shifting in his chair. He wants to take control of this interaction again, but he can't quite figure out how.

"I saw the banners out there. Are you fan?" Decker asks, his easy grin sliding into place. God, he really is good at this charm thing.

"Oh yes, I was at your Stanley Cup win over Dallas," Mr. Brentwood says. "What a game!"

"It was. I'd be happy to offer your family tickets to a game or two this season. I can put you in my suite," Decker says, maintaining his stranglehold on the room.

Mr. Brentwood practically lights up, and I can't believe it. My plan is working.

"And now I'm going to turn things over to Grace, because she's the brains behind this operation. I'm just glad she's letting me help out," he says.

If Mr. Brentwood knows that Decker was sentenced to help out thanks to the punch, he keeps that to himself. With great effort, he drags his gaze over to me, and his face takes on the look of someone getting ready to watch to a bunch of third graders perform *Death of a Salesman*.

But I don't let the set of his jaw or the way he's already starting to zone out get to me. Instead, I focus on the way Decker is leaning back in his chair, pivoting his body to face me. *He's* paying attention. He's listening like I'm about to lay out the strategy for his third Stanley Cup win.

"As you know, the library will experience some unfortunate budget cuts in the upcoming fiscal year—"

"Well, I do appreciate that our government can balance a budget," Mr. Brentwood says.

"Of course," I say, even though every bone in my body wants to start shouting about the value to the community of every dollar budgeted for the library. I could give the most hysterical TED Talk right now, but I don't think that would do much for my cause. Instead, I decide to play Mr. Brentwood's game. "And because we at the library know exactly where our bootstraps are, we're prepared to do our part to pull ourselves up. We're planning to relaunch the Cardinal Springs Book Festival the first week in August, the weekend before school starts. It promises to be a wonderful community event that will encourage literacy, creativity, and a joy of reading. We're going to have a silent auction, an opening night gala, and a full day of author panels and readings, all to raise money to support our programming for the upcoming year.

"But because it takes money to make money, as you know, and because we have an accelerated schedule this first year, we'll need some support to get the festival off the ground. And we'd love nothing more than to have Brentwood Automotive be our banner sponsor this fall."

There's a long pause while Mr. Brentwood folds his arms over his chest and leans back in his chair, the ergonomic monstrosity creaking so loudly it sets my teeth on edge. But I do my best to hide that as I endure the torture of waiting for his response.

Finally, finally, *finally*, he lets out a long breath and gives me a smile that sends a shiver up my spine.

"Well, Grace, if you don't mind taking a little advice, it sounds like you've gotten out over your skis a bit."

"Excuse me?" I say.

Beside me, Decker shifts in his chair.

"Perhaps you should be thinking about ways to tighten the library's belt instead of scrambling to throw together a fundraiser at the last minute."

"I'm not scrambling—" I say, but he holds up a meaty hand, gently shaking his head like he's scolding a small child.

"I know you didn't get the chance to go to college, so you missed out on the opportunity to gain this important knowledge. But a budget is a big responsibility, one you clearly—"

My face heats up as he starts to ramble. I bite down on my cheek—*hard*—to keep my eyes from watering. I will *not* let this man make me cry, even if he is delivering surgical strikes to my softest, weakest spots. As he drones on about business plans and budgets under the bullshit paternalistic guise of "educating" me, I let myself zone out, actively working to bat away the voice in my own goddamn head saying, *He's right—you don't know the first thing about running a business. Your bookstore dream is more like a fairy tale. You'll need magic beans to pull it off.*

"I'm gonna stop you right there," Decker says, cutting the man off mid-sentence and yanking me out of my misery spiral. I snap back to this glass-and-chrome office and blink as I watch Mr. Brentwood's face redden at the interruption. "Thank you for your time."

"Excuse me?" he sputters.

"You're obviously a busy man with cars to sell and sports memorabilia to dust, so we'll let you get back to it," Decker says. He rises from his chair, subtly jerking his chin at me. I jump up and follow him; somehow he's already holding the door open for me. He glances up at the framed Grinders jersey on the wall, covered in signatures, with a little brass plate below it explaining that it was signed by the championship team. "By the way, that jersey? It's a fake. Buchko doesn't have a *t* in it, and Hornik didn't join our team until two seasons later."

As soon as I step out of the office, Decker takes my hand, pulling me past an open-mouthed Molly, whose fingers pause over her keyboard. He drags me through the dealership at a breakneck pace, not stopping until we're out on the hot sidewalk.

"What the hell was that?" I ask.

His brown eyes are fiery, his jaw tight. "I'm sorry to be another man in your life telling you what to do, but I'm willing to fall on that grenade just to make sure you don't have to ask that mother-fucker for a goddamn *penny*," Decker growls.

I scoff. "That's very gallant, but I need that money. Begging smug assholes is just part of the game."

Decker's eyes flare. He steps closer, the proximity forcing him to look down at me. "I'm a smug asshole. Ask me for the money."

I don't know if it's how close he is or the intensity of his gaze, but I have to swallow hard before I can speak. "What?"

"Ask me," he says. His fists clench at his sides like he's trying to keep himself from running back into the dealership and swinging at Mr. Brentwood. "I've got money. Probably more than him. And I'll write you a check without making you feel small just to make myself feel big."

"Decker, I—"

"*Ask* me, Grace." It's part challenge, part plea.

My breath shakes when I open my mouth. "Would you like sponsor the book festival? I can show you all the details—"

"*Yes*," he says, nodding. "I'll have the check sent today."

We stand there on the sidewalk, surrounded by shiny new cars and red banners flapping in the summer breeze, and I don't know what to do with myself—there's too much adrenaline fizzing through my body, too much tension. Before I know it, I'm launching myself at Decker, making contact with his hard chest, throwing my arms around his neck. He locks his arms around my waist, pulling me up and into him, my feet lifting off the ground. His biceps flex as he squeezes me, and I sigh into his cheek.

I don't know what happened in there, how it all went so side-ways. But now I have the money I need, and I don't ever have to speak to Burch Brentwood again.

Decker loosens his grip on my waist, and I slowly slide down his front, my body reading the ridges and muscles there like a topographic map of desire. When my feet hit the pavement, I have to force myself to unwind my arms from his neck. I take a step back, and even though I've put a few feet of space between us, I still feel everywhere he touched me, like if I looked down, I'd see those places lit up.

"Thank you, Decker," I say, my words coming out on a surprised laugh. "Honestly. We really need this."

"No need to thank me," he says. He reaches for the passenger door of my MINI. "Just meet me at the Northern Arena tomorrow morning. Eight a.m. Now, unless you'd like to talk to that asshole about getting a full-size car, I guess I should start folding myself up like an old T-shirt so we can get the fuck out of here."

Right. The skating lessons. Which means I have until tomorrow morning to untangle this ball of emotions I'm feeling for him. The gratitude crossed with desire. The misfiring hormones mixed with my desperation to save the library. The boardwalk magic trick of his good looks, his firm body, and that goddamn smirk.

I very much look forward to wiping that smirk off his face tomorrow.

# CHAPTER 19

## DECKER

The Frank Northern Ice Arena is silent, save for the sound of a baseball game blasting from the tinny speaker of an iPhone. Darren Essex, the manager of the arena since before I was born, is parked in the front row of the bleachers, his gray hair flopping over his eyes, which are locked on his screen.

"You're not going to like the ending of that one," I say as I approach the old man.

"I heard," he replies with a huff. He taps the screen and the action pauses. "Couldn't stay awake till the end last night, and from the headlines, seems like I made a good choice."

"The Cubs are very good at disappointing you," I say.

His eyes flicker to life. "Ah, but that's what makes the wins even sweeter." He rises from his seat and digs in his pocket for a silver key ring that he passes to me. "You're gonna act your age now, right?"

Darren's known me since I first learned to skate here, so he's got some stories to tell. Before this summer, the last time he saw me was when I was a senior at Cardinal Springs High School, pulling pranks and talking shit. That year, I used my parents' Amazon Prime account to order a metric ton of those plastic ball pit balls and filled the practice rink. It looked amazing, but it was an unbelievable pain in the ass to pick them all up.

"Just a skating lesson," I assure him as I tuck the keys in my pocket. During the winter, there would be league practices and open skates all day on a weekend, but today Grace and I will have the place to ourselves and I'll lock up when I'm done.

The creak of the ancient door echoes through the empty arena, and Darren and I both turn in time to see Grace emerge from the tunnel between two sets of bleachers. She's wearing a pair of black leggings with seams that should be warnings and a red long-sleeved athletic shirt that curves around her breasts like a taunt: *Wouldn't you like to have your hands right here, Decker Brooks?* And here I thought upside down with her panties in my face would be the most tempting she'd ever be. But turns out Grace in full-coverage spandex is infinitely more appealing. If she asked me for another ten thousand dollars right now, I'd give it to her. I'd give her anything she wanted after that moment on the side-walk in front of that fucking gaudy car dealership.

"Just a skating lesson, huh?" Darren mutters under his breath, his eyebrows arching toward the ceiling. I give him a look that says, *Zip it, old man*—but, you know, respectfully. He just laughs. "Got to call your brother. The wife wants to do a kitchen remodel," he says to Grace.

"I'll let him know you're interested," she says, sidling up to us. "Felix loves a good kitchen job."

"You kids be good," Darren says, and I don't know if it's the wink he throws us or the cold of the arena, but Grace's cheeks pink up in a way I like.

When Darren is gone, I gesture to the front row of the bleach-ers. Two pairs of skates are waiting. Twenty-five years of hockey means I don't go anywhere—even Cardinal Springs, Indiana in the summer—without my skates. These are scuffed from the final games of the season, but that's the only play they've seen, since I usually wind up with new skates every dozen games or so. I probably should have tossed them directly into the nearest dumpster after that last game to rid myself of the bad luck clinging to them, but apparently I'm a masochist, because I brought them home from the arena. They sat in the corner of my condo while I packed my bags, and then I slung them into the back of the Bronco just before I hit the road. Just looking at them makes my stomach feel like fifteen gymnasts are doing flips inside it. But they're all I have, and I didn't have time to get new ones after proposing this half-baked scheme to spend time with Grace.

And let's be honest, that's exactly what this is: a plot to get some time alone with her. I know nothing can happen, but that doesn't mean I can't just...*be* around her. I feel better when she's with me, like maybe I'm not a fuckup, like I'm more than just a bad hockey season or a smile. I could have asked her to dinner, or to a movie, or to take a drive in the Bronco, but those all felt a little too close to dates. And that's a line we can't cross, a line *I* can't cross. So instead, we're standing here in a dank, empty ice arena while I watch her toe off her sneakers.

I texted Grace last night to get her shoe size and arrived early to find the least abused pair of rental skates. I chose hockey skates for her because I thought it would be sexist to assume she'd want figure skates, and also the balance on those things is all wonky. If I'm actually going to teach her to skate—and I *am*—then I need to stick with my skill set.

I brush away the questions about why I want to show off in front of Grace and instead press down on her shoulders until she sits on the bench. I crouch in front of her and reach for one of her skates. I slide my hand gently up her calf to lift her leg, enjoying the feeling of her muscle flexing beneath my touch.

"I can do it, Decker," she says, her voice a little airy, but she doesn't pull her leg away. I have to keep my eyes down, focused on the skate, because I hear the way her breath picks up, and I don't trust myself not to watch her chest rise and fall. Don't trust myself not to wonder what it means.

I have to clear my throat before I can speak. "I know, but if the laces are too loose, you'll break an ankle," I say. "That'll really fuck with your half marathon training."

I wait for her to yank her foot back, to show me the stubbornly independent girl who's in control of every moment. But she sits still, her leg growing heavy in my hand, trusting me to take care of her. Just like she did yesterday when she swallowed her pride and asked me for the money for the festival. I was going to write her a check regardless. There was no *way* I'd make her beg other assholes like Brentwood. But I also knew Grace needed to do the asking, needed to feel in control. I didn't want to take that away from her.

I get her feet securely into the skates, then make quick work of lacing them through the foot and ankle. I allow myself one quick glance up at her face and catch her watching my busy fingers. Her cheeks are pink, and she gently bites the edge of her bottom lip as she studies my movements. I stifle a groan at the thought of sinking my teeth into that pillowy lip, then following it with a swipe of my tongue, getting another taste of her strawberry lip gloss.

If she were any other woman, this would be an incredible start to a skating lesson. But this is Grace McBride. Lacing up her skates should not feel like this, like an invitation. And after she leapt into my arms yesterday, thrilled to leave that stupid fucking prick Burch Brentwood behind, just being *near* her feels indecent. Holding her calf in my palm feels pornographic, and a low thrum of *I want her, I want her, I want her* beats like a drum in my mind.

But she is not mine to have.

My thoughts are a tangle of frayed skate laces. I need to get control of them. I'm about to take this girl out on the ice, after all. I need to make sure she doesn't get hurt. I need to make sure she's safe.

And I'm starting to think that means safe from *me*.

*Don't fuck this up, Brooks.*

Just as I think that, I reach the top of her skate, yanking the laces tight hard enough that a little squeak escapes her lips.

"S-sorry," I say.

"It's fine." She finally pulls her foot away and stands, testing the blades on the rubber mats by the bleachers.

I busy myself with lacing up my own skates, a task I could do upside down in the dark and still be ready for sixty minutes of regulation play and a few overtimes. At least now I feel like I'm on firm ground. With this, I know exactly who I am, what I'm doing, what's expected of me.

But as soon as I stand, Grace beside me, that feeling flees. I don't mean to stare at her body—I just want to be sure she doesn't wobble—but unlike her brothers' favorite nickname for her, there's no gracelessness that I can see. She stands firm on the rubber mats, her shoulders back, her core engaged. With strength and posture like that, this skating lesson probably isn't going to be so hard for her.

"So, are we doing this?" Grace asks.

"Yeah, let's do it," I say, because for some reason I can't manage to volley back one of my trademark smartass replies. And if I can't tease Grace, I don't know how to be around her. What does that even leave on the table? *Sincerity?* Jesus Christ. That's not a program I have in my operating system.

And if I keep thinking about this, I'm going to short-circuit. *I'm* going to fall down and bust my fucking ass. So I turn my back to her and walk to the open gate of the rink.

"Okay, keep your knees bent. You don't want to lock them, or you're going down like a sack of rocks," I tell her, shooting my left foot out to show her. "And keep your eyes up. Wherever you look is where you're going. If you look at the ice, that's where you're going."

I watch as Grace toddles gingerly to the edge of the ice. I step out onto the surface and glide about a dozen feet, then turn, plant my blades, and hold my arms out.

"Okay, push off with one foot, out to the side, and just glide," I tell her. My muscles tense, prepared to grab her in case she comes out flailing like Bambi. I almost hope she will so I can come to the rescue and pull her to me.

I let out a shaky breath and plaster on a smile—my best all-American grin.

"Okay, let's see what you got," I say.

Her face is totally impassive, the blush in her cheeks her only sign of emotion. Then she suddenly breaks into a grin and arches an eyebrow. "You gonna catch me?"

"Of course," I say with a gentle smile. My heart picks up its tempo, going from gentle ballad to pop-punk frenzy, and my breath hitches. "I'll catch you."

Her eyes narrow slightly. "We'll see about that."

And then she steps out onto the ice. In an instant, she's gone, sprinting away from me down the straightaway. When she hits the turn at the far end of the arena, she leans, her left arm tucking neatly into the small of her back as she digs deep for some of the most beautiful crossovers I've ever seen. Coming out of the second turn, she tucks her right arm back to meet her left, knees bending as she pushes side to side. She looks far too relaxed for the amount of speed she's got under her feet, as if she's out for a casual stroll and not putting up speed that would impress at the NHL Combine. When she leans into the third turn, her crossovers look damn near elegant. Out of the fourth, her skates make the most delicious *schick, schick, schick* sound that lights up every nerve in my body. On the final straightaway, she turns it up to eleven, finding even more speed. I nearly step out of her way as she barrels toward me, but at the last second she leans back, throwing her skates out in front of her for a hockey stop that showers me in freshly shaved ice.

I'm half hard by the time I blink the snow out of my eyelashes. I swallow, watching her chest heave, warm little puffs of breath coming out of her mouth.

It takes me entirely too long to find my words, as the first ones that enter my mind are way too X-rated to say out loud. I finally settle on, "What the *fuck* was that?"

She rolls her eyes. "What the *fuck* made you think I needed skating lessons?"

Her cheeks are pink, her mouth stretches into a wicked grin, her hands are resting on her hips, and holy shit, she's never looked so beautiful. As much as I've tried to pretend I don't want her, I can't do that anymore, not with that expression of pure satisfaction on her face. Then she bites her lower lip, trying to tone down the gloating, and that's even worse. My entire body feels pulled toward her, like she's a powerful magnet. I practically have to dig my blades into the ice to keep from wrapping my arms around her and planting my lips on hers. *My god*, this woman. She is an absolute wonder.

A wonder who fully conned me.

"In my defense, in all my years of club and high school hockey, I never once saw you on the ice," I say. "You were always bundled up in a million layers, sitting at the top of the bleachers with a book."

"Yeah, because hours of hockey tournaments are so fun for a nine-year-old who isn't allowed her own pair of skates because Dad was afraid I'd fall and my heart would shatter," she says matter-of-factly, like the statement itself isn't shattering. She gives a little stomp to clear her skates of ice and then squares her shoulders. "Last year I joined a speed skating club in Bloomington. It was too cold to run outside, and I wanted some good cardio that I didn't have to do by myself. It was fun, and it turns out I'm kind of good at it."

"Fuck yeah, you are," I say. I can't hide the awe in my voice, nor do I want to. She deserves to hear how incredible she is. "Did you compete?"

"Just one club meet. The only real meet I could make was up in Gary, and I couldn't figure out a good way to explain the trip. But maybe this winter," she says. She shrugs and pushes off, leaving me to trail after her like a needy puppy.

"Grace, you gotta. You're really good, and fucking fast. Don't you want to feel the weight of a medal around your neck?"

She pivots so she's skating backward, facing me. "We'll see," she says with a half grin that feels like a brush-off. She's very good at telling people what they want to hear, or telling them just enough that they *think* they've heard what they want to hear. But I'm not letting her off the hook so easily.

"How about this? Next winter, when that Gary meet comes around again, just tell everyone you're visiting me. I'll be your cover."

Her eyes widen, and her skate slips slightly. I throw my arms out, but she manages to get her blades under her right away, steady as a table.

"I'm not sure which would freak out my family more—me joining a speed skating team, or me voluntarily spending a weekend with you," she says before elegantly whipping back around.

"It wouldn't be *so* crazy," I say, letting the image unfold in my mind. Her packing a bag into that tiny, ridiculous car of hers and coming to see me. Me watching her skate. Her jumping off the podium directly into my arms. It suddenly doesn't feel crazy at all.

Her head tilts like she's trying to guess my angle. "What do you mean?"

I shrug. "I mean, I'm not the ogre you thought I was. Maybe we're even friends now." *Maybe we could be more.* The words are right there on the tip of my tongue, foreign and strange but ready to come out nonetheless. "Right?"

She bites her lip, nods. "Yeah, okay. We're friends, I guess."

I skate closer to her but leave a respectable distance between us that I absolutely don't want.

"If we're not friends, then what are we, Grace?" God, I like the sound of the word *we*, the way her name feels in my mouth.

She doesn't answer, but her lips turn up, her nose wrinkles, those fucking freckles dancing, and a tiny giggle escapes her lips on a puff of air I can see thanks to the cold of this cavernous, empty arena. My breath catches as I watch it curl into the air and disappear.

This girl who runs in secret, who skates like her perfect ass is on fire and reads the smuttiest books I didn't even know existed… She built all my furniture. She cooked for me. She fixed my fucking sink.

She keeps surprising me over and over.

And suddenly, all I want is to surprise *her*.

And so I push off the ice, closing that respectable distance, and grab her hand. Her fingers thread through mine like we've done this a thousand times, and I instantly want to do it a thousand more. I tug her into me. She braces herself against my chest, but she doesn't waver. I wrap my arm around the small of her back, resting my palm on the curve of her hip. It feels as good, as right as I imagined.

I pause, a question, and then she goes and surprises me again.

We're still gliding slowly across the ice when her lips brush mine, but as soon as I feel the press of her against me, taste the hint of strawberry on her lips, I dig my blade in hard. We stop, because I know that kissing Grace McBride will demand every ounce of my attention.

She may have started it, but now it's my turn.

I cup the nape of her neck, my thumb pressing into her jaw as I angle my face to take her in more fully. I part her lips with my tongue and swallow the hum of pleasure that vibrates through her. My other hand coasts along her rib cage, my thumb stopping just beneath the swell of her breast. She arches into my touch, pulling a groan from deep into my chest that she tastes with her tongue. My cock stiffens in my sweats, and I know she feels my desire for her because she rolls her hips slightly, yanking another groan out of me.

And then a creak echoes through the arena like a crack of lightning, followed moments later by the slam of the metal door. Grace's hands, which just seconds ago were clenching the fabric of my sweatshirt, suddenly press hard against my chest, propelling her backward, away from me. She comes to a stop with about six feet between us, her eyes wide, her chest rising and falling quickly. I blink, trying to make sense of being yanked out of her warm embrace and thrust back into the cold. Our gazes lock, a series of silent questions passing between us. Or maybe it's just her asking, because there's no question about what I want.

Not until Archer emerges from the tunnel between the bleachers.

# CHAPTER 20

## GRACE

"What are you two doing here so early on a Saturday?" Archer asks as he steps out onto the ice in his sneakers and walks toward us. That's a thing that always surprised me growing up—how easy it was to walk across the ice in street shoes. Every time someone did it, I expected them to go full Wile E. Coyote, skidding into a dramatic split. It wasn't until I joined the speed skating club that I finally learned that walking on indoor ice is fairly easy, so long as you take steady, sure-footed steps. "And why are you on skates?"

My heart is still racing a thousand miles an hour, my breath coming in heaving gasps, to say nothing of the sting where Decker nipped at my lips. I'm afraid that if I open my mouth to answer my big brother, the only words that will tumble out are *Holy shit, I just kissed Decker Brooks.*

And boy, did I.

I don't know what possessed me to rise up on the tips of my blades and taste him other than pure, unadulterated craving. And maybe a healthy dash of *What could this hurt?*

But now, with Archer standing there holding a mesh bag full of pinnies that smell like dryer sheets and rank body odor, my thoughts are bouncing around like they've been loaded into a dryer.

"Uh, I mean, I'm just—" I stammer, shifting my feet forward and back on the ice.

"Just getting in a little morning skate and decided to drag my jailer along," Decker says, and while his voice is doing that laid-back, *Hey, man, who's got worries?* thing, his eyes are still laser focused on mine. His tongue darts out to swipe at his lower lip, and his fingers twitch at his side like he wants to pull me back into him.

Or maybe that's wishful thinking.

If I have no idea what *I* think of the kiss, I have not a shot in hell of figuring out what *he* thinks.

"Well, I was just dropping off the pinnies, and then I'm headed to the diner to meet Owen for breakfast," Archer says. "You guys want to join?"

Decker's brows rise in question, letting me take the lead.

The last thing I want to do right now is have breakfast with two of my brothers and the man I'd prefer to yank behind the bleachers like some horny teenager, but I don't know how to say no to Archer without raising a whole lot more questions that not even Decker's relaxed smile and easy excuses could answer.

So I put on a smile and say, "Sure," watching Decker carefully for a reaction. But I don't get one, or at least not one that tells me anything. Just a small nod, a lock of his blond hair flopping onto his forehead.

"Breakfast sounds great," he says.

———

Sometimes living in a small town really fucking sucks. Like when the ice arena is so close to the diner that your brother proposes you all just hoof it together, which means you don't even get a tiny window of travel time to ask your hookup what the hell your kiss meant. Does this mean we kiss now? Were there feelings attached to that kiss? We established that we were friends just moments ago; what are we now?

And can we kiss again? Like, right now? Maybe if we duck behind the mail truck for a second while Archer bends down to tie his shoe?

Instead, while Archer squats on the sidewalk to fix his laces, Decker and I just share a silent film's worth of wide-eyed stares, a flurry of questions bouncing back and forth between us so quickly that I'm surprised they don't create a breeze. So I guess it's good that we can't have this conversation immediately, because I have absolutely no idea what I would say.

My whirring thoughts are interrupted by the jingle of the bell on the door of Pete's Diner, which Archer is holding open for us. Decker gestures for me to go in first, like he's some kind of gentleman or something.

He sure doesn't kiss like one.

"You feeling okay, Grace? Your cheeks are all red," Archer says, sending my hands flying up to my face, as if I'll be able to feel my sexual frustration written across it like braille. A welcome blast of cold air from the diner does nothing to cool me down.

"Just the skating," I say. "It's harder than it looks, I guess."

Decker cuts me a sidelong look, but Archer is too busy studying me. "You wearing your heart rate monitor?" he asks.

"Yes, Dad," I reply in my favorite snotty sister tone, holding up my wrist to show him my Apple Watch.

"Hey, guys, back here," Owen calls from a booth by the window near the back of the diner. Pete's is an old-school place with a counter stretching from one end to the other and booths lining the window, almost like an old train car. The smells of toast and coffee and griddle grease fill the space, and on a Saturday morning, it's bustling, a few people waiting outside for a table.

I head for the back, aiming to take the open seat next to Owen. He's in shorts and a sweaty T-shirt, clearly fresh from the gym. The thought of sitting pressed up against Decker in a booth while we face off against my brothers makes my heart rate kick up so fast I'm surprised my watch doesn't buzz with an alert. But then Archer shoulders past me with his long legs and takes the seat by Owen, leaving the opposite side of the booth for Decker and me. And Decker is roughly the size of a Clydesdale, so even when I slide all the way against the window, his muscled thigh still presses against mine on the cracked seat cushion. I press my hands to my cheeks again, because if the flood of warmth between my thighs is any indication, I must be blushing the color of summer tomatoes.

"I ran into these two at the arena this morning and figured I'd drag them along," Archer says to Owen, who is busy stirring creamer into his coffee. He looks up, and his eyes narrow. For a second, my breath catches, but then I realize his gaze is focused over my shoulder at the door. I swivel just in time to see Cannon step inside. He's wearing khakis and a polo, a ball cap pulled low over his brow; he's probably headed to the golf course. He's alone, and he scans the counter, looking for an empty stool. When he doesn't find one, his eyes land on our table. They stop at me, then flick over to Decker, who has also turned to see what has drawn my brother's ire.

Cannon's shoulders stiffen slightly, his eyes flitting back to me for a fraction of a second before he turns and walks out.

"Well, hell, you really are an honorary McBride brother," Archer says, reaching across the table to slap Decker's shoulder. Decker returns his grin, but I notice it takes some effort. "Glad to finally be rid of that guy. No offense, Grace."

"None taken," I lie, because it actually does rankle that apparently my brothers have hated Cannon for quite some time. After the breakup, this news came out slowly at first, then all once, like water from a fire hose. Seven years worth of complaints and jokes all came flooding out, and I know they're not nearly done yet. And yeah, Cannon turned out to be a real shithead, but I'm still not exactly pleased that everyone was rolling their eyes and gritting their teeth behind my back for all those years. It makes me feel small and stupid, like I'm still the clueless kid sister tripping through life. I think I would prefer their normal brand of butting in, telling me what to do with my love life like they do with everything else.

A warm hand covers my knee beneath the table, the fingers pressing into my skin on a silent squeeze. I look over at Decker, but he's got the menu in his other hand and is pretending to study it. And as quietly as it arrived, his hand slips away.

"Seriously, Grace, you need a glass of ice water?" Archer asks, concern that I don't want etched across his face. "She looks weird, right, Owen?"

Owen glances up from his coffee, his eyes wide. Of all my brothers, Owen definitely has the softest heart. He's the most gentle, always the last to join in on the teasing. And I've always appreciated that despite my family's attempts to make him use his medical training against me, he does his best to hold back.

"She looks happy," he says. He says it casually and accompanies it with a little shrug, but it warms every part of me.

I cut my eyes over at Decker and catch the tiniest twitch at the corner of his lips.

"I think I'm just warm," I say, and reach for the hem of the long-sleeved Lululemon running top I wore to the ice rink. I peel it up and over my head, tossing my hair over my shoulder. Beside me, Decker shifts, his hand clenching around the menu. "Also I forgot sunscreen yesterday when I did an outdoor program. Maybe I just got a little color."

A lie, but Archer doesn't need to know that. He doesn't need to know anything about how I've been spending my time. Especially my time with the "honorary McBride brother."

Ugh.

Suddenly Owen presses his face to the window, squinting into the sun.

"Holy shit," he says, and when I follow his gaze, I spot a man across the street. He's hard to see at first because he's tucked in the narrow alley between two buildings. He's obscured by a shadow and also by the woman pressed up against him, her arms wrapped around his neck as she gives him what looks like a hell of a kiss.

"Is that Dad?" I squeak, leaning so far toward the glass that my forehead thunks against it.

Decker leans toward the window, too, his whole torso pressing against me. I nearly forget that I'm watching my dad engage in a public make-out session.

"Who's he giving mouth-to-mouth to?" Decker asks.

I can only see the back of the woman, but her silver-streaked curls pulled up into a messy bun give her away immediately.

"That's Corianne, his trainer," I say, eyes wide.

"What the hell is he doing?" Archer says as we all watch them kiss like one of them is shipping off to war. Archer turns to Owen. "Is that…ethical?"

"I mean, she's not his doctor," Owen says, his brows knitted. His cheeks flush, and he finally has to look away. "It might be a gray area? But, I mean, they both look like they're consenting."

"Consenting all night long," Decker says with a laugh.

"Gross!" I swat at him, but that just sends a shock of heat up my arm at the feel of his biceps. "Should we bust him?"

"Leave the old man alone," Decker says.

"But he's a grown adult! He can't have sneaky make-outs on street corners with random women!" Archer sputters.

"She's hardly random, Arch," I say. "They've been working out together for years."

"Yeah, which is weird. I swear that's a conflict of interest or a breach of trust or something," Archer says.

"You think Corianne is abusing her power over dad? For what reason?" I ask.

"Orgasms," Decker says.

"That's my *dad*, man," Archer says, his voice low. "And, I mean, if he feels like he has to hide it, that's a red flag, isn't it? Why wouldn't he tell us?"

"I don't know, maybe he's worried you'll freak out?" I say, leveling him with a look.

Out on the street, Corianne and Dad pull apart, and Dad takes one of her hands in his. He lifts it to his lips and plants the most delicate kiss on her palm. Then he lets her hand go, and they step out onto the sidewalk. Had I not seen what they were just doing, I might have missed how close together they're walking, their shoulders nearly bumping as they chat and laugh. They're trying to hide whatever's happening between them, but it's pretty obvious if you're looking for it. They seem…happy.

Across from me, Archer looks baffled and maybe a little bit furious. He's usually so in control of his emotions, toggling between congenial and stoic. It's weird to see my big brother so ruffled. "Archer, what's going on?" I ask.

"I just think he needs to be careful," Archer grumbles, reaching for his menu. "Dad doesn't date, so whatever that was is a big fucking deal. Suddenly there's another chair at the dinner table, another stocking on the mantle at Christmas. Do *you* want a new mom?"

I suck in a breath, and Owen stiffens.

"Christ, Archer," Decker says. "Calm down."

"This is serious! I can't believe you guys don't get that," Archer grumbles.

As Dad and Corianne disappear around the corner, I realize I've never seen that look on my father's face before. My whole life, he's gone on only a handful of dates, none of them amounting to anything. Most of them seemed more like obligations, like he thought he should be getting out there, but ultimately he was happier in the store or working on projects around the house. He's happy with all of us kids, too, obviously, but it's a different kind of happy. It's not the smile I've only seen in photos, with him pressed up against my mom, their twin grins a mile wide.

There's one photo, my absolute favorite, of the two of them standing in front of an ice cream truck in the late nineties. They're both holding enormous ice cream cones, both of them with white blobs of vanilla soft serve on their noses, their heads tossed back as they laugh, their eyes closed at the hilarity of it. It's the only picture of my mom that makes me cry every time I look at it, because I can't hear her laughter. I have no memory of it, not even an echo of one. I never heard her laugh.

I don't even realize tears are forming in the corners of my eyes until I feel Decker's hand on my thigh again. This time his thumb traces slow, firm circles on the fabric of my leggings, leaving a trail of heat everywhere he touches. Though his eyes are back on his menu, I can feel every bit of his focus on me, like he knows what I'm feeling. And in an instant, I'm pulled back from the ledge. The tears retreat, and the lump in my throat recedes. I'm as safe and secure with him now as I was that very first day when he held me tight against him and pulled me out of that blasted urn.

But across the table, my big brother is a frustrated tangle of emotions, terrified that our family is about to change. Terrified that one kiss could pull everything apart.

And suddenly that kiss on the ice feels like it's much bigger than just Decker and me.

# CHAPTER 21

### DECKER

"Guys, I gotta go," Owen says, eyes on his phone. His eggs are growing cold and congealed on his plate.

"Everything okay?" Archer asks.

"Yeah, just a patient. I think he's having an allergic reaction to an antibiotic I prescribed. I told his mom to meet me at my office." Owen reaches for his mug, downs half his coffee in a single gulp, then grabs a triangle of toast as he rises from the booth.

"Isn't your office closed on Saturdays?" Archer asks.

"I'm not making his mom drive him to Bloomington when I can just as easily walk four blocks and unlock my office," Owen says. He shoves the wedge of toast in his mouth and drops some bills onto the table. "Besides, urgent care will bleed you dry. See you guys later." He doesn't wait for goodbyes before he's out the door.

"He works too hard," Archer mutters.

"What crawled up your ass and died?" I ask.

"Seriously, first you freak out about Dad, and now you're mad at Owen for helping a patient?" Grace says.

"Hey, I don't need the two of you teaming up against me," Archer says, pointing at us with his fork. "It's fucking weird."

The idea of being on a team with Grace is too fucking good,

even if Arch looks like someone pissed in his coffee. So I hold my hands up in surrender, and Archer sighs into his pancakes.

"Sorry," he mutters, but he doesn't unclench.

The rest of the meal is tense. I keep my eyes on my veggie omelet, half terrified that if I look over at Grace, I'll pull her into my lap to continue what we started. It's all I can think about as I chew and swallow. That, and what Archer would do to me if he saw. He already damn near caught us back at the rink.

After the way he melted down over his dad and that yoga lady, I'm pretty sure he'd remove my arms from my body and beat me with them.

And I think I might have to let him.

I let my eyes wander away from my plate and over to Grace, who's sitting beside me in those goddamn leggings and a tight tank top. Her dark hair is pulled into a ponytail that falls over her milky-white shoulder. My gaze drifts down to her breasts, which swell with each breath. It takes real effort to drag my eyes back to my breakfast. But I do it, because if Archer crawls out of whatever funk he's in and notices the way I'm ogling his sister's truly incredible tits, he will put me through the window of this diner.

For the rest of the meal, I have to force myself not to kiss her.

But I cannot force myself not to want to.

When the plates are empty and the waitress drops the check, I lunge for it before Archer can swipe it. "My treat," I tell the two McBrides still at the table.

Grace bumps my hip, trying to wedge me out of the booth. I comply, and she slides out and jumps to her feet.

"Where are you headed in such a hurry?" Archer asks.

"Why, you want to criticize my Saturday plans, too?" she retorts.

Archer throws up his hands. "Excuse me for worrying about my family."

Grace rolls her eyes. "I'm going home. I've got a list of admin tasks to do for the book festival," she says.

"Anything I can help with?" I ask, because I want nothing

more than to follow her home. I'll do anything to spend more time with her, to find out how she feels about that kiss, to find out if she wants another.

Because even though her very big, very grumpy brother is standing in front of me reminding me that I absolutely should not, *I* very much want another. And at home, there would be a door we could lock. No interruptions. I nearly groan just fantasizing about what our afternoon could be like.

But Grace isn't on the same page. "Nope, all good," she says. She turns back to Archer. "I hope that by the next time I see you, you've managed to cool your jets a little bit."

"No promises," Archer replies, then looks at me. "Hey, I'm headed to the gym. You want to lift with me?"

*No, I want to go make out with your sister.* "Sure," I say, trying not to watch Grace's ass in those leggings as she heads out. Without even thinking about it, I follow her. "I'm going to head home and change. Into shorts. I'll meet you there."

And then I'm out the door, single-minded in my pursuit of Grace. She's already half a block away, but with my long stride, I catch up to her in no time. I fall into step beside her.

"What are you doing?" she asks, looking stubbornly forward like we're in some Soviet spy flick and she doesn't want to be seen talking to me.

"I'm going home to change and then meeting Archer at the gym." I brush the backs of her fingers with mine, and she jerks her hand away like she's touched a hot stove.

We walk, the silence between us growing heavy. She flings open the door that leads to our apartments and charges up the stairs, but then she pauses on the landing and doesn't unlock her door. I stop in front of mine so that we're toe-to-toe in a space roughly the size of a New York City elevator. The tension between us feels like a long fuse, the flame creeping steadily toward an explosion.

Grace's ice-blue eyes bore into mine, an army of thoughts battling behind them. And I just wait. I know what I want. I want to press her up against that door and finish what we started. I want to see where it goes. I want to see if her body goes pliable against mine.

But more than that, I want to know what *she* wants.

"That was a mistake," she says.

*Fuck.*

"I mean, it was good. *Really* good," she continues.

*Okay. Say more.*

"But it can't happen again," she says.

*Goddammit.*

"Okay," is all I say.

"I mean, you saw how Archer reacted to seeing my dad with Corianne. He would lose his fucking mind if he thought you and I were fooling around," she says.

I nod.

"And besides, I'm basically your boss, so it's kind of inappropriate for anything to happen between us," she says.

"Probably," I say.

"So we'll just move on." She worries her keys in her hand, the metallic rattle an audible manifestation of her anxiety.

"Okay," I say.

"Okay," she says.

I stare at her for one more beat, maybe to give her a chance to change her mind. But I know she won't. Not right now, anyway. Grace is stubborn. I'm not going to push her. If *she* wants to forget about that kiss, I won't mention it again. I'll let her play this however she wants.

But *I* won't forget about it.

Because I can't help but notice that although Grace has a list of reasons why nothing can happen between us, *because I don't want to* isn't on it.

———

Archer's gym is a few miles from downtown, out near the highway, so we drive there in the Bronco. He's still tense, a low-simmering enigma as we drive in silence. Once inside the brick box of the gym, Archer bolts for the leg press machine, skipping his warmup, maybe out of spite. At who or what, I don't know.

I don't have that luxury, though, so I park myself on an open mat and start working on mobility and activation, warming up my sleepy, creaky muscles before I reach for the weights. Since I lifted heavy on Thursday, I don't plan to do anything too wild today.

"Yo, can I get a spot?" Archer calls, lying down on a bench. He's got some hefty plates on the bar, so I hustle over before his mood gets the best of him and he does something epically stupid. Which is weird, because that's usually *my* job.

He blows through six reps, face reddening, sweat pricking his temples, then drops the bar on the rest with a heavy clang. He sits up, elbows on his knees, panting.

"Hey, man, you wanna, uh—" I pause, glance around. We're far from downtown, but the notorious gossips could be anywhere. We're clear, though—the only other folks in the gym are a pair of older gentlemen in jeans, walking slowly on treadmills. "You wanna talk?"

"About what?" Archer grunts, then flops back onto the bench. He reaches for the bar, and I move into position to spot him.

"About why you seem like you wish you could throw these weights through the front window?"

Archer lets out a bitter-sounding chuckle.

"Yeah," is all he says as he hits his fifth rep. The weight is starting to get to him, and the sixth is a struggle, but he makes it. The bar lands on the rest with an even louder clang than before, and Archer is back up, eyes on the floor, chest heaving.

"Okay, good talk," I say. I move to take some weight off for his last set, but he shakes his head.

"Leave it," he says.

"Sure," I reply. I give my shoulder a roll just in case I need to catch this thing. He may not need any weight dropped, but I might.

He lies back, gripping the bar, his knuckles white. When he puts up his first rep, he pauses.

"Cassie's pregnant," he says, lowering the bar to his chest. My eyes go wide, but I don't have time to react, because Archer lets out a growl and throws up his second rep. "She just got engaged to that asshole, the smug fucker on the LA Gold? Saw it on Instagram."

"Johanssan?" I ask. When my press got bad, I handed off my social media to an assistant, but I know Anders Johanssan. He's so pretty the LA Gold treat him like a mascot. He's the king of thirst traps, but his play is only mid.

"Yeah," Archer grinds out on the third rep.

I don't know what to say. The truth is, Cassie and Anders are probably the perfect couple, so long as they have separate walk-in closets and bathrooms for their beauty routines. But I don't think that's what Archer wants to hear.

"I'm sorry, man," I tell him, my arms out, my legs braced, because that fourth rep isn't coming easy.

I think Archer wants to say something else, but he wants a fifth rep more. He grinds his molars as he works, his back bowing off the bench. And I want him to get it, too. I'm trying to will it, but it's not coming, and finally I reach for the bar, gently helping to guide it back onto the rest.

"Fuck!" Archer cries, dropping his arms over his face.

"It's okay, Arch," I tell him, reaching down to pat his shoulder.

"It's *not*. The whole thing has me fucked up. I thought I was over Cassie. I mean, I think I knew we weren't going to work out as soon as we left Boston. But seeing her with a big fucking rock on her hand, holding an ultrasound picture? It really threw me."

"Do you still love her?" I ask.

"No," he says. He sits up and swings his legs around so I can sit down beside him. "Really, I don't. I think it's that…I mean, I'm just…I'm lonely, man. I'm fucking *lonely*. I thought when I moved back here that I was going to settle down. The NHL was never my dream—you know that. It was awesome, but the most important thing to me has always been having a family. And when I moved back here, I thought at least I would still get that. I've got a house and a job I love, but I'm still fucking *alone*. And I hate it."

His voice catches on that last part, his shoulders bunching as he works to calm down. I throw an arm around him, tugging him toward me. And I feel like a total fucking asshole. Because this summer was supposed to be about Archer and me. I could have been helping him with this shit. I could have been taking him out. *I'm* staying out of trouble, but that doesn't mean we can't try to find some trouble for him. But instead I've been distracted by his little sister, including kissing her behind his back.

"I'm sorry, Archer. But it's not too late," I tell him. "You're a great guy, and I know you're going to meet someone who will love you like you deserve to be loved. And hell, you know that whatever Cassie puts on Instagram is ninety percent bullshit. She may have a picture-perfect life, but she's never going to be as happy as you are."

"Yeah," he says, his voice gravelly. "But how the fuck am I supposed to meet someone?"

"Grace is on the apps," I tell him. "You should try it."

Archer turns his head slowly, his eyes narrowed. "Grace is *what*?"

*Fuck.* I don't even know why I brought that up. Maybe to make sure Arch doesn't suspect anything? Maybe to convince myself that no matter how badly I want her, she's not going to be with me? Nor should she—I've already been a shit enough friend to Archer. He doesn't need to deal with this on top of everything else. And I need him. He's the only guy in my life who's not obligated to put up with me because of his job. I love my teammates, some more than others, but we don't have the same kind of bond. So many of the guys I started with have retired or been traded.

Archer's lonely now, but he won't be forever. He's got a family that adores him, and I know he's going to meet some incredible woman and shower her with all the love that fills him. She'll be one of the luckiest women on the planet, because she'll have strong, solid, kind Archer McBride beside her.

But without Archer, who do I have? My parents, who barely tolerate me? Grace, who doesn't want me? Archer's all I've got. I owe it to him to be a better friend.

"You better tell me everything you know about my sister and these app idiots," Archer says, interrupting my spiral. "I bet this is Wyatt's doing. She's a bad influence on Grace."

Yeah, she's not the only one.

# CHAPTER 22

## GRACE

I spend the rest of the weekend hiding out in my apartment, pretending to read. In reality, my brain is fully occupied with thoughts of storming across the hall, bursting through Decker's front door, planting my lips on his lips, and seeing what happens next. I keep getting a chill, the ghost of his thumb resting just below my breast, his warm palm pressing against my ribs. Decker may not be in my apartment, but I feel him *everywhere*.

I finally give up on the reading charade when I realize I haven't turned a page in twenty minutes; I'm just staring at the same paragraph, my eyes completely glazed over. I dog-ear the page of the new Alexis Hall, then reach for my laptop.

I was lying when I told Archer I had admin tasks to do for the book festival. My to-do list is well in hand. In fact, I have infuriating little to accomplish this weekend. So when the screen glows to life, I glance around furtively, as if there might be someone hiding behind the fiddle-leaf fig in the corner of my apartment, ready to jump out and bust me for googling Decker Brooks.

I click on the image tab and start scrolling. Nearly all of the first results are of Decker in his orange-and-black Grinders uniform, a stick clutched in his gloves. I haven't actually seen him play hockey since Archer was in the league. Decker is a center, a position that requires an incredible amount of speed and finesse. In every photo, he looks laser focused on the game, the puck, the play.

There are suggested topics across the top of the search screen, and I click on "Decker Brooks suit." That brings up photos of him arriving at various arenas on game day, his shaggy hair pushed back, well-tailored suits hugging every muscle, every inch of his height. Even in the still photos, I can see the ease with which he moves. Whether on skates or in loafers, he exudes confidence with every motion.

My mind starts going on very vivid little imagination safaris, thinking about what Decker could do to *my* body with *that* body.

A new suggestion is at the top of the screen now, and even though I know I shouldn't, I click on "Decker Brooks girlfriend."

These pictures weren't taken by team PR reps or sports photographers. These are paparazzi photos, some of them from red-carpet events, some snapped from across the street or inside dark clubs. In each picture, he's got a different woman on his arm, every one of them beautiful. Some of them I recognize, like Imani Menendez and that brunette singer who recently won a Grammy for Best New Artist—I can never remember her name, but all her songs sound like she's having very quiet orgasms. Others are just miscellaneous beautiful women, the kind you see on Instagram prancing across busy streets in New York in haute couture or holding up jars of pickles that cost thirty-seven dollars in LA grocery stores. Their makeup is always perfect, their hair beautifully tousled, their clothes expensive.

These are the kinds of women Decker usually kisses.

And suddenly his willingness to forget all about the kiss we shared makes a whole lot of sense.

I wasn't lying when I told him that letting anything more happen between us would be a mistake. Archer's reaction at the diner yesterday when he saw Dad kissing Corianne was only a little bit out of character. When I started dating Cannon, it took Arch a good year and a half to stop glaring at him, and he only ever made it as far as careful indifference. It takes a lot to earn my brother's approval, and he's been even less willing to give it since Cassie left him.

Finding out that his best friend is sneaking around with his little sister would be a double betrayal.

And now that I'm looking at pictures of Decker at movie premieres and club openings with the most beautiful women on the planet, I sort of can't believe I ever thought the two of *us* together was even a possibility. Decker is one of the most famous hockey players on the ice today, maybe even a Hall of Famer if he doesn't fuck up his legacy by acting like an idiot. He's a literal multimillionaire who looks like a Greek god.

Cannon's words echo in my ear unbidden. *Decker Brooks has had fucking supermodels, Grace. Supermodels. You think you stand a chance in hell of pleasing him?*

I squeeze my eyes shut, trying to call up a meditation mantra or a song or *anything* to drown those words out. They fade away, but my own voice takes their place, asking if I seriously think I'm going to tame Decker Brooks. It's not even about whether or not I'm good enough for him. The man runs through women like they're protein shakes. He's not relationship material, and even if he was, I live in Cardinal Springs, and he lives at the business end of a paparazzo's lens. This whole thing is a ridiculous thought exercise.

I slam my laptop shut and reach for my book, determined to make good on my promise to forget about that kiss.

---

On Monday morning, I trudge into the library, bleary-eyed and clutching a triple espresso. Necessary, since I woke up at four a.m. gasping from a dream in which Decker did very interesting things to me with his tongue, and then I couldn't get back to sleep.

Fortunately, Decker's not due in for another hour. That gives me time to come up with tasks that will keep him far away from me and my horny impulses until I can get my hormones under control or he finishes his community service, whichever comes first.

"Grace, are you free for a check-in?" Suzanne calls from her office behind the circulation desk. "I'd love an update on where we are with the festival."

Okay, this is good. Focus on the festival, not on the extremely tall, handsome man who kisses like he's looking for the secret to eternal life inside your mouth.

"Yep," I say, and head into the tiny office. I drop my tote bag on the carpet and sink into one of the chairs across from Suzanne's desk. I take a long pull of my coffee and reach into my tote for the brown paper bag I brought from Crimson 'n' Cream, already spotted with warm, buttery grease. I offer it to Suzanne. "Double chocolate cherry? I got two."

"I'm trying to cut down on sugar in the mornings," Suzanne says.

"You've started your day with a fountain Coke the size of your head for as long as I've known you," I say. "Maybe start there?"

"But the fountain Cokes are the only things stopping me from committing murder, honey," she says, reaching for the sweating cup on her desk and taking a long sip from the straw. "I'll drink my sugar, thanks. I had eggs for breakfast. Now, tell me where we're at with the festival."

I update her on everything I've accomplished so far. I've got sponsorships well in hand—there's Decker's check, of course, and I managed to secure smaller amounts from most of the local businesses, including the McBride contingent. Dad donated on behalf of the hardware store, Owen gave through his practice, and Felix even gave five hundred dollars from his fledgling contracting company, plus they've all promised to do manual labor during the event. I hand over the envelope of checks so Suzanne can deposit them, because pretty soon we're going to need to start spending.

Suzanne grabs a windowed business envelope from her desk, extracts her purple reading glasses from the top of her head, and squints through them at the small print. "We did get this one for fifteen thousand dollars from Top Deck LLC. That's not Brentwood, though, right?"

I blink several times. "Wait, fifteen thousand? From *who*?"

"Top Deck LLC," she repeats.

"Who the hell is that?"

Suzanne arches an eyebrow, her expression saying, *Do keep up, Grace, dear.*

Top Deck LLC...*Deck.* "Holy shit, did Decker give us *fifteen* thousand dollars?"

"That would be my guess, based on the return address in Chicago," she replies.

My mouth drops open. "But I only asked for ten."

"That boy is generous," Suzanne says.

God, he's making it infuriatingly hard to forget about kissing him on Saturday.

"Speaking of," she says, glancing over my shoulder, "that boy seems to be pacing back and forth outside my office."

I turn and see Decker strolling past the door with practiced ease. His hands are shoved deep in his pockets, like he's just out for a morning stroll, but when he catches me watching him, he quickly picks up his pace and disappears. Seconds later, he passes by again, going the other way.

"He's not a boy, Suzanne," I say.

"No, he's very much not," she agrees, her lips curling up.

"Suzanne!" I have to work to keep my voice low, partially because we're in the library and partially because I don't want Decker to hear.

"Oh, don't get me wrong," she says with an eye roll, "he'll always be a smelly teenage hockey player to me, practically my own kid. But he's not that to *you*."

I narrow my eyes at her. "He's nothing to me," I say, trying my best to mean it.

She smiles. "I don't think that's true, Grace."

"Are you trying to play matchmaker?" I ask, and that's when

several puzzle pieces snap together in my mind. Suzanne was the one who volunteered Decker for community service at the library. She assigned him specifically to me. "Wait, *have* you been playing matchmaker? This whole time?"

She shakes her head, but the move is exaggerated, like she's acting out a stage direction. "As your supervisor, it would be deeply unethical for me to get involved in your romantic life."

I raise my eyebrows. "I notice that you're very diplomatically not denying it."

"I always thought I would make a good diplomat," she says.

I point at her. "You're *still* not denying it."

Suzanne flutters her eyelashes, the picture of innocence. "What was the question, dear?"

I huff out a sigh. "Fine. But no matchmaking. Or no *more* matchmaking. There will be no match made between Decker and me, okay? We're friends, and that's all." I say it like I mean it, even if I'm only about a third of the way there.

"Well, when Decker first arrived here, you weren't even that," she says.

I throw up my hands. "Okay, then—yes, maybe you were right to smash us together like a five-year-old playing Barbies. We've become friends. But that's as far as it's going to go."

Suzanne studies me from across her desk, brows knitted, fingers tented beneath her chin. Her gaze is so intense that I begin to withdraw, to cower, like she'll be able to tell that I'm lying.

It's already gone further than that.

But it definitely won't again.

It *won't*.

It's can't.

"If that's your story, I'll accept it," she finally says, and honest to god, I'm not entirely sure the woman can't read my thoughts. "Now, as for the festival, it sounds like you have everything under control. But don't be a hero, Grace—tell me when you need help. Just because you're heading this project doesn't mean you need to do everything on your own. Please delegate."

"Great, then you can help me by sending Decker down to the basement to count the folding chairs," I tell her. "I need a full inventory."

She laughs. "You can't be serious."

"I am," I say, then pull a list from my tote bag. "And when he's done, he needs to go the Baptist church, the Episcopal church, the Presbyterian church, and the synagogue and count the chairs there, too. Oh, and the community center. I need to make sure we won't have borrow any from Bloomington or Martinsville."

"And you can't ask him to do this because…"

"Because I'm delegating," I say with a cheeky grin. I rise, hoist my tote bag onto my shoulder, and take a pull from my coffee cup. The caffeine sends a zing of excitement through me; it's the first time I've felt like maybe I *do* have everything under control. "I'll be in the nonfiction stacks going through emails and finalizing our author list."

I stride out of Suzanne's office and come face-to-face with Decker, who is still wearing holes in the carpet with his pacing.

"Suzanne has your assignments," I tell him. "Should take you all day, so I'll sign your form tomorrow. Enjoy!"

And then I march toward the stacks, ready to distract myself with kicking this book festival's ass.

———

When I leave the library at the end of the day, I have a list of confirmed authors and a rough sketch of the schedule. This book festival is actually happening, and I feel *fantastic*. The deep dive into planning worked, and I've managed not to think about kissing Decker at all.

Well, not very much. But I feel more confident that we can be friends.

On my way home from the library, I stop at the market and pick up ingredients to make lasagna. For the first time since

Decker arrived and shook my life up like a snow globe, I feel like things are settling. I'm in my routine again.

And then I get home, and there he is, standing on the landing outside my apartment. He's leaning against his own door, one foot kicked up behind him, his arms crossed over his broad chest. When I get to the top of the stairs, he doesn't move, forcing us to stand practically toe-to-toe.

Decker reaches into his back pocket and pulls out a folded piece of paper. "Your chair inventory," he says. "Unless the entire population of Indianapolis shows up to this book festival, you should have twice as many chairs as asses. Reverend Halliwell at the Presbyterian church says you're welcome to use the sanctuary or the fellowship hall, dealer's choice. Rabbi Meisner says you can do setup after sundown on Saturday or he can unlock the doors for you early on Sunday, just let him know. And Pastor Scott would like assurances that the books featured at the Baptist church will be"—he make air quotes—"clean enough for Baby Jesus."

Being this close to him is making it a whole hell of a lot harder to remember why I thought we could be just friends.

"Can you put all that in an email?" I ask him, turning to my front door. I'm desperate to get away from him, because apparently I can only be friends with him if I don't have to look into his eyes, or glimpse his corded forearms, or take in his tall frame. God, in just shorts and a T-shirt, his hair flopping over his eyes, day-old stubble dotting his sharp jaw, he looks absolutely delicious. I have to get the fuck away from him *immediately*.

I adjust my grocery bag on my elbow and try to shove the key into the lock, only I miss, and my key chain clatters to the floor. When I bend over to get it, the bag slides down my arm, throwing my balance off, and I overcorrect, sending my ass directly into Decker's crotch. His large hands grab my hips, and he rights me in one swift movement. Then he bends down to scoop up my keys and unlocks the door.

I step inside, and he follows me.

"Whatcha making?" He nods at my grocery bag before settling onto one of my barstools like he's a regular.

"Lasagna." I start unpacking and lining up all the items on the counter, then pull the other necessary ingredients from my cabinets. I decide to focus on cooking, in hopes that horny mode will power down or run out of memory.

"Yum. My favorite," he says. He leans his elbows on the counter and watches me preheat the oven, but when I rise onto my tiptoes to pull my lasagna pan from the cabinet over the fridge, Decker is up and around the island in a flash. He sidles up behind me, placing a hand on the counter by my hip and reaching over my shoulder for the pan.

"You know, I, too, am tall," I say, taking it out of his hands.

"That thing is heavy. I didn't want you to drop it and mess up my dinner," he says with a devilish grin.

I scoff. "What are you doing? We're just friends, remember?"

"I remember," he says. "That's why I'm here. To have dinner with my friend. Unless—"

"Nope. No unless. Just friends," I say in my most authoritative, firm tone.

"Cool. But I think after what you did to me today, you owe me some lasagna." He smirks.

"What the hell did I do to you?"

"You banished me to the Miracle Mile, and I had to spend an entire day trying not to swear. Do you know how fucking hard that is for me?"

"Jesus wept," I reply. I start layering my lasagna in the pan.

"The chairs at the Episcopal church are in a closet in the choir room. I had to listen to an hour of handbell practice, and let me tell you, God did not give with both hands when distributing musical talent to the Episcopalians," he says. He bats his eyelashes, adopting an expression more suited to shelter dogs and orphans. "Feed me. Please?"

I groan. "Fine. But first you have to tell me why you wrote a check for fifteen thousand dollars to the book festival when I only asked for ten."

He shrugs. "I told you, I didn't want you to have to ask any smug assholes for money. You know, other than me."

I roll my eyes.

"The extra five is a buffer, and if you don't need it, just throw it into the library budget. You work hard—you deserve it," he says.

I want to be mad at him, but I realize that being pissed at someone for giving you an extra five thousand dollars is ridiculous, and also what he just said was really sweet.

"Thank you," I say.

He just waves me off, then takes the jar of sauce out of my hands and pops the lid with a quick flex of his forearm. And oh my god, my entire body is in flames.

I take the jar back and throw myself into the recipe. Unfortunately, it's pretty simple and doesn't require much focus. I don't even have to parboil the noodles, and I'm cheating with jar sauce. Sure, I bought the good organic jar sauce, but today is going to be more Rachael Ray than Nigella Lawson. Which leaves a whole lot of mental attention for the rangy, grinning hockey player draped over my kitchen island.

I'm so distracted, I trip over his splayed leg and drop a spatula covered in marinara on the floor, splattering my cabinets and my shoes.

"You okay?" Decker asks, bending to pick up the spatula.

I reach for a dish towel, then point at the couch. "Do me a favor and go in the living room? Your interference is making a mess."

Decker skips the couch and plants himself in front of my bookshelves, which are stuffed full, the books perilously stacked. "Have you read all these?"

"Most of them. But I maintain a pretty robust TBR section." When Decker raises a questioning eyebrow, I clarify. "To be read."

"Wow," he says. He scans the spines like he's looking for something in particular. He pulls a blue paperback off the top shelf, and I recognize it immediately: *It Happened One Summer* by Tessa Bailey, one of my favorite romances of the last few years. "Why do you keep books you've already read?"

"Because sometimes I like to reread them," I say. I look up from sprinkling shredded mozzarella on my lasagna just in time to see him flip the book open and scan a page. He blinks, then shudders out a nervous laugh, his mouth dropping open.

"*'High-maintenance pussy'*?" he mutters. "Jesus Christ, Grace."

Hearing him say those words causes something to glitch in my body, and I freeze, my hand, still clutching a wad of shredded mozzarella, hovering in midair. But he doesn't notice because he's too busy reading, his eyes growing wider and wider. His lips part, and a little huff of breath escapes.

I wonder what part he's at.

As warmth gathers in my belly, I realize what a mistake it was to let Decker into my apartment. Catastrophic! Right up there with getting bangs after a breakup (thank you, Wyatt, for talking me out of that one). It obviously hasn't been nearly long enough since the kiss and our agreement to ignore it. I haven't had time to send the message to my hormones that Decker Brooks is off limits. In fact, I'm pretty sure my hormones have an out-of-office message on, because as I watch him read—Decker Brooks *reading* in my living room, *oh my god*—I have the sudden urge to leap over this island in a single bound and climb him like a tree.

I'm lost in those dirty thoughts when his eyes dart to mine, his lips quirking up into a smile.

"Grace, there's a sticky note in here," he says, pointing at the pastel pink slip. "You bookmarked this."

I swallow hard, my voice coming out on a whisper. "Yeah."

He groans, and the sound goes directly into my panties. Holy shit, I need to get this under control.

"Unless you want to hand over your phone and let me check out your search history, I will not be talking about my favorite scenes with you," I say, then force my eyes back to my lasagna.

"Scenes? Plural?"

I reach for the aluminum foil, using it to gesture at the book-shelf, eyebrows raised. "Sure, not every one of those books is open door. I like a good closed-door swoony romance. Sometimes leaving things unsaid is just as sexy," I say. "But sometimes…you just want someone to say it."

Now it's Decker's turn to freeze, the book looking tiny in his big hands. He glances back down at the page, and what I would give to know what his eyes land on when he says, "And you like this."

I nod. "Yes."

His eyes go back to mine, and a tether of heat forms between us, even clear across the room. "Like, in real life," he says. His voice is low scrape that makes me shiver. "You want this."

I nod again. "Yes."

The corner of his lips quirks up. "Have you ever had it?"

"Like that?" I ask, my eyes dropping down to the book. "You mean the way they talk?"

"Yeah. Like this."

I can't bring myself to say it. I can't believe I've let this conversation go so far astray. So I focus on covering the lasagna with foil, crimping every edge perfectly, and placing it in the exact middle of the oven rack. By the time I close the door, I'm confident that I can speak without my tongue hanging out of my mouth.

"I'm not talking about this with you," I say carefully.

"Why not?"

My voice rises what feels like six or seven octaves in exaspera-tion. "Because you're…*you*!"

He rears back. "What does that mean?"

I roll my eyes. "It means I've had exactly one dick, and you've had a cavalcade of pussies. Discussing my sexual experience with you feels like asking the world's greatest violin player to saw out 'I'm a Little Teapot.'"

I don't know if it's my confession that I've only ever slept with one guy or my use of the word *pussies*, but Decker's mouth drops open, and when he closes it, he swallows hard. "First of all, thank you. Having my sexual prowess compared to the world's greatest violin player is going in my player bio. Second of all…that's a no, then?" His voice is back to that low, gravelly scrape. "The sport-o didn't do it for you?"

I sigh. Do I really want to get into this with him? Cannon would never talk dirty. Not to me, anyway, though I shove *that* thought away because it stings like alcohol on a paper cut. When Cannon and I had sex—which wasn't very often by the end—it was like a silent film. Only instead of a raucous piano soundtrack, Cannon would throw a country slow jams playlist on his smart speaker, and I'd have to pretend I could get it up for the dulcet tones of Morgan Wallen singing about liquor and trucks.

*I bet Decker's good at dirty talk.*

The thought zips through me like an electric shock so intense I'm surprised my hair doesn't stand on end.

He's still waiting for my answer. "There's a difference between a good hamburger and a great hamburger," I finally say.

Decker's brown eyes turn molten. "And you've never had a great hamburger."

I shake my head. "Not as of yet, no. But someday, some guy is going to throw me over his shoulder and whisper every one of his filthy desires into my ear."

There's a heavy silence between us as I process what just fell out of my mouth. Have I been drinking? Am I high? Am I drunk *and* high?

"You can't say stuff like that to me," Decker says, his voice husky.

"Why not? We're friends, aren't we?" God, I sound like I've been huffing helium, the way my voice squeaks.

"I don't know if we'll be able to stay friends if you talk to me like that," he says, then goes back to the book.

He finally moves to the couch, dropping his enormous frame onto the cushions. We exist in silence for the next few minutes, him reading while I chop garlic for a quick vinaigrette, then dress the bagged salad I bought. Every once in a while, I glance over to find his mouth hanging open. Finally, he interrupts the silence with a small laugh, one filled with awe.

"And to think the road map has been here all along," he mutters. He closes the book and taps it on his thick thigh. "Can I borrow this?"

I don't know what's more shocking—the conversation we just had, or the fact that Decker Brooks wants to borrow a book from me. We have officially entered the Upside Down.

"S-sure," I sputter. "But I want it back. I've annotated that one."

His eyebrows rise. "You've *what?*"

"Highlights," I say.

He nods, not even trying to suppress his grin. "Okay, then."

# CHAPTER 23

## DECKER

"During one game that went into *six* overtimes, we wound up eating packets of ketchup between OTs. The calories kept our energy up, and the sodium kept our muscles from cramping," I tell the group of little kids gathered at my feet.

"*Ewwwww!*" they chorus. They gag and scream, barely keeping their butts on the industrial carpet. Their enthusiasm is infectious, and I find myself shouting and groaning along with them, because yeah, eating plain ketchup *was* pretty fucking gross. But at that point, I was so ragged I'd have eaten a puck if I'd thought it would keep me going.

"I love ketchup!" Nora, the little redheaded girl who knows a shocking amount about hockey's more obscure rules, grins. I notice she's got a new missing tooth.

"Mom, can we have ketchup for dinner?" Nimesh says, bouncing so hard on his knees that I'm sure he's doing permanent damage.

I hold up *Eat Your Superpowers*, the picture book we just read. "Remember, just like a car needs gas, your body needs fuel. That's what food's for. And every food has a job to do. So make sure you put all your foods to good work, okay?" I point at the bouncing little boy in front of me, and he drops back down onto his butt. "Nimesh, that means some protein and vegetables, too, okay?"

Nimesh wrinkles his nose and opens his mouth like he's going to protest, then pauses and shrugs. "Okay, *fine,*" he says, and at the back of the room, I see his mother's mouth drop open in surprise. I'm guessing Nimesh doesn't usually agree to eat vegetables without a Congressional level of debate.

The parents are lined up along the back wall, some of them making sure their kiddos don't talk too loud or interrupt or bolt from the room. A few are focused on their phones, probably using story time to deal with work tasks or simply decompress a little. I don't blame them—just an hour with these kids sucks the energy right out of me. Sometimes I feel like I've done sprints by the time I finish. Tired, but also filled with their enthusiasm.

As an only child, I've never really thought much about kids. Several of my teammates have them. They sit by the glass, bouncing on their mothers' laps in tiny jerseys that say DADDY on the back. I always sort of took for granted that I'd have them someday. It was an abstract idea that existed somewhere in a hazy future, like retirement—it would probably happen to me eventually, but it wasn't something I needed to concern myself with now. But this summer, the threat of my career ending and these weekly visits with a room full of five- to nine-year-olds has me thinking about them more and more.

Of course, I'd never have kids with the women I've been dating, if you can even call it that. Up until now, my life has not been designed for meeting the kind of woman you could start a family with. But maybe this summer will change all that, change the way I approach dating.

*Maybe…*

Ms. Suzanne strolls into the children's section, a stack of books under her arm. Her purple reading glasses are tucked into her gray curls. She smiles as she does a sweep of the room that has me sitting up even straighter.

I turn back to my audience. "Okay, kiddos, that's it for today. Will I see you all back here next week?"

"My mom says we have to go visit Grandma and Grandpa since they complain about not seeing us but refuse to make the effort to come here," Nora says. In the back of the room, a woman with matching red hair puts her hands over her face.

I cover a laugh and tell Nora to have fun visiting her grandparents, then remind Nimesh to please walk (like a big boy, not like a monkey) as he leaves the library. But before they head out, he and his mom stop by the table where I'm cleaning up.

"Nimesh's skates came in last week, and we went to our first open skate at the ice arena," she tells me, her pride evident in her wide smile.

"Hey, that's great, little dude," I say, ruffling his hair. I look back up at his mom. "You might want to get him a helmet if he's going to be speed-demoning around the ice like he does in here. And maybe some wrist guards."

"Already ordered," she says with a rueful grin. "He's begging to sign up for youth hockey, but holy heck, the gear is expensive! I think we're going to try a few more practice sessions to make sure he wants to stick with it before we commit. But I'll tell you, I've never seen him so hyped about anything other than Minecraft, and if he really loves it, we'll make it work, whatever it takes. Anyway, I just wanted to thank you for doing all this for the kids. You're really getting them excited about sports and moving their bodies in new ways."

I feel my cheeks flaming. "Thank you, I'm really happy to be here," I say. And it's true. Three weeks ago, when I was first assigned to the library, I was just happy not to be in the newspapers or in jail. But now I can't imagine spending my time in Cardinal Springs any other way. I really love seeing the kids' eyes light up, watching them literally vibrate with excitement.

Still, I can't stop thinking about what Mrs. Joshi just said. I was lucky when I started hockey. My parents had money and were willing to drive me wherever to try and get my boundless energy out, even if they desperately wished I was more interested in books than pucks. The kids I played with had that same kind of privilege. It shouldn't be that way. And maybe there's a way I can help make sure more kids get a chance to feel the exhilaration of shooting down the ice on skates, of a perfect pass, the satisfying crack of a good slap shot.

"Did Mr. PB&J seriously just do a story time about eating your vegetables?" Ms. Suzanne makes her way over to me.

I shrug. "I ran out of hockey books, and I only know so much. Figured it's never too early to start teaching them about how good nutrition benefits an active body."

She can't hide her surprise. "I'll admit, Decker, this is not at all what I imagined when I cooked up this community service plan with the sheriff. I figured you'd be good for unloading the book drop and cleaning out the basement storage rooms."

I laugh. "Trust me, it's a shock to everyone that I'm useful for more than just manual labor."

She scoffs. "Oh, I always knew you were good for more than that. But this particular skill set is quite the surprise. These programs for the kids are excellent. I've heard from several parents whose children can't wait for story time every week. You're a hit."

I'm dumbfounded. "Really?"

"Yes," she says matter-of-factly. "I wouldn't make that up. I'm proud of you, Decker."

It's been a long time since I've heard anyone say that. Not since—

"And Coach would be, too," she says, reaching out to pat my arm. "I think he would have really loved seeing you here. He always said his hardest hitter had the softest heart."

I stiffen like I can hold back the swell of emotion with sheer brute force, but I can't stop the lump that forms in my throat. I can only clear my throat to try to work past it.

Sensing my discomfort, Ms. Suzanne takes a step back. "Speaking of manual labor, there are two cases of bottled water sitting outside my office. Could I trouble you to carry them upstairs to the staff lounge?"

I nod, the lump starting to dissolve. "Not a problem. Do you want them in the fridge?"

She shakes her head. "You can just leave them on the counter."

"I'll do it as soon as I clean up here," I say.

The last of the kids and parents are trickling out, leaving me to put all the tiny chairs back at the tiny tables in the main reading room. I sweep the plastic fruits and vegetables I used for a game into a box and return them to the little play kitchen by the children's circulation desk. Then I head to the nonfiction shelf and scan for 613.2, the Dewey decimal number for *Eat Your Superpowers*. The shelves in the children's section are low, so I have to squat down to find the exact spot to slide the book in. Before heading to Ms. Suzanne's office, I make a pit stop in the fiction section to see if *Hockey Night in Kenya* has been returned. Hockey is a depressingly white sport, and it would be great to show the kids some diversity. It's not back yet, though, so I may just order my own copy and bring it in. Otherwise I'm going to have to do some serious brainstorming about what to do with the kids next.

I find the water bottles outside Ms. Suzanne's office and hoist both cases onto my good shoulder, then start for the stairs. What I'd really love to do is organize an open skate for the littles. I put a bug in Archer's ear about it, but he said there aren't enough rental skates for small kids at Frank Northern. In fact, they only have one pair in each size, and with a group like this, there's bound to be overlap. I can easily solve that problem—I can just place an order with our team gear sponsor and have dozens of pairs here within a week. But the root of the problem remains: hockey has an incredibly high barrier to entry. And that barrier contributes to a lot of the diversity problems in the sport, especially in America and other more diverse countries, where it's less ubiquitous than in Canada and the Nordic region. It's absolutely wild that Cardinal Springs produced *two* NHL players, but there are barely any others from the entire state of Indiana.

I'm lost in thought about how quickly I can put together this open skate and what else I could maybe do to expand access to hockey in Indiana when I arrive at the staff lounge, tucked in a back corner of the second floor by the nonfiction stacks. There's a tall, narrow window in the door, and as I reach for the knob, I catch a glimpse of dark brown hair, milky-white fingers threaded through it. It's Grace, sitting on the couch, elbows on her knees. I can't see her face, but everything about her posture says *stress*.

I pause before I enter. I haven't seen much of Grace since our dinner Monday night, when she fed me lasagna and filled my mind with images of her in those romance novels she loves. The one I borrowed, about a fisherman and a socialite who fall in love and engage in some intensely steamy, well-described sexual escapades, was—pun absolutely intended—a real banger. I stayed up late several nights reading it and took extra-long showers in the mornings, my fist and I working out some of the intense mental images the book inspired. Only it wasn't the flighty redheaded socialite character I envisioned. It was Grace and those intense ice-blue eyes and that thick, dark-chocolate hair.

The images come roaring back to me now as I stand here on the faded carpet of the library, two cases of water on my shoulder and the object of my fantasies just a room away.

I know I said I could forget the kiss we shared on the ice, but I was lying. I was lying through my teeth, and I honestly can't believe she even bought it. I've definitely *tried* to forget, but no part of me can let that image go. My brain has been filled with that kiss twenty-four hours a day since it happened. That kiss is like a one-hit wonder with lyrics about her strawberry lip gloss and my fingers pressed into her skin. There are times when I worry that song has become so much a part of me that if I open my mouth, the only words that will tumble out are *I kissed Grace McBride, I kissed Grace McBride, I kissed Grace McBride*—a real showstopper of a refrain.

But I understand her argument. I don't want to lose Archer,

and he would *not* be okay with me thinking any of these thoughts about his baby sister, much less acting on them.

And then there's the rest of our conversation that night, when Grace confessed that she'd never had a great hamburger. I have no doubt I could satisfy that particular craving for her. Sex and hockey: those are my talents. But the thing about Grace is that she deserves *more* than just the great hamburger. She deserves the whole damn meal. And I'm just a bum hockey player, traveling for half the year, living and breathing my sport three hundred miles from here. In just two months, I'll load up my Bronco and head north. I'm due back in Chicago for training camp a month after the book festival, and if we have a good season, I won't get off that roller coaster again until the middle of June.

That's not what Grace needs.

*I'm* not what Grace needs.

That doesn't stop me from wanting her, though. And so I adjust the cases of water on my shoulder and push through the door.

"Hey, girlie, how's it hangin'?" I say when she doesn't look up at the sound of my footsteps on the linoleum floor.

She only groans in reply, so I put the water down and lean back against the counter, crossing my arms over my chest. "Seriously, are you okay?"

She finally lifts her head, revealing dark circles beneath her eyes, her hands pressed to her cheeks. "Just trying to psych myself up for the rest of my day," she says.

"It's three p.m.," I say. "Your day is nearly done. What could possibly be left on your agenda that has you looking like you're about to get a root canal?"

She lets out another long groan. "I woke up in the middle of the night and realized I'd put the romance panel in the Baptist church, and if you'll recall, Pastor Scott requires that the books featured there be—"

"Clean enough for Baby Jesus," I finish, shuddering at the memory of the pastor, with his slicked-back hair and obvious veneers, smiling at me like a televangelist. "Well, shit, I've only read one romance novel in my life, but if the rest of them are like that, Baby Jesus is going to be blushing pretty fucking hard."

"Exactly," she says. "But the romance panel is sure to have the biggest attendance, and the Baptist church is our biggest venue. The only one that comes close is the community center, but it's not available on Saturday morning because there's a Zumba class. So I had to change the *time* of the romance panel, which meant contacting all the authors in case they needed to adjust their travel plans. Then I finally crawled back into bed, but I woke up again at four a.m. with cramps and didn't manage to get any more sleep."

I grimace. "Tell Suzanne you're not feeling well and go home."

"I would, except I have a meeting with the city manager at four thirty to finalize which streets we're closing for the festival," she says, dropping her head back into her hands. "It's in an hour, so I don't have time to go home, take a nap, and then get to City Hall."

I glance at the couch, a worn brown leather number that frankly looks perfect for a snooze. "Take a nap here. That couch looks mighty comfortable," I say.

She throws her hands up in frustration. "I'll be so freaked out that I won't wake up in time that I'll never actually fall asleep."

I know I'm supposed to keep my distance. But I also told Grace we could be friends. So I pull out my phone and set an alarm. Then I cross the floor and take the cushion next to her, throwing my arm over the back of the couch behind her. I gently tug on her shoulder until she begins to lean back, melting into my side. The feeling of her pressed against me is so good—*too* good— but I shove that thought down and repeat, *just friends, just friends, just friends.*

"Power hour," I tell her. "Close your eyes, catch some z's, and I'll wake you up in time for your meeting."

"Seriously?"

"Seriously. I do it all the time when I have to sit around on set for media day or photo shoots or whatever. You would not believe the incredible naps I've managed in the Grinders locker room with just thirty minutes to spare." I give her shoulder a squeeze, and she takes it as an invitation to rest her head on my biceps. I force myself to breathe normally even as her silky soft hair brushes my jaw. "I'll catch up on emails while you sleep. Do the Wordle. Watch game tape. I've got earbuds. It's no big deal."

"I doubt I'll be able to fall asleep," she says, but she nestles closer, adjusting her shoulder so it tucks under my arm. She fits just right, like a puzzle piece.

"Close your eyes and see what happens," I say, my voice low and soothing.

"Your alarm is set?" she asks, her eyes fluttering shut.

"It's set," I assure her, then double-check that I actually did it right. Sure enough, it'll chirp loudly in an hour to wake her.

Before I've even closed the clock app, Grace's breath steadies and slows, and she drifts off to sleep.

Forty minutes later, I'm staring at the *New York Times* crossword puzzle and wondering why I know way fewer words than I thought when the lounge door creaks open and Ms. Suzanne pokes her head in.

"Is she okay?" she whispers, nodding at Grace, who is drooling on my shoulder. "She's meeting with the city manager in forty minutes."

I hold a finger to my lips, nodding. "I'll wake her in time," I mouth back, not wanting to disturb one second of Grace's rest.

Suzanne smiles, but she doesn't leave right away. She lingers, her eyes flitting back and forth between Grace and me. I know what this looks like. It certainly *feels* like that to me. But if this is all I get of Grace McBride—the feel of her breath against my chest, the weight of her head on my shoulder, the knowledge that she feels safe enough with me to fall asleep—then that will have to be enough.

# CHAPTER 24

## GRACE

I slept with Decker.

Literally.

He woke me up by stroking his thumb across my cheek. I blinked my eyes open to find myself snuggled—*snuggled!*—into the crook of his arm, my palm pressed to his chest.

"Time for your meeting," he whispered, his breath hot on my cheek. It sent a zing through my body that made me feel like I'd licked a nine-volt battery.

In seconds, I was on my feet, swiping at the drool—*the drool!*—on my cheek, staring in horror at the evidence of it on his shirt. I simultaneously wanted to climb back into his lap and sprint from the room.

I slept with Decker, and it left me with more satisfaction coursing through my body—even now, two days later—than any orgasm Cannon ever gave me.

Which is why I'm fleeing town on Saturday morning.

Okay, not *literally* fleeing town. I'm simply sneaking out of my apartment and closing my door as quietly as I can so I can creep down the stairs, sprint down the block to my car, and drive two and a half hours north to scout food trucks for the book festival.

At my meeting with Miranda Jin, the Cardinal Springs city manager—the one where I arrived very well rested, thanks to Decker, but still fairly addled, *also* thanks to Decker—she approved closing all of Main Street. That leaves us with two extra blocks, and I decided that having a bunch of food trucks would keep people at the festival all day and draw in folks who might not ordinarily come. And today, the city of West Lafayette is hosting a food truck festival, so my plan is to go up, eat myself silly in the name of research, and try to drive the feeling of Decker's heavy palm resting warm on my hip clear out of my mind with hot cheese and ice cream.

And if I don't manage to drown out all the lusty thoughts pinging around in my mind like the loudest, most obnoxious pinball machine on the planet, at least I'll be too far away to do anything stupid.

My car is parked in a small lot a block down behind my building. I climb in and turn the key, but nothing happens. Not even a cough or a hiss or a little electric click. My battery is totally dead. Again.

"*Uuuuggghhhh,*" I groan, and drop my head onto the steering wheel. It bounces off the center with a little toot of the horn.

"Need a jump?"

I jerk upright, hands pressed to my pounding heart, and turn to find Decker peering into the driver's side window. I reach for the button to lower it, then remember that my battery is dead. "What are you doing out here?" I yell through the glass.

He holds up a grease-spotted brown paper bag from Crimson 'n' Cream. "Strawberry banana muffins," he says. Then he reaches for the door handle, pausing to lift his eyebrows in question. I nod, and he pulls it open. "Do you want a jump? My car's just down the street."

I shake my head. "It's just going to die again when I get where I'm going. I need a new battery."

"Good thing your dad owns a hardware store," he says, and

then smirks. "Unless you're trying to avoid him finding out that you blew off his offer of help and wound up with a dead battery."

I shoot him a dirty look.

"Where are you headed?" he says. "I could just give you a ride."

"West Lafayette. They're having a food truck festival."

"Well, that sounds delicious." He reaches deep into the pocket of his worn khaki shorts, and I force myself not to stare at his pants places, remembering the feeling of him against my hip when I kissed him at the ice rink. My fingers twitch with the desire to follow his hand into his pocket, and oh my god, I cannot do this with him.

"Don't you have other stuff to do? This is going to be an all-day thing."

He shrugs. "It's Saturday. I don't have hours at the library, and Archer's on a date."

My eyebrows fly up into the atmosphere. "He's *what*?"

Decker grimaces. "Shit, I wasn't supposed to tell you that." He scrubs at his forehead. "For such a close family, you McBrides sure do have a lot of secrets."

"Spill," I demand.

He sighs. "Fine. But you can't tell him I told you."

"Throw in a muffin and you've got a deal," I say, reaching for the bag, but he pulls it away and holds it over his head. I may be tall, but he's taller, and I refuse to jump for it, partially because I don't trust myself not to jump directly into his arms.

"You know, I'm the one with the information here. Information *and* muffins. I could simply not tell you," he says with a smirk.

"And I could simply assign you to work senior hour every day until you finish your community service," I reply.

He blanches, then lowers the bag and shoves it at me. "Take them all. Anything but that," he says, but I take only one muffin before I pass the bag back to him. "Molly Black."

The muffin nearly falls out of my hand. "Molly Black? *Seriously?*" I screech.

Decker's head whips around to make sure no one heard me. "Hey, keep it down. And yes, Molly Black. They matched on that app you use. It's just a first date."

"You are seriously failing as a best friend if you're letting him go out with Molly Black," I say. "In our yearbook, she quoted her favorite song, "Free Bird" by 'Leonard' Skynyrd. *Leonard*."

Decker laughs. "Hey, I'm just happy he's willing to go out with anyone. He's been a hermit since Cassie left him. And anyway, we both know he's not going to wind up with Molly Black. They probably won't even have a second date. Archer just needs to shake the rust off. Molly will help him do that. Let the man get laid."

"Ew. Gross."

"You asked," he says. He holds up his keys and jingles them right in my face. "Now, are we going?

I should say no. I should eat crow at the store and buy a new battery or simply walk the hundred miles to West Lafayette. Anything is better than climbing into Decker's Bronco. Because that might force me to look my feelings for him right in the face. Right in *his* face. His chiseled, tanned, smiling face. If I want to maintain this friendship we've built, spending a day with him would be a mistake of epic proportions.

"Do you need directions?" I ask.

———

Decker's car is a baby-blue vintage Bronco so shiny and beautiful that it looks like it should be used in LL Bean ads or country music videos. It looks like it probably shouldn't have an engine inside, it should simply be filled with backpacks and parked on top of a big fake rock inside an REI. The interior is a buttery leather the color of a caramel macchiato, soft as the expensive swaddle blankets Ms. Kinicki uses for baby Isabelle.

And holy shit, does he look incredible behind the wheel. I keep sneaking glances at him, his shaggy blond hair pulled back into a low messy bun that should make him look like an asshole but instead makes him look like he came to fix your washing machine and also star in a porno. His muscled arm is outstretched as he rests his hand on the steering wheel, his long, strong fingers tapping along to the beat of music I can barely hear. In worn, frayed khaki shorts and a navy T-shirt, I can't *believe* he has the audacity to be this hot.

Fortunately, he's got the top down, and the roar of the wind as we fly down Highway 231 means we don't have to talk. I don't think I know how to talk to Decker unless he's teasing me about something. It was weird enough when we became friends and I started spilling my secrets to him. But ever since he walked out of my apartment with a copy of *It Happened One Summer*, I can't stop my mind from writing all manner of smutty scenes. Only instead of a grumpy, beanie-wearing fisherman doing unspeakable things to me, it's Decker with that cocky grin.

The drive is two and a half hours, but it passes in a flash. Probably because I'm sitting stock still, trying to ration the number of times I allow myself to look over at him, to watch stray strands of hair whip around his stubbled jaw, the way his muscles flex when he turns the wheel. By the time we pull into West Lafayette, I'm wound so tight that when Decker hits a pothole, I let out a small scream.

"Little jumpy?" he asks, glancing over at me.

"My car is more comfortable," I lie, as if the shocks on the Bronco are the problem and not the fact that between the vibrations from the road and the dead-sexy man sitting next to me, I swear I'm four seconds and one smoldering look away from an orgasm.

"If we'd driven here in your car, it would've taken me six days to pull my knees out of my neck," he shoots back.

I know I should banter back. The teasing is the only thing that feels normal between us since that kiss, but I can't come up with anything. For the first time, I can't keep up. It's infuriating, because Decker seems to have had no problem forgetting our moment on the ice. He managed to sit there in front of me reading one of the filthiest sex scenes Tessa Bailey has ever committed to paper and not look like he wanted to drag me off to bed. When I woke up pressed against him, he was watching game tape on his phone. I was having a crisis of lust while he was studying hockey plays.

I'd do well to catch up with him.

I wrack my brain for something to say that's in the ballpark of normal, but all I can come up with is, "So, have you ever been to West Lafayette?" I quickly look out the window so he can't see me grimace. Seriously, I went with *come here often*? Could I be more of a fucking goober?

"For hockey tournaments and stuff back in the day," he says. If he clocks my awkwardness, he mercifully ignores it, but it's hard to tell what he's thinking with his eyes hidden behind his sunglasses. "And my dad spent a year as visiting faculty at Purdue, so I came up a few times then."

Family. Okay, good, I can work with that. That's neutral and not at all related to what it would be like to climb into the buttery-soft back seat of this Bronco and pretend we're teenagers at the drive-in. I mean, the leverage I could get using the roll bar alone...

"How are your parents? Still working?" I ask, just now realizing how infrequently Decker brings them up. I'm not even sure if he's seen them since he's been back in town. It's frankly a little weird that he's rented and furnished a whole apartment when his parents have a mansion out by the lake that looks like it must have at least five bedrooms.

Decker gives a laugh that has a bite to it. "Pretty sure my mom's going to keel over in her office at a hundred and ten years old. I can't imagine them retiring. It's probably why they're always pestering me about what I'm going to do when I retire from hockey."

"You're thinking about retiring?" This is news to me. I can't imagine Decker anywhere but the NHL. It's like imagining the lions at the zoo opening the gates and heading to the mall for smoothies.

"Fuck no," Decker says, and I notice his grip on the steering wheel gets tighter, the veins in his tanned arms growing visible. Then he takes a deep breath and visibly relaxes. "I mean, any player my age thinks about it, but for me it's more like thinking about how to avoid it."

"How much longer do you think you have?"

And there's that flex on the steering wheel again.

"I don't even want to speculate," he says. "I mean, you know how fickle the hockey gods can be. Archer should have had a long career. Potential Hall of Famer. But anything can happen in an instant, and it's all gone."

I nod. "True, but I think Archer's happy where he is."

"Are you sure about that?" I can tell from his tone that Decker doesn't believe me.

"Yeah. I mean, he loves hockey, but he never seemed to have the same drive in the league that you did. That killer instinct that kept him on the ice every second. He was talented, but it wasn't everything to him. He likes the game, but not necessarily the playing. I think coaching suits him. And working with the kids. Though I wouldn't be surprised if he moved to something bigger. College maybe. Or the AHL. He could definitely level up."

"Yeah, his Hockey IQ is off the charts," he says. "I wonder if Cassie would have stuck around for a big time coaching gig?"

I scoff. "Are you kidding? I saw online that she's already engaged to the goalie for Los Angeles."

"Yup," he says. His jaw flexes. "Archer deserves better."

And then he does that thing where he presses the flat of his palm to the steering wheel and turns it one-handed, pulling the car into an open spot near the park. It shouldn't be sexy, but it absolutely is. Across the street, there are dozens of trucks in a parking lot across from a big open area where people are spread out on the grass, enjoying their food.

"Okay," Archer says, giving a game-time clap. "What's the plan?"

"Get something from every truck, eat ourselves silly, and then rank everything so we can decide who to invite."

"*Fuuuuuuck*," Decker groans, the sound so sexual that I worry we're going to be asked to leave. He locks eyes with me and grins. "I'm so glad I got invited on this trip."

"I think you invited yourself. But you can count these hours as community service, since this is for the book festival."

When I mention his community service, something flickers in his eyes, but his smile never wavers. "Excellent," he says. "Let's eat."

We take a quick inventory of all the trucks and decide to save the two dessert trucks for the end. We'll order as much food as we can carry in one trip, then settle in for our first taste test. We get in line for a black truck called Dumpling Is Up. We're about three people from the window when the guy in front of us turns around. He's young, with fraternity letters on his T-shirt and a backward ball cap covering shaggy brown hair. He scans the crowd, and when his eyes land on Decker, he does a double take.

"Holy shit, are you Decker Brooks?" he says, his voice starting loud and high but quickly dropping into a quieter, more *hey man, it's cool* tone.

"Sure am," Decker says, and his lips spread into a grin. It's one I'm starting to recognize, the smile he throws on for strangers he's trying to impress or anyone he's trying to woo. It's intensely charming, but I also know it's fake as all get-out.

"Oh man, that's so cool," the guy says, his face lighting up. "I got up to Chicago for three Grinders games this season, and I saw you in Boston over winter break. You're the most badass guy in the league, seriously. The Grinders need more players willing to throw hands, you know?"

"I make it physical when it needs to be," Decker says, that smile stiffening just a little, not enough for the guy to notice.

"I have your sweater—fuck, I wish I had it. I'd get you to sign it. You've been my favorite player for forever. Seriously, since I was a little kid. I'm going to cry real tears when you retire," he says, the words running out like water overflowing from a bucket. "Please never retire. Play forever. Like, until you drop dead on the ice."

A muscle in Decker's jaw ticks, just the smallest betrayal of his true emotions, but he holds on to that smile like a life raft. "I'll do my best, man."

"Hey, can I get a picture?" The dude's eyes cut over to me, like he's finally noticed there's a whole other human being standing in front of him. "Sorry, I don't want to interrupt your day out with your girl."

I open my mouth to say I'm not his girl—I'm not his anything, no matter what my body thinks. But Decker's smile just widens. "No worries. We can do a quick selfie."

I watch as Decker takes the guy's phone and stretches out his long arm, his grin perfectly in place. He takes a couple of photos, then passes the phone back. By the time the transaction is done, the frat boy is next in line and Decker is free.

"That was intense," I whisper. "Do fans often bring up your death?"

"Only the ones who *really* love me," he whispers back, the smile melting off his face. "Sorry about that."

*"Oh my god, that's Decker Brooks!"*

This time the voice is female, and it's not directed at us. The speaker is somewhere nearby, trying to be subtle and doing a spectacularly bad job of it. Decker tenses, and I scan the area around us. I find a trio of college girls, lithe in head-to-toe Lululemon and oversize sunglasses, all perfectly tanned and high-lighted.

"Sorority girls at four o'clock," I say. Decker glances in that direction, and I hear gasps and giggles.

"Ask for his number," one girl says.

"Grab his ass," says another.

"Flip for him?" says the third.

Beside me, Decker starts shifting back and forth, his eyes boring into the back of the guy ordering his dumplings, as if he can Jedi mind trick the whole operation into moving faster.

There are more giggles and whispers, quieter this time, but it sounds like the girls are forming a plan of attack. Decker is growing more agitated by the second, and just as I hear the sound of a pair of Hokas approaching from the right, I reach over and take his hand. He hesitates for only a second, and then his fingers thread through mine, his hand warm and strong. It makes my palm feel small and delicate, and then he lifts it to his chest and caresses my fingers with his free hand. My breath catches in my throat like a frantic butterfly trying to escape. Heat gathers in my core, and it's only the flash of blond beach waves in the corner of my eye that reminds me that this is just for show. I look over in time to see the tallest of the three girls approaching. Her eyes go to my hand cradled in his and pulled to his chest, and she strolls right on past us.

"That was a close one," I say, my traitorous voice trembling.

"Yeah," he says, his voice gravelly. "Thanks."

Ahead of us, the window opens up, and Decker steps forward. He lowers my hand but doesn't let go, pulling me along with him. He holds it as he orders, as he taps his phone to pay. He holds it as he steps to the side, his thumb rubbing a gentle pattern on my wrist. I'm not even sure he realizes he's doing it. Maybe he's just putting on a show for anyone else in the crowd who might be thinking of approaching.

My body doesn't give one single solitary fuck what his motivations are. My body just wants him to hold me, to never let me go. When he finally unthreads his fingers to claim our order at the pickup window, I swallow back a sad little sigh.

No one else bothers us as we move through the parking lot, and we don't discuss either of the fan encounters. Instead, we focus on our smorgasbord: tacos and barbecue and arepas and mac and cheese and burgers and hot dogs and fried chicken. We load ourselves down with paper plates and boats and boxes, stacking them high until we can't carry any more. Then we find a spot on the grass, where we use the food as an excuse to ignore what happened at the dumpling truck.

But the warm spot on my wrist bears the memory of it, and it shows no sign of forgetting.

# CHAPTER 25

## DECKER

aid out before me is an assortment of the greasiest, most delicious fair food I've ever had, and all I can think about is holding Grace's hand.

Holding her *hand.*

On a scale of one to sexual, this should be a solid two and a half, and yet my entire body lights up at the memory of her soft palm against my calloused hand.

If this were a date, it would easily be the best of my life.

But—and I have to keep reminding myself of this—it's not a date. Even though we're sitting on the flannel blanket I keep in the back of the Bronco, enjoying a picnic while all around us kids run and squeal, parents sip beers, and couples lean in for first and fourth and fortieth and four hundredth kisses. I find myself jealous of the people who can so freely show the ones they're with how they feel. If I let my emotions take over, I'd probably have Grace flat on her back, her raven hair spread out in the green grass, her ice-blue eyes reflecting the clear blue sky. I'd cover her body with mine, pressing her into the earth as I kissed her, and hell, we'd probably be asked to leave within seconds.

But I can't do that, because even though she let me hold her hand, it wasn't real. This thing between us, this thing I can't ignore? It's just a fantasy.

My phone buzzes in my pocket, and I slide it out. "It's Archer," I say.

"Guess his date isn't going well," Grace says.

ARCHER

Talked to Darren. If you can get some extra pairs of skates, we can do an open skate for the little kids the Saturday morning after the 4th of July.

The text is totally innocuous, but my shoulders jump as if he can see me out here with his sister, read the lust all over my face. It's a good reminder of why I have to stay on my side of the blanket.

Across from me, a respectful distance away, Grace wads up the last of the greasy napkins and deposits them on top of a stack of empty paper boats.

"I think we should go with the Afficianadoughs pizza truck," she says, pulling out her phone and taking notes. "Indy-pendent Pizza only sells Pepsi products, and frankly, that should be illegal."

Grace, apparently, has not been overtaken by the same lust monster that I have been. And I guess I'm grateful for that. Her casual conversation keeps me from doing something monumentally stupid, like getting arrested for public indecency and pissing off my best friend all in one go.

"You don't like Pepsi?" I ask.

Her eyebrows shoot up. "You *do*?"

I shrug. "I mean, I don't drink a lot of pop, but every once in a while a Diet Pepsi can be really refreshing."

She looks like I've just told her I like to recreationally snort jalapeño peppers. "I'm sorry, *Diet Pepsi*? Ugh, straight to jail."

"Seriously?" I can't help but laugh. I love that she has capital-O Opinions and isn't afraid to tell me how wrong she thinks I am. It's not something I often get from women, unfortunately.

She levels me with a deadly serious look. "I don't even believe in the carceral state, but these streets are not safe with a Diet Pepsi fan running free."

"Well, they don't call me a bad boy for nothing," I say with a smirk.

"Yes, when the tabloids discuss your exploits, they definitely focus on your soft drink preferences," she says wryly.

I roll my eyes, but a prick of unrest zips through my chest. I hate that she knows all the worst shit that's been said about me, that maybe she even *believes* all of it. But maybe it's okay if she does. It'll just remind her of what I already know is true: I'm not good for her.

"Is it time to head back?" I ask, trying hard to hide the disappointment in my voice. I'm not ready for this day to end. It's so good being far away from Cardinal Springs and all the prying eyes that mean we can't be more than friends.

"Actually," she says, looking down bashfully, "there's this bookstore in Crawfordsville that I was planning to stop by on the way home. It's okay if you need to get back, but—"

"Yeah, let's check it out," I say, thrilled that I've been granted more time with her. And I didn't even have to scheme to get it, like when I invited myself on this trip this morning. "I finished that book you loaned me, so I could use another."

Her cheeks flood with crimson. "Are you telling me you finished *It Happened One Summer* and that you want *more*?"

*I'm telling you that I've reread the highlighted passages enough times that I can recite them from memory.*

"It's a better way to pass the time than watching ESPN highlights," I say with a shrug. I pull my keys out of my pocket. "You've got directions to this bookstore?"

She waves her phone. "On it."

Another Page is located in an old filling station on the edge of downtown Crawfordsville. It's dinnertime, so the shop is fairly empty, but because Grace and I just ate enough food for six football teams, the last thing we need is another meal. She has a box of cannoli in her purse that she assured me she'll share if we get hungry, but at this point I can't imagine wanting to eat again until Monday.

"Okay, don't let me walk out of here with more than one book," she says, glancing around the store with wide-eyed wonder. "Two, max."

"Why?"

"You've seen my bookshelves. My apartment is small, and it's already overflowing with books I haven't read," she says.

"Then why buy more?"

"Because I can't not! I mean, look at this one." She pulls a paperback off a table near the entrance. The cover has a vibrant mosaic design, and the title looks like it's been hand stitched onto the cover. "It's gorgeous, and it's enemies to lovers, which is my favorite trope. And, I mean, no one gives the side-eye to a wine collector who buy bottles they don't plan to drink until the time is right. They just build their wine cellar, and then on a random Thursday night, they get to browse the racks, trying to figure out what goes with their meal, or their mood, or the weather. That's how my bookshelves feel to me. If it's stormy, I want something cozy to curl up with under a blanket. If it's a gorgeous spring day, I want something happy I can read while lying on a blanket in Henry Park. This one will be perfect for the first snow, when I have a steaming mug of hot chocolate and a pot of soup bubbling away on the stove."

And oddly enough, I get it. I know I've only read that one book—honestly the first I've read since college, and if we're being *truly* honest, I didn't actually read many of the books that were assigned to me then, either. But the book she gave me suited my mood perfectly: funny and hot as fuck. It was what I needed to exorcize some of the frustration I've been feeling, both because of my sexual hiatus and because of the intense heat I feel whenever I'm around Grace.

We start to move through the store, no section left unbrowsed.

"I would put the children's section in the back," she whispers as we approach a set of low shelves filled with picture books near the front of the store, accented with a small rainbow rug by the window. "Parents feel better browsing the rest of the store on their own if they know they're between their kids and the door. Plus, putting the gifts near the front makes for more impulse purchases."

I raise my eyebrows. "Seems like you've thought about this a lot."

She makes a humming noise but keeps her eyes studiously on the display in front of her.

I reach out and run a finger from her shoulder to her wrist. "Do I sense another Grace McBride secret?"

She squares her shoulders and lets out a long breath. "I've sort of maybe been thinking about opening my own bookstore. In Cardinal Springs."

My eyebrows shoot up. "Wow, seriously? That sounds amazing. And you'd be really good at it. What's stopping you?"

She tucks another book under her arm. "Money, obviously. The startup costs are enormous, and I don't have any collateral that would qualify me for a decent loan."

"I'm sure your dad would cosign. Or any of your brothers."

She shakes her head. "I don't want to bother them. And a small business is a risk. They'd be too worried or too involved."

I poke her in the ribs. "You're doing it again."

She shakes me off with a laugh. "What?"

"Hiding. From them. From yourself."

She scoffs. "When did you get so enlightened?"

"Despite all evidence to the contrary, I do see a therapist."

"Seriously?"

"Yes, Grace, it's the twenty-first century," I say. "She specializes in sports psychology."

"To teach you to be one with the puck?"

I shrug. "Yeah, kind of. To deal with anxiety and stress. To manage aggression. To keep from going even further off the deep end. Truth be told, I should probably be seeing her this summer. Might help me deal with the disaster my life has become."

"You're not a disaster, Decker," she says. "You need to stop doing that."

"Doing what?"

"Letting the story people tell about you become your truth," she says, and when I cock my head, she sighs. "You let everyone think you're this big dumb disaster who smooths everything over with a wink and a smile, but you're not. You're smart, you're sweet, and I've seen you with the kids at the library. They look up to you, and they should. Maybe you should start seeing yourself the way they see you."

My heart clenches. I know that in a different world, I would work my ass off to be the man Grace just described. I'd do it for her. But in this world, where she's got dreams and a life in Cardinal Springs and I have a hockey career in Chicago, I can't. And even if we could make that work, the door cracked open that day we kissed on the ice, and then she closed it, hard. And I'll respect that. But my god, do I want her.

Instead of pouring all that onto her, I say, "Tell me more about your store. What would it be like?"

Her cheeks flush, and her smile is so warm and bright I'm surprised the books she's holding don't ignite. "It's not going to be a specialty shop, like a children's bookstore or a romance bookstore. I want it to be a true community space, to really serve all of Cardinal Springs. We'll have a diverse selection—fiction and nonfiction, novels and poetry and picture books. But I do want a really good children's section, since that's my area of expertise."

"One of them," I say, tapping the romance novel in her hand.

"According to Ms. Tingle, you've got quite the recommendation list."

"True," she says. "The romance section will definitely be robust, which can be unusual in indies. They tend to be a little snobby about commercial fiction, but I think reading is meant to be joyful, and my store is definitely going to celebrate that. I want to put it in the old Quinn Camera building."

It takes me a beat to remember that place. It's where we got our disposable cameras from prom developed. My dad used to get his old Kodak film camera serviced there. It's a great building. I didn't realize it had closed.

Grace weaves up and down the aisles, running her fingers over spines in a way that makes me wish it was my skin she was touching. She smiles and sighs, sometimes pulling a book off a shelf to read the back. The stack in her arms grows—so much for that two-book limit. Not that I plan on stopping her. I can't imagine telling this girl there's a single goddamn thing she can't have.

"I hate having to choose," she whines as she pulls some of the books off her stack.

"Okay, well, pick something out for me," I tell her, because I know I can't talk her into buying more books for herself. "Something like the one you gave me."

"First of all, I *loaned* you that book. I definitely want it back," she says, leveling me with a serious look that quickly morphs into sparkling delight. "Second of all, *yes*. Picking out a book for someone is my very favorite thing, so thank you for this incredible gift."

In her excitement, she grabs my hand and practically skips back to the romance section. I trot to keep up with her. She drops my hand to pull a book off the shelf, and my heart lets out a sigh at the loss of contact. She holds out a book with a pale pink cover featuring a couple sipping coffee.

"What's this one about?" I ask.

"Oh, this one is for me. Or at least it's in the running. Sorry, I'm still shopping for us both."

The word *us* does dangerous things to my insides.

She adds two more to her stack before reaching for a third. "Okay, did you like the heat level of the Tessa Bailey?"

My cheeks warm. "Yeah, uh…" I cough. "That was, uh, good."

She smirks. "Okay, then, he likes the queen of dirty talk," she says in this warm-honey voice that makes me shift so she won't notice the situation in my boxer briefs.

She pulls two books off the shelf, one with a blue illustrated cover and one with a photo of two people. "This one," she says, holding up the smaller paperback featuring an older white man embracing a beautiful Black woman, "is super hot but less high jinks-y, if that makes sense. Alyssa Cole is the master of sexy romance. And this one is a little bit more of a rom-com, and oh my god, the pages basically catch on fire in some scenes."

I tuck *A Duke By Default* and *This Kiss Quotient* under my arm. "Sold," I say. "Now, what are you going to get?"

She looks down at the stack in her arms, then quickly adds another three so it nearly reaches her chin. "I need to think about it. Ugh, it's so hard to choose! It's like picking out a puppy at the shelter. They all deserve to come home with me, you know?"

She carries the stack over to a table and lays them out, intermittently flipping books over to read the backs or opening to the first pages. I watch her brow furrow, her lips moving slightly as she reads. I can't take my eyes off her. I never knew watching a woman shop could be so goddamn sexy. The way her fingers dance across the covers makes my skin light up with need. The plump lower lip she's biting as she tries to narrow down her selection begs for my tongue. When she juts out a hip, deep in thought, all I can think of is sinking my fingers into the skin there while I roll my hips into her. I bite back a groan at the thought.

I can't hide it anymore—not from myself, at least. I'm completely gone for this girl.

And then her phone rings. She glances at the screen. "It's my dad. I'm going to step outside and take this." She picks up a purple paperback and hands it to me. "Will you put the others back for me? We should hit the road soon. It's getting late."

"Sure," I say to her retreating back as she answers the call.

As soon as she's out the door, I scoop up all seven of the books she's been perusing. Brother's best friend and enemies to lovers and friends to lovers and only one bed, all the tropes I wish could be ours. All the love stories I wish we could have. I feel the weight of them deep in my chest, where I'm holding all my feelings for her.

If I can't have her, then I'll have to settle for giving her everything she could ever want.

"Well, this is quite a haul," the woman behind the counter says when I set the books down with a thump. She starts scanning the barcodes. "You've got quite the reader on your hands."

"She's actually thinking about opening up her own bookstore," I say, the pride pouring out of me. "She's a little nervous about the financing, though."

"Where does she want to put the store?"

"Cardinal Springs."

The woman's face lights up. "Oh, that would be a great market. Very bookish community, lots of local pride, and not a single bookstore for miles in any direction. She'd do very well, I bet," she says. She plucks a bookmark off the counter and scrawls a phone number and an email address on it in purple pen. "I'm Sue—I own this place. Tell her to contact me if she has any questions. Some incredible booksellers in Indianapolis supported me when I was getting started. I'd love to pay it forward."

I take the bookmark, an idea starting to form. "So you're doing well?"

"Small businesses are always touch-and-go, but the book business is booming these days, and as long as you build a strong connection with your community, you can make it through the lean times," she says. She passes me two paper bags stuffed with my purchases. I slide the bookmark into one of Grace's selections.

"Thanks, I'll definitely pass this along," I say with a smile, this one genuine.

Out on the sidewalk, Grace is leaning against the brick wall of the bookstore, her phone pressed to her ear. She takes in the bags I'm carrying, her eyes going wide.

"Yeah, Dad. Uh-huh. Yup, you were right," she says, then rolls her eyes. "Okay, talk to you later. Love you."

"How did he find out about your car?" I ask.

"Small towns," she replies. She peers into one of the bags. "What did you do?"

"I couldn't help myself. Once you called them puppies, I felt like I was leaving behind little fuzzy golden retrievers," I say. I transfer her purchases into one bag and pass it to her.

"Can I Venmo you?" she asks.

I shake my head. "My treat," I tell her. "You paid for all the food."

"No, *you* paid for all the food, because I expensed it using the sponsorship money for the festival," she replies. I can tell she's trying to scold me, but her smile is bright. I would do fucking anything to make this girl keep smiling at me like that.

"Just take the books," I tell her. "Call it payment for the recommendations."

"You still have to give *It Happened One Summer* back," she says. Which is fine, because there's a brand-new copy of that book in my bag. And when I get home tonight, I'm going to mark all the spots in my copy that she marked in hers. Every moment with her is becoming like that. I've memorized them all. The way she lets loose those great big belly laughs, her wide smiles. The way her hand felt in mind. All the knowing smirks and gentle teasing. I'll put it all away so I can take it out and look at it later when I'm back in Chicago, back in my real life.

When this is all just a memory.

# CHAPTER 26

## GRACE

We're about fifteen miles outside of Crawfordsville and an hour and a half from home when the engine of the Bronco coughs. Then it rattles and lets out a grinding thud, and our speed suddenly drops.

"What the hell was that?" I yelp, my heart in my throat.

Decker eases onto the brake, carefully steering us toward the shoulder of the two-lane rural highway lined with dense trees. We bump over the edge of the pavement and onto the gravel, where the Bronco gives one final wheeze before coming to rest.

"I don't know," he says. He jumps out of the car and walks around to pop the hood. It releases a hissing cloud of steam. I climb out and hurry over to look at the overheated mass of engine parts. "Shit."

"What happened?" I ask.

"I don't *know*," he says. He leans in, sort of sniffs around, then rocks back on his heels, his hands sliding deep into his pockets.

"Can't you fix it?" I ask.

Decker glares me like I've just asked him to recite the owner's manual in Latin. "Does it seem like I know how to fix cars?"

I shrug. "I mean, you're tall and burly, so yeah, kind of." I trail off, because I'm not in the mood to compliment him at the moment. Not when we're standing on the side of a desolate rural highway as the sun inches closer towards setting, staring into the steaming guts of his car. "And, I mean, you own a vintage car. I figured you spent years restoring this thing yourself, pouring your blood, sweat, and tears into it or whatever."

"I bought it from a vintage car dealer because I thought it looked badass." He doesn't even have the good sense to look sheepish when he says it.

I slap his arm. "What the hell, Decker?"

He leaves the hood open and steps away from the car, digging his phone out of his pocket. "It's fine. We're going to call a tow truck and have it hauled to a mechanic who can fix it."

He searches for the number, then holds the phone to his ear. Meanwhile, I pull out my own phone, but I have only a couple of bars of service. I tap the Uber app, but nothing appears. Not one single little animated vehicle, no matter how far I zoom out.

"How are we going to get home? It's not like we can call an Uber in"—I pause and peer at the map—"Lapland, Indiana."

Decker sighs and has the nerve to seem annoyed. With *me*. "Grace, this has been happening for approximately two and a half minutes. Can we try to solve the problem before we freak out?"

"I'm not freaking out!" I yelp, and a small flock of birds takes flight from the copse of trees beside me.

"You're scaring the wildlife," he deadpans.

Okay, maybe I'm freaking out a *little*. It's getting dusky out, and his car is steaming. My heart is still pounding from our impromptu swing off the road. And yes, I know my car is also dead, but that's a dead *battery*. This is catastrophic. Decker and his vanity ride have stranded us. I'm going to have to bump down the road crammed into a tow truck with Decker and a stranger, and who knows how long it'll take to fix the car. We could be out here half the night, and I *hate* feeling out of control like this.

I emit a combination of a growl and a shriek that makes Decker's shoulders jump up to his ears. He shoots me a look. "Hey, Grace?" he says.

"Yeah?" I grind out.

He smirks. *"Relax."*

And out comes another shriek that sends something in the woods skittering. Decker just chuckles and turns away, wandering a few steps down the road. I hurry after him, and when someone picks up the call, I lean in so I can hear both sides of the conversation.

"Lou here."

"Hey, yeah, I'm out on two thirty-one about fifteen miles south of Crawfordsville, and my truck just broke down. Any chance I can get a tow?" Decker says.

"Sorry, man, I'm at my kid's Little League game, and we've got about six innings left. My wife is out of town, so I don't think I'll be able to make it until tomorrow," the guy on the other end of the line says.

Decker presses his palm to his forehead and looks up and down the road, but he sees what I see, which is nothing. No cars coming. I can't even remember the last time we passed any kind of structure that wasn't sinking into the desolate Indiana farmland.

"Is there anyone else you can recommend?" Decker asks, his voice tight.

"Whelp, Antonio's got the only other truck for about fifty miles, and he left to visit family in Honduras this morning, so I think you might be shit out of luck until tomorrow," Lou says. "If you're willing to walk a piece or sleep in your car, I can get you first thing in the morning."

Decker lets out a deep sigh. "I'll call you back."

Luckily, I'm already in problem-solving mode. "There's a motel two miles up the road. According to Google image search, it might be the place we meet our death, but I'm not sleeping in a car with no roof when there are things rustling around in the underbrush."

Decker nods. "Fair enough. Then we better start walking."

I turn and head back to the car, pulling out my purse and the two bags of books.

"I don't think we'll need the books," he says. "We won't be at the motel long."

I narrow my eyes. "What if it rains?"

He lets out a theatrical sigh, but he can't hide the quirk of his lips as he takes the bags from me. "Okay, let's get going."

I don't speak for most of the walk. Not to Decker, anyway. I occasionally mutter phrases like "looked badass" and "wouldn't know his ass from a Phillips-head," and Decker knows better than to chime in.

It takes just under an hour for us to reach a clearing in the trees. The motel—an old 1950s single-story strip of rooms, red brick with bright blue doors and trim—sits behind a gravel parking lot. There are at least two dozen motorcycles, old-school Harleys with the tall, curved handlebars and shiny chrome coated with dust, lined up in front of the rooms but only a handful of cars. The window of the small main office is lit up, but there's no one inside.

"My car disaster, my treat," Decker says as we approach.

The door has a little bell on it, and as soon as we walk in, a woman emerges from the back. She looks like she's in her midsixties, like her curly hair is probably a silvery gray beneath the bright red dye. She's wearing a floral Hawaiian-looking muumuu in a cacophony of neon colors and gold door knocker earrings. Her nails are long and red and as fake as her hair. She gives us a wide grin.

"Well, y'all don't look like you're with the Disciples of Doom," she says with a crackly smile.

"The what?" I ask.

"No, ma'am," Decker interrupts, and I'm temporarily struck silent by his use of *ma'am*. "We were actually headed home to Cardinal Springs from West Lafayette when my car broke down. Unfortunately, we can't get a tow tonight—"

"Antonio's in Honduras, and lemme guess...Lou is at Hunter's baseball game?"

"Yes, ma'am," Decker replies.

I don't like the way Decker's manners send a flood of heat to my core, not when I'm still pissed off that he got us into this mess.

The woman rolls her eyes. "Lou's convinced that kid's headed to the pros, but he couldn't hit a fastball if he were watching it in slow motion," she says, shaking her head. "I'm Lana. So, y'all need a room?"

"Two, please," I say, leaning on the counter.

Lana's eyes sparkle. "The good news is, Snakes got picked up on a weapons charge, so he's spending the night in county lockup. Bad news is, the rest of the Disciples managed to keep their noses clean this month, so I've only got the one room."

"Snakes?" I say, my mind conjuring all kinds of terrifying images of convicts and murderers.

"Oh, he's a sweetie. All these guys are, so long as you keep on their good side. And a pretty young thing like yourself should have no problem with that," she says with a wink.

My face must betray my terror, because Lana tosses her head back and cackles a hard, nicotine-laced laugh.

"Oh, honey, I'm just teasing. They're good guys," she says. Then she leans across the counter and whispers, a serious look on her face, "You're not cops, though, right?"

"No, ma'am," Decker says.

"He's a professional hockey player," I say. I don't know why. Maybe I feel the need to emphasize to her and the two burly, grizzled men in leather vests who just walked in that I have someone with me who knows how to fight.

"Is that right?" Lana says, giving Decker a once-over so brazen that I nearly blush on his behalf. "Never got into hockey. I love me some bruisers, but it always seemed a little too yuppie for me. I like MMA, myself. If they're gonna fight, no sense in doing it in helmets and pads. No real blood in that."

"I've got some scars that would beg to differ," Decker says, laughing. He pulls his wallet from his back pocket and holds out his credit card.

"Well, here's your key," Lana says, ignoring it and passing him a large blue plastic keychain with an honest-to-god brass key attached. "You're in room nine. Enjoy your stay at the Last Stop."

"But we haven't paid," Decker says, still holding out the card.

Lana waves him off. "Room's already paid for. No refunds just because you *forgot you were on probation*." She directs that last part at the two men, who are standing in front of the vending machine.

"Piss off, Lana, the boy learned his lesson," the taller man says.

"And these two fine stranded folks will benefit from it," Lana says.

Decker turns to the two men. I notice he's standing up to his full height but also lowering his chin to signal respect. "We're happy to reimburse you, honestly."

"Not taking your money, pretty boy," the older man says, his gruff voice sounding like it's tangled in his chest-length gray beard. Then his eyes catch mine, and a hint of a smile appears.

"Well, thanks," Decker says, sliding the key off the counter. He reaches for the two bags of books and signals for me to head out the door.

"Sleep tight, y'all!" Lana calls after us.

# CHAPTER 27

## DECKER

'm on high alert as we make our way to room nine. The two guys in the lobby seemed nice enough, but you don't fuck with guys who call themselves the Disciples of Doom. I stay close on Grace's heels the whole way.

We find room nine midway down the line of doors. The space inside could be best described as vintage but at least seems blessedly clean. The walls are paneled in dark wood like a 1970s basement, and the carpet is brown and ancient. But the bathroom is spotless, if spare, with two sets of fresh towels on the rack. The sheets are white and starchy and free of any stains, the quilt on top emitting the strong scent of dryer sheets.

And there's only one bed.

"I can sleep on the floor," I say as Grace stares at the bed that may not even be a queen.

"That's ridiculous," she scoffs. She sits down on the edge, the mattress bouncing and giving a small squeak. "I'm not some virgin made of candy glass who can't share a flat surface with a man lest her virtue be compromised."

Fuck, that sentence does weird things to my brain. I don't want to think about her virtue...or what havoc I could wreak on it.

I clear my throat. "I mostly thought you'd be too mad at me to let me share the bed with you."

She pauses, her eyes on the popcorn ceiling. "Good point. I *should* make you sleep on the floor solely for driving a vanity vehicle you haven't maintained," she says. "Luckily for you, I'm forgiving. And also a little bit nervous about all those bikers. So you can sleep next to me if you take the side closer to the door."

"So I can protect you?"

"So I have time to climb out the back window while they murder you first," she replies.

As if on cue, a fleet of motorcycles roars to life in unison. The sound is deafening, and I slide the curtain aside with a finger to watch as one by one, they peel out of the gravel parking lot and onto the highway. Soon the room is silent again, Grace's growling stomach the only sound.

"You're seriously hungry again?" I say. I am a little bit, too, but I also have a hundred pounds on her.

"Anxiety makes me hungry," she says sheepishly.

I sigh, hating that I've put her in this spot but also not hating that I get to sleep beside her tonight. All day I've been looking for ways to stretch this trip out as long as possible, to have more time with her away from the prying eyes in town. Maybe I manifested this, not that I believe in that shit. Although looking at how narrow this bed is, I might just start.

"Want me to hit the vending machine?" I ask

"I have cannoli in my purse, remember?" she says. She reaches for her leather tote and pulls out a white pastry box tied with blue-and-white string. "There's nowhere in Cardinal Springs that makes it, and it's one of my favorite desserts." She pulls her legs up onto the bed, leaning back against the pillows, the box balanced on her stomach. "You want one?"

"Yes, please," I say. I take a seat on the other side of the bed and lean back against the two thin pillows that are destined to ruin my neck in a single night. There's very little space between us. I try to stay as close to the edge as possible without falling off.

When the cannoli is almost gone, Grace yawns. I look at my watch. It's barely nine p.m., but it's been a long day, and we did walk a couple of miles from the car.

"You want to just head to bed?" I ask.

"Sure," she says. "How do you want to do this?"

"Uh, what?" I cough, and powdered sugar explodes from the last bite of my cannoli.

She rolls her eyes. "I mean, do you want the bathroom first? To change?"

"I figured I'd just sleep in my clothes."

She pauses, as if picking her words carefully. "You don't have to. It probably wouldn't be very comfortable."

"Okay." I stand. Maybe I should go into the bathroom to undress, but she's watching me, and suddenly I want to give her something to see. So I reach back for the collar of my shirt and tug it over my head. I drop it on the floor next to my shoes, then unbutton my shorts and let them fall to the ground, too. I'm left standing on the matted brown carpet in only my black boxer briefs.

When I turn, Grace is staring at me in open-mouthed wonder. It feels like standing in a sunbeam.

"Jesus Christ, Decker," she says.

I glance down. "What?"

She half laughs, her eyes roaming over my body. "It looks like someone typed 'hot hockey disaster' into an AI generator and you popped out."

I furrow my brow. "I...thank you?"

She rolls her eyes. "Don't act surprised. All of that"—she gestures up and down my body from across the bed—"is what got you into this mess. Imani Menendez doesn't fuck around with scrubs."

I blush.

"The truth is, Imani and I just kissed once when we were drunk at a club. There were pictures, so it looked like more than it was. She was way too good for me and I knew it. She was too good for Perrault, too, as is evidenced by his fucking mouth."

Grace's curiosity is piqued. "You never slept with her?"

I shake my head. "Nope. She's just a friend."

"Huh," she says, running her finger through a blob of cream in the pastry box before popping it in her mouth. The way she sucks on it is downright pornographic, but her eyes look like she's doing a mental word problem.

"Go ahead. You can ask," I say.

"What about the others? The singer? The actresses?"

I sigh. "Are you asking if I slept with them?"

"I'm asking if you *dated* them," she says.

"Yeah. Not seriously. Just a little bit of fun," I say. I plop down onto the bed with a heavy bounce. "My life isn't really conducive to anything serious, with all the practice and games and travel. And meeting people is hard. At least I know those women aren't after me for my fame or my money. We have an understanding."

"Have you *ever* been in a serious relationship?"

I stare up, tracing the edge of a large brown water stain on the popcorn ceiling with my eyes. I want to ask her what she means by "serious," but I don't like what that says about me. This conversation is already making me feel gross, like it's confirming all her worst suspicions about me. That my life is defined by paparazzi cameras. That I'm a player who runs through women like I run through hockey sticks. That I can't be serious, can't be trusted, can't love anyone.

I don't like that it all might be true.

"I don't know what to tell you, Grace. My personal life is a disaster. Not quite the disaster the press makes it out to be, but it's not that far off." I sigh as I reach for my clothes, fold them, and lay them atop the chipped bureau. "Hockey is my life. Everything else comes second."

Her brow furrows like she wants to challenge me, but instead she just nods. Thank god. I can't keep talking about my hookups with her.

She shoves the last broken, gooey bite of cannoli into her mouth and stands. I'm about to tell her she has powdered sugar on her nose when she reaches back and unhooks her bra, tugs the straps down over her arms, and then pulls the whole thing out the bottom of her tank top.

I nearly choke on my tongue.

"What?" she asks, flopping onto the bed beside me.

"Is that bra trick one of the things they teach you when they divide the boys and girls up for sex ed in middle school?" I ask.

"Sleepovers," Grace replies, and unbuttons her shorts. She slides them slowly down her shapely, toned thighs, then stands and neatly folds them. When she turns to set them on the chair, the hem of her tank top rises so I can see her panties. They're pale blue cotton with drawings of bacon and eggs all over them.

I bark out a laugh.

"What now?" she asks, spinning around and tugging down the hem of her tank top. And fuck, somehow that's even better, that shy, modest pose. I don't know where to look—her shapely legs, the prick of her nipples against the thin fabric of her tank top, or her lush pink lips. I focus on her blue eyes and pretend she's not about to bring me to my knees.

"What's with the panties?" I ask.

Grace freezes. "What?"

"All your panties have cartoon drawings on them. The cherries from the park that day. Pretty sure I saw goldfish on the ones you were wearing when you made me soup. And now bacon and eggs?"

"I like fun underwear," she says, her cheeks crimson. She holds the tank top down with one hand, then uses the other to pull back the covers. She gives the sheets a cursory glance, and then, satisfied that there are no spiders or snakes (biker or otherwise) hiding in there, she slides in. She quickly pulls the covers up over her lap, then shrugs. "And they're comfy. I don't want to spend my whole day feeling like my underwear is creeping up my butt."

As soon as she's settled, I slip in next to her. I lean back against the pillows, my feet nearly hanging off the end of the tiny bed. Despite my best efforts to stay as close as possible to the edge, I can feel the heat coming off her skin. It feels as if there's barely a whisper of space between our thighs.

"You good?" Grace asks.

*No.* "Yup."

She pulls the chain on the little bedside lamp, plunging the room into darkness. Silent darkness. What I wouldn't give for the roar of those motorcycles right now. Or some grumbled conversation outside our door between Snakes and Bullet, or whatever those guys call themselves. Even some crickets or cicadas would be good right now, but nature is conspiring against me, and the room is deathly silent.

Grace is frozen beside me, and from the quickness of her breath, which I can absolutely hear, I know she's not close to falling asleep. I wonder if I'm destined to lie here awake all night with a hard cock, blinking at the stupid popcorn ceiling.

"So, when you talk about heat levels, what's the scale?" I ask, because I can't do this. I can't lie here next to her in the dark, not talking. "In the books, I mean."

There's another stretch of silence, and then she sighs. "I cannot have this conversation with you right now." *While we're in our underwear in bed,* she doesn't say, but I imagine it.

"Sorry, just trying to make conversation."

"Maybe we should just try to go to sleep," she says. She rolls over onto her side, her back to me, the bed bouncing and squeaking with her movement. "We'll get up first thing and deal with the car."

If that's what she wants, fine. I'll lie next to her, quiet and chaste, willing all the blood out of my cock, pretending I don't want to know what her bare skin feels like under my palms, pretending I'm not imagining sliding those ridiculous bacon-and-eggs panties down her thighs. Pretending I don't want to taste every inch of her. I have to tense to hold myself still, because every nerve in my body feels pulled toward her. But Grace was clear. She doesn't want to start anything with me. She just wants to go to sleep. I'll do anything this girl asks of me. Hell, I'll sleep on the roof if she wants me to.

"Yeah, first thing," I say.

"Good. Well, good night, Decker."

I let out a long, quiet breath, willing my heart to slow down, my muscles to relax. But my control in this moment hovers right around zero. Despite years of training to develop heightened awareness in every inch of my body, to teach it to do exactly what I want even in the most intense situations, it has finally crapped out on me in this quiet motel room on a desolate stretch of Indiana highway. It's all I can do just to keep breathing.

"Good night, Grace," I say.

# CHAPTER 28

## GRACE

'm sure I'll never fall asleep, not with the tension vibrating through my body and the screaming silence of the motel room. But at some point, the long day in the heat, all the food, and the walk to the motel get the best of me, and I drift off.

Some time later, my eyes flutter open to darkness, the glowing red numbers on the digital clock reading 1:17 a.m. It takes me a minute to remember that I'm in a motel in a tiny town in Nowhere, Indiana. With Decker. Who's down to his boxers, next to me in this far-too-small bed.

No, not just next to me.

I freeze, realizing that I'm curled into Decker's side, my body pressed up against him, one of my legs thrown across his hips. At some point, I migrated across this tiny mattress in my sleep. At some point, his body welcomed me in, his arm snaking around my back, his large, warm palm resting on the curve of my ass.

I tense and start to move away, but his hand presses into my skin, his fingers kneading me. A quiet groan escapes his lips, his eyes still closed.

"Don't go," he whispers, and I can't tell if he's awake or if he thinks this is all a dream.

"Decker," I whisper, still draped over his body. Beneath my

knee, his cock swells, and I suck in a breath. My god, how did those ESPN photographers use just a hockey stick to cover all of *that*?

Feeling him, his desire, I have to know if he's awake. I have to know if it's me he's thinking of as he grows hard, or if it's Imani Menendez or another one of the many gorgeous women he's had on his arm. I lightly stroke the dusting of blond hair on his carved chest. I tilt my chin, my lips near his ear, and whisper again. *"Decker…"*

His free hand slides across his body and grasps my waist, pulling me even closer, the ridge of his hip delivering the most delicious pressure to the apex of my thighs.

"Are you awake?" he murmurs, his eyes fluttering at half mast. He turns his head until those deep brown eyes are boring into me.

"Yes," I hiss, unable to mask the pleasure curling through my body like smoke. My poker face is gone. All rational thought left with it. I want him. Desperately. And it's only by the grace of god and the wheezing of the anemic air conditioner in the window that I'm able to hold myself back.

But then Decker snips each string of my control with the sharpest of scissors.

"Stay," he says, his voice a low rumble beneath my palm. "Please. I want to feel you. Just for a minute. Then we can go back to forgetting."

My heart squeezes in an extra beat, a flood of heat gathering low in my belly.

"I don't want to forget," I tell him, and suddenly I can't contain it, any of it, the feelings and the desire and the raw truth of it all. "I never did."

Any question as to whether Decker is awake is answered when the hand on my hip moves to my cheek, gently brushing back the hair that rests there and tucking it behind my ear. His fingers linger, then trace a delicate line along my jaw. I roll toward him, delighting in the way his body lines up with mine. Every point of contact is an injection of heat, a pool of desire. And then his lips cover mine, the kiss picking up right where we left off back on the ice. There's nothing tentative there. No questions, just answers. His kiss says, in no uncertain terms, that there will be no forgetting. Not this time. He kisses me like he's trying to burn the memory of his lips and tongue into me, and I am consumed with the heat of it.

And emboldened.

My hand goes to his hip, tugging him toward me. He follows, rolling until his body covers mine, the evidence of his desire for me pressing into my sex. My hands snake up his back, and I drag my fingernails against his skin as I roll my hips into his.

"Fuck, Grace," he says, finally breaking the kiss. He presses up, his biceps flexing, his hair flopping over his eyes as he gazes down at me.

"Do you want to stop?" I whisper.

He freezes, the only motion the quick rise and fall of his chest. "Do you?"

I shake my head against the pillow. "No," I say, finally telling him the truth. Finally telling *myself* the truth. That I've wanted Decker for a long time, before we started talking about romance novels, before I kissed him on the ice. Maybe even as far back as the day I watched him sit in that absurdly tiny chair and entrance a crowd of tiny humans, a picture book held aloft in his enormous hands. Hands that are now stroking my skin with all the care he used to turn those delicate, colorful pages. "Please don't stop."

"Thank fuck," Decker says, dropping his lips down to the sensitive spot behind my ear, drawing lazy circles with his tongue. He follows that with a line of kisses down my neck, and I arch against the pillow to urge him on. His tongue dances in the valley of my collarbone, his fingers matching the motion on my belly, playing with the hem of my tank and the waist of my panties. Every nerve ending in my body lights up, and I don't even know where I want him to touch me first. What I want the most.

Him. Just him. Anything he wants to give me.

His body, fine-tuned and sculpted, flexes above me, tension radiating off his muscles. He looks like he's doing everything he can to hold himself back, to reel himself in.

But I want to see him break.

"Touch me, Decker," I whisper.

His groan turns into a growl.

"Greedy girl, asking for exactly what she wants." And then his mouth crashes into mine, his tongue parting my lips. But my attention is on his fingers, which are tracing a line down my hip, curving across my thigh, and teasing the edge of my panties. I heave a sigh into his mouth, and when his fingers slip beneath the cotton and find the warm, sensitive center of me, I toss my head back into the pillow. His lips move to the shell of my ear, and he whispers my name.

"Look at me," he says. "I need to see you see me touching you."

I open my eyes and meet his, his brow furrowed as his fingers part my folds. He studies my face as he explores, gliding through the wet slickness, teasing my entrance. Every time my eyes start to drift closed in ecstasy, Decker pauses until I return my focus to him.

"That's it," he says, his hot breath sending another rush of wetness between my legs. "Let me in, Grace. Let me feel you."

It's not until that whispered request that I realize I'm tensing my thighs, holding myself taut against the thrill of his touch. But when his thumb turns a slow, soft circle around my clit, I let out a long breath, my thighs falling open against the mattress.

Decker hums his approval as one of his long, thick fingers slips inside me, and immediately I know it's not enough. Not when I can feel the hard outline of his erection, desperate against his boxer briefs, pressing into my thigh.

"More," I beg, arching into his touch, and he adds a second finger. The fullness is good, but I want *more*. I thread my fingers through his hair, pulling him down to me. I kiss him, our tongues tangling, then pull back and demand again, "*More.*"

Decker growls, and a third finger slides in, curling against the spot inside me that sends sparks shooting up my spine. All the while, his thumb works my clit, slipping across the bundle of nerves until my cries crescendo.

"Come for me," Decker says, half order, half plea, and it's all I need to shatter underneath his hand. "Fucking come for me, Grace."

"Decker!" I cry, whining his name in a tone that would embarrass me were I not so fucking thrilled by what he's doing to me, so out-of-my-mind obsessed with his touch and the orgasm he sends rocketing through my body.

"Goddamn, you're beautiful," he grinds out, his jaw flexing, watching me come apart. As the last shudder wracks through my body, he lowers his forehead to mine, pressing into me, his chest heaving. "I could watch you come forever," he mutters.

Decker moves like he's going to roll off of me, but I can still feel the desperation of his erection, the long, thick maleness of him. And I am not letting him out of this bed until I undo him as well.

# CHAPTER 29

## DECKER

As Grace pants below me, I hear the whoosh of my blood, feel it running hot through my veins. My whole body is a skate lace pulled taut, tied into knots, ready to break.

And then she rolls her hips beneath me.

"More," she says, her eyes heavy-lidded. *Fuck*, she looks like the dirtiest dream, her panties wet and shoved to the side, her pussy glistening and swollen beneath me. I can't believe I just held her pleasure in my hand, coaxed it out of her with my fingers, the evidence of it coating my palm. Goddamn, seeing her shatter like that, hearing my name tripping off her pink lips like a prayer—it's better than any orgasm I've ever had. Seeing her satisfied is my greatest victory, a buzzer-beater slap shot of a win.

And she wants more.

"Please, Decker," she pants. "I want you."

Those words are so goddamn sweet, I have to taste them, devour them, and I cover her mouth with mine. I would give her anything she wants, and she wants me. This girl who fights me about everything, who is so tough when everyone treats her as fragile. She's asking *me* for something, and like fuck I'm not going to give it to her.

Except.

"Grace, baby, I don't have anything," I say as the swollen, dripping head of my cock makes contact with her entrance. I'm straining against the fabric of my boxer briefs, my shoulders bunching with the realization that this is as far as we can go tonight. That this may be as far as we ever go, if she wakes up tomorrow and remembers that I'm a walking disaster, that she has no use for me. "I don't have any condoms."

But she doesn't stop. She presses herself into me, wrapping her legs around my waist and pulling me down with her heels, begging for the invasion. Her eyes are wide, her lips full and bitten. She grinds out a moan, her chest heaving.

"I'm on birth control. And I got tested after—" She breaks off, her brow furrowing, not wanting to bring that fucker into this. I reach up and stroke her cheek, pulling her back to me, to this bed, to *us*. She nuzzles into my touch, her lids heavy as she sighs. "It was clear."

She waits, a question hanging in the air. I scan my memory, just to be sure, because I am not about to bring my mess anywhere near this incredible siren of a woman. But I had a physical right before the playoffs began, and there was no one after that. During the playoffs, I kept my eye solely on the game, not that it mattered. And after the playoffs, I was too fucked up to go looking for anyone.

And that's when I found Grace upside down in a planter and my whole world turned upside down with her.

"I'm safe," I tell her, meaning it in every possible way. "I'll always keep you safe."

I drop kisses on those perfect freckles, because I need a pause. The notion that she's going to let me fuck her at all is blowing my mind, but the fact that she wants me to fuck her *bare*? The thought is almost too much. I nearly come before I can even get inside her. Before I can even slide those ridiculous soaked panties down her thighs.

But then I remember what Grace said that day I borrowed her book. What she wants, and what she's never had. What no one has ever given her. I gaze down at her, her raven hair fanned out on the white pillow, her icy eyes wide, her pink lips swollen and parted, her tongue raking along the bottom of her teeth. I've faced some of the biggest, baddest, most bloodthirsty players in professional hockey, but I've never been as nervous as I am right now, staring into this woman's big blue eyes, trying not to break her.

Praying she doesn't break *me*.

I suck in a breath to steady myself, to keep my hands from shaking as I hook my fingers into the waistband of her panties and slowly drag them down her thighs, planting kisses along her smooth skin as I go. Grace, impatient with need, tugs her tank top over her head, tossing it onto the floor, and when I sit back on my heels, I'm gazing at a blessedly naked, absolutely beautiful Grace McBride. Her breasts are milky white, her nipples taut and pale pink. I palm them, and they fit perfectly in my hands as my thumbs swipe across their pebbled tips. I revel in her gasp, in the way she arches into my touch, her hands fisting the sheets at her sides.

I slide my waistband down to free my cock, taking myself in hand and loving the way her eyes grow wide at the sight of me. I can't help the smirk that spreads across my face.

"Tell me what you need, Grace. Talk to me."

"I…" She hesitates, looks up at the ceiling, a flush climbing her neck.

I lower my lips to the shell of her ear, dragging my tongue over the spot behind it that I already know she likes. She lets out the softest, sweetest sigh. I whisper, "Like the books, Grace. Let me give it to you like in the books."

She lets out a whimper that lights me up, but it's nothing compared to the feeling of the head of my cock slipping along her warm, wet folds. I want inside her with a fierceness, but I also know I need to take my time. I want to make this good for her. And it's partially selfish. This might be the only chance I'll ever get with her, and I want to ruin her for everyone else. I want her to feel only *my* touch on her pebbled skin forever, even if it can't ever be me again.

She bucks against me, but I reach down and grasp her hips, slowing her down. Stilling her.

"Patience," I hiss, and when her brow furrows and she gives me the sexiest little glare I've ever seen, I can't help but chuckle. But something about her fury comforts me. It reminds what this is. Because even though I can barely contain my feelings for her, I know she doesn't feel the same way about me. When I told her about my history with women, she barely seemed surprised. She probably sees me how everyone else sees me—as a good time, a good fuck. This, whatever is happening between us in this quiet, dark motel room? It can't be anything more.

And I believe that, right up until the moment I lower my lips to hers, notching my aching cock into her entrance. I give the slightest shuddering press of my hips and know immediately that this is bigger than a good fuck. And even if she doesn't know it or can't admit it, I won't pretend with her. Not here, not now, not while she's splayed out beneath me, her lips parting as I slide into her slowly, inch by inch.

"*Fuck,*" I groan as her legs wrap around my waist, sealing me to her.

"It's so good," she murmurs into my neck. "How is it so good?"

*Because I was made for you.*

The thought invades my brain unbidden, riding a wave of euphoria, and it hits me harder than any check I've ever taken into the boards. It rattles me all the way to my core, and I grit my teeth to stop it from tripping out of my mouth.

I slide out of her and immediately press myself back in, reveling in the little whine that escapes her throat. I should have known being with Grace would be different. *Everything* about her is different, from the way she refuses to take shit from me to the way she gives me every part of her, even the parts she hides from everyone else. But I'm unprepared for just how deep my feelings for her go until I'm inside her.

My mind spins as I pick up my pace, and I distract my lips from saying all the things I can't say to her by kissing every freckle across her chest, laving the flat of my tongue across her nipples, the silvery puckered scars from her childhood surgery, trying to wring every last ounce of pleasure from her. Every single muscle in my body is tense from holding myself back, from not saying what I'm thinking or driving into her as hard as I want to.

And then she digs her heels into my ass, pulling me in deeper. It sends an electric shock skittering up my spine, and I look down, trying to read her.

But she doesn't make me read. My beautiful girl, my open book, blinks those wide baby-blue eyes at me, her full lower lip plump and pouting, when she begs, "Don't be gentle with me. *Please.*"

Jesus fucking Christ, I'm gone for her.

Will go anywhere for here.

Will do anything to give her what she needs. What she *deserves.* What no one else has ever given her.

"I know what you can take, Grace," I reply, then drop my lips to her ear and whisper, "so go ahead and *take it.*"

She hesitates for only a second before taking control of her pleasure, taking control of *me.* She arches, thrusting against my cock, taking me deeper, urging me faster. Demanding. She's so fucking confident. It's like when she took off skating that day at the ice arena. She knew exactly what she was capable of, and she let me see it, reveled in surprising me. And knowing how often she hides, how often she pretends, the fact that she's letting me see how strong she is, that she's letting me in, *pulling* me in, is nearly too much.

It feels like glimpsing a shooting star.

I meet her thrusts with my hips, sure to drag my pelvis over her clit with every movement. I feel my cock bottom out inside her, feel her muscles clench, her nails dig into my back as her cries grow desperate, just a litany of prayers and pleas and my name uttered over and over. I can feel my orgasm building, feel it trying to break, but I force it back. I focus on her pleasure, on making sure she takes hers first.

My biceps start to burn as I hold myself above her, watching the flush climb her chest, her breasts bouncing as she meets me with every thrust.

*Mine.* I can't say it, because it isn't true. But I think it every time I slide into her. *Mine. Mine. Mine.*

"Fuck, Decker, I'm coming!" she cries, her chin tipping up, urging me on.

"Fucking take it. Take my cock in that perfect pussy," I growl. Sweat rolls down the back of my neck as I work over her and work to make myself wait. I'm standing right on the edge, holding her, waiting for her to go first, and when she does, it rushes across every inch of her skin.

Her eyes fall closed. I can only imagine the explosion of stars that must occur behind those eyelids, because watching her here, now, beneath me, enveloping me, quaking and heaving as her innermost muscles clamp down on my cock, causes a full Fourth of July fireworks display in my brain. It's only because I practice focus for a living that I'm able to watch her through the rush of my own oncoming orgasm, see every moment of her peak, the rise and float and fall of it.

And the second I know she's gone, I let go of my tether, crying out as my own orgasm rockets through me, pouring deep into the velvety warmth of her.

"Grace," I cry out, uttering it over and over like a prayer. "Grace, Grace, Grace, Grace."

*Give it to me. Please, give me Grace.*

*I don't deserve it.*

*I don't deserve you.*

*You're all I want.*

*Grace.*

# CHAPTER 30

## GRACE

The morning sun blazes through the gap in the curtains, warming my face and rousing me from the most incredible dream.

And then, as I pry my eyes open and throw my arms out, stretching my sore muscles, I realize it wasn't a dream at all.

The night comes back to me in delicious flashes: Decker's lips, his hands, the feel of his warm breath as he whispered dirty things in my ear. I close my eyes and sprawl out in the beam of sunlight that falls across the bed, enjoying the tingle that travels across my body. I've never felt *anything* like the orgasms that crashed over me last night, my body thrumming under Decker's control. Just the memory has me on the edge of coming again.

But when I roll over to curl up with the man who played a finesse game with my body, all I feel are cold, bare sheets.

Decker is gone.

I pause, listening for the sound of the shower running or anything else that might reassure me that he hasn't fled, but there's nothing. Of course, a six-foot-five, two-hundred-pound athlete can't possibly hide in this dusty shoebox of a motel room.

He's *gone.*

And I'm panicking.

Suddenly I see the previous night through a very different filter. How I threw myself at him, literally waking him up with my body wrapped around his. How I begged him to touch me, begged him to fuck me. He was happy to give me what I wanted in the heat of a dark, quiet night, but I guess in the cold light of morning, he's experiencing some regrets.

Panic gives way to irritation that his way of dealing with all this—the complications, the embarrassment, the regret—was to run away. What was he thinking? He's not a child, no matter how often I've seen him act like one. He wasn't coerced. He just followed his dick. And then he *bolted*? Like a fucking *coward*?

And I just keep spiraling from there. I probably have six or seven emotional breakdowns in the few minutes before the door creaks open.

I bolt upright, yanking the rumpled sheets up over my bare chest. Because of course I'm still completely naked. By the time I was done screaming his name last night, I was far too tired to search for my underwear. I'm regretting that now as I watch Decker stride into the room, somehow looking fresh in his clothes from yesterday. His hair is pulled back in a sun-streaked bun at the nape of his neck, and his shorts and T-shirt are only slightly wrinkled. He's holding a white pastry box in one hand, two paper coffee cups balanced on top.

"Morning, sunshine," he says with an easy smile as he kicks the door shut behind him.

"Where did you go?" is the first thing that flies out of my mouth, and I hate that it comes out sounding slightly accusatory. Then again, I did have the best sex of my life with the most confusing man I've ever met and then woke up *alone*. I have some serious questions, so I might as well start there.

Decker comes around the bed and lowers his large frame onto the edge next to me, then passes me a coffee cup. It's still hot, and the smell goes a long way toward reviving me. I had no alcohol last night, but I'm fuzzy-headed nonetheless.

"I woke up early, thanks to every single spring in this mattress digging into my spine, and since you were still snoring like a longshoreman—"

"Lies," I interject between sips of coffee. The cream and sugar ratio is almost perfect.

"Sure." He smirks, then takes a sip of his own coffee—black, I know from the short month we've spent in each other's orbit. "So I ventured out to see if I could deal with the truck."

Oh, right. The Bronco, which is still parked two miles down the highway and in need of a tow.

"And?" I ask.

"And just as I was leaving a message for Lou, the tow truck driver, one of the motorcycle dudes shuffled out of the room on the end. He told me his name is Nickel because he did five years in prison. I didn't ask what for, but I don't think it was white collar crime," he says, and I can't help but laugh. "Anyway, he asked me a few questions about the Bronco, loaded me onto the back of his bike, and drove me out there, and the next thing I knew, she was running again."

"What was wrong with it?"

Decker blushes. "Look, I'd like to bolster my manhood by explaining it with technical words, but all I can tell you is that he stuck his head under the hood and did something with what I *think* was a wrench, but I'll be honest, I can't be sure. There was some clanging, and then he said it was good to go. I drove it back here and it was fine. She's parked right outside the door." He looks down, remembers the box, and drops it into my lap. "Oh yeah, and then I ran into Lana, who told me about a donut shop a mile up the road, so I picked up sustenance. There's a bacon, egg, and cheese sammy in there for you."

My stomach growls, and I yank open the box to find a foil-wrapped sandwich, cheese oozing out the seam, and half a dozen glistening glazed donuts.

"I already ate mine," he says with a sheepish grin. "Worked up a bit of an appetite fucking you senseless last night."

And then he puts his coffee down on the chipped bedside

table and pulls me in for a kiss. There's no hesitation, no obvious regret. No disgust that I haven't brushed my teeth in twenty-four hours. And, I think as his palm skates across my breast where I've dropped the sheet, certainly no disappointment that I'm not dressed. Just Decker and his lips and tongue and a groan that rumbles up through his chest and into my mouth. Decker kissing away every anxiety I cultivated while he was gone.

Rude, I worked hard on those anxieties.

I pull back slightly, and Decker blinks as if I've startled him out of a dream. He takes in my furrowed brow, the way my teeth are sinking into my bottom lip. "Are you okay?" he asks.

"When you weren't here, I got a little worried," I admit.

"About what?" he asks, so sweetly oblivious to the waves of questions swirling through my brain.

"That maybe you had regrets," I explain.

And this asshole—this infuriatingly sexy *asshole*—has the nerve to grin his trademark *aw shucks, ma'am* grin, which quickly turns into something slightly more devious. "Oh, I have plenty of regrets, Grace McBride, but my biggest one is waiting so long for you." He leans into me again and flicks his tongue over the tender spot where I worried my lip with my teeth. His hands thread into the tangled hair at the nape of my neck, and he groans into my mouth as I part my lips for his tongue. And he damn near kisses away all of my anxiety in one fell swoop, but there's still enough sense in my brain to wonder what comes next.

Decker's groan turns into a growl when I pull back slightly.

"Should we talk about last night?" I ask him, tugging the covers back up over my bare chest.

His eyes drop down, his expression morphing into an adorable little pout of frustration. "I think technically it was this morning," he says, his flashing eyes returning to mine.

I roll my eyes. "What I mean…" I say, then pause to summon a little more courage. "I really enjoyed last night."

He arches an eyebrow. "This morning."

I swat at his arm. "Yes," I reply. "I liked it. A lot."

He grins. "I did, too. Am I sensing a *but*?"

I shrug, the sheet slipping, sending his eyes back down to my chest. "I don't know. I'm a little freaked out, to be honest."

To his credit, he drags his eyes away from my nipples and back to my face, his gaze softening.

"Talk to me," he says.

"I just...I don't know what it means."

"It can mean whatever we want it to, Grace," he says. "What do you want it to mean?"

"What about Archer?"

Decker sobers. "Well, your brother would thoroughly and completely kick my ass if he found out, and I think I'd have to let him," he says. He pauses, fiddling with the sheet. "Do you want him to know?"

Do I? That would certainly bring a whole new dimension to what happened between Decker and me. It would take us from friends with benefits to something else entirely. Would we be in a relationship? Would that make him my boyfriend? It's all too much to think about.

"I feel like we have enough to deal with without bringing Archer into it," I say, this time only a half truth.

He pauses. "So..."

I shrug, the answer obvious to me. "So...maybe we don't have to tell him?"

Decker nods like I've given him the answer he was waiting for. "If that's what you want."

I mean, if we're talking about wants, that's a different matter, because what I *want* is a repeat of last night. What I *want* it explore with Decker even more. "Okay, but..."

He laughs. "Spill it, Grace."

I let the words rush out fast, all on one quick exhale. "So, we just don't tell him about this one time?"

The corner of his lips quirks up. "Or?"

Oh god, this absolutely *infuriating* man. How am I naked and wet and wanting, and yet I still sort of want to wrap my hands around his throat? "I guess I'm asking if this was a one-time show or if maybe there's a chance for...I don't know, an encore?"

Decker grins, and there's a look of victory there that tells me he was playing with me just a little bit. "I don't love the idea of an audience, but if you're into it, I guess we could have a conversation..."

I huff out a sigh of frustration, half charmed, half infuriated that he can't just give me a straight answer. "No, I mean...do you *want* an encore?"

Decker slowly runs his eyes over the length of my body, a low rumble in his chest. He reaches up and takes my cheeks in his hands, his thumbs stroking my skin. He lowers his mouth and takes the sweetest sip of my lips.

"Grace, when it comes to you, I am made of want," he whispers. And then he pulls me in for another knee-melting kiss that has me sinking back into the bed, Decker stretching out over me, the pastry box shoved aside as he presses his hips and the evidence of that want directly into my core. "I want to experience you coming apart in my arms as many times as you'll let me. So yes, I am very much hoping for an *encore*."

With one exquisite roll of his hips, my legs fall open, ready to welcome him back inside. And then two sharp knocks on the door jolt me out of my reverie.

Decker's fingers, which are threaded through my hair, press into my scalp in frustration. "Goddammit," he mutters.

"What?"

"Lana threatened my life if we're not out of this room by ten. Which is a problem, because if I keep kissing you like this, we're not leaving this bed until tomorrow," he growls. "Fuck, why did we wait so long?"

"Because my brother is your best friend and he'd probably display your severed head on a hockey stick in his front yard if he knew what happened last night," I remind him. And myself, to be honest. Because at this moment, Archer's reaction feels a whole lot less important than what Decker could do to me in this bed if we kept going.

But at the reminder of my big brother, Decker stiffens. And not in the fun way. He props himself on his elbows, his biceps flexing by my ears.

"Just so I'm clear, you're saying we should keep going, but keep it to ourselves," he says. A statement, not a question. Or maybe a suggestion? All I'm sure of is that last night, I felt sexy and wanted and powerful. I can't remember the last time I felt that way. As I lay beneath him, Decker saw me. He read me like a book.

*Keep it to ourselves.*

I just wish I knew what *it* was. The sex we had and have agreed to repeat? Or is he talking about feelings? A relationship? I want to ask him what comes after the sex, or along with it. But I'm too scared. Partly because I don't even know what I want, if I'm even ready for another relationship. And even if I *do* want more than just sex, the reality is that Decker and I have an expiration date. He's going back to Chicago in two months. The hockey season will begin, and whatever this is will be over. Am I seriously going to sit here in this dingy motel room the morning after hockey's bad boy rocked my world and ask if he wants to have a long-distance relationship with me?

Absolutely the fuck not.

And anyway, Decker doesn't do relationships. He told me so himself just last night, before he rang my bell so hard I can still hear the echo. What, do I think I have a magical vagina that convinced Decker to change his entire philosophy on relationships in one night?

God, he really did fuck me stupid.

So even though I'm not entirely sure what I'm agreeing to, I nod, his palms still resting in my hair.

"That sounds like a plan," I reply.

His lips curl into the grin I see only sometimes, the one I've learned to look for. It's not the one he shows to the cameras, or the parents at story time, or whoever he's trying to convince of something. No, this is the real Decker Brooks smile, and when he shines it down on me, I forget everything else.

"Ten a.m.!" Lana screeches through the door, and Decker and I both burst out laughing.

"I'm not entirely sure she won't send the Disciples of Doom in after us," he says, planting a gentle kiss on the tip of my nose. "But let's continue this conversation later, okay?"

It takes us very little time to clear out of the room, since we have only the clothes on our backs, my giant bag of books, and a box of donuts. I climb back into Decker's Bronco feeling like I've lived six or seven lives since yesterday morning. My body is alive and my mind is spinning, and just like yesterday, the wind rushing through the car is as loud as my thoughts.

The main difference is that for the whole ninety-minute drive from the Last Stop to Cardinal Springs, Decker holds my hand, his thumb rubbing lazy circles across the back. I'm filled with questions, but I focus on the only answer I have: I want his hands on me again. I want to feel the ridges of his muscles, the heat of his moans against the shell of my ear. I want the shuddering evidence of his desire. Anything beyond that feels like too much to hope for.

Still, there was a moment last night when he was deep inside me, his gaze boring into me, when I thought he was going to confess something. I don't know what, but it looked like he was working to hold back words with every muscle in his body.

As the Bronco cruises past the sign welcoming us to Cardinal Springs, the one that touts Decker's hockey glory, his grip loosens on my hand. He pulls it away to rest it on the steering wheel, his eyes focused on the road ahead.

# CHAPTER 31

## GRACE

"Haven't you always wanted to make out in the library?"

It's Thursday, just four days since Decker and I left the Last Stop, and we've had encores every single night since. Mostly in his bed, because he says my full-size mattress is made for "half-size people," and it hard to complain now that I know all the things he can do to me in a California king. We've kept it all behind closed doors, as we agreed, but it's getting harder and harder to keep our hands to ourselves when we're outside our apartments.

Especially when we're deep in the nonfiction stacks.

Decker is supposed to be reshelving books, but instead he's got me pressed up against the oceanography section, his firm hands prepared to do some serious exploring. And it's hard to push him away like I know I should, because I *have* always wanted to make out in the library. Another item Cannon never marked off the sexual checklist, up there with dirty talk and consistent orgasms.

Decker, on the other hand, has ticked every box.

I let him kiss me so hard I nearly forget where I am until Ms. Tingle rounds the corner, her sparkly cane creaking as she leans on it. Decker springs back like he's been tased.

"Oh, don't stop on my account," Ms. Tingle purrs. She cocks one hip and gives us a once-over.

"We weren't—" I start.

"I was just helping Grace find a book," Decker volunteers, his hair flopping over his reddening cheeks.

"Inside her mouth?" Ms. Tingle arches an eyebrow. "Don't get yourselves all in a wad. I'm no gossip. And lord knows Mr. Tingle and I got up to some hanky-panky in the library a time or two. Though we preferred the last study room on the end. A little bit more private."

She winks, and Decker barks out a laugh. I know I'm blushing like a summer tomato, my cheeks so hot I'm surprised there's not steam coming off them.

"Do you need something, Ms. Tingle?" I ask. I'm unsuccessful at keeping the squeak out of my voice.

"I can't remember the name of that book you were telling me about. The one with the chastity belt?"

Decker's eyes go wide. "The *what?*"

"Shut up," I mutter, then smile at Ms. Tingle. "*The Professional* by Kresley Cole. But we don't have it, so you'll have to order it online."

Our romance section is woefully small. We have the budget to order *New York Times* bestsellers and to continue acquiring series we've started, with a little money left over to fulfill patron requests. Half the books I've recommended to Ms. Tingle are ones I've donated to the library from my own collection. But a lot of the really popular, really smutty romances that I know Ms. Tingle and readers like her would eat up are out of reach for us. When I think about my own bookstore, I dream of a romance section bursting with books that people can otherwise buy only from internet behemoths.

"Thank you, dear. I love a Mafia romance, so I'll put that one on my list. Maybe I can get it from Red Books next time the senior center organizes a bus trip to Bloomington," Ms. Tingle says, and my heart sinks, because I know those bus trips happen only every other month. I'm glad Ms. Tingle has absorbed my anti-Amazon rants, but I hate that it means the books she wants are out of reach.

Beside me, Decker taps at his phone screen. "What are you doing?" I ask.

"Adding it to my Goodreads."

"Okay, well, I'm going to go see if Marjorie has returned the new Kennedy Ryan. Might as well read that one again while I wait!" Ms. Tingle cuts her eyes between Decker and me, then chuckles, waving her papery hand at us. "As you were."

She turns and toddles slowly away, and as soon as the sounds of her cane and her orthopedic shoes fade, Decker hooks his fingers through the belt loops of my jeans and drags me toward him. His lips hover over mine, sending zings of arousal rushing through my body. "You heard the lady," he says, then covers my mouth with his. His hand snakes around to palm my ass, his fingers kneading as he slants his mouth over mine, making me hum against his tongue.

And then my phone vibrates against his hand in my back pocket. His long, strong fingers pickpocket me, spinning the phone to face me.

"You've got a text," he says, his eyebrows rising as it vibrates a second, third, and fourth time. "Someone's persistent."

I glance at the screen and see texts from both Carson and Wyatt.

CARSON

SOS—need my girls

WYATT

I have a shift at The Pint tonight. Come to
the bar?

CARSON

YES. Because I need my girls AND tequila

WYATT

Just put a brand new bottle of Patron on the shelf. All for you baby girl

CARSON

Thank god. You in Grace?

WYATT

Do we need to put out an APB on your ass? Where the hell have you been?

CARSON

I'm starting to worry you're dead in a ditch somewhere. Seriously. Text back

I scan the messages, then start tapping frantically.

GRACE

Sorry sorry sorry! Not dead! I'll be there!

"Everything okay?" Decker asks. He could easily read over my shoulder, since he's still pulling my hips tight against his in a way that feels delicious, but his eyes are only on my face.

"Yeah, I've just been, uh, *occupied* these last few days? And my friends are freaking out," I explain.

The grin that spreads over his face could light up an arena. "Occupied, eh?" He does a little thrust with his hips that nearly has me dragging him to the floor.

"Yes, you menace," I reply with absolute no venom. I have no more venom for Decker, just desire. How the fuck did we get here? "Looks like I'm spending the evening at the Half Pint providing emotional support and drinking tequila."

"No worries. I should probably text Archer back, too." At the mention of my brother, Decker releases his hold on my belt loops. His name is like an air horn, a reminder of why we shouldn't be making out in the stacks, even if we're in a spot where no one ever goes. A reminder that maybe we shouldn't be doing any of this at all. But Decker quickly shakes it off—literally gives his head a shake, tossing his hair back. "You go hang with the girls, and I'll meet up with your brother." I step back, but he pulls me in again. "You're not meeting them *yet*, though, right? Maybe we can check out that study room. The last one on the end? I'd love to see you bent over one of those tables."

I reach around and pinch his round, muscled hockey ass, swallowing a groan at the memory of this morning, when I gripped that ass to pull him deeper into me. "We replaced the wooden doors with glass ones last year," I reply. "It was mostly because of the high schoolers, but I'm not surprised that Ms. Tingle took a few spins in the study rooms, too."

Decker chuckles, then brushes his lips over mind. "Man, the library is so much hornier than I thought."

———

I head over to the Half Pint just before five. Carson is already there, perched on her usual stool, the one on the end next to the wall. She's already got a drink in front of her, her face tipped forward as she takes a long sip from the straw.

"Don't get too far ahead of me," I say, sliding in next to her.

"Hey, stranger," Carson says, and I'm glad to hear she's not slurring. I don't know why she needs an SOS, and she's not too far gone to tell me.

"Sorry, life has been nuts," I reply.

Wyatt pops through the swinging door to the back and sidles up to us. The Pint doesn't have a full kitchen, just a few snacks, so it's still pretty quiet in here while everyone grabs dinner elsewhere before popping in for their evening drinks.

"Aren't you a sight for sore eyes," Wyatt says. "Would you like a margarita, too?"

I glance over at Carson's half-finished drink. But I know how hard Wyatt's margaritas hit, and I'm already thinking about crawling into bed with Decker when I get home, so I don't want to get too blitzed.

"Just a cider tonight," I reply.

She nods. "Coming right up."

"So, tell us how we can help," Carson says between sips.

"What? Aren't we here for you?" I ask.

"Yeah, but you're obviously underwater with the book festival," she says, and it takes me a second to realize that she thinks *that's* why I've been MIA for the last week, not because I've gone into hiding with Decker and all the things his muscular, shockingly flexible body can do to me. "I stopped by the hardware store yesterday, but your dad said you ditched your shift to stay late at the library."

That *is* what I told my dad. Since I only work half days at the library on Wednesdays, I usually cover for him at the store so he can run errands or do admin work. But lately he hasn't needed much help, so I begged off to watch a movie with Decker. We saw approximately nine minutes of it before we shed our clothes and set about testing the strength of the countertops in Decker's kitchen.

Putting together the book festival has actually proven to be fairly easy. We're just over three weeks out, and our lineup is set. We've got Annabeth Zhou, an up-and-coming author of cozy mysteries, as our keynote speaker and an impressive slate of authors from different genres and backgrounds. I've successfully delegated tasks to my committee. Using the blueprints from past festivals has been like having a cheat code. All I have left to organize is the opening night gala.

"Things are going really well, actually," I say. I hate that I have to hide what's happening between Decker and me. "Anyway, we're here for you, Carson."

Wyatt reappears with my drink. "Out with it," she says.

Carson groans. "It's almost too humiliating to repeat," she says. She pulls out her phone, taps it a few times, and then slides the glowing screen toward us. The dating app is open, the same one I signed up for and then promptly ignored. I'd gotten no further than exchanging a handful of awkward DMs that led me to believe I wasn't remotely ready for a new relationship. So I guess this thing with Decker is perfect, since he's not offering me one.

On the screen is a new DM. The sender has included a screenshot of one of Carson's profile pictures from a New Year's party where the three of us are hoisting champagne glasses. We're all dolled up, even though we never left my apartment. Wyatt's in a black bustier we found at a thrift store in Indianapolis, her curly bob dyed a vibrant lavender, her tattoos snaking inky black across her pale skin. I'm wearing a pink sequined dress with thin straps that was so tight it made my B-cup breasts look closer to a C+. I picked it up cheap from Target, and those sequins cut my arms to ribbons and fell off in chunks—definitely not my favorite fashion moment. After about an hour, I ditched it for pajamas.

Carson is between us in the photo, her blond hair in beachy waves falling over a forest-green velvet dress we called her "returning home from the war" dress. It was cut in a vintage forties style with a high Peter Pan collar and little white pearl buttons down the front. It was shockingly short, swishing over her curves and showing off her shapely legs. She wore it with fishnets and black patent-leather heels, and she looked like a fucking knockout, a dirty fantasy in a prim little package. But in this photo, you can't see the hemline or the fishnets or the heels, just the high neck and the way the dress stretched across her ample bosom.

Underneath the screenshot, the guy she matched with has written, *Are either of your friends single?*

Wyatt snatches the phone off the bar to glare at the message, as if maybe upon closer examination it will say something different. "Are you *fucking* kidding me?" she screeches when it remains the same.

Carson reaches up. "Please don't throw my phone. I already

did once this morning, and I don't know if it can take another collision."

"I'm so sorry," I say, rubbing her back. "But seriously, fuck that guy."

She sighs. "I know. I wouldn't want to date a shithead like that. But *all* the guys on this godforsaken app are like that. The 'nice' ones just want to hook up with me in secret, and the assholes message me directly to tell me that I'm just barely hot enough for them."

"If this guy or anyone like him has ever managed to trick a woman into bed, I will eat my shoe," Wyatt snarls. "Fuck the apps."

"But then how am I supposed to meet anyone?" Carson says, her eyes watery. "It's not like guys are walking up to me in the Half Pint."

"Beers! My brother has returned!" Archer's voice booms through the nearly empty bar, and my stomach immediately performs five backflips. Because if Archer is here... I spin on my stool, and there he is, his hair pulled back in that lazy bun I love, his biceps straining against the sleeves of his T-shirt. But Archer and Decker aren't alone. Behind them, stone-faced in a starched long-sleeved dress shirt and shorts and sporting a fresh buzz cut, is my brother Dan, apparently home from New York.

"Danny!" I cry, jumping off my stool and racing toward him. He scoops me up into a strong hug, then drops me back onto the wooden floor.

"Hey, Baby Gracie," he says, his voice quiet.

Decker snorts, and I shoot him a glare over Dan's shoulder, then I press my lips together to keep them from curling into a smile.

"I'm going to let that slide," I say to my brother, jerking my knee in warning. "You get *one* because you've been gone. What are you doing here?"

"Showed up on my doorstep this morning," Archer says, throwing an arm around Dan.

"How long are you here for?" I ask, but Dan just shrugs. He's always been a vault, and I know that if he's not in the mood to share right now, no amount of grilling will make him crack. That doesn't mean I won't try later, though.

Instead, I grab his hand and drag him toward the bar. "Wyatt, you haven't met my brother Dan. He's in finance in New York and never visits." Dan, standing a half step behind me, just grunts, then pulls his hand away and shoves it into the pockets of his khaki shorts. I glare at him, but the truth is, Dan has always been the quiet one. A grunt is practically effusive coming from him. "And you remember Carson."

"Tell her she's hot," Wyatt says, narrowing her eyes at Dan like she wants him to make up for the stinking pile of humanity that is the central Indiana dating pool.

"Wyatt!" Carson screeches, shooting our friend a horrified glare.

Dan turns, leveling his gaze at Carson. Her cheeks flush under the scrutiny, and I'm about to crack a joke to defuse the moment when Dan nods. "She's a knockout," he says, his voice low. He keeps his eyes on Carson for another split second. Then he turns to Wyatt and says, "Beer, please," before heading off to an empty table in the back.

"What the fuck?" I ask Archer, who shrugs.

"You know Dan. He'll tell us when he tells us," he says with a puzzled shake of his head. "Sort of like how you didn't mention that you and Decker took a little road trip and wound up in a hotel room together."

"What?" I practically yelp, and shoot Decker a panicked look. He gives me the smallest shake of his head that I hope means *I didn't tell him shit.*

"Why you two idiots didn't call me to pick you up instead of crashing in a fleabag motel is beyond me," he grumbles, and holds up two fingers to order his own beer. Wyatt, just a few steps away filling Dan's pint glass, is intently listening to this conversation, and her thick eyebrows lift. "Then you wouldn't have had to spend the night on some dank motel floor," he says to Decker.

Now it's Carson's turn to raise her brows. "You made him sleep on the floor?" she asks, her eyes sweeping over Decker's hulking form.

"You better have," Archer says, his voice a low warning.

"Not his best night of sleep, I'm sure," I say, forcing a laugh and hoping my face isn't doing anything like what my mind is doing.

"No worries, man," Decker says, hands up like he's being confronted by the cops. All I can see is those hands all over my body under the sheets at the Last Stop. My cheeks heat, and I immediately reach for my pint glass and take a long pull.

"You want a beer?" Archer says, apparently satisfied that no funny business occurred.

"Yeah," Decker croaks, and Wyatt reaches for a third pint glass. She fills it and slides it across the bar, her eyes narrowing as she silently gathers intelligence. Decker takes his beer and throws me one last quick, wide-eyed look before following Archer back to the table where Dan is already sitting in the shadows.

As soon as they're gone, Wyatt leans forward and slaps her hands down on the bar. Mercifully, she drops her voice low before she says, "What in the actual fuck was *that*?"

"I know that man didn't sleep on the floor, Grace Addison McBride," Carson hisses. "You shared a bed with Decker Brooks and didn't tell us?"

Wyatt arches an eyebrow, a Cheshire Cat grin spreading over her face. "I think they shared a lot more than that."

"Oh my *god*, spill!" Carson squeals.

"Shush!" I whisper, then glance over my shoulder. Archer, Dan, and Decker are sprawled out in their chairs, sharing easy conversation and sipping their beers. None of them is looking over here, so I turn and lean in. I know I can't keep lying to my friends. I don't *want* to keep lying to them. And they're not the ones we're trying to hide from, anyway.

"Archer can't know. He'd freak out," I whisper, then lean in even closer. Carson and Wyatt lean in until we're all practically nose to nose. "But Decker and I, we, uh…"

"Had an only-one-bed situation?" Carson says, and I can tell she's working hard to keep her voice from rising several octaves.

"Yes," I confirm.

"I'm sorry, you're going to have to spell it out for me," Wyatt says.

"They slept together." She turns to me. "Right?"

"Yes," I admit.

Wyatt nods. "Ahhhh, and I'm going to guess that's why you've been MIA? You're a sexual expat thanks to the hot hockey god over there?"

Now I can't hide my smile. All I can do is nod. Carson squeals, and Wyatt's mouth drops open as she absorbs my news.

"Holy shit," Carson sighs.

"So, what, are you guys dating now?" Wyatt asks.

"No!" I say, and now it's me who can't keep my voice down.

"Then what's going on?" Carson asks.

"Fuck buddies," Wyatt says, crossing her arms and nodding sagely.

"I mean, I guess?" I say, though I hate that term. "We're just… having fun."

Wyatt and Carson share a glance.

"What?" I point a finger between them. "What was that?"

Neither of them speaks at first, but finally Carson cracks. "Are you sure that's a good idea?"

"Hey, you're the one who was encouraging me to jump into bed with him!" I say to Carson, then turn to Wyatt. "You were all, *Have fun, Grace, loosen up*! That's what I'm doing."

"Just be careful," Wyatt says. "A one-night stand is very different from a friends-with-bennies situation. That can get messy, especially when you're hiding it from your overprotective big brother."

"Not to mention that you're not exactly a no-strings-attached kind of girl," Carson says.

"But what if I am? I spent six years with Cannon. I don't even know what kind of girl I could be," I shoot back.

"Okay, maybe you are," Wyatt says. "But what if *he's* not?"

I bark out a laugh, not even bothering to keep that quiet. But when I speak, I drop my voice low again. "Are you serious? You think *Decker Brooks* is going to get attached?"

"Why wouldn't he? You're amazing, Grace," Carson says.

"We're just telling you to be careful," Wyatt says. "Have all the fun you want, but keep your eyes open."

"Trust me, my eyes are wide open," I reply.

I turn and peek over my shoulder. Decker is leaning back in his chair, his beer bottle at his lips. He's laughing at something Archer has said, but his eyes? Those are on me.

# CHAPTER 32

## DECKER

t's the morning of the Fourth of July, and the library is closed. Which means Grace and I can sleep in, tangled up in each other after a night of me making her scream my name as she comes. I'm standing in a scalding-hot shower and taking advantage of the homemade steam room, gently stretching my muscles. I feel surprisingly good. My hip flexor, which I tweaked in the last game of the season, is feeling fine. Loose, even. My knee is less mad at me, because I ordered a Peloton and have been riding that in my apartment instead of running. Even my shoulder, which should hurt from all the hours I've spent holding myself above Grace's panting, writhing body, seems to welcome the workout. Aside from a few scratches from Grace's fingernails, nothing hurts at all.

I should feel like shit. I'm a thirty-three year old professional hockey player who has spent the last week getting far too little sleep, thanks to the insatiable brunette who shares my bed. And when I do sleep, it's with my arm thrown out so she can tuck into my shoulder, her body curled around mine. Sometimes I don't even sleep then, just lie in the dark, staring up at the beams that cross my ceiling, listening to her breath and the soft little sighs she makes when she's dreaming. Sometimes I wonder what she'd say if I confessed to her that this is more than just sex to me.

But Archer's warning at the Half Pint is still loud in my ears. Grace says he's the reason nobody can know about us, but in my lower moments, I wonder if that's actually true. I wonder if he's just an excuse so she doesn't have to tell me the truth, that she doesn't want me for any more than this. I love Archer like a brother, and I know he'd be pissed as shit if he knew what was going on between Grace and me. But sometimes when I'm with her, I'm so happy that I think I'd be willing to make him mad and force him to get over it.

But immediately my rational mind pipes up, asking what would happen next. Would we date? And when I go back to Chicago for training camp in September, would we be long distance? I could ask her to come with me, to leave her family and friends, but for what? So she could sit alone in my apartment while I play an eighty-game season, half of them on the road? What about her plan to open her own bookstore, a dream she tends to like it's an injured baby bird? I can't ask her to give that up for *me*.

And so as I reach for the soap and a loofah, scrubbing my exhausted but happy muscles, I come back around to the same conclusion as always: this will have to be enough for me, because I'm not enough for Grace.

Even though the thought is hardly a warm one, *all* thoughts of Grace turn me on, and my cock is stubbornly erect. Especially because when I turn off the water, I hear sizzling coming from the kitchen and smell browning sausage. Knowing that wonder of a woman is out there in my barren kitchen, cooking me breakfast? Fuck, I don't think there's anything sexier. I give up and wrap a towel low around my waist, the evidence of my desire for her obvious. And I'm rewarded for it with a wide smile when I walk into the kitchen.

"I cannot take care of that and also cook sausage," she says, using the spatula to gesture at the bulge under my towel.

I grin at her and stride over to the stove. I turn the burner off and then grab the pan handle and slide it aside.

"Sex first, then breakfast," I growl, grasping her hips and kissing her. She's wearing one of my Grinders T-shirts, the one from a charity kickball game we did a couple of summers ago. It's adorably oversize on her, the hemline skimming low on her thighs. It's got my name and number on the back, and holy shit, I want to spin her around and bend her over my counter, see her wear my number while I fuck her.

But I've got other plans.

I reach beneath the billowy hem and grasp the waistband of her panties, dragging them down her bare legs. I pause only to take in the pattern: black with glasses of red wine and wedges of cheese—brie, I think. I will never understand how this woman makes ridiculous cartoon panties so sexy.

As soon as she steps out of them, I grab her hips and lift her onto the counter. I let my towel fall to the floor and use it as a cushion as I drop to my knees in front of her.

"I thought we were taking care of you," she says, her voice breathy.

"Taking care of you *is* taking care of me," I tell her. "What I want right now is to taste this perfect pussy." Then I dip my tongue into her glistening folds, brushing the tip of my nose along the dark curls there. I suck in a breath, the scent of her intoxicating. But the taste of her is even better. All thoughts of breakfast are gone as I begin to devour her, laving my tongue over her clit, planting my lips over it to gently suck, reveling in the feel of her fingers snaking into my wet hair and tugging, a moan raking out of her throat. I look up, and she's watching me intently with those ice-blue eyes. I smile into her deliciously wet pussy.

But when I reach up and slide two fingers into her tight heat, her eyes flutter closed, her head dropping back as she releases a loud moan that echoes off the empty walls of my apartment.

"That's it, baby, open for me," I say. Her knees spread wider, giving me room to tilt my head, to run my lips across her at a better angle, coaxing her toward another orgasm. I'm getting pretty good at making Grace come. I study her like a playbook, noting every movement that elicits a quiver or a shiver or a gasp. Or my favorite—

"*Fuuuuuuck*, Decker, *yessss*," she hisses when I suck her clit into my mouth, releasing it with a pop. My girl really likes that. I do it again, feeling the quiver in her thighs and the clenching inside her pussy that tells me she's close. But I don't let up.

"As soon as I come, I want you to fuck me," Grace whines, leaning back on one arm, her other hand still in my hair, still pulling me close, exactly where I want to be. *"Hard."*

I love it when she tells me what she wants. I think I might be the only one who gets to see this demanding side of her, and it's hot as fuck. Not to mention that the things she wants from me are things I'm all too happy to give.

I curl my fingers inside her and glance up, watching the ruby red flush climb her neck. "Come for me, Grace. I want it. I want it so *fucking* bad," I growl, and then I drop my lips back down, my tongue tracing figure eights over her swollen clit.

I feel her orgasm the second it hits, her inner muscles clamping down on my fingers, a scream tearing from her throat. She jerks forward, folding her body over me, her panting breath hot in my hair. I know she's not done, that she wants more—that she can *take* more—but I let myself revel in this moment, in the fact that I get to be the one to make her feel like this. I dig my fingers into the fleshy curve of her hip and focus my breathing, focus on *her*. Learning her body and what makes her scream? Nothing else has ever made me feel like this.

"Oh my fucking god, my ears are ringing," she whispers between heaving sighs.

I laugh, because I know what she means. An orgasm with Grace McBride lights up parts of my body I never knew existed. I love that wrung-out, turned-inside-out, outside-my-body feeling of being with her, and I love making her feel it, too.

I rise from the floor, taking my aching cock in my hand. "I

believe you made a very specific request," I tell her, lining up the head of my cock with her dripping pussy. And I'm just about to do exactly what she asked of me, exactly as hard as she begged me to, when there's a knock at my door.

"Nooooo," Grace whispers into my ear, her fingers digging into the taut muscles of my back.

"They'll go away," I pant, my control reduced to the thinnest thread as I long to slam into her. But I know how my Grace likes to scream, and I'm not about to give that show to whatever chuck-lefuck is standing outside my door at ten a.m. on a federal holi-day. "Just wait a minute."

"Deck, you in there?"

Grace's body stiffens, and I jerk away from her at the sound of Archer's voice booming through my door. I hope to Christ I locked it.

"Fuck," Grace whispers, and not in the fun way she said it just moments ago.

"Bathroom," I say, lifting her off the counter and planting her gently on the floor. She grabs her underwear and disappears into the bathroom, closing the door with a near-silent click.

I reach down for my towel, then decide to leave it and head for the door. I flip the lock (thank god, that was a close one) and open the door a crack, poking my head out.

"Hey, man, what's up?" I ask.

"Can I come in?" Archer asks.

"No. I'm naked," I reply.

"Why?"

"Because living alone means I can walk bare-assed out of my own shower," I reply. "Do you need something?"

Archer seems to take the explanation at face value. "Yeah. I'm throwing a little last-minute Fourth of July party this afternoon. I need you there."

I blink at him. "You pounded on my door at ten a.m. on the Fourth of July to tell me you decided—*today*—to throw a party *tonight*? Why didn't you just text?"

"I did. You didn't answer, and I couldn't risk you sleeping through the whole thing." He's shifting from foot to foot, dragging his hand through his dark hair like he's nervous.

"Archer, what the fuck?"

He huffs out a sigh. "I've got this new neighbor. Single mom, little kid. They don't know anyone, the kid wants to see fireworks, and the mom seems, I dunno, sort of sad? I just figured…" He trails off.

"Uh-huh," I say, my brows knitting together as I read his raised shoulders, the slight flush in his cheeks.

"Dude, don't be fuckin' weird. I'm just trying to be neighborly," he snaps. Then he glances over his shoulder at Grace's door. "Speaking of, have you seen my sister?"

"Your sister? What? No," I say, and then I cough to keep any other suspicious-sounding denials from coming out of my mouth. I'm suddenly flashing back to the time campus police asked me if I was smoking weed when I smelled like I'd hotboxed a Taco Bell.

"I knocked on her door, but she didn't answer," Archer says.

"She must be out doing stuff for the festival," I reply. At least now I'm doing better than my weed stop, when I walked away with a ticket because I'm a shitty liar when I'm stoned.

"On a holiday?" Archer asks.

I shrug. "She's working hard on it, man."

Archer's brow furrows, his lip curling. "I feel like she's seeing someone," he says, and my heart damn near stops. "Carson and Wyatt have her on those apps, and if she's meeting random guys from the internet, I want to know about it. That shit is sketchy as fuck."

I let out a breath and try to bring my heart rate back down out of the red zone. "I'm sure she's fine," I say.

Archer nods, like he doesn't believe me but is willing to end the conversation. "Well, if you see her, tell her she's coming to my thing, too."

I let myself imagine Grace's reaction if I demanded her presence anywhere, and the thought goes straight to my cock, still half hard despite this conversation. I fucking love it when Grace shoots her mouth off at me.

"*I* haven't even agreed to come to this thing," I remind Archer.

"What else do you have to do?" he asks.

*Your sister, all day and all night.*

"Right," I reply, clearing my throat and hopefully that thought from my brain. I can come back to it when Archer's gone. "What time?"

"Five? I'll grill, and I picked up a bunch of fireworks to shoot off when it gets dark," he says. Satisfied that he's completed his mission, he turns, then pauses to call over his shoulder, "Oh, and bring something. Food or whatever."

"Okay."

"Don't be late. And wear clothes," he says.

"Thanks for the reminder, asshole," I laugh. And then Archer takes the stairs two at a time.

I shut the door and then flip the lock *and* the deadbolt. I look out the peephole to make sure Archer isn't coming back with another request or reminder, and when I don't see anything, I call out, "He's gone."

Grace emerges from the bathroom, looking like she's been holding her breath the whole time. "Fucking hell, that was close," she says, hands to her chest.

"It wasn't, actually," I remind her. "The door was locked."

"Yeah, but you know my stubborn-ass brother—he could have just barged in," she says as I wander over to a laundry basket by the bed and pull out a clean pair of underwear. Then I go back over to her and pull her to me, palming the back of her head, the other hand resting on her ass.

"We're good, Grace," I say. "And there's a Fourth of July party at your brother's, apparently." I fill her in on Archer's plan and his mysterious new next-door neighbor.

"So, we're going to this," she says. She moves to the stove and restarts the burner, putting the sausage back on the heat. There's a pair of homemade English muffins sitting on a cutting board beside the hot pan, each one split open and topped with a thick slice of cheese. The sausage patties, which Grace made by hand, are a test for next month's cookbook club. I could get used to this life, except for the fact that by the time September cookbook club rolls around, I'll be gone.

"Sounds like it," I reply.

"No, I mean together," she clarifies. "Are we going to this thing *together*?"

God, I wish. I'd love to live in the universe where Grace and I get to attend family parties together. Where I could spend the whole night by her side, soaking in the throaty sound of her laugh, resting a hand on her hip, sneaking as many appropriate kisses as I could. But Grace was clear. She doesn't want Archer to know, and I'm not going to push her on that.

I shrug. "I mean, as far as Arch knows, we're friends now. We live across the hall from each other. I don't see any reason not to show up at the same time."

"Okay. But we have to bring two separate things. Showing up with just one side dish is very coupley," she says, flipping the sausage patties expertly.

"Okay, then I'll bring beer," I say.

She arches an eyebrow. "Seriously? That's not a side."

"He said 'food or whatever.' Beer definitely falls into the 'whatever' category." I grin. "Unless you want to cook a side for me?"

Grace rolls her eyes. "You mean, do I want to do your homework?"

"I'll carry your books," I say, waggling my eyebrows at her. "And also the orgasms."

She swats me in the arm with the greasy spatula. "I think you'll give me orgasms whether I make potato salad for you or not."

"Correct," I say, then lean down and pull her to me for a kiss. "But I'm pretty sure I can just bring beer. It'll give us more time for the orgasms."

Just to prove it to her, I retrieve my phone from the bedside table. Sure enough, I've got a handful of texts from Archer about this mysterious Fourth of July party. I text him back while she assembles the breakfast sandwiches. By the time she's done plating, I've got my proof.

DECKER

Should I bring beer?

ARCHER

Obviously.

I flash my phone screen at her. "See?"

She laughs. "Fine. Then I'll make hash brown casserole."

My stomach growls. "Can I help?"

"You mean, can you be my taste tester and pull crunchy brown bits off the top as soon as it comes out of the oven?" She grins, the freckles on her nose dancing. "That's a privilege you have to earn."

So I reach for our breakfast plates and push them aside to make room on the counter for her tight little ass.

"Challenge accepted," I say, and get to work.

# CHAPTER 33

## GRACE

"Are you sure this thing can make it all the way to Archer's?" I ask as we roar down Main Street in Decker's Bronco.

"Nickel swore to me he fixed it," Decker says with a grin, "and the man had an incredibly trustworthy face tattoo."

The engine rumbles as we bounce over the entrance to the gas station, where Decker pulls up to a pump. "I'll fill her up, then run in for the beer," he says, climbing out.

"How about I pump the gas and you get the beer?" I ask.

Decker shakes his head. "Nope. Ladies don't pump gas when I'm around."

"Is that what I am? A lady?" I scoff.

"Not so much this morning—just ask the bite mark on my shoulder," Decker says with a wicked grin. My eyes go to the spot, but of course it isn't visible beneath the button-up shirt he's wearing, the sleeves rolled up on his corded forearms. I gulp, because with his hair loose in the breeze, his hockey ass squeezed into a pair of navy shorts, he's practically one of my dirtiest fantasies come to life.

"Let the record show that my feminism is going to let this one slide," I say. I sink down into the buttery leather seat and scroll on my phone. The hash brown casserole is covered in foil and safely tucked between my feet, even if it is missing a few too many crunchy brown bits. But I forgive Decker for pillaging my side dish, because he pillaged a few other things while it was in the oven. I have never been so spoiled in my life.

I'm working on the Wordle when a shiny silver Mercedes pulls up to the pump next to us. A tall man in a starched white Oxford tucked into khaki pants climbs out. The gold of his belt buckle catches the sunlight, drawing Decker's attention away from the pump.

"Oh, hey, Dad," he says.

I nearly drop my phone. I glance first at Decker's father, then at his mother in the passenger seat. The last time I saw his parents was his and Archer's high school graduation. They look almost the same now—just as put together, though a little grayer. They look like they bring a dinner party with them wherever they go, and I always feel underdressed for the occasion.

His dad blinks, like he's surprised to see his son in the small town where they both live.

"Oh, hello, Decker," he says. His gray hair, once blond like his son's, is cut short and perfectly gelled like he just stepped off the set of *Mad Men*. His shiny leather loafers match his belt, and I wouldn't be surprised if the combined cost of them exceeded what I've spent on my entire wardrobe. It's weird seeing the two men standing so close to each other. They're both tall with broad shoulders and sharp jawlines, but Decker looks like a punk rock cover of his father's classical piano piece.

After a beat of silence, his dad seems to realize that he should speak a little bit more, so he smiles and says, "Happy Fourth of July. Your mother and I are headed to the club for the fireworks."

"The club" is Idle Hour, a country club on the edge of town with a golf course, a full tennis center, and its own small lake. They shoot off an impressive display from a barge in the middle, and growing up, we used to park on the side of Highway 31 with the other yokels and try to see it over the trees.

"Right, right," Decker says, rocking back on his heels, a muscle in his jaw flexing in a way that tells me he's uncomfortable. And I don't blame him. This interaction feels less father-and-son and more like when a congressman gets confronted in an airport for his shitty voting record. So I jump in and try to rescue Decker.

"Hi, Mr. Brooks," I say, leaning through the window of the Bronco. He's clearly struggling to place me, so I say, "Grace McBride," pointing at myself like he might think I'm introducing someone else.

"Oh, right," he says, breaking into a very political-looking smile. I remember that Decker's dad is some bigwig at Indiana University, but I can't remember exactly what he does. Something that requires him to shake a lot of hands, I'm guessing. "How are you?"

"I'm good," I reply.

He nods and turns to the pump, tapping buttons. But as soon as the gas begins to flow, we're back to our awkward interaction. "So, where are you two off to?" Mr. Brooks asks.

"Archer is having a get-together. For the Fourth. I'm giving her a ride," Decker says, nodding in my direction. And I kind of hate that he's talking about me like I'm just some tagalong. It takes me back to being a kid, back to when I couldn't stand Decker. Back to a time long before I knew all the ways he could make me scream his name. But he's definitely not thinking about that right now. Right now I'm just someone who needs to be hidden. From Archer, and now from his parents.

*Which is what you want, you idiot.*

The passenger door to the Mercedes opens, and Decker's mom climbs out. She's wearing a shirtdress, the same starchy white as her husband's Oxford, and a red-and-blue silk scarf. She smiles, slightly less distant than her husband.

"Grace, hello. How's your brother? Still working for Merrill Lynch?" Dan worked as a research assistant for Dr. Brooks for two summers during undergrad. She wrote him a recommendation for his MBA applications.

"Uh, no, he's actually working for a private equity firm," I tell her, though it occurs to me that Dan hasn't said word one about his job since he showed up in Cardinal Springs. He's been staying at Archer's, so maybe I'll get the story tonight at the party. But knowing Dan, probably not. "I can't remember the name. Fisher something?"

"Oh, Fisher Donovan! That's an incredible firm. They do good work," she says.

I have no idea what work they do, much less how good it is. They could be corporate raiders or robber barons, for all I know. Dan has never explained it, and I'm not sure I'd understand it if he did. But I guess Dr. Brooks would know, so I just smile and nod. "He's actually in town visiting."

"Oh, tell him to come by and see me. I keep my same office hours," she says.

Out of the corner of my eye, I see Decker tense.

"And how's the rest of your family? Your other brother is a doctor, right?"

"Yes, Owen's a pediatrician here in town," I say, and then, even though she didn't ask, I rattle off the rest of the McBride Christmas letter. "Felix is a contractor and started his own business last fall, and Archer is teaching AP history at CSHS. And I'm still at the library."

"Well, that's lovely," she says, though I can tell she has stopped listening. "Your father must be so proud."

Decker looks like he wants to start walking away down the road.

"I think he just wants us all to be happy," I tell Dr. Brooks.

Her smile grows tighter, and the gas pumps clicks to signal that the Mercedes is full.

"Well, it was good running into you, son. You'll have to stop by for breakfast one of these days," Mr. Brooks says.

"Yes, dear, you've been a stranger this summer," his mother adds.

"Just busy," he replies tersely. His mother's tight smile is reflected on his face.

After a few more businesslike goodbyes, Decker's parents slide back into their Mercedes and speed off toward the club.

Decker finishes up at the gas pump, then mutters something about grabbing the beer before disappearing into the store. But as soon as he returns with a case of Upland IPA, I say, "Uh, why did it seem like that was the first time you'd seen them in years? You all live in the same town. And not a big one, either."

"We're not that close," is his only explanation. He shoves the key into the ignition with a little too much force.

"You don't talk to your parents?"

"Not really," he replies.

"Seriously? Not even when you're here?"

He shrugs. "I had breakfast with them right after I got arrested."

I gape at him. "That was more than a month ago. How can you not see your parents for a *month* when you're in the same tiny town?"

He huffs out a bitter-sounding laugh. "Not everyone's family is as close as yours."

"But you're their only son," I protest.

The engine roars to life, and Decker shifts, the Bronco jerking out of the parking lot. "I don't think they really get me," he says. His eyes are on the road, his wrist resting casually on top of the steering wheel, but I can tell he's tense. He's not comfortable with the reality or this conversation about it. "I mean, I'm their son, and they love me. I know that. But they don't really know how to be around me."

"How is that possible?"

Decker throws his hands up, then drops them to grip the steering wheel again, his knuckles white. "My parents are college professors. They imagined raising a kid who would follow in their footsteps, go to Princeton or Yale, get a PhD, and sit around the table discussing scholarly articles or doing the *New York Times* crossword puzzle. Having a son who's a college dropout and plays sports for a living is literally their worst nightmare."

"But you're super famous! You're the best, most-feared center in the league, you've won the Stanley Cup *twice*, and you were named the playoff MVP. You were Rookie of the Year, and you've been an All-Star five years running. There's already talk of the Hall of Fame. How can they be ashamed of that?"

Now he smiles, finally glancing at me, an eyebrow raised. With his hair whipping across his forehead in the wind, he looks incredibly rakish. "You know my stats?"

I shrug, but I know the heat in my cheeks gives me away. "I googled you. I had to make sure you weren't a serial killer before I left you with the children." We pull up to the red light at the end of Main Street, just a block from Archer's, and I tug his chin until he's looking directly at me. "Decker Brooks, in case nobody's ever told you, you're incredible. You work hard, you're a valuable player, and most importantly, despite what the tabloids may say, you're a good man. You should be proud. I know I am."

Decker's eyes widen, something flickering across his face. His hand snakes over to my thigh, under the hem of my sundress, and squeezes. "Just so you know, the only reason I'm not kissing you senseless right now is because this is Mrs. Eberle territory. It feels like she might jump out from behind that trash can any second. But fuck, that's the nicest thing anyone's ever said to me."

I bite my lip, nearly sinking my teeth into the skin, I'm trying so hard not to lunge at him.

"I guess you should be happy. I mean, you could have a family like mine, overbearing as hell and all up in your business, constantly telling you what to do," I say.

The light changes, and Decker stomps on the gas. "Come on, Grace. You know which one is worse," he says, and my cheeks immediately blaze with shame. "Your family loves you, and the only reason they're overbearing is because you refuse to tell them when to step off. You never stand up for yourself."

"Hey," I say, but it's a weak defense. He's right.

But knowing the truth and doing something about it are two very different things.

Decker pulls the Bronco up to the curb in front of Archer's house and shuts off the engine. "I'm sorry if that was harsh, but I also want you to know how much I wished I could be a McBride growing up. Watching you all pile into the stands to cheer for Archer…I wanted that so much. They'd all be there cheering for you, too, if you'd let them."

"I hate when you get all wise on me," I grumble. If I sit in this moment too long, I might start to cry. I might realize how desperately I need to follow his advice. And I can't walk into a family party with tears in my eyes and Decker Brooks beside me.

I reach down for the casserole dish, gathering it into my arms. "Okay, time to put our game faces on. In there, we cannot talk about bite marks or kissing anyone senseless."

"Harder than a face-off against a seven-foot Russian," he replies. But then his phone rings, and the display on his dash lights up. Whoever restored this vintage car—definitely not Decker—added a state-of-the-art Bluetooth stereo. The screen reads BRIELLE ANDREWS, and my stomach drops. My mind is suddenly filled with a gallery of paparazzi photos of Decker and various beautiful women.

"Uh, I'll, um, leave you to—" I stammer, scrambling to get out of the Bronco, but Decker's hand closes around my wrist.

"She runs PR for the Grinders," he says. He taps the button to answer. "Hey, Brielle. What's up?"

The voice that comes out of the speakers has a heavy Chicago accent. She sounds young, in her twenties, and like she is very much not to be fucked with. "I haven't heard anything from you, so I figured you were either following orders or dead," she says.

Decker laughs. "Believe it or not, follow orders. Laying low, just like you told me to."

"So it's true what they say—puppies are trainable," she says, but I can hear the smile in her voice. I like her already.

"I've been a very good boy," Decker replies, shooting me a devious grin.

"I'll be sure to have some Snausages on my desk when you get back. Speaking of, September fifteenth for media day," she says.

"Right," he replies, a short, hard reminder that he's due back in Chicago eventually. A reminder to me that my new favorite recipe taste tester and orgasm dispenser isn't staying forever. In fact, he's staying just eight more weeks.

Which is fine. Surely this thing will have run its course by then. It hasn't even been two weeks since Decker first rocked my world in that motel room. This is new and fun, but it's not permanent, and I'd do well to remember that.

"I know this is probably too much to hope for," Brielle says, "but have you been up to anything worth mentioning in the media lately? Anything to burnish your reputation?"

Decker shakes his head even though she can't see him. "Nah, not really," he replies.

Brielle sighs. "Okay. Keep doing what you're doing, and I'll work up some good charity moments for you during preseason. I'll make you into a reformed bad boy if it kills me."

*He already is one*, I want to shout into the phone. *I don't think he was ever actually a bad boy!* But I stay silent. Beside me, Decker shifts in his seat.

"Don't put yourself out," he says, keeping the smile in his voice even though it's fallen off his face. "The press is going to write what they're going to write."

There's a pause, and then Brielle says, "It's my job, Brooks."

Decker sighs. "Yep. You know I'm always up for charity." He pauses. "Something with kids, maybe? I'm good with kids."

"We can do that. Children's Hospital always loves visitors. And we're starting a relationship with an after-school program on the South Side. We can definitely use you there," she says. I'm deeply grateful that she's so open to his suggestion, that she seems to see what I see. Decker needs more people in his life who don't shove him into boxes. He's been playing the bad boy role for so long that I think sometimes even *he* forgets that he's more than that.

"I gotta go," says Brielle. "I've got half a page of calls to make."

"Thanks for checking in," Decker says.

"Later, Brooks." And then the line goes dead.

"You should have told her about big kid story time," I tell him.

Decker shakes his head. "Nah. It's not a big deal. And besides, then I'd have to admit that I punched your ex-boyfriend and am doing community service." He pulls the key from the ignition and shoves it into his pocket. "Best to keep it all quiet."

"And you were just lecturing me about telling people the truth?" I tease him.

"It's just story time, Grace. If I tell them, they'll want to send a crew down here, film content, interview me, interview you. I don't want any of that," he says.

He climbs out of the car, and it takes me a second to move, because I'm too busy trying to shake off the sting. I know that keeping what's going on between us from Archer was my choice, but then it was Decker's parents, and now he wants to make sure *no one* finds out about me. I don't know why I'm surprised or why it makes my chest ache.

I follow him out of the car, the casserole warm in my arms, and remind myself that this is good. This is what I want—sex with no strings attached. It means no one gets hurt.

No one's *supposed* to get hurt, anyway.

# CHAPTER 34

## DECKER

Grace follows me up the stone path that leads to Archer's porch. I want to fall back next to her, but we're supposed to be pretending we're just friends. And besides, I need a minute. I'm still rattled from the phone call with Brielle. Because suddenly it's like someone has started a game clock on whatever this thing is with Grace. I've got just two months left with her before I have to go back to my real life. Talking to Brielle definitely reminded me of that. And the idea that the press could get wind of this, of her? It sort of terrifies me. It just serves to remind me that Grace doesn't belong in my world, because my world isn't just mine. If she showed up in Chicago with me, a spotlight would immediately be pointed at her. She'd have to deal with hockey commentators who pin every weakness in my game on the women I'm seen with, gossip sites that trade in worthless nonsense based on grainy photos and social media posts. To say nothing of the fans and haters alike who'd flood her social media.

*Fuck.* Just thinking about the harassment she could face simply for being associated with me makes me want to put my fist through Archer's front door.

"Are you okay?" Grace asks when she steps onto the porch beside me.

I steady myself with a cleansing breath. "Yeah," I say, then raise my fist for what I hope is going to be a gentle knock, but Grace grabs my arm.

"McBrides don't knock," she laughs, then shoulders through the front door.

Inside, the bright living room is empty. I trail after Grace through the small dining room at the center of the house and into the kitchen at the back. She deposits her casserole dish on the kitchen table alongside two open bags of chips and a store-bought salad, and I throw the beer in the fridge. There are voices coming from the back deck. Everyone else must be outside.

Then Archer bursts through the back door, practically body-checking me away from the fridge door.

"Thank god you're here," he says, reaching for a plate of premade hamburger patties. His voice is tight, his shoulders drawn up around his ears. "So far it's just Dan, and he has the conversational skills of the Sphinx. Owen's supposed to be here, but a kid stuck a marble up his nose, so he rushed off to his office, and Dad and Felix are both running late."

"This is just a cookout, right?" I ask, glancing over at Grace while Archer attacks the burgers with little jars of spices. "You sure it's not a covert op?"

"What?" Archer snaps, not looking up from the meat.

"You're a little high-strung, Arch," Grace says, shooting me a grimace. I know Archer's going through some shit, what with Cassie's announcement, but this seems a little over the top.

"This was a mistake," Archer grumbles. He slams a jar of garlic powder down on the counter. "I should have invited other kids. Hey, Grace, can you call some of the library kids?"

Grace and I share a look of two people wondering how they're going to defuse a bomb.

"No," she says gently. "I'm not going to call children and invite them to your house."

Archer sighs. "The kid looks bored, and I think Dan is freaking out her mom," he says, and that's when I remember the new neighbor, the single mom and her daughter.

"We can go out there and make conversation," I reassure him. "Grace is good with kids, and I'm charming as shit."

Archer rolls his eyes, but he seems to unclench a little bit. I move toward the door, and Grace follows me.

"What the hell is going on?" she whispers as we step out onto the deck.

"I think your brother has a little bit of a crush," I reply.

"Shut *up*," Grace says, but she can't say more, because the party, such as it is, is before us. Dan is sitting at the patio table, peeling the label off his beer bottle, his eyes hidden behind a pair of Ray Ban aviators that make him look like a Secret Service agent. Across from him is a woman with brown hair pulled through the back of a University of Alabama baseball cap. Beside her is a little girl around the age of the big kid story time kids. She has the same dark hair as her mother, but hers is short and jagged, and I wonder if maybe the haircut was self-inflicted.

Grace immediately slips into librarian mode, a wide smile spreading across her face that puts everyone at ease. It works on me, at least. Between that smile and Archer's freak-out, I've mostly shaken off the phone call with Brielle.

"Hi," Grace says, pulling out the chair next to Dan. "I'm Grace, Archer and this guy's little sister." She nods at Dan, who gives what I think is supposed to be a smile but leans more toward a grimace.

"How old are you?" the little girl asks.

"Betsy," her mom chides. "That's rude."

"Sorry," Betsy says.

"It's okay. I'm twenty-four," Grace says, a gut-punch of a reminder that not only am I fooling around with my best friend's sister, she's his *much younger* sister. "And how old are you?"

"I turned eight in May," the little girl replies.

"I'm Madeline," her mother says, offering a hand to Grace. "And I'm twenty-five."

Jesus Christ, I feel ancient.

I must make a face, because Grace lifts her eyebrows in my direction. I try to school my expression so I don't come off as rude.

"I'm going to go grab a beer," I say. "Anyone want anything?"

"I'll take a beer," Grace says, and Madeline asks for a bottle of water. Betsy requests a Coke, but after a stern look from her mother, she asks for water, too.

I grab the drinks from the kitchen, moving around Archer, who is standing over the sink, struggling to open a package of hot dogs. "Do you have a thing for this woman?" I ask.

"I barely know her," he grunts.

"But you have eyes," I reply. Madeline is unquestionably beautiful, with green eyes, pale skin, and a willowy figure.

"She has a kid," Archer says, as if that's an answer.

"Who seems perfectly nice and not possessed by a single demon spirit."

Archer sighs. "I don't know. Yes? She's sweet and smart, and she talks fast, and a lot, and I want to hear what she has to say? But I don't know how to do this. I've been on one date since Cassie left, and it was a disaster. I spilled red wine in Molly's lap and spent half the meal giving her a play-by-play of the Indiana State High School Hockey Association playoffs. She faked an emergency text and left before dessert."

I grimace. "Maybe it was a real emergency?"

Decker eyes me. "She said her friend's cat was stuck in a tree," he says, and I can't control my face. Poor guy. "Anyway, Madeline is gorgeous, but she's also a single mom and new in town, and I get the sense that things have been a little rough for her. I'm just trying not to be weird."

He gives the edge of the hot dog package a hard yank, and it bursts open, raining hot dogs onto the black-and-white tile of his kitchen floor.

"And succeeding beautifully," I say as we watch a hot dog roll under the fridge.

"Fuck," he moans.

"Hey, man, chill. We'll rinse them off, and then you'll cook them real good. They'll be fine," I say, squatting down to pick them up. "As for your new neighbor, just be yourself. Be her friend. If something grows from there, great. If not, you've got a friend and she does, too."

Archer looks at me askance. "Jesus, when did you become Yoda?" He shakes his head, digging the hot dog out from beneath the fridge. "That all sounds good, even if taking relationship advice from Decker Brooks is something one would usually only do after losing a drunken bet."

"Thanks," I say, trying to keep my voice light even though the quip stings like a bitch.

"I'm just kidding," Archer says. "Though you've got to admit, you're good at a lot of things, but relationships aren't on the list."

"Fair," I reply. He's right. I've never had even one real relationship, unless you count going on three or four consecutive dates with the same woman or flying off to Mexico for a weekend of sex and cocktails on the beach. Which is why the thought of trying to make things between Grace and me work long term is completely ridiculous. I don't have any experience with relationships, and I'm seriously going to practice with Grace McBride? She deserves more than that.

"What are you boys doing with those hot dogs?"

I glance up and see Mr. McBride walk in. Next to him is that yoga teacher I saw him sucking face with in an alley. Now her hand is in his. I clock it at the some moment Archer does, and he tenses anew.

"Hey, Mr. McB," I say. I hold up one of the hot dogs. "Just seasoning them."

"I'll stick with the burgers," he says with a chuckle. "Decker, this is Corianne Hathaway. Corianne, this is Decker Brooks."

"So nice to meet you," she says with a warm smile. "I'm a big

Grinders fan. I'm from Naperville, and growing up, my dad drove us in for a game every year for my birthday. That was long before your time, though."

"Back in the Browning era?" I ask, glancing over at Archer. It's clear he's still wound too tight, so I try to do him a solid and be his social buffer. "Those were good times. He's a legend."

Despite my efforts, Archer seems determined to be in a bad mood. "Corianne is Dad's physical therapist," he says.

Mr. McBride coughs. "Not for a couple of years now," he says, his cheeks reddening.

But Archer doesn't read the cues. "Then what exactly have you two been doing together twice a week all this time?"

Mr. McBride's face clouds, and Archer's expression flickers. He looks just like he did when he was a little kid, about to be chastised by his father.

"Well, she was my personal trainer for a while, but now we just work out together for fun," he says, squeezing her hand. "Corianne and I are dating."

Archer lets out a bitter-sounding laugh. "Glad you've finally stopped sneaking around. You're not very good at it," he says, tossing the refrigerator dog into the trash. Then he takes the plate of meat and shoulders through the back door. "If you'll excuse me, I need to go check on my guests."

"Sorry," I say when he's gone, rubbing the back of my neck. "He's going through some stuff. And we saw you two a couple of weeks ago in the alley, so…" Mr. McBride's face goes crimson as he fills in the blank with the memory. "Anyway, congrats. And if you want to come up to a game this season, let me know. I can get you guys good seats behind the glass."

Corianne smiles, and Mr. McBride slaps my back. "Thanks, Decker. I should probably go talk to him."

"I think just give him a little time," I say. "He'll come around."

"Yeah, okay. You're a good friend."

Am I, though? Because despite running interference for him

and giving him what I'm pretty sure was excellent advice about Madeline, I'm still keeping a big secret from my best friend. And if that interaction with his dad's new girlfriend is any indication, this secret could end our friendship.

# CHAPTER 35

## GRACE

When Decker returns with our drinks, I've got my phone out and am deep in the *New York Times* Spelling Bee game with Betsy. I can already tell she's smart, a good speller with a vocabulary larger than the average second grader. When she starts at Cardinal Springs Elementary this fall, I'm pretty sure she's going to wind up in the gifted program.

As we work our way from Great to Amazing in Spelling Bee, Felix shows up with more beer and a story about an inquiry he got about building a "giant monstrosity" out by the lake. Owen returns from his office, having successfully extracted the marble from his patient's nose. Carson and Wyatt show up together, Wyatt with a bottle of tequila she probably took from the bar and Carson with one of those cakes with berries laid out in the shape of the American flag. Betsy remains the only kid in attendance, but she doesn't seem to mind. Like a lot of only children, she seems perfectly comfortable talking to grown-ups.

Throughout the evening, I keep an eye on Decker, watching him help Archer grill burgers and hot dogs. When we sit down to eat, he takes a spot at the far end of the table next to Corianne, who arrived with Dad in what appears to be the hard launch of their relationship. Archer is taking this development with all the grace of a man who's being asked to chew glass, but he manages to mostly keep his attention on Madeline. She seems nice, and she's good at carrying on lively conversations. She's one of those people who has never met a stranger, and it makes her a good party guest in a crowd of McBrides.

Across the table, Wyatt is making Owen inspect her new tattoo, which she claims is "more red than any other one she's gotten." The tattoo is just above her left breast, so she's pulling her tank top way down to show it off, and Owen is trying to look professional while also blushing red as a cherry popsicle. And next to me, Carson and Betsy are engaged in a debate over which of the original American Girl books is the best. (Neither of them is sticking up for Molly, who is the obvious pick.)

"Oh, hey," Wyatt says, looking down at her glowing phone. Owen has apparently assured her that her tattoo isn't infected, or at least he's managed to gracefully extract himself from the conversation, because he's taking a very long pull from his beer bottle. "My sister is coming to visit. Tonight. I told her to come over here when she gets into town."

"Seriously?" I say. "Hasn't it been forever?"

Wyatt's half sister, Hazel, is away at college. Wyatt's been her surrogate mom ever since their birth mother was arrested and sent to prison for check fraud. That's why Wyatt moved back to Cardinal Springs when Hazel was fourteen. It was either that or Hazel would go into foster care.

"She hasn't been back since last summer. She stayed on campus for the holidays, and over spring break she was working on some big paper," Wyatt says, her brow furrowed.

"Where's she studying?" Madeline asks.

"She's at Cornell. She's double majoring in biology and landscape architecture," Wyatt says, her smile proud. "She's amazing with plants. The only reason my front yard doesn't look like an abandoned lot on Mars is because Hazel planted everything and sends me detailed care instructions."

"Her yard looks like *Eden*," I gush.

"Is your house the one over on Mulberry with the gargantuan hydrangeas out front?" Madeline asks.

"That's me," Wyatt crows.

"I've admired it on my runs," Madeline says.

"You're a runner?" I ask.

"Yeah. I'm training for the Indy Marathon in October," she says.

"Wow, that's amazing. Your first?" I ask.

"Third. I ran Indy two years ago and Nashville the year before that. I took some time off after some injuries, but I'm getting back into training. This town is great for it—lots of flat road. We moved from Brown County, where it's all hills."

"I'm training for my first half, and I'm pretty slow, but if you ever want a running buddy, let me know," I tell her. "There are a bunch of great trails just outside of town."

"I thought we decided you weren't doing that," Dad says, apparently yanked out of his new relationship bubble by the news that I've been running. And I don't know where it comes from, but righteous indignation bubbles up in my chest. For the first time, I open my mouth and let it spill out.

"I'm not sure why you think my training is a family decision, considering I'm twenty-four years old," I say.

Dad sighs, a long-suffering sound that makes me grit my teeth. "Grace, you need to be realistic. It's not good for you to be stressing your heart like that."

"It is, actually," I say, squaring my shoulders. All around us, other conversations trail off as my voice grows louder. "And you know how I know? Because I've been running for years—trail running outside of town so no one would see me. Dr. Pincushion says my heart has never been stronger. He encouraged me to try the half." I sit up straight, feeling energy race up and down my spine as my dad gapes at me.

"You're running in the woods by yourself?" Felix asks, his brow furrowed.

"Yes. I use Strava, and Carson is my emergency person," I say. I let my eyes pass over Decker, and he tilts his chin in a subtle encouraging nod. "And in the winter, I'm a member of the Central Indiana Speed Skating Club."

"Seriously?" Archer says.

"Last year I finished third in my age group at an open meet in Indy."

"Wow," Owen says.

"Yeah," I say. I nod, having made my case.

I glance around the table and catch Decker biting his lip to suppress a smile. Nobody says anything for a beat. Then Felix leans back in his chair. "Well, let us know when the next meet is. We'll make signs."

"When's the half?" Archer asks, pulling out his phone. "I'll add it to the calendar."

"We can do signs for that, too," Owen says. "Really embarrassing ones."

Beside him, Dan suppresses a grin.

I don't let myself look at Decker because I know he's gloating. I can't believe it took me so long to tell them all the truth.

I smile and turn back to my dad, the only person at the table who still looks frustrated. "I know you worry. I get that. But maybe in between the worrying, you could support me a little, too?"

The table is quiet, gazes darting back and forth between Dad and me. Finally, he sighs. "You're never going to get me to stop worrying about you, Gracie Girl," he says, his voice hitching, but he clears his throat and charges on. "But the support I can manage. If you say you're being safe, I trust you."

I let out a breath, one I've perhaps been holding for a very long time.

"Thanks, Dad," I say.

"But please do team up with Madeline or take one of your brothers. I don't like this running alone in the woods thing," he adds.

"That's fair," I reply.

"Let's trade numbers," Madeline says, passing me her phone.

"Okay, it's almost time to set up," Archer says, rising from the table. "Who wants to help me open the fireworks?"

Felix and Dan rise from their seats at the exact moment that Betsy throws her hand in the air.

"I don't think that's a good idea, honey," Madeline says, looking up at Archer.

"She could help unpack boxes, if you're cool with that," he says, standing up straight like a Boy Scout. "I'll send her back up here when it's time to light the fuses."

"Okay," Madeline says, then levels her daughter with a mom look. "No fire," she says.

Betsy scampers off after the guys, and I expect Decker to follow them, but instead he pauses beside my chair. He bends down like he's clearing my plate, but he whispers in my ear, "Wait a few minutes, then meet me in the laundry room." Then he whisks my plate away and disappears into the kitchen.

My gaze darts around the table, but everyone is involved in conversations except for Madeline. Since I apparently need to kill a few minutes, I turn to her.

"So, what brought you to Cardinal Springs?" I ask, pressing my hands into my lap to keep them from shaking. Something about the scrape of Decker's voice in my ear, his instructions to meet him in secret, have my entire body electrified.

"I got offered a job teaching at a dance school on Main Street," she says.

"Miss Vanderbilt's School of Dance?" I ask. "I took tap there when I was five!"

"That's the one. I teach ballet and modern," she says. "I got an offer from a studio in Indianapolis, too, but when I looked at rentals up there, it was crazy. Our house costs the same as a one-bedroom in Indy, and here Betsy gets her own room *and* a yard. I couldn't pass it up. And Angie Vanderbilt is looking to retire in the next couple of years, so if things go well, maybe I can take over the school."

"That's so cool," I say. "Do you have any family nearby?"

"My parents are in Birmingham, but we don't see each other too often," she says, and I hear what's unsaid in that statement—that her relationship with her parents is strained and that Betsy's dad isn't in the picture.

"I'm sorry," I say.

"That's okay. It's Betsy and me against the world. We like it that way," she says with a tight smile.

"Well, if you need anything, Archer is a great person to know. You've made a whole table full of helpful friends tonight," I tell her. "Owen's a pediatrician, Felix is a contractor, my dad owns the hardware store, and Archer is the most protective galoot you'll ever meet. Between us, you've got basically every emergency covered."

"Thanks, I appreciate that," she says, her smile growing warm. Then she looks down at her watch. "It's been a few minutes. You should probably head to the laundry room."

I breathe in so fast that I hiccup. "What?" I sputter.

"Don't worry, I'm good with secrets," Madeline says with a wink. "But for the love of god, don't leave that man waiting."

The guys are down in the grass lining up a truly obscene amount of fireworks, Archer hovering over Betsy to make sure she doesn't somehow spontaneously make fire with her bare hands and blow her little fingers off. Dad and Corianne are deep in conversation, and when I catch Carson's eye, she nods toward the kitchen door. She may not have heard Decker's request, but she doesn't miss a thing. I roll my eyes, scoot my chair back, and quickly slip into the kitchen.

Archer's laundry room is at the front of his house, a little annex built off the porch and added sometime in the house's hundred year history. It's small but private and—most importantly—has a door that locks.

And as soon as I step inside, Decker closes the door behind

me, flips the lock, and presses me back against it, his lips covering mine. When he breaks away, his voice is a low, delicious gravelly scrape. "That was the sexiest fucking thing I've ever seen."

"What?" I ask, breathless.

"You standing up for yourself."

"Ohhhh," I say, my understanding melting into a puddle of desire as Decker reaches beneath my dress. "What are you doing?"

"I was hoping to fulfill your request from this morning. I was instructed to fuck you. *Hard.*" He punctuates the word with a light slap to my ass that sends heat and wetness pooling between my thighs.

I open my mouth to protest. Because, here? In my brother's laundry room? With my entire family outside? Then Decker drops his lips to my neck, his tongue tracing a hot line across my collarbone.

"They're about to start lighting explosives out there," he whispers into my skin. "We've got time."

"Hmmmm," I moan, thrusting against his hand.

"We can stop," he murmurs. "Or...we can do it like in the books."

*Oh god.* Something inside me snaps, or unravels, my grasp on logical thought fraying, and I shimmy out of my panties.

"Fucking fireworks—of course," Decker chuckles as he helps me step out of the black undies with neon bursts of light all over them. I hear the clink of his belt, the drag of his zipper, and drop my gaze just in time to see him take his cock, thick and straining, into his hand. "Tell me what you want, Grace. Say it again."

"Fuck me, Decker," I say in my quietest voice but with all the conviction I can muster. *"Hard."*

Decker grips my ass and lifts me, walks me over to the dryer, and sets me down. I hiss at the feeling of cold metal on the backs of my thighs, but it's quickly forgotten—with one swift thrust, he's deep inside me.

I grit my teeth against the scream the climbs up my throat.

The first firework explodes outside the tiny round window high on the wall of the laundry room. Fractals of yellow-and-blue light glitter and frizzle across the wall as Decker pulls back and drives into me again and again, his pace picking up, meeting my request for *hard*. One of his arms flies up to the cupboard mounted on the wall behind me, pressing into it just beside my temple. His muscles flex, sweat pricking at his sideburns as he surges into me, an exquisite drag that stokes a fire deep within me. I watch his jaw flex as he keeps his focus on me, his eyes on mine. And he never takes them off me as he lifts his thumb and dips it between my lips. When I suck hard on it, he bites back a growl.

"Fuck, Grace, you're going to undo me," he grits out. I love watching him struggle with the frayed end of his control. But I lose my focus when he drops his hand between us, his thumb circling just above where we're joined. I lose track of whether the crackling light on the wall is a firework or my own ecstasy. My orgasm coils low in my belly, roiling with each thrust, on the verge of bursting out of me.

"Oh god, I'm going to come," I whine, and it takes everything I have to keep my voice low. When he pinches my clit between two long, strong fingers, I bite down on his shoulder to keep from screaming out his name.

"Give it to me, Grace," Decker growls, thrusting so hard I can't believe the dryer beneath my ass isn't banging into the wall. "I want it. It's *mine*."

"Yes," I hiss as my orgasm sizzles up my spine. I feel the moan before I hear it, or maybe Decker puts his mouth on mine and swallows it before it can explode out of me. Soon our sounds of pleasure are tangled up in our tongues, each of us helping the other to tip over the edge and fall, fall, *fall* without drawing the attention of the crowd outside. My fingers dig into his back, his hair, tugging him flush against me, feeling his chest rise and fall with his heaving breaths.

"Good girl," he whispers, his breath hot on my neck. He kisses me, then pulls back, our foreheads pressed together as we work to catch our breaths.

"What the fuck was that?" I mutter.

"What you deserve," he says.

And suddenly I'm breathless again.

Decker slides out of me and reaches into the cabinet over my head, pulling down a roll of paper towels. He takes one and folds it, then bends to clean me up before reaching down for my panties, abandoned on the floor. He holds them out so I can step in, and it's not until I'm put back together that he attends to himself.

My ears are still ringing, my body buzzing from the orgasm, but there's something else. Something in my chest, just behind my breastbone. I'm blown open, like some part of me is ready to pour out, or fill up. I can't quite tell what it is yet, but I know some part of me never wants to be anywhere but in this laundry room with Decker.

"You go first," he says, nodding at the door. He fastens his belt, then reaches out to flip the lock. Outside the window, the crackles and pops of the fireworks are still going, punctuated by the whoops and cheers of my family and friends. "I'll wait a beat. I don't think anyone'll notice."

"Okay," I say.

And all at once, I don't know what to do with myself. I want to kiss him. Fuck, I want to hug him, but all of a sudden that feels too...intimate? He was just inside me, whispering the dirtiest things in my ear, controlling every inch of my body with his, but the thought of pulling him to me, resting my cheek on his chest, listening to his heartbeat even for a minute feels like standing on the stage of my high school graduation stark naked.

Instead, I turn and walk slowly out of the room.

For the first few steps down the hall, I'm not sure I remember how to walk. By the time I'm in the living room, feeling starts returning to my fingers and toes, and as I make my way through the kitchen, the ringing in my brain quiets. I step out onto the deck, tilting my head up to watch the fireworks bloom in the air, feeling almost normal.

Except for that opening in my chest. It's starting to feel like a part of me now. Like nothing will ever fill it.

"You okay?"

Wyatt sidles up to me, her eyes on the sky. Archer's backyard is a cornfield that's part of a small family farm, which is why he's able to shoot off such an impressive fireworks display.

"Yep." I nod, hugging my elbows to my chest, but it does nothing to dull the ache inside me.

"I hope you just got railed enthusiastically by a man who knows how," she says with a low laugh.

After glancing around to make sure no one is nearby, I smile. "You have no idea," I whisper.

"Good," she says, glancing at the door, which Decker has just opened. He gives her a mild smile, heading toward the stairs. As he brushes past me, he doesn't say a word, but he snakes his hand out and discreetly pinches my ass. I can't contain a laugh, and Wyatt groans. "You're so totally gone."

"Shut up," I tell her. "It's fine."

"I hope so," she says.

The last of the fireworks explodes in the night sky, a burst of red and blue with white sizzles raining down from the middle. Everyone breaks into applause, Dad giving his signature whistle, and Betsy tears away from her mother to race down into the grass and examine all the tattered bits. Archer holds out an arm to keep her from touching anything hot, then picks up a fuse to show her the exploded end.

Owen walks over, phone in his hand. "Patients okay?" I ask as he stares at it.

"Yup, just answering a question about a fever," he says, tapping the screen.

"Are you ever off duty?" Wyatt asks him.

"Nope," he replies, as if that's normal. And for Owen it is, or it has been ever since he finished his residency and came back to practice in Cardinal Springs.

"Hey, y'all. Did I miss the show?"

I turn around and see Hazel emerging through the door. Her long blond hair is braided over one shoulder, her cheeks rosy and round.

And that's not the only part of her that's round.

"Holy shit, is she—" Wyatt gulps, her eyes wide as saucers as she stares at her sister's belly, Hazel's hands supporting the swell of it. Wyatt turns to my brother, whose attention is finally off his phone. "Is she fucking *pregnant?*"

"I'm not an OBGYN, but…" he says, implying *but I have eyes.*

Hazel spreads out her fingers, making jazz hands near her belly. "Um, surprise?"

# CHAPTER 36
## DECKER

'm getting smoked by an eight-year-old.

In my defense, he got a head start, and I'm carrying two hockey sleds.

"I won! I won!" Nimesh cries as he careens across the blue line. "I beat an actual NHL player!"

"Well done, bud." I shift the sleds in my arms so I can pat the top of his helmet, which tips down over his eyes.

It's the middle of July, and being on the ice feels amazing, even if it's to wrangle a bunch of enthusiastic eight-year-olds. We finally managed to organize the open skate for the library kids, and nearly everyone has shown up for it. We've got a dozen skaters on the ice with Archer, Grace, and me. Their parents are spread out in the bleachers, watching as their kids, all in the brand-new skates and helmets I ordered and donated to the arena, race and spin and trip and splat all over the pockmarked ice. Nicola Coughlin is buckled into one of the sleds I special ordered, using a pair of short hockey sticks to drag herself across the ice. She's wasted no time getting her balance and figuring out how to adjust her weight to turn, and now she's faster than most of the kids on two feet.

When we started, only two or three of the kids could stay

upright, but after about half an hour of coaching, they're all on the move. A few of them are even working on their crossovers, big grins on their faces, even when they trip over their own blades and go Superman-sliding across the ice. We gave them all youth-size hockey sticks, which help with their balance, and they spend the second half of the hour slapping pucks around, pretending to achieve NHL glory.

It's among the most fun days I've ever had on the ice.

Grace, who no longer needs to hide her skating skills from me or anyone else, is wearing her own hockey skates, a scuffed black pair that is clearly well loved. They only serve to elongate her athletic legs in her black leggings, and were it not for the fact that we're surrounded by tiny humans, their parents, and her big brother, I'd drag her off to the locker room.

"Can I try a sled now?" Betsy asks, careening up to me with as much speed as Nimesh.

"Sure." I special ordered the sled for Nicola. Her wheelchair is parked by the bleachers, and she's spent the day darting around the ice propelling by a pair of half-size hockey sticks. I ordered three sleds, because I knew there would be other kids who'd want to try them after they saw Nicola's. This way, she's not the only one out there perfecting her sled hockey game. "Nicola, come show Betsy how it's done!"

Nicola races over, and sure enough, as soon as Betsy straps herself in, they take off, passing a puck back and forth.

When our ninety minutes are up, I blow my whistle and call the kids to center ice to take a knee.

"Okay, that's it for today," I tell them. I'm immediately hit with a wall of groans that bounce across the ice. "But the good news is, we have all this gear now, so I think we can probably do this again soon. I'll let your parents know when."

Those groans turn to cheers. I need to talk to Darren about ice time, which I'm happy to pay for. I had no idea how much fun it would be to get out here with a bunch of kids, some so little they can barely pronounce the *s* in *skate*. Most of them are just out here to have fun, but Nimesh looks like he could have some heat under his skates, and I'm definitely going to look up info on the youth sled hockey league up in Indianapolis for Nicola's mom. She's an ace on that thing.

"Okay, since we're not in the library, I want today's *hockey* on three to be as loud as you can make it," I tell the kiddos, and boy, do they deliver. They shout so loud I'm surprised the banners overhead don't blow back.

As they return to their parents with tales of their morning, Archer skates over and showers me in a spray of ice with a perfect hockey stop.

"That was great, man," he says, planting his stick and leaning on the handle. "You were really amazing with those kids."

"You sound surprised," I say. I push off, bending to pick up the little orange cones I scattered across the ice for our drills.

"I just didn't see this journey for you. Grace says you're kicking ass at story time, and now you're on the ice with a bunch of kids acting like Mr. Youth Hockey? Working with kids is a really specific skill set, but you've got it, man. Seriously."

I can't help but think back to my first day in Cardinal Springs, when I stepped out onto the ice with Archer's team and they asked if I was going to coach them. I'd scoffed at the idea. Archer had, too. Me working with children? Might as well ask Kid Rock to be your nanny. But now here I am, already plotting the next ice time, thinking up stick handling drills we can do and skating skills we can work on. Even if most of these kids never play a single minute of hockey, the hand-eye coordination and the phys- ical confidence that comes from skating will serve their growing brains and bodies well.

I just wish I could give them more than a few skating lessons.

Archer skates over and holds open the mesh bag for me to dump the cones in, then ties off the drawstring. "I gotta get going," he says. "I promised Madeline I'd have Betsy home in time for her ballet class."

"We can skip it! I hate ballet!" Betsy calls from the bench

where she's taking off her skates. Apparently on top of being a pretty strong skater, she has the hearing of a bat.

"You're going," Archer calls back, but I notice the corners of his lips curling up. He swings the mesh bag over his shoulder and turns to me. "You good to lock up?"

I nod, patting the master key ring in my pocket.

"I'll help," Grace calls. She's next to Betsy on the bench, her skates already sitting beside her. She was mostly just an assistant today, but I did have her demonstrate speed skating and crossovers for the kids, so she got a bit of a workout. She's got one long, lean leg extended along the bench, her lithe body bending over it. I swallow hard and make myself look away.

Archer nods, apparently only fully trusting me when I have a babysitter. But I'm just glad he's not worried about me spending alone time with Grace. He seems to have gotten used to seeing us together, even if he doesn't know what kind of together we are.

Fuck, *I* don't even know what kind of together we are. I feel incredible when I'm with her, and I think I make her happy, too. But I can't ask her what this is when I have nothing to offer her. I'm leaving in six weeks.

As Archer heads out with Betsy, he pauses to plant a kiss on the top of Grace's head. "Happy birthday, little sis," he says. Her cheeks heat, and she mutters something I can't hear.

When we're alone, I drop down on the bench beside her. "It's your birthday? Today?"

"Yes," she says, sort of terse, and reaches for her skates. She jumps up and starts checking under the bleachers for anything the kids might have left behind. I slip off my own skates and put my sneakers on, catching up to her just as she's retrieving a pink beanie from the floor.

"Why didn't you tell me?" I ask.

She doesn't look at me. "Because I have plans," she says. "I told you I was going out with Carson tonight. We have a whole birthday tradition."

"Yeah, but you didn't say that last part. You just told me you were going out with Carson."

"Which I am."

"Okay. Well, I don't want to impose on your tradition, but I would have done something for you. You're making me feel like a deadbeat."

Grace waves me off. "Don't worry about it. That's not what this is, anyway," she says. She's been doing that a lot lately. It's a gut punch of a reminder that I'm not her boyfriend, that this unnamed situation we've got going on is just temporary.

And I don't need the reminder. Every time I wake up, my first thought is that I'm one day closer to leaving her. Media day will be here before I know it.

So I'm very aware that I'm not her boyfriend, that I *can't* be.

Still, she deserves a fucking birthday present from me.

"Do you want to get lunch, or—"

Grace whirls around, her jaw set, her brow furrowed. I know that look. It's the one that tells me she's about to put her foot down, about to get stubborn. It's a look she used to give only to me before she started standing up for herself with other people.

"I have plans, Deck," she says. "My whole day is spoken for. Seriously, don't worry about it. My birthday isn't a big deal to me."

There's something familiar in the way she's brushing me off, like how she holds her cards so close with her family. I'm missing something, but I know her well enough now to know that I can't push her.

"Okay, heard," I say, holding up my hands in surrender. I know not to fight with her. I like when she stands up for herself. Still, my mind is whirring with ideas for something small I can get here. Something that can stay here with her when I'm gone.

---

Later that night, I'm in my bed in my boxers, eating leftover chicken salad that Grace made. "The secret is to use a rotisserie chicken and a shit ton of sweet pickle relish," she told me, and she wasn't wrong. This is the best fucking chicken salad I've ever had.

Unfortunately, I'm eating it while torturing myself with video of the final playoff game. On my television, I watch the embarrassing breakaway in the first period where I lost an edge and a chance to score, falling spread-eagle on the ice a dozen feet from the goal. I watch my sluggish play in the second period, when my hip flexor started acting up, probably from that stupid fucking fall in the first. That was when my patience with Perrault started to wear thin. I watch my penalty early in the third when I cross-checked him after a collision into the boards. Even though you can't hear it in the broadcast, my ears ring with every word Perrault chirped at me, his comments growing increasingly vile.

And when the clock ticks down with just over three and a half minutes left in regulation, the game tied, I watch my face-off with Perrault. I remember the lightning pain in my hip, the ache in my shoulder, the tension vibrating through me. I remember glancing up into the stands and seeing Vipers fans holding up signs with my picture on them that said TAKING OUT THE TRASH and BROOKS, TELL IMANI TO CALL ME. And then Perrault leaned in, his voice low enough that the official couldn't hear, and released a stream of misogynistic, slur-filled shit.

I remember throwing down my stick and gloves and launching myself at him, a full-body slam into the ice. I caught him off guard, and the fucker didn't fight back. He wanted to draw the penalty, and he could see that I'd reached the frayed end of my control. I played right into his fucking hands.

My fingers itch to turn off the game, or maybe punch Perrault again right through this fucking television. But instead I force myself to watch the whole thing, the way the officials dragged me away from him and I accidentally took a swing at one of them in my rage.

I was forced off the ice and sent to the locker room. The Vipers scored with a minute remaining, and the Grinders had nothing left. No gas to answer. No goal to force an OT.

When my phone buzzes, I answer it before I even process that it's a number I don't recognize.

"What?" I snap, my nerves jangling with tension.

"Decker? It's Carson."

My blood skids to a halt in my veins, my brain conjuring all the worst possible scenarios.

"Is Grace okay?" I picture the pair of them drunk, stranded somewhere, maybe some godforsaken club in Indianapolis or a roadside bar. Grace seemed so keyed up earlier. I knew something was off. I should have listened to my gut, shouldn't have let her run away from me.

"I think so?" Carson says, then swallows hard.

I sit up so fast the remote goes flying. "You're not with her?"

"That's why I'm calling. I came down with the stomach flu around lunchtime. I've been barfing all afternoon, so I had to cancel our plans. She said it was fine, but...she has this thing about her birthday, and I don't want her to be alone. I'd call Wyatt, but she's got her hands full with Hazel, and I figured you—"

"I've got it," I say, already off the bed and tugging on a pair of sweatpants.

"You're sure?" she says, then burps into the phone.

"I'm going to find her right now." I tug a shirt over my head and look around for my sneakers.

"Hey, Decker?" Carson's voice is wobbly, and I can't tell if it's her stomach or something else.

"Yeah?"

"I know you've got a shitty reputation, but I also know that I've never seen Grace as happy as she's been with you these last couple of weeks."

I pause, not sure what to say. I didn't realize Carson knew about us, whatever we are.

"But Decker, if you hurt her, I will remove your testicles with a rusty skate blade and use them to score goals on Grinders ice, you hear me?"

I half laugh. I've never heard such a creative threat, and I spend most of my time with professional athletes. We talk shit for a living.

"You don't have to worry," I tell her. "Grace is safe with me."

She sighs. "Okay. Go take care of our girl. And I don't mean fuck her brains out, okay? Unless that's what she wants and enthusiastically asks for." She pauses to take another long, deep breath. "Grace hasn't spent her birthday alone in…well, ever. I have no idea what you're walking into."

"I'll text you an update," I assure her.

"Thank you. I'm going to hang up and go barf now."

"Feel better," I say, and I'm pretty sure I hear her retching before the line goes dead.

I find my shoes underneath my couch and step into them, sprint to the bathroom to brush my teeth, and then race across the hall. I knock, but there's no answer.

"Grace?" I call, knocking again. "Grace, are you in there?"

There's shifting behind the door. It opens a crack, but she doesn't show her face.

"What are you doing here?" she asks.

"Carson called me. She told me she got sick. She didn't want you to be alone."

"I'm fine," she says, but her voice hitches at the end. I hear a sniffle behind the door, then the sound of a tiny little sob.

"Grace, baby, let me in," I plead. "I'll just sit with you. We don't have to talk or anything." My heart's already pulling at the seams, knowing she's been over here all day, hurting. Hearing her so upset makes it crack.

There's a pause, and then the door swings open. Her back is to me as she shuffles over to the couch. She drops down onto it, and when I follow her, I see that her eyes are red and swollen, her gaze slightly unfocused. Probably because there's an empty bottle of wine on the table, a second one open beside it, along with a glass.

And next to that is a white bakery box, the pink-frosted cake inside it half gone, a fork stuck in the top like a threat.

"Are you—" I start to ask.

"You said no talking," she snaps, her words slightly slurred. She hiccups, and that's when I realize she's blitzed out of her goddamn mind. I've only ever seen Grace have one beer, maybe two. More than a bottle of wine is a *lot*. She's tall, but she's still no bigger than a minute.

I head over to her well-stocked kitchen, filling a tall glass with water. I set it on the coffee table in front of her, where she eyes it like it's a trap.

"I don't want to be taken care of," she says. I can tell she's trying hard to keep her voice from shaking. "I just want to be left alone."

So I lower myself down beside her and don't say a word. We sit in silence for long enough that we bypass the awkwardness and I start to get comfortable with it. Finally, she reaches for the water glass. She takes a tentative sip, then grimaces.

"Too full," she mutters, flopping back against the cushions.

I stay quiet, waiting patiently. And then she starts talking.

"I hate my birthday," she says.

"I'm sorry Carson got sick," I try.

She shakes her head, a strand of her dark hair sticking to her tear-streaked cheek. My fingers itch to brush it back and kiss every hurt away with it. But I know she doesn't want that, doesn't need it. So I sit still and give her my full attention.

"It's not that. I always hate it. It's the worst. Every year I put my head down and just try to get through it. Carson and I have the same birthday, did you know that? We were born on the same day. That's how we became friends. Her mom swept in when I needed someone who wasn't a dad or a brother to help me, and that included planning my birthday parties right alongside Carson's. Because my dad and brothers were always too shattered to celebrate another year that she'd been gone. Another year I'd kept her from them."

She breaks off, burying her head in her hands, drunken sobs seeping through her fingers. I reach out to pull her to me—I can't fight the urge anymore—but she shrugs me off, so I drop my hands into my lap. Fuck, knowing she's been torturing herself with this guilt about her mom, that this is why she hates her birthday…it kills me.

"Grace, honey, you didn't do any of that," I say, begging her to hear me. To believe me.

She looks up, her cheeks wet. "Every year, my birthday just marks another year I didn't get to know her. And I'm just so…" She breaks off, searching for words. "I'm just so *sad*."

This time when I reach for her, she lets me pull her in. I wrap an arm around her waist, squeezing her so she knows I'm here, my other hand cradling the back of her head, stroking her hair. I rest my chin on the top of her head and have to swallow twice, hard, to keep the lump in my throat at bay. I will be strong for her, goddammit.

"You don't have to do it like this, Grace," I whisper.

"Like what?" she hiccups.

"Alone. Hiding. You could talk to them—your family. About how you're feeling. About her."

She lets out a bitter laugh. "My mom died, Decker. I'm here, and she *died*. She died *because* I'm here. I don't deserve to talk about her with them."

I pull back and stare directly into her watery blue eyes. "Grace, I don't know how to get it through your head that you deserve *everything*. Everything you need, everything you want should be yours. And I wish I could give it all to you. But this is a thing *you* need to do. *You* can talk to them, just like you did on the Fourth. You can be honest with them. They'll surprise you, I know it. I know you can do it, my brave girl."

Her eyelids flutter as she looks down. "I'm not brave," she says. "I'm terrified."

I reach down with a finger and tip her chin up until her eyes are back on me. "Naming the fear is the scariest part. Owning it.

And you've done that. But maybe now it's time to give it away, to let the people who love you hold on to it for you."

*I'm one of those people*, I don't say, but it's true. I want to steal into her heart and take every fear, every hesitation, every ounce of pain so she never has to feel it again.

She seems to think about what I've said, her eyes on me the whole time. I don't break her gaze.

"Stay with me, Decker." Not a question. It never was.

"I'm not going anywhere," I promise her. Then I scoop her into my arms and carry her to her bed. I toe off my shoes and slide in beside her, folding my body around hers.

"I'm sorry," she cries, her shoulders shuddering as I squeeze her to me.

"You don't have anything to be sorry for. I'm here for you no matter what."

I hold her as her cries turn to sniffles, her breathing slowing. Soon she's quiet. Then her body goes heavy in my arms, the tension in her muscles releasing as she drifts off to sleep.

When I know she's fast asleep, I kiss her hair, breathing in the scent of her shampoo.

"Everyone thinks I'm the bad boy," I whisper, finally letting my own tears fall. "But you're the one who's gonna ruin me."

# CHAPTER 37

## GRACE

'm not sure which thing wakes me up: the feeling of an ice pick burying itself between my eyeballs, or the flavor of sour dryer lint on my tongue. Every nerve ending in my body is screaming, which is what happens when you drink a bottle and a half of pinot noir and eat the better part of a birthday cake.

I swallow, and a wave of nausea rolls through me. In an instant, I launch myself out of bed and into the bathroom, dropping to my knees just in time to release the contents of my stomach into the toilet.

I'm mid-retch when I feel my hair being pulled away from my face.

"Let it out, baby," Decker murmurs as he rubs soothing circles on my back with his big warm hand. Not soothing enough, unfortunately. I heave again.

"I'm sorry, I wanted to get more water into you last night, but you passed out too fast," he says.

"What are you doing here?" I croak, spitting into the toilet bowl and wishing the floor would open up and swallow me whole. Decker is maybe the last person on planet Earth who I want to see me like this.

"You don't remember?" His brow furrows. "Carson sent me over."

Right. Carson, who is also barfing her guts out, though her illness is likely not self-inflicted.

"I remember," I mumble. I flush the toilet, rise shakily to my feet, and shuffle over to the sink, reaching for my toothbrush. "But why are you *still* here?"

I catch sight of Decker in the mirror, standing sentry behind me. He flinches like I've slapped him.

"Sorry," I say. "I just mean that this is so gross. You don't have to be here for any of this."

"I wasn't going to leave you last night," he replies. "When you're done brushing your teeth, there are some Saltines and Gatorade on the island. Plus ibuprofen, but eat the Saltines first or the meds will make your stomach feel worse. I also picked up ginger ale and coffee—I wasn't sure which your stomach would prefer. And I got you an egg sandwich, in case you're like me and prefer to soak up alcohol with grease."

"Ugh," I groan, my stomach turning a somersault.

He gives me a sympathetic grimace. "Saltines it is, then. Listen, I'm supposed to meet Archer at the gym—"

"Don't tell him," I say, spinning around so we're face-to-face. "About last night, and what I said about…my mom."

Just the mention of her makes the emotions of last night start crawling up my throat again. That was the worst it's ever been.

When I was a little kid, I didn't understand what my birthday meant for my family. I just knew it was a day I got to spend with my best friend, enjoying a joint birthday party at her house, or the bowling alley, or the skating rink. As I got older, as I learned more details about my mom's death, the day took on a different meaning. But those birthday parties with Carson, which we started planning with the precision of generals going into battle, distracted me.

When we got to high school and moved past the party stage, Carson still stayed by my side every birthday, distracting me with karaoke and, later, alcohol. Our tradition is now well worn. We find the loudest club we can in Bloomington or Indianapolis; once we went all the way up to Chicago. We drink and dance and yell over the crowd, everything too loud and chaotic to let my grief through. We finish the night at the nearest karaoke bar, choosing the screamiest music on offer, singing our voices raw. Then we tumble into a hotel room, exhausted, and when I wake the next morning, I've missed the anniversary of the moment I entered this world and my mom left it. It still hurts, but it's all a little bit dulled by the noise, the alcohol, the idea of fun. And most of all, by my best friend.

But last night it was just me and that fucking birthday cake. I don't know whether to be pissed or grateful that Carson sent Decker after me.

"I won't tell Archer anything," Decker says carefully. I can tell I freaked him out last night. Whatever I did, whatever I said, this isn't what he signed up for. This was supposed to be just a summer fling. It was supposed to be fun and easy. And then I went and treated him like my boyfriend.

*Fuck.*

If I didn't feel like week-old roadkill, I might jump him just to try and get things back to normal. But the thought of letting anyone touch my body right now makes me want to walk into the ocean. So instead I reach for the Gatorade.

"Thank you," I say, and pop the lid. I throw a single Saltine into my mouth, but it tastes like sawdust. I wash it down with a swig of Gatorade and brace for its return. Fortunately, my stomach accepts the offering. I swallow three ibuprofen and sink onto one of the barstools, waiting for relief or death, whichever comes first.

"But in the privacy of this apartment, I'm going to reiterate my advice," he says carefully. Like he's trying to talk a tiger down from mauling him.

Bits of our conversation come back to me, fighting through the fog of my hangover. And even though I can't string it all together perfectly in my pounding head, I remember enough to know he's right.

And I'm also still too fucking terrified to admit to my family that I feel this crushing guilt.

"Yeah," I say. The boulder of emotion sits heavy on my chest.

Decker pulls out the stool next to me. "Hey, I can cancel on Archer and stay here with you."

I shake my head. "No. Go. I need to shower and eat..." I grimace at the thought. "Eventually. Once the memory of wine and strawberry frosting fades."

"Okay. But I'll be back after," he says.

"You don't have to take care of me, Decker," I tell him. I vaguely remember saying the same thing last night.

"I know I don't have to," he says slowly, "and I know you don't need it. But I want to, because it's what you deserve."

Those words also sound familiar, but I can't quite place them. I look up at him, trying to put together the memory, and Decker leans in and kisses me. It's chaste but tender, somehow more intimate than any of the times he's put his tongue in my mouth.

"Eat and drink," he says. "You'll feel better soon."

When he's gone, my apartment feels too empty. I immediately miss his hulking frame on my couch or leaning over the island while I cook. I glance down at the array of hangover supplies. I'm not surprised he's good at dealing with this sort of thing. It's the advice that shocks me, and the fact that Decker is so good at caring for me. If you'd asked me back in May, I would have described him as oblivious at best, self-centered at worst. But after the way he held me while I slept, held my hair back while I barfed, held my heart while it shattered, it's clear I was wrong. He's capable of so much more than I knew, and so much more than I think even *he* realizes.

As I reach for the bag from the diner, I know I can't deny it any longer. I want much more than just a fling, more than just sex. Hell, I feel closer to him now than I did yesterday, and last night was the first night since the Last Stop that we *didn't* have sex.

And from the look of this spread, maybe his feelings for me are bigger, too.

It feels like too much to hope for. And what if I'm wrong? What if I tell him how I feel and he doesn't feel the same? What if I tell him and he leaves anyway?

I don't know if it's that thought or just the smell of the egg sandwich seeping through its foil that sends me running back to the bathroom.

# CHAPTER 38

## DECKER

My nemesis stands before me, and I take a deep centering breath as I prepare to do battle.

It's time to empty the book return.

The hulking metal container on the sidewalk in front of the library is like the world's worst jack-in-the-box. Anything could pop out at any moment. In the six weeks I've been working at the library, I've found books in here, obviously, but not always library books. There's been plenty of trash, mostly crumpled napkins and wadded-up fast food bags. I've found two diapers, lots of gum, three stuffies, a Cardinal Springs Debate Team T-shirt, and—on one especially shitty Monday morning—the remains of a chocolate milkshake.

So as I stand on the sizzling concrete, the morning heat already oppressive, I brace myself for the unexpected. Someday I fully expect to find an actual child in there. I take the brass key from my pocket and turn it in the lock, close my eyes, send up a prayer, and peer in the open door.

Just books.

Thank the library gods.

"Find anything good today?" Grace bounces down the sidewalk, her sandals clip-clopping on the concrete. She's smiling, her cheeks pink and her blue eyes clear. There's no trace of the girl who fell apart on her birthday, who chafed when I tried to put her back together. She hasn't spoken another word about that night, and I haven't brought it up. Part of me is afraid that if I do, she'll tell me it's not my business, that I'm not her boyfriend. That this is just sex. And I know all that's true, but hearing her say it might just break me. So I've let everything go back to the way it was, except for my feelings for her. I can't shrink those back down.

"Just books today. But the cheese bandit has returned." I hold up a Zadie Smith book, which has a Kraft single sticking out of it. "At least this one has the plastic wrap on it."

Grace rolls her eyes. "I've talked to Mr. Martinez *four times* about his choice of bookmarks. Apparently he only reads when he's having his afternoon snack of cheese and Ritz crackers, and according to him, 'things get confused.'"

"Get ready for conversation number five," I tell her, removing the cheese and tossing it into a trash bag—I now know to bring one out with me when I perform this daily task.

Grace leans back against the book drop, apparently unbothered by the heat. Her dark hair is pulled up in an artfully messy bun, a few strands escaping and blowing across her pink cheeks. She's wearing the same light-blue sundress she wore to Archer's party, the one I dragged up her hips so I could fuck her in the laundry room. The rush of that moment comes roaring back to me, and I wonder if I can convince her to stay at the library after closing and finally christen the nonfiction stacks.

"Oh fuck," Grace groans as she peers at her phone. Her finger flicks the screen as she scrolls.

"Everything okay?" I ask, straightening the books on the rolling cart I dragged out here.

"Annabeth Zhou, our keynote speaker for the festival, has to pull out. She had a death in the family. Fuck fuck *fuck*."

"Oh man, that sucks," I say. "Can we get someone else?"

"In less than two weeks?" She groans again. "We've already sold a ton of tickets for the keynote. We'll have to replace Annabeth with someone just as big to keep people from asking for refunds, and this close, that's going to be damn near impossible!" She pushes off the book return and starts pacing back and forth in front of me. "If we were Chicago, maybe even Indianapolis, we could probably find someone, but how am I going to convince a *New York Times*–bestselling author to drop everything and come to Cardinal Springs, Indiana in exchange for two hundred and fifty dollars and a night at the Holiday Inn out by the highway?"

I reach out and grasp her shoulders, stopping her pacing before her shoes catch fire. "Anything I can do to help?"

She sighs and shakes her head. "I need to think," she says. "I'll go talk to Suzanne. Maybe she knows someone and can call in a favor."

She hurries into the library, and I start stacking books on the return cart again. But now I'm wracking my brain, trying to come up with ideas for how to help her. I could obviously write her a check so she could offer more money to an author. But that wouldn't solve the time crunch problem. It's probably going to come down to calling in a major favor. Hopefully Ms. Suzanne knows someone.

I'm about to charge into the library and offer her a stupid amount of money—anything to ease her mind—when I pull the last hardcover from the bottom of the return box. It's got a misty coastal mansion on the front with the title—*Reckless Redemption*—in shiny gold letters. A sticker declares the author, a *New York Times* bestseller, "beloved."

But what draws my eye is the author photo on the back of the jacket, large and in full color. The woman looks to be in her late sixties, her silver hair cut to her chin, bangs blunt across her forehead, her lips painted a bright ruby red.

And I know her.

Usually when I see her, she's wearing an orange-and-black Grinders jersey. Usually she's sitting behind the glass just to the side of the home bench, swearing up a storm at the officials.

I tuck the book under my arm and drag the cart inside,

moving so fast I nearly dump all the books onto the carpet when I bump through the door. I abandon it at the circulation desk and make my way into Ms. Suzanne's office, where she and Grace are huddled around a laptop.

"I've got it," I say, holding up the book.

Ms. Suzanne peers over the top of her purple reading glasses. "Finally starting your Janice Andrews journey, dear?"

"I know her."

Grace cocks her head. "Who?"

"The author." I glance at the front cover. "Janice Andrews. She's a *massive* Grinders fan. Rinkside season tickets every year I've been on the team, sponsors our community outreach, comes to every player meet-and-greet. I've had my picture taken with her at least a dozen times. I think she's friends with our owner. She's a serious VIP."

Grace's mouth drops open as she looks from me to the book and back again.

"Do you think she'd—" She cuts herself off, like it's too much to even consider.

"I can get her contact info from Brielle. She's got all the contact info for our VIPs. I'll call Janice personally to ask," I tell her. "Like I said, I've met her several times. She's a real firecracker."

I pull my phone out of my pocket and start tapping out a text to Brielle.

"Even if she agrees to do you a favor, she might still want a big stipend," Ms. Suzanne says.

I wave her off. "Whatever she wants, I'll write the check. But knowing her, she'll just want a signed jersey and a meet-and-greet."

Within seconds, Brielle responds with a thumbs-up, and a few minutes after that, a phone number appears in my messages.

"You're seriously telling me that all this time, you've been buddies with the most popular romance author *of all time*? The woman who single-handedly keeps Rivercrest Books afloat with her sales? The woman who has hit the *New York Times* bestseller list more times than Stephen King?" Grace shakes her head. "How did you not say something?"

I shrug. "I didn't know."

Ms. Suzanne's eyebrows furrow. "You didn't *know*?"

"I'll be honest—before this summer, I don't know that I've ever read an entire book, even for school. I don't know the names of famous authors. She could have *been* Stephen King, for all I knew."

"How the hell did you get through Cardinal Springs High without ever reading an entire novel?" Ms. Suzanne mutters.

"CliffsNotes," I say, and she throws up her hands. I don't think I've ever seen the woman this disgusted, and that includes the time Archer dared me to snort Pixy Stix before our home opener senior year. (I sneezed blue raspberry dust all over my jersey.)

"I've got the number," I say, holding up my phone. "Should I call?"

Grace races around the desk and throws her arms around my neck, squeezing. "Thank you," she says, her voice right by my ear. Over her shoulder, Ms. Suzanne looks entirely too pleased with herself.

"She hasn't said yes yet," I tell Grace.

She pulls back and grins at me. "She will. I know how hard it is to say no to you."

# CHAPTER 39

## GRACE

Decker has become a regular fixture at our Monday-night family dinners at Dad's house, just like he was when he was a teenager. But back then, he and Archer spent those meals trying to flick peas into my milk cup or gross me out with belching contests. Now Decker's sliding his sneakered foot up my calf beneath the table. He still sits next to Archer, since he's there ostensibly on my big brother's invitation. But we arrive together. He helps me cook. He sneaks kisses or swats my ass when no one is watching and feeds extra bites to Puck, who seems to recognize that our new guest is a softie.

It's all very...domestic.

In my weaker moments, I imagine the truth coming out, everyone finally knowing about Decker and me. I think about what it would be like for him to take the seat beside me at the table, to hold my hand during dessert, to be *mine*.

The thing about spilling the truth about the marathon training to my family is that it only served to highlight all the other secrets I've been keeping: Decker, my feelings about my mom, my plans for the bookstore. My private thoughts used to feel weightless, but they're getting awfully heavy these days. Maybe Decker is right. Maybe it's time to offload some of them.

"Grace, this chicken is incredible," Corianne says, reaching for the platter to fork some more meat onto her plate.

"Thanks," I tell her. "It's an Ina Garten recipe. I can give it to you if you want. Lots of butter, but it's worth it, I think."

Corianne is another new regular guest at family dinner. She sits to Dad's left, and he holds her hand, stroking the back of it with his thumb. Archer has even stopped grimacing when he notices it, and I've never seen our father happier.

"So, Grace, where are things with the book festival?" Dad asks, pouring gravy over his mashed potatoes.

I sit up straighter, my to-do list always on the tip of my tongue these days. The festival starts a week from Friday, just under two weeks away, and whenever Decker isn't kissing all my stress away, my brain is whirring with prep and plans.

"Well, we got the signed contract from Janice Andrews this morning," I say.

Corianne lets out a little squeak. "I cannot *tell* you how excited I am to meet her. She's been my favorite author since college, when I picked up the first book in the Clyne Family series. They're so soapy and swoony. I love them!"

"And it only took a signed, game-worn Winter Classic jersey and the promise of a private dinner with me to get her to agree," Decker says with a laugh.

"But she refused your giant check and told you to send it to the food bank!" I point out.

"She's a classy broad," Decker says.

"As soon as we announced our new headliner, ticket sales exploded. People are coming in from out of state to hear her speak," I tell everyone. "We had to move the keynote to the Baptist church."

"Apparently the draw of Janice Andrews was too great for Pastor Scott to worry about the sex scenes in her books," Decker says wryly.

"Honestly, the boost in sales is going a long way toward us meeting our goals. It could still rain or there could be some other disaster, but it looks like we're going to make up the budget short-fall and then some," I say.

"That's great, honey," Dad says. "Have you given any more thought to library school? I imagine Suzanne will start thinking about retiring soon. I know she'd love to recommend you for her job when she does."

I immediately deflate. Of course I haven't thought about going back to school—a requirement if I were to take over as the librarian when Suzanne retires. Because I don't *want* to take over as the librarian when Suzanne retires. I want to buy the old Quinn Camera building and open my bookstore, where I can hold story times and recommend books and serve the community without making minimum wage and spending half my time cleaning French fries out of the book return or lecturing old men about using cheese as a bookmark.

But they don't know that, because I haven't told them.

"No," I say, then take a deep breath. I glance across the table at Decker, and he seems to know what I'm thinking, because he gives me a tiny nod that says *I've got you.* "I've actually been toying with the idea of opening a bookstore here in town."

I let out a breath and brace for the onslaught.

"Seriously?" Dan asks from the far end of the table, the first thing he's said since we sat down.

"Not just toying with it, actually," I say, because if I'm going to be honest, I need to go all in. "I've made plans. I took a couple of online business classes through the community college, and Deva at Red Books in Bloomington has been helping me draw up a business plan. I joined the American Booksellers Association and have done several webinars. I feel ready."

Dan nods. "Sounds like you've done your due diligence. How are you financially?"

Dad sits up straighter, his mouth opening, but Corianne squeezes his hand and cuts him a look, and he closes it again.

"Well, that's going to be the hard part, but there are some small business grants through the chamber of commerce that I qualify for. I've got a little bit of savings, but not much. Definitely not enough. I'm going to make an appointment at the credit union to talk about small business loans."

I fold and unfold the cloth napkin in my lap, waiting for the explosion of warnings, of advice.

But there's just silence. Everyone is watching me. Waiting for me to keep going.

"I'd really like to put it in the old Quinn Camera space," I continue, "but Mr. Quinn wants to sell the building, not rent it, and I think that might be out of reach for me."

I feel the toe of Decker's sneaker on my ankle, rubbing a little circle. When I look up, he's smiling down at his plate.

"I've got a little bit of cash saved up," Dad says. "You're welcome to it. As a loan, since I know you're too stubborn to take it as a gift."

Immediately, tears prick my eyes.

"I can do whatever build-out you need. Call it a birthday and Christmas present. I make some mean bookshelves," Felix says.

"I'm up for whatever grunt work you need," Archer says.

"And I'm happy to go over your financials," Dan says. "If you want."

The first tear rolls down my cheek, and I swipe at it. Decker tenses like he wants to shove back his chair and race around the table to me, but I shake my head. I'm not ready for *all* my secrets to come out. Not yet.

The tension shatters when the front door slams and Owen comes careening into the dining room. He drops into the last open chair and reaches for the chicken.

"Sorry sorry sorry, had to stay late to do stitches. One of my patients tried to cut her own bagel and narrowly avoided removing one of her fingers," he says. "Are we talking about the book festival? Because the supplies arrived today for the cast booth."

My sweet brother volunteered to set up a booth to give kids fake casts for five dollars, all the profits going to the library fund.

The kids are going to love it, especially since Dan is going to set up next to him and draw designs on them. Despite his financial wizardry, he has always been the artistic one in the family.

My family chatters around me for the rest of the meal, the meal I made for them, and I realize Decker was right. My fears were of my own invention, as most fears are. My family is learning how to support me without running me over because I'm showing them how. I'm letting them in and then setting the boundaries I need. And because they love me, because they only mean well, they're able to be here for me in exactly the ways I want.

I look up from my plate at the man across the table who told me all this, who begged me to see what he saw, who told me I could show the people who love me the real me. That they'd support me anyway.

I wish I could make him see that that's true for him, too.

# CHAPTER 40

## GRACE

The day has arrived. Tomorrow is the Cardinal Springs Book Festival, and all the hard work I've put in—to say nothing of the insane amount of work that still awaits me—will hopefully pay off.

But tonight?

Tonight, we party.

To kick off the festival, I've planned an opening night cocktail party. All the authors will be here, and we sold tickets to the public so folks can come mingle with them. The dress code is cocktail attire, and even though there's still so much for me to do between now and tomorrow night, when I can finally collapse, I'm giddy with excitement.

I lean toward the mirror to wipe a stray blob of mascara from beneath my eyebrow, then stand back and take in my dress. It's a gorgeous little silver chiffon number by a designer I've never heard of, and I got it for fifty dollars on Poshmark. The thing apparently retails for almost four hundred dollars, and it looks like it's worth every penny. It's one-shouldered with an open back, a nipped-in waist, and a skirt that flutters dreamily just above mid-thigh. It's best described as ethereal, and I feel like a Greek goddess in it.

But it's nothing compared to how I feel when Decker finally catches sight of me in it. He stands in my doorway, leaning against the frame, his deep chocolate eyes sweeping up the length of my body.

"Good god, woman, are you trying to kill me?" he asks, charging forward and pulling me into his arms.

"I could say the same about you." He's wearing an incredibly well-tailored navy suit with a white dress shirt open at the collar and leather loafers with no socks. His blond hair, usually so unkempt, is slicked back and tucked behind his ears. On my many illicit Google adventures into Decker Brooks, I've seen him look just like this in dozens of game day arrival photos, and once in a very sexy slo-mo video made by a fan (do not ask me how many times I've watched that video—I admit nothing). But seeing him like this now, in real life? It's something else entirely. To be in his arms. To be kissed by Decker Brooks in a suit.

I highly recommend it.

"Okay, this is your last chance," I murmur into his full lips. "Once I put on lipstick, no more kissing."

"Can't you skip it tonight?" he begs, then nips my lower lip. "A whole night with you in this dress, and I'm not allowed to kiss you? That's torture."

"You're not allowed to kiss me tonight regardless, because every single person in this town is going to be in the room."

Decker licks the spot he just bit, and I melt a little bit more into his arms. "Surely there will be coat closets or something," he says with a wicked grin.

"Down, boy." I swat at him, marveling at the firm planes of his chest. He's been upping his workouts lately now that he's only about a month away from training camp. Five weeks, to be exact. Not that I'm counting.

(I'm totally counting.)

But at least once we get past this weekend, crazy as it will be, we'll have more free time together.

"Oh, by the way, I have something for you." I walk over to my kitchen island, a little slower than normal since I'm still getting used to my delicate gold heels with straps that wind up my calves. I snag the piece of paper on top and present it to him with a flourish. "Once you sign this, you will have completed your community service. Congratulations, your record will soon be expunged. Cardinal Springs thanks you for your work."

"Wow," Decker says, taking the pen I offer and scribbling his name on the bottom line. "Does this mean we can't make out in the stacks anymore?"

"It means that what you do with your free time is no longer the court's business."

Decker dips his head, meeting my lips once more, one hand skimming up the back of my thigh to squeeze my ass. Then he flips up the back of my dress and peers over my shoulder.

"What are you doing?" I giggle.

"Just want to know what panties you're rocking tonight."

I don't say anything, letting him squint. I know the exact moment he sees them, because a groan tears from his throat.

"The cherries," he growls. Then he spins me around and starts marching me toward my bedroom.

"What's happening?" I laugh.

"I have been dreaming about these cherry panties for months. I'm going to enjoy the *fuck* out of you wearing them," he says. "Pun intended."

"We have to go, you menace," I say, barely containing my laughter and also barely managing to make myself spin out of his grip. I want nothing more than to fall into bed with him, to peel that suit off of him, to enjoy every inch of him on every inch of me, but we have one last hurdle to clear before we're free. To say I'm looking forward to spending the last few weeks of summer with Decker is an understatement. "I'm running this thing. I can't be late."

Decker groans and drop his head, a lock of hair escaping from behind his ear and falling over his face. "Tonight," he says, trailing after me like a hungry puppy. "Tonight, you, me, and those panties have an appointment."

"Noted," I say, swiping my lipstick from the counter and dropping it into my purse. I have a feeling that despite my warnings, I'm going to need a reapplication.

———

The party is being held in the old fire station at the far end of Main Street. It's a stately brick building that was renovated about twenty years ago to be an events space. It's gorgeous inside, with creaky wood floors and soaring ceilings. Earlier today, Decker and my army of volunteers and I set up for the evening: tall cocktail tables scattered around, two open bars, and a buffet donated by Crimson 'n' Cream and Pete's Diner. There's a long table in the back for the silent auction, and at the far end of the space, Sheriff Woods is in a tuxedo with his DJ equipment—he moonlights as a wedding DJ and donated his services.

It seems like nearly everyone in town has bought tickets, even Burch Brentwood, who finally did end up donating a paltry $250. I'm pretty sure it was just to avoid the gossip that was sure to happen if his company logo didn't appear in the program.

Speaking of gossip, Mrs. Eberle comes rushing up to me in a black faux-Chanel dress as soon as I'm in the door. "Grace, this event is just *lovely*," she gushes, her eyes going back and forth between Decker and me, who is standing behind me. "And your dress is absolutely gorgeous. Don't you think so, Decker?"

"Grace is always beautiful," he says, and I don't dare turn to look at him for fear that the amount I love this man is written all over my face. "If you'll excuse me, I'm going to go make sure the bar's set up properly."

Mrs. Eberle and I both watch him go, neither of us pretending not to stare as that round hockey ass struts away.

"Bless the tailor who made those pants," Mrs. Eberle says before making the sign of the cross.

"Amen," I add.

I know I shouldn't engage with her. I know she's going to buzz around the room telling everyone I said Decker has a hot ass. But first of all, that's just a fact—every woman in this room agrees with me, and some of the men, too, if the lingering stares that follow him through the ballroom are to be believed. And also, I'm starting to not give a fuck what people think about me being with Decker. I know all the reasons we're not supposed to be together. I know I said Archer would lose his mind if he found out, and he probably would at first. But Archer is over in the corner right now, holding a beer and laughing with Dad and Corianne. It took him a little time to warm up to her, but he seems to have gotten over his initial discomfort with our dad dating.

I watch Decker join them, easing into the conversation like he's slipping into a warm bath. My whole family already loves him, which is much more than I can say for Cannon, whom they tolerated like an awkward foreign exchange student they couldn't wait to be rid of. It was one of the things that made my relationship with Cannon so hard. He never made an effort with them, and they never made one either. But surely Decker being with me would just make my family love him more? His reputation may be shit, but it's also bullshit. If they don't know that already, they'll figure it out as soon as they see the way he treats me, how happy he makes me.

Right?

I picture telling them about the marathon training and the bookstore, all the things I've done to show my family who I am and what I want. Because I've opened up, the way they treat me has changed for the better. Dan has already gone over my business plan and made a few small but very smart suggestions. Archer has offered to go running with me, because even though he's cool with my training, he doesn't want me in the woods by myself. Dad has even invited me to work out with him and Corianne because, as he's reminded me several times now, "good strength training is the foundation of cardio."

Across the room, Decker must feel my gaze on him, because he looks up and meets my eyes, a smile spreading across his face that takes my breath away. My god, that man. That sexy, ridiculous, delicious disaster of a man.

"If you don't go jump into that man's arms right now, I will kill you myself," Mrs. Eberle says, staring at me sidelong.

"Mrs. Eberle!" I cry, wide-eyed.

"Oh, hush. I know I'm a relentless gossip, but I'm not saying anything that's not true. I don't know why the two of you think you need to sneak around, and frankly, I don't know how your family hasn't realized what's going on yet. The pair of you give off vibes for days. But that's men for you, I guess. They never notice anything unless it's printed, framed, and handed right to them." She grabs my arms, giving me a squeeze. "You're a good girl, Grace McBride. You do so much for everybody. I mean, take a look around. This night is spectacular *and* it's going to save the library. You deserve real happiness, and I think that man can give it to you."

"It's all a little more complicated than that," I say, because the sneaking around is only the first hurdle.

She waves me off. "Yes, yes, hockey and long distance and all the baggage, but none of that lasts forever. Nothing good comes without a few sticky parts. It's just a matter of how hard you're willing to work."

Across the room, Sheriff Woods fires up "Cha-Cha Slide," and the crowd, which until now has been quiet, maybe even a bit sedate, erupts. Nothing like a group dance with easy-to-follow instructions to get a bunch of middle-aged Midwesterners out on the dance floor.

"Oh, excuse me, honey, they're playing my song," Mrs. Eberle says with a little shimmy. "Good luck to you!"

Across the room, Dad and Corianne have joined the dancers in a "right foot, let's stomp." Betsy drags Madeline and Archer onto the dance floor, laughing as she forces Archer through the movements.

And Decker is left alone holding his beer.

And looking at me.

I cross the floor to him, weaving between Mrs. Eberle and Daphne from the bakery cha-cha-ing real smooth. Even though I have to duck a few enthusiastic jazz hands and I can hear people greeting me and telling me what a great party this is, I can't take my eyes off Decker. He stands there in the corner, one hand in his pocket, his rascally hair already rebelling against whatever product he used to try and tame it. My fingers twitch at my sides, aching to sink in that hair, to really mess it up as I go in for a kiss.

"Hi," I say, suddenly shy as I stop in front of him. I'm on the precipice of something, at a hinge point. I don't know what's around the corner, but I'm desperate to look.

"Hello, gorgeous," he says, his voice low, the grin on his face easy. And I know I'm blushing; I can feel the heat pulsing in my cheeks and chest. Who needs blush when Decker Brooks has eyes only for you?

I'm suddenly completely unable to be normal. I wish I had a drink, something to do with my hands besides using them to drag him off into the nearest dark corner. I fumble around in my brain for a G-rated thought.

"Everything seems to be going pretty well, huh?" I say, gazing out at the dancing crowd. I can feel his eyes on me, but I can't look at him. I'm afraid that if I do, he'll see the way I feel about him all over my face, as if my freckles will move to spell out I LOVE YOU, DECKER BROOKS across my cheeks. So I babble on. "I think the extra twinkle lights around the buffet were a good idea. I just hope nobody spills on them. You don't think they could start a fire, do you? If water gets on them? Surely that's not a thing that happens. I mean, people hang those lights outside, and it rains outside. I'm sure it's fine."

Beside me, Decker lets out a soft chuckle, but I just keep going. "Do you think there are enough pens over by the silent auction? I should have brought an extra box. People are always walking off with pens. I'd hate to miss out on bids just because there's nothing to write with."

He squeezes my arm slightly, just enough to get my attention. When I look up, I see him gazing back at me with a smile and soft eyes. He bends down and whispers, "As soon as the sheriff plays something a little slower, I'm going to ask you to dance. We'll pretend we're just friends, and I'll keep my hands in appropriate places, but just know that I won't want to."

I breathe out a long sigh that I have to work to keep from turning into a moan. God, I'm so in love with this man I feel like the force of it could lift me right off the ground. And yet, even though I'm full of fizzy thoughts I can't let out, he still manages to make me feel completely at ease.

"I look forward to it," I tell him, and my heart honest-to-god sinks when the song changes to Taylor Swift's "Shake It Off." Would it kill Sheriff Woods to spin a ballad? At this point I'd take the national anthem. *Anything* to spend a few minutes swaying in the arms of Decker Brooks.

"Mr. Brooks, always a pleasure." The voice, gravelly as a country road and syrupy as sweet tea, cuts through my thoughts, and I spin around to see the one and only Janice Andrews. She's wearing an emerald-green sheath dress with a deep V-neck. Her hair is perfectly curled, and her makeup is snatched to the heavens. She looks *fabulous*, and I immediately want to be her when I grow up.

She slides right up next to Decker and winks at him, not hiding for a second that if given half a chance, she'd take him to bed and smoke the world's most fabulous cigarette afterward.

"Ms. Andrews, good to see you again," Decker says, ever the charming gentleman. His all-American grin slides into place. "You need to meet Grace McBride, the mastermind behind this whole thing."

She turns to me, her smile wide. "Well, aren't you a pretty little thing?"

"Ms. Andrews, oh my goodness, it's so great to meet you," I

say, taking her hand. Her nails are polished purple. "I'm Grace McBride—we've been corresponding these last two weeks. I can't thank you enough for jumping in at the last minute. Truly, it means so much to me and to the library."

She waves me off. "Oh, honey, I was free, and I love helping libraries." She takes a sip of what looks like straight scotch. "When I was a broke single mama, the library was the only thing that kept me sane. I wrote my first book in a study carrel at the local branch library in Brownsville, Mississippi. You call me anytime. And when you do, you call me Janice, okay, hon?"

My mouth drops open. I still can't believe I'm talking to *the* Janice Andrews. I remember checking her books out in middle school and hiding them under my pillows, reading them at night by flashlight, completely enraptured by the rich settings, the sassy characters, and the *drama* of it all. I'm pretty sure I didn't understand a good chunk of what was happening, as I was twelve and reading about thirty-year-old divorcees getting second chances at love, but the details didn't matter. I was swept up by the language, the rhythm of her dialogue, and the yearning.

I may not have understood yearning back then, but I sure as shit get it now.

"So tell me, are you two a thing?" Janice asks, waving a finger between us.

I open mouth to say yes, partly because lying to Janice Andrews feels like lying to a priest or the president and partly because I just want to. But Decker cuts me off.

"Just longtime friends," he says. He smiles at me, because this is what we do. We obfuscate. We hide. Because I asked him to.

Janice eyes us like she's judging livestock at the fair. "Well, I love me a good friends-to-lovers story."

She takes a last very unladylike swig of her scotch, the ice cubes rattling. "If you'll excuse me, I'm gonna go get another one of these. But let me leave you with a bit of advice," she says. "Slow burns are sexy as hell, but don't drag it out for too long. Readers can only take so much waiting."

# CHAPTER 41

## DECKER

"And now, for the lovers in the crowd, a little Etta James," Sheriff Woods says, and a new slow song, a plea for a Sunday kind of love, oozes through the sound system.

I turn to Grace and admire the flush high on her cheekbones and the way her dark hair rests over her bare shoulder. "I believe you said you'd dance with me?"

"Only if you ask me real nice," she says with a wink that damn near ends me.

I finish my beer and deposit the empty bottle on a nearby table. Then I hold out my hand, the other tucked behind my back like one of those dukes on the paperback novels Ms. Tingle checks out.

"Grace McBride," I say, keeping my voice low, "would you make me the happiest man in Cardinal Springs and do me the honor of dancing with me?"

"Hell yes, I will." She grins the grin that makes her nose wrinkle and her freckles dance, the grin that makes me want to kiss her senseless. Instead, I take her hand and lead her to the edge of the dance floor. I slip one hand around her waist, loving the way her hip fits perfectly in my palm. I pull her as close as I can without drawing suspicion, but not nearly as close as I'd like.

"I love this song," she sighs, her head tipped back slightly.

"It's a good song," I reply, but honestly, "What's Your Fantasy" by Ludacris could hit the speakers right now and I'd keep holding her tight, swaying in this dark corner.

"I don't think I've actually thanked you," she says.

I cock my head. "For what?"

"For everything you did this summer. At the library. And for the festival." She lowers her eyes, her dark lashes brushing her cheeks. "For encouraging me to finally speak up."

I scoff. "You don't need to thank me. I was support staff at best. You did all the heavy lifting on your own."

She looks up at me, nearly knocking me back with the depth of the blue. "That's not true. I needed someone to push me out of my comfort zone."

"I am good with the big hits."

She narrows her eyes in faux fury. "Can you be serious for a minute?"

"Almost never," I say, because I fucking love to tease her. All these weeks later, after all the times I've had her splayed out naked beneath me, all the times I've tasted her, teasing her is still my very favorite thing. "But for you, I'll make an exception."

I spin her, her flouncy little dress swishing around her thighs, the silver threads running through the fabric catching the light. All those pinpricks of light shoot through my chest. Fuck, watching her smile in the midst of this party she pulled off for the library she gives her all to, the library she's going to save…it's almost like looking at an eclipse, too bright to gaze at head-on. An absolute wonder.

The song ends, and I slow to a stop as Etta James wails one last time for a perfect kind of love. And I know for sure that I have just that in my arms right now. If only things were a little bit different. If only I could be good enough, lucky enough.

"Leave room for the Holy Spirit, you two," Archer says as he dances by with Madeline. They're laughing, and there's no accusation, but still I let Grace go. I step back, watching her turn as another admirer begins to sing her praises for tonight, for this weekend, for saving the library. She's incredible, and I love that tonight she's getting all the recognition she deserves.

"Decker! Don't you look dapper." Mrs. Joshi, Nimesh's mom, dances up beside me with a man who must be Nimesh's dad, if the matching mop of dark curls is any indication.

"I've got to thank you for getting Nimesh into skating," the man says, shaking my hand. "We were starting to get worried we'd never peel him off the couch. Not that he needs to compete or win or anything—we just want him to be active. To have fun moving his body."

"And thanks to you, it looks like I'll be driving him to Bloomington every Saturday this fall. He begged to join youth hockey, and that's the closest league." She says it with a lighthearted grimace. "It'll just be a few years before he goes to middle school, though. Then he can play for Cardinal Springs and I can save the miles on my minivan."

"Hey, that's great," I say. "Not about the commute, but that he's found his niche."

"It was all you," Mr. Joshi says. "You really inspired him."

"I just wish we could keep you around longer! When do you head back to Chicago?" Mrs. Joshi asks.

"Media Day is September fifteenth, so I'll probably head up a couple of days before that."

I can't help it—my eyes go to Grace, now surrounded by admirers. Someone hands her a glass of red wine, and I watch her eyes go wide with horror. She's been off red since her two-bottle night on her birthday. I'll have to discreetly trade it out for white.

"Well, you'll be missed, that's for sure," Mr. Joshi says. "We're thinking we're going to get Nimesh Grinders tickets for his birthday in November. It'll be a long drive, but worth it."

I drag my attention back to the Joshis. "I can get you guys tickets. Just let me know what date you're thinking. We can do an arena tour, and I'll introduce him to some of the other guys," I tell them.

"He would die of happiness," Mrs. Joshi says, grinning from ear to ear. She grabs my biceps, shaking it theatrically. "Ugh, don't leave!"

I laugh, but my mouth tastes sour, that beer I drank dancing around in my stomach.

"If you'll excuse me, I'm going to go grab some water. But you have my email. Just let me know about that game," I say.

I slip away into the crowd. It's remarkably easy to do. Grace and the authors are the main attractions tonight. Everybody's too wrapped up in them to pay any attention to me.

# CHAPTER 42

## DECKER

As the night continues, my mood sours. People keep asking me when I'm leaving, prying to see if I have any insider information about the season. It's not that I don't want to talk about hockey. It's that every conversation is a reminder that I'm getting closer and closer to leaving Grace behind.

I try to focus on her as she works the room, getting showered with praise. I've never been so happy to be in the background. To be the number two. Of course, it would be easier to keep my negative thoughts at bay if I could spend the night by her side, pulling her into me, peppering her delicate neck with kisses and whispering dirty plans for later into her ear.

But that just brings me back to the fact that we're *not* together. Not like that. Because I'm leaving her.

So I joke around with Archer and Madeline. I sit with Ms. Tingle and let her give me book recommendations. I listen as Wyatt's sister, Hazel, tells me all her worst pregnancy symptoms while Wyatt buries her head in her hands. I let Janice Andrews flirt with me shamelessly.

And still I find myself watching Grace win the night and half hating myself for planning to drive away in a month.

And then I spot him.

Cannon fucking Brentwood.

He's alone at a table at the far end of the ballroom, a full rocks glass in front of him. He's staring intently into the crowd, looking like he's either talking himself into or out of getting up. And when I follow his gaze, it leads straight to Grace. She's deep in conversation with Janice Andrews, and he looks like he's trying to psych himself up to go over there. To do what, I have no idea, but there's no way in a frozen hell I'm going to let him near her on her big night.

"Over my dead, rotting corpse, motherfucker," I mutter.

I slide my all-American grin into place, adding just a hint of menace at the edges. Then I amble over to his table. He jumps when I pull out the chair beside him, and I slide into it with relish. I take pleasure in the fact that he leans away from me.

"Hey there, chief," I say, suddenly very relaxed. I can already tell this is working. My body hums with the need for a fight, an old feeling I almost don't recognize. I thought maybe it had disappeared entirely, but as I watch Cannon shift in his seat, his eyes narrowing like maybe he wants to mix it up with me, I realize it's as fiery as ever.

Grace's laugh rings out across the ballroom, and both Cannon and I turn toward the sound. Her head is thrown back at something Janice Andrews has said, the two of them thick as thieves. She looks as happy as I've ever seen her. Cannon cannot screw this night up for her, but neither can I. And getting into it with her ex would be disastrous.

"What do you want?" Cannon grunts.

"Just to make sure you're not about to do something stupid like bother Grace on her big night."

"What, you gonna punch me again?" His words are clear, no slurring this time. Looks like he hasn't started in on that whiskey yet.

"I'll do whatever needs to be done," I reply with a casual shrug.

He scoffs. "Since when are you her guard dog? Pretty sure she couldn't stand you when we were kids."

"Things change," I reply.

"Right," he says, turning to me with a rancid smirk. "But you don't."

"What the fuck?" I say, working hard to maintain my air of indifference. But that flicker of desire for a fight returns, intensifies, glowing warmer and brighter inside me. I remind myself that this little prick doesn't deserve my ire, even though I've got it in spades.

"I've been asking myself the same thing every day since you showed up in this town." He laughs. "What. The. Fuck. What the fuck is Grace doing with an asshole like Decker Brooks?"

*Making up for all the orgasms you failed to deliver*, I want to say, but instead I grit my teeth and force a smile.

"Look, I understand. Life didn't turn out how you planned. You wanted to be a professional athlete. And I get it, I do, because being a professional athlete is really fucking fun." I pause, reaching for his glass and take a long swig. Then I tip it toward him in a mock toast. "I speak from experience."

I slam the glass back down onto the table, the liquid nearly sloshing over the side. Cannon narrows his eyes and pushes it back toward me.

"Yeah, you're right. I'm just a washed-up has-been. I let my misery about that infect everything. I ruined what I had with Grace because I was a sad fucking sack of shit. My bitterness pushed away the best thing that ever happened to me." He slides his chair back from the table and stands. "I may be just a washed-up has-been, but you know what? Soon, you will be too. Sooner than you think, your hockey career will be over, and then what? What will you do when it's all gone? You think you're going to be okay? You think you're going to handle it well? Are you going to make Grace pick up the pieces of *that*?"

He turns to walk away, then stops, turns back. "You think your story ends differently from mine, but it doesn't. It just lasts a little longer."

He turns to look at Grace, and I can't tell if he's planning to go over to her or not. My fingers twitch, my body wanting to hit him, to lay him out just like I did back at the Half Pint. Just like I did Perrault. Just like I'm good at. But I force myself to sit still and flash him a sinister grin that might bear more resemblance to bared teeth.

"Leave her alone, Brentwood," I say, my voice full of acid.

He laughs. "If you care about her at all, you will, too."

———

About an hour later, I'm lost in my own misery, sitting on a bench outside the entrance to the ballroom. The music is muffled, quieter than the persistent buzz of the overhead fluorescent lights. I look up when I hear footsteps and see Grace standing in front of me. Even in the shitty fluorescent light, that dress sparkles. *She* sparkles.

"I've been looking all over for you," she says. She drops down onto the bench beside me, a manilla folder in her hands. Her grin is a mile wide. "We closed the silent auction. Looks like Ms. Tingle won the skating lesson with you. She said she just wants to watch you skate around for an hour, but she asked if she could pick what you wear."

"Whatever she wants," I say, my voice a croak.

I try to find my smiling, happy self again, but he's too busy replaying the conversation with Cannon. I've been stewing out here since he walked away from me, his words pinging around in my head like a toddler high on Pixy Stix. I've been trying to calm my thoughts, force them to make some fucking sense. But I just keep coming around to the same black hole of doubt.

"The party's winding down," Grace says. If she notices my dark mood, she's ignoring it, bending herself to accommodate me. I fucking hate it. "Do you think I could get one more dance?"

And maybe this is what I need—Grace back in my arms. It felt so good earlier. It felt right, like I was exactly where I needed to be. But then I let that asshole get in my head, and I ran from Grace when I needed her most.

So I let her tug me off the bench and lead me back into the ballroom and onto the dance floor. Resting my hands around her waist lifts my mood slightly, as does watching her smile up at me. This is all fine. I didn't punch Cannon. I let him talk his shit, but I kept him away from her. She's fine, and I'm fine.

Except I'm not fine. I still want to fight Cannon. If he walked up to me right now, I'm not sure I could keep my fist out of his face. And then what? More charges? Pictures on the internet? Ruining the night Grace worked so hard on with my mess? Maybe Cannon's words bug me so much because they're exactly what I've been telling myself for weeks. That I'm not good enough for her. That I'll only let her down. Fuck things up. Hurt her.

"Hey, are you okay?" Grace asks, her arms tightening around my neck, pulling me closer.

"I'm fine," I lie.

I know I'm a better man than Cannon Brentwood, but that bar is basically on the ground. Clearing it doesn't mean I come anywhere close to being a good enough man for Grace.

"Decker, come back to me," Grace murmurs. She rises up on her tiptoes, her pouty lips drawing close to mine. Here in the middle of this dance floor, in front of her family and friends and damn near the entire town.

I immediately take a step back, releasing her, and look around. The crowd has thinned, but that just means it's easier for everyone who's still here to see us. Archer's gone—he left a while ago with Madeline to take Betsy home. But Felix and Owen are still here, chatting at the end of the buffet table. Grace's dad is across the dance floor, Corianne in his arms. As soon as she kisses me, this thing we're doing will go public, and I won't be able to protect her. Not from the judgment of her family, and not from everything else that comes with...well...*me*. The spotlight and the scrutiny, the loneliness and the distance. Because my life is hockey. There's nothing else. With it, I can't be with her, and without it, I don't know who I am. Just another washed-up has-been? A bitter retiree? Lost? That's not what Grace needs. It's not what she deserves.

But if she kisses me right now, in front of all these people, that's what she'll get.

"What are you doing?" I ask.

She pauses, biting her lip, trying to find her words. Then her cheeks flush and her lips tug up, and I want to stop the words I know are about to tumble out of her mouth. I let this all go too far. I've been selfish, I wanted her too much, and now I've gone and set her up for heartbreak. "Kissing the man I lo—"

"*Grace,*" I interrupt, her name coming out harder than I intend. But I have to stop her before she says something she can't take back. She has no idea what being with me would mean, what she'd be opening herself up to. She knows offseason Decker, laying-low Decker. These last few weeks have only happened because I'm far away from my real life.

"Sorry," she says, her smile dimming, the light going out of her eyes, and in that moment, I hate myself.

"It's fine," I tell her, reaching for her again. The music is still playing, an old Green Day song from the nineties. The one they always play at graduations. The one about turning points and mistakes.

About having the time of your fucking life.

That's what this summer has been, but summer doesn't last forever. Soon it'll be over.

I think it already is.

"So, tomorrow," Grace says, leaning into me, resting her cheek on my chest. My heart feels the weight of her and cracks beneath it.

"I'm actually going to go tomorrow." The words are out of my mouth before I even test their weight.

Grace reels back like I've slapped her. "What?"

My heart may be breaking, but there's still time to mitigate the damage to hers. So I charge on.

"My community service is done. The press frenzy has died down. My team is happy. So I should probably head back to Chicago. I can lay low in my condo, focus on my workouts. Get back to PT. I need to make sure my hip isn't going to crap out again as soon as training camp starts. I mean, once we get going, it's nonstop. Eighty games, weeks on the road, longer if we make the playoffs. That's gotta be my focus."

Her brow furrows. "But you have another month. At least. Media Day isn't until September fifteenth. I thought we had time after—"

I cut her off. "This has been a great vacation, but I need to get back to my real life."

She's studying me like I'm a puzzle, this girl who knows which smiles I fake. I've caught her off guard, and I hate it. I've worked so hard to let her know me, and I'm actively destroying all of that now. But I have to, because she can't ask me to stay, and I won't ask her to wait. This thing we're doing? It has to end now. For her sake.

Grace gapes at me in open bewilderment, blinking rapidly. It takes me a beat to realize that she's trying to blink back tears. In my head, I hear an entire arena full of fans booing me, just like they did when I got ejected in Game 7.

And I hate myself more now than I did in that moment.

But while looking at Grace's expression right now hurts worse than losing a dozen Stanley Cups, I know I'm doing the right thing. The longer I stay here, the worse I'll hurt her when I leave. The longer I stay here, the more I risk blowing up her life for nothing. Our lives don't fit together. The sooner she realizes it, the better.

"So this is it? It's all over? This? Us?" Grace laughs, a bitter sound that's covering a sob. Every muscle in my body wants to grab her, to pull her to me, to apologize, to take it back.

But I'd just be doing that for me, to avoid having to look at her pain. I can't put off the hurt forever. It's coming like a hit from a six-foot-seven 250-pound defenseman. All we can do is brace for it and hope we can still get up when it's over.

This is me trying to make sure she can still get up.

"There was never an *us*, Grace," I tell her, breaking my own heart into a million pieces as I break hers.

Her jaw flexes, and she takes another step back from me. That beautiful dress catches the light, and she shines like an avenging angel. *Give it to me good, my beautiful, brave, wondrous girl.*

"Fuck you, Decker," she says, then turns and walks away.

"Atta girl," I whisper as I watch her go.

# CHAPTER 43

## GRACE

The festival is a blur. I throw myself into the work, hoping it'll distract me from the hollow feeling in my chest that is Decker's absence, the ragged edges where he ripped my heart out as he left.

It barely works.

The festival is a massive success, but I barely remember any of it. Afterward, everyone keeps telling me how wonderful it was, and the proof is there in the returns. We've made up every penny of the budget shortfall plus a couple of months extra. That means that when we plan next year's festival, we won't be starting in the hole, and that should be a good feeling.

It's not until the weekend's over and Decker's long gone that I truly feel the full brunt of the blow.

"You were dicknotized," Wyatt tells me, but it was more than that. It was the way he encouraged me. Believe in me. Fought for me.

Until he didn't.

Until he walked away.

I spend most of August oscillating between abject fury and distant hope. Every time I walk out of my apartment, I glance at the door that used to be his. I imagine knocking, or maybe just finding him waiting there, leaning against the doorframe with that smirk I used to love. I find myself skulking around the nonfiction stacks, hoping to find him in a dark corner, a romance novel in one hand for inspiration, a devious grin on his face. Every time I hear the rumble of a particularly loud engine, I search the road for his baby-blue Bronco.

I'm always disappointed.

The only sign of him arrives a week after his departure: a box addressed to the library filled with tiny Grinders jerseys, each one with a personalized nameplate and number. The kids, who are disappointed by his absence, are ecstatic over the gift.

There's no jersey for me, which is fine, because I'm much less forgiving than an eight-year-old.

With time, my anger gives way to sadness. That he left. That he's not coming back. That I let myself care this much. That I'm even surprised.

By the end of August, the hurt has subsided. Now I'm just numb and trying to ignore the wound. I throw myself into every task that's put before me, from reclaiming story hour to filling out small business grant applications.

When Dad asks me to help him bake a birthday cake for Corianne, I agree. It took me a few weeks after Decker left to want to cook again. Every time I stood in my kitchen, all I could think about was him draped over the island, stealing bits of food. On my worst days, I felt the ghost of his arms wrapping around my waist, pulling me in as he licked the shell of my ear, peppered my neck with kisses.

I tell Dad we should bake the cake at his house.

"Dad, don't eat that, there's raw eggs," I say, swatting at his hand as he tries to dip it into the bowl of homemade cake batter. His original plan included a box of Duncan Hines, so I've had to take over.

"I'm an old man," he says, going in for a second attempt. Puck's tail thumps the tile floor at his feet. "I can think of worse ways to shuffle off this mortal coil than eating cake batter."

"Have you ever had food poisoning? It's not a delight." I reach for the greased cake pans and begin pouring the batter in. We're doing a classic yellow cake with dark chocolate buttercream frosting and a caramel drizzle. "Besides, you won't get to enjoy this cake with Corianne if you're barfing your guts out."

"Fair," he says. He checks the oven to make sure it's the right temperature. He's definitely not the worst helper I've ever had in the kitchen.

"Things seem to be going pretty well between the two of you," I say. While Corianne has become a permanent fixture in Dad's life, we haven't had much of a chance to discuss it. And considering this is the first time in my entire life I've seen my dad date, it probably bears talking about. "Hey, Dad? Why did you hide your relationship with her at first?"

He looks up from the beaters, which are sticking out of a bowl of fudgy frosting. He opens his mouth, and I think he's about to play it off, maybe make a joke, but then he just sighs.

"I was scared," he says, resting the hand beater on the edge of the bowl. "I loved your mother so much. I didn't know if I could open myself back up to that again, or if I even knew how. Plus, I was worried about you kids. I didn't want you to think I was trying to replace her."

At the mention of Mom, I feel my throat start to close up, tears threatening to fall. Puck, sensing tension, ambles over and flops at my feet, his tail wagging gently.

"I'm sorry, Dad," I say, keeping my eyes on the mixing bowl in front of me.

"For what? I was never worried about you, Gracie Girl." He chuckles. "It was mostly Archer, if I'm being honest. He's never been very good with change."

I let out a little laugh, but half a sob escapes with it.

Dad comes around the island and wraps me up in a hug. "What is it, honey?"

"I just..." The explanation is right there on the tip of my

tongue, the one I poured out to Decker. But Decker's gone, and I'm scared.

"Talk to me, Grace," Dad says, stroking the back of my hair as I cry into his flannel-clad shoulder. My tears are flowing freely now, and I can't hide it anymore. I just let it all out.

"I'm just sorry," I say between sobs. "That she's gone."

"Oh, honey, you can't go putting any of that on yourself," he says. He squeezes me, then reaches for a box of tissues on the counter, plucking one out for me.

"I know," I say, dabbing at my eyes, which does nothing to slow the tears. "Like, intellectually I know. But also, she died because of me."

Dad levels me with a look, the same one he used when I was thirteen and tried to tell him that Lululemon leggings were an essential part of my gym uniform at Cardinal Springs Middle School.

"Grace, she died because of a postpartum hemorrhage no one predicted. It was a tragic, terrible fluke. It was nobody's fault, least of all yours. And not for nothing, but she was *so* happy she was going to have a daughter. She loved all you kids, of course, but she was so giddy over your arrival. Her last few months were filled with joy because of you, and that's how I'll always remember her." He pulls out a tissue for himself. "Anyone can die of anything at any time. I could have died in that car crash. It's just the way life goes. So we make the most of the time we have. But she died so happy, Grace, and that was because of you."

I throw myself back into his arms, letting the flannel of his shirt warm my tear-streaked cheeks.

"I'm just so sorry we never talked about this, that I never told you," he says between sniffles. "I should have realized it wasn't right, the way you disappeared on your birthday every year."

"To be fair, I worked really hard to make sure nobody noticed," I say with a wan smile.

"We'll do better. No more McBride family secrets, okay?"

"Thanks, Dad," I say, and let out a long breath that sends with it the last of the weight that's been sitting on my shoulders for so long. I didn't realize just how heavy it was.

"In that spirit, do you want to tell me what went on between you and Decker Brooks this summer?" Dad asks.

I snort. "Not much of a secret, I guess."

"No, that one you were pretty terrible at keeping."

# CHAPTER 44

## DECKER

The tunnel is dark, save for the orange LEDs that give it an ominous, cave like feeling. The Grinders are lined up along the sides while the crowd's frenzy builds. All around me, my teammates are backslapping as we wait for our cue to hit the ice for our home opener.

I've played more than eight hundred NHL games, and never once have I failed to feel the thrill that comes from getting ready to take the ice.

This? A crowded ice arena being rocked off its foundation by the cheers of our fans? The pounding music, the flashing lights, the adrenaline coursing through my body? This is where I live. It's what I live *for*.

Or at least, I used to.

"Kick some ass, boys," Hornik, our goalie, shouts, trudging up and down the line in his heavy pads. He gives us all backhanded slugs right on the crests of our jerseys. When he gets to me, he looks me dead in the eyes. "Let's go, Brooks. Home ice. We own this shit!"

I roar back at him, but it takes more effort than I'm used to. I work to keep my game face on as the social team swarms around us with cameras, shooting content they'll post throughout the game.

"You good, Brooks?" Brielle is standing beside me in all black, the Grinders logo stitched on the pocket of her fleece.

"Fuck yeah," I reply, because I know that's my line. I could play my part in my sleep. It's always been easy, but today, for the first time, it feels like work.

"You did good this summer," she says. "You made my job easy."

"Happy to help," I tell her, and tap my stick on the rubber mat to try to keep myself here in this moment. Anything to stop myself from thinking about the summer.

The first few weeks I was back in Chicago, that was all I did. I sat alone in my apartment and replayed every single moment I'd had with Grace, from finding her upside down in the park to the kiss on the ice to holding her hand at the food truck festival. All those moments when I thought I was in control.

What a fucking idiot I was.

Outside the tunnel, the crowd roars, and my teammates start spilling onto the ice. The announcer calls names and numbers, and when it's my turn, I fly out of the tunnel, the spotlight following me as I skate a lap. The ice feels good beneath my blades, and the roar of the crowd, cresting just for me, propels me forward. I try to sink into the familiarity of it all.

I thought that once training camp started, things would get easier. I'd have something to focus on that wasn't Grace crying, walking away from me, hating me. Practice and drills and workouts and team meetings would fill my mind. This was what I was here for, after all.

And they did, at first. I was busy in the training room and on the ice and in coaching meetings. Brielle filled my free time with appearances at schools and hospitals and head start programs. It worked.

At first.

But it didn't take long for me to realize that something was missing. And it wasn't just Grace.

It was me.

Every night, I went home to my empty condo. I ate whatever nutritionally complete prepped meal was waiting in my fridge. I wrestled with sleep, simultaneously relishing every memory of Grace and wincing at the stinging pain of thinking about them. And every morning, it got harder to slap on that all-American grin.

I take my place on the blue line with my teammates, the Vipers lined up opposite us. The anthem singer warbles her final notes, and we break. I'm in the first line tonight, taking the first face-off at center ice.

Against Perrault.

I drop down into position, ready to strip this puck off him as soon as it drops.

He looks at me from beneath his visor, his lips curling.

"You took the bitch, I got the cup," he sneers, crouched low and ready like a coiled spring. I know he means Imani, and I know he knows that was all a stupid fucking tabloid lie. But he did take my cup.

Too bad for him, that's not the most important thing I lost this year.

"Enjoy it, you bastard," I say, and feel all the tension bleed from my body. There's no fight left in me, not for him. For the first time since I shrugged on my jersey, I smile. "It won't last forever."

"What the fu—" he mutters, but he barely gets the words out before the official drops the puck. And I'm ready. I lunge, catch it on my blade, and execute a perfect pass to Buchko.

The game begins.

Finally, I'm focused.

———

We win 3–0, and I come off the ice with one goal and two assists. It's one of my best games in a few seasons, and the locker room is rocking. It feels fucking great to destroy the team that destroyed us in the finals. It's like an answer to a long-asked question. Celebrating Hornik's shut-out, we've got the fire as we talk about Thursday's road game in Toronto.

I'm slumped on the bench in front of my locker, exhausted and peeling off my pads, when Brielle walks up. She gives me a once-over and arches an eyebrow.

"What?" I ask, still panting from the game.

"You seem—" She pauses, cocking her head.

"Old? Tired?" I quip.

She shakes her head. "Sad."

I scoff. "What, are you my therapist now?"

"Just a friend. Speaking of, someone's here to see you."

My heart stutters. I swear to god I lose three full beats thinking for just a moment that it could be Grace. Then Brielle says, "Should I send him in?"

Of course it's not Grace. I made damn sure of that, and when I take a shot, I don't intend to miss.

Archer strolls into the locker room. "Hey, man, nice game," he says. He's wearing a Grinders T-shirt beneath his Bearcats fleece. "That was an incredible short-handed goal in the second."

"Thanks," I tell him. That one did feel good. But not good enough. "What are you doing here? You could have told me you were coming."

"And risk psyching you out with my killer good looks behind the glass? Nah," he chuckles. "You up for a drink?"

Early in my career, the younger guys and I used to hit a club after a win. We'd drink and dance and find people to take home. But my plans tonight are simply to slink back home and fall into bed, spend another night alone with my misery. Even after our win, the thought of going out turns my stomach. A quiet bar with Archer would be okay, though.

It takes me half an hour to shower, get my shit packed up, and check in with the equipment manager. I get to bypass the post-game press since I'm still on a restricted PR schedule, this time at my own request. I have no patience for the press right now. If I never speak to them again, it'll be too soon. Just seeing their cameras and microphones reminds me of Grace and the reasons I did what I did.

I meet Archer at a bar on the Near West Side, a quiet pub with low lighting and quiet music, where most people are nursing beers, not downing shots. Nobody recognizes me, so I shed the ball cap I'm wearing pulled low over my eyes and slide into the booth across from him.

"So, what's with the surprise appearance?" I ask, signaling the bartender for one of whatever Archer's drinking.

"It wouldn't have been a surprise if you had answered any of my texts," Archer says. "You want to tell me what that's about?"

Absolutely the fuck not.

"Sorry, man, you know how preseason can be," I say.

"I do. Which is why I was surprised when you bolted from town without a word a full month before it even started," he says. Goddamn, best friends suck when they're calling you on your shit. "Then I show up to one of the best games you've played in years and find you sitting in the locker room, moping like the Vipers just ate your lunch. If you were going to crush Grace, you should at least be living your best hockey life. What the hell is going on with you, man?"

Wait, what?

The beer I'm swallowing takes a detour into my lungs, leaving me sputtering.

"Yeah, I knew," Archer says, rolling his eyes. He reaches for his pint glass and takes a long pull. "You're not that slick."

My throat burns from the beer and the revelation. "But...I mean...how? *When?*"

"I don't want a single fucking detail about where you two slipped off to during the fireworks," Archer says, "but needless to say, it didn't go unnoticed. Plus one night at family dinner you rubbed my ankle with your foot. Between that and all the moony looks, it wasn't hard to put together."

I had a great poker face until she came along. But of course I couldn't hide my true feelings for Grace.

"Sorry, man," I mutter.

"Hey, you guys had your reasons for keeping things quiet. I was no treat this summer," he says, his fingers tightening around his glass. "But I'm working on that."

"With Madeline?" I ask, cocking an eyebrow at him.

He levels me with a look. "Keep her name out of your mouth."

I raise my hands in surrender. "Okay, how about I don't call you on your shit and you don't call me on mine."

"The problem there, oh best friend of mine, is that your shit involves my sister. And that I cannot ignore." He tips the last of his beer into his mouth.

I swallow hard. My heart is pounding, and my voice shakes when I finally ask, "How is she?"

"She's fine," he says, looking me dead in the eyes.

And yeah, of course she's fine. She's Grace fucking McBride. When I left her, she told me to go fuck myself. She saved a library and conquered her demons this summer. She can do anything. It would take more than *me* to break her.

"I mean, she was a wreck when you left, if you call being a quiet, focused robot a wreck. That was a really shit thing to do, walking out the weekend of the book festival. Frankly, I should kick your ass," Archer says.

"And here I was worrying you'd kick my ass for sleeping with your sister," I say, and from the way Archer's fist tightens around his glass, I can tell we're not *quite* at the joking-about-it stage.

"Look, I'm not sure what I would have done if I'd found out about it at the beginning. But now I just want to know why the fuck you walked away from her," he says. "She was great for you. I'd never seen you so happy, with the kids at the library and the family dinners and her. What the hell happened?"

"She *was* great for me," I concede. "But I'm shit for her."

Archer's eyebrows lift. "What the hell are you talking about?"

"Look, the summer was great, but that was because I was outside my real life. It was always going to end. I had to come back to Chicago. Back to hockey. Back to shitheads like Elias Perrault. Back to the cameras and constant press. And just because I managed to keep my shit together for a summer in Cardinal Springs doesn't mean I'm not going to fuck up again. And hell, even if I don't, who's to say the press won't make something up? Being with Grace was amazing, but her being with me? That's a fucking mistake."

Archer sighs. "You are way more fucked up than I thought."

"I think I'm exactly as fucked up as you thought. I had a good summer, but I haven't changed. Not really. That night? The night I left? I nearly punched Cannon Brentwood. Again." My hands fist on the table just thinking of that little shit.

"So? First of all, he probably deserved it. And second of all, you *didn't* punch him, unless I really wasn't paying attention at that party."

"I didn't," I concede. "But I wanted to."

"But you *didn't*. I saw you. You put the fear of god in him, as you should have, and then you both walked away." Archer takes a second beer from the waitress with an easy smile, but when he turns back to me, his face is serious. "Look, I'm not going to gloss over the last ten, twenty years of your life. You've made some shitty decisions. That supermodel at my wedding? Mistake. Letting yourself get photographed walking out of every club in Chicago with a different famous woman? Mistake. Letting the tabloids and Perrault goad you into that ejection? *Enormous* mistake. But Decker, all of that's in the past. You *have* changed. The Decker of last year would have laid Cannon Brentwood out a second time and then taken a selfie with his unconscious body. But you walked away because that was Grace's night and you didn't want to fuck everything up for *her*."

The words spin around in my brain like those little cartoon

birds after you've been hit on the head with a really big mallet. And then Archer delivers the final blow.

"Do you love her?" he asks.

"*Yes.*" The answer comes out before I even have time to think about it. It's like a reflex. It's the first time I've admitted it out loud, though, and it's killing me that I'm saying it to her brother and not to her. "I'm sorry."

"I don't know why you're apologizing to me," he says with a shrug.

"It's just…I didn't mean for it to happen at all, and I shouldn't have lied to you about it," I say. "I was a pretty shitty friend this summer."

"You shouldn't have lied, but I get why you did it," he says. He starts peeling the label off his beer bottle, a little pile of shreds forming on the table. "I'm sorry for that. *I* was a shit friend this summer, too. I was going through my own stuff, and I hate that it forced you guys into that spot."

I wave him off. "Nah, I think you held me back from making things even worse. Hiding it is what kept me from trying to drag your sister into a relationship with me. I mean, seriously, can you imagine? Me trying to have a relationship? That would have been a fucking disaster. At least she got a clean break from the Decker Brooks hot mess express."

Archer eyes me, his brow furrowed. "Are you serious with this shit?"

"What? You think she'd be better off if I'd roped her into a long-distance relationship with me, hockey, and the press?"

Archer rolls his eyes. "Grace is a grown-ass woman, and I think she deserves to make that decision for herself." He takes a long pull of his beer, but he keeps his eyes on me like he's waiting for me to solve a puzzle.

"I was just trying to protect her," I tell him.

"Yeah, ask all of us McBride men how much she likes that," Archer says with a wry chuckle.

Now I'm scrambling. Archer's taking apart my reasoning brick by brick, and if the wall I've built disappears, I don't know what I'll do. "But that doesn't change the fact that I live here and she lives there."

"For *now*. But how much longer are you going to play? Two seasons? Three? You think you can't get through that if you want a real future with her? You're seriously going to throw away an entire lifetime of happiness because you can't handle a couple of seasons of FaceTime calls and quick getaways? Take it from me, hockey can end at any time. You may be planning for another few years, but it could all be over tomorrow. You have no idea. I'll be honest, dude—you gave up a person you love for a sport, and it didn't even look like you were having a whole lot of fun out there tonight."

My heart pounds as I try to process what he's saying. It can't be right. Because if it is, if I'm not the fuckup I thought I was, if I'm not toxic, if I *am* good enough for Grace, then—

"I made a huge mistake," I say.

"And now we're cooking with gas," Archer says, rolling his eyes. "The only question is, what are you going to do about it?"

# CHAPTER 45

## GRACE

"Okay, so, looking forward to the October calendar, Halloween is on a Saturday this year," Suzanne says, adjusting her reading glasses to look down at her notebook. "Should we do the library trunk-or-treat on Saturday afternoon, or should we do it earlier in the week in the evening?"

"I think the parents would prefer Saturday afternoon," I tell her. "Keeps the costuming to a single day, and the teachers will thank us for not getting the kids all sugared up on a weekday."

"Okay, I'll put that in the next newsletter," she says. She caps her pen and sits back in her desk chair, tugging her cardigan tighter around her. It's the first week of October, but we're having a cold snap, and the heat in the library isn't on yet. "Anything else?"

I take a deep breath, feeling the fizzy adrenaline of this moment rush down to my fingertips. "Actually, there's one last thing," I say. "I'm working on plans to open a bookstore here in Cardinal Springs."

Suzanne's eyebrows rise, her mouth dropping open. "Really?"

"Yes. I mean, it's still a ways away. I just got approved for a small business grant from the chamber of commerce, but I won't hear back from the governor's office grant program until next month, and then I'll need to go back to the bank to talk about my loan options. And of course I can't secure a location until the money comes through, so yeah, definitely months away, maybe more," I say. I let out a shuddery breath. I've been so nervous to tell her this news, but now that I've said it, I'm exhilarated. This is definitely—maybe—happening. "I wanted you to know because it means I'm going to be leaving eventually, and I know how hard it can be to find good employees. I can try to do both for a while if you need me to, and I'll definitely help you fill the—"

"Grace," Suzanne says, raising a gentle hand. "Breathe."

I suck air into my lungs, then let out a nervous giggle. "I'm sorry. I just, I don't know. This is sort of strange."

She smiles. "New beginnings are exciting *and* nerve-wracking," she says. "But I'm so proud of you. You're smart and talented and organized as all get-out, to say nothing of your passion for reading. Your bookstore is going to be such a welcome addition to the community." She rises and comes around her desk, pulling me into her arms. "If there's anything I can do to help, please let me know. You have worked yourself to the bone for the library, and I would love to try to pay you back."

"I mean, you *do* pay me," I joke.

"Yes, and we both know it isn't nearly enough for the effort you put in." She winks at me. "The book festival alone—my goodness!"

"And I fully plan to partner with the library for that going forward. The entire bookish community will support the library, I swear!"

"I don't doubt it." She glances down at her watch. "Now, you should get going."

It's just barely five, and while that is technically the end of my shift, I'm not usually a clock-out-on-time kind of person. "There are a few books I want to reshelve in early readers, so—"

"It's dark, you've been here all day, and as we just established, we don't pay you enough. So go, treat yourself to a nice evening," she says, shooing me out the door.

"Okay, if you insist," I say.

I tuck my notebook into my tote bag and sling it over my shoulder. As I stroll out the front door, I'm already thinking about what I have in my fridge to make for dinner. This month, cookbook club is doing *Night + Market*, this incredible Thai cookbook, which means my cupboard is full of some really fun spices and sauces. I could pick up some veggies on the way home and do some experimenting.

But first, as has become my habit, I head down the block to stroll past the old Quinn Camera building. I started making these pilgrimages after I submitted my first grant application. They became more regular after I met with the credit union. When I got my first grant, I started walking by almost every day. I love to stand in front of the building, staring at the FOR SALE sign and imagining the space lit up and full of books. I picture where I'll put the register and what kind of story time rug I'll get. I imagine opening day, when everyone I love will crowd into the shop, choosing stacks of books and walking out with heavy bags. Call it wishing, call it manifesting, but whatever it is, it's helping me with the long wait as I sort out funding. Buying the place is going to be a real stretch, if it happens at all. I've already talked to a commercial real estate agent, and sitting in my inbox is a list of other possible locations I could lease. But I haven't looked at them yet, because I'm not willing to give up on my dream of Quinn Camera.

I approach the building, already letting my imagination unfurl with ideas, then skid to a halt on the sidewalk.

Because the FOR SALE sign is gone.

And in its place is a big red SOLD sign.

"No," I whisper, trying to peer through the darkened windows for any evidence of who might have stolen my bookstore. But the space is pitch black, the windows still dusty, and I can't see anything.

Until the lights flicker to life.

I jump back, startled. It's as if the building is trying to talk to me.

I see now that the space has been mostly cleared out. The old glass cases and the hulking film developing machine are gone. The old Kodak ads that were taped to the walls have been removed, and the worn brown carpet has been pulled up to reveal the old hardwood below.

And in the center of the space, beneath a spotlight, is one bookshelf, five shelves high and made of a rich, dark wood. It's stuffed full of candy-colored paperbacks.

Romance novels.

And standing beside the shelf is Decker Brooks. He's wearing jeans and a dangerously fitted olive-green Henley that brings out the gold flecks in his brown eyes. His hair is loose, but he has attempted to tuck it behind his ears. When his eyes meet mine, he gives me a nervous smile. Not his all-American grin, but a new smile I've never seen before. He looks…vulnerable.

I suck in a breath so hard my chest hurts.

He steps forward and opens the door. I hear a little bell tinkle to announce him.

"Hey," he says, then looks at his shoes, chuckling, like he meant to say something else but has already fumbled it.

"Hi," I reply. Not my smoothest line, either, but I'm still trying to get oriented in a reality where Decker Brooks is standing in *my* building next to a bookshelf full of romance novels.

"Come in." He holds the door open for me, and I walk through it. The space smells like lemon Pledge and Murphy Oil Soap. The floors, though they need refinishing, gleam under the lights.

"What is all this?" I ask.

"You haven't figured it out?" He takes my hand and leads me over to the bookshelf. "It's your bookstore."

"What?" I ask, looking around, still bowled over by being inside the space after peering through the glass for so long. I can't even begin to process the fact that Decker is here with me.

"It's yours," he says simply. "I bought it for you."

Now my focus is entirely on him. "Wait, what? *Why?*"

He smiles, but it doesn't quite reach his eyes. "I probably missed my chance," he says, his voice quaking slightly. "Of all the stupid things I've done—and you know there have been a lot—leaving you tops the list. Number-one dumbass move: Decker Brooks walks away from the love of his life. I will spend the rest of my days kicking my own ass for the way I hurt you."

I press my lips together, because if I don't, I'm afraid the whimper sitting at the back of my throat might escape.

"I don't deserve it, I know that, but still…" He sucks in a deep breath and takes both of my hands. "Still, I'm asking. Give me another chance. If you do, I won't make the same mistake again. I will spend every single moment of the rest of my life proving to you that there's nowhere on this planet I'd rather be than by your side. Right here in your bookstore. In your bed. In your heart. Please, Grace, I'm begging you. Please let me be yours."

Tears are rolling down my cheeks, and I drag my eyes away from him to give myself a moment to think. I gaze around the space, at the dream I've had for so long. The dream I thought was getting closer but still so far away. And now he's saying…

"You bought this for me?"

Decker nods. "And it's yours no matter what, whether you take me back or not. I'm giving it to you, but if that freaks you out or makes you uncomfortable or you just plain want to do it on your own, we can get a lawyer and work out a lease-to-own agreement. If you want to buy it from me, that's cool, too. I'll do whatever you want. But Grace, I've always said you deserve everything, and this is me giving it to you. Whether you want me or not."

I turn back to him, blinking, trying to get my bearings. He bought me a bookstore. He bought me a *bookstore*. And he wants me back.

"But if I open this bookstore, that means that you…I mean, I'll be here, and you'll be—"

"I'm staying," he says, never taking his eyes off me. They bore into me with that famous focus that means he never loses the puck, can swipe it into the net from the most wild of passes. That attention is all on me.

"What?" I croak.

"I'm staying. Not yet, not until the season is over," he says. "But then I'm all yours. If you'll have me."

"Are you serious?" He's *retiring*?

"Grace, for so long, hockey was the only thing that understood me. That accepted me. That…loved me back. I thought I had to hold on to it with everything I had, because once it was gone, I'd be left with nothing. But then I found you. And you helped me find me."

"So you're retiring and moving…*here*?"

"After the Grinders win the Stanley Cup this year," he says, reaching out to knock twice on the side of the wooden bookcase. "After that, I'm coming back here. I've been talking with Brielle about starting a youth hockey foundation. It'll be based in Cardinal Springs, but we'll do fundraising and outreach nation-wide. I want to help bring hockey to kids who wouldn't otherwise have access. It'll take some time to get it off the ground, but after I retire, I'll have the time, money, and contacts to get it done. And I can't wait. Working with the kids at the library this summer changed my life. *You* changed my life."

"Oh my god," I whisper. It's all too much. The bookstore. The foundation. Him.

"And I couldn't have done any of this without you. Baby, you showed me what I'm capable of. You saw me, even when I didn't see myself. I'm just so fucking sorry it took me so long to catch up."

"Okay," I say, because it's the only word I can think of. I'm still processing. When he walked out on me, I was devastated, mostly for me, but also for him. Because he was so clearly hiding behind his bad reputation and that all-American grin. Because even though I knew he was more than that, *he* didn't. But now, standing inside this dream he's made come true for me, the joy on his face when he talked about starting his foundation, the strength in his voice when he announced his retirement? *That's* the Decker Brooks I always knew he could be. Knew he already *was*.

And now he knows it, too.

Decker laughs nervously. "Grace, you're gonna have to give me a little bit more than that."

"You're seriously retiring from hockey?"

He nods. "I'm going out on my own terms while I can still walk unassisted," he says, laughing sheepishly. "Oh, and there's one more thing."

He reaches for a bright blue book and slides it off the shelf with one of his long, strong fingers. It's a new copy of *It Happened One Summer*. He hands it to me. "Open it," he says.

I flip to the title page, and there in purple Sharpie is a large scrawled signature. And above it, Tessa Bailey has written, *Grace —If he groveled real good, I say go for it.*

I bark out a laugh. "Where did you get this?"

"She was at this bookstore in Chicago two nights ago. Thanks to you, my social media serves me all the latest romance novel news, and I figured maybe if the bookstore didn't do it, Tessa Bailey could?"

"I don't need all of this, Decker," I whisper, placing the book back on the shelf. "I just need *you*."

Decker reaches out, quick like he's trying to sneak in a goal, and pulls me to him. His arms wrap around me, warm and sure, his lips at my ear. "I love you so much, Grace."

Okay, I lied. *That's* what I need.

"I love you too, Decker."

# EPILOGUE



## DECKER

The singer begins the national anthem. This is the last time the crowd will be quiet for the next sixty minutes of play. It's Game 7 of the Stanley Cup Finals against the Boston Bearcats, and I feel oddly calm. Would I have liked to put this thing away in four? Sure. But it's hard to complain about a few extra games. No matter what happens tonight, this will be the last professional hockey game I'll ever play.

And I feel good about that.

I scan the first row behind the glass and find her just beside the Grinders' bench. Janice Andrews is on her left, my parents on her right. All four of them are wearing my jersey, orange with black-and-white thirteens on the sleeves, my name and number on the back. The rest of the WAGs are in custom varsity jackets tonight, but Grace has hers draped over the back of her seat.

"I only get one season to rock your sweater, Brooks. I'm not missing a single second of it," she told me before the game. And I love it. I'll love it even more after the game when I can bend her over my bed, lift my jersey over her hips, and show her just how much I liked seeing her in the arena, cheering for me.

She catches me watching her, and her smile turns up to eleven. It's like a spotlight shining right on me. Like a moth, I want to drift across the ice to her.

And then she holds up a small sign on white posterboard, pressing it to the glass.

I'M JUST HERE FOR THE HOT DOGS.

Our anthem singer hits a warbling high note, and I tip my head back and laugh. But when I look back over, she's flipping the sign.

#13 IS MINE.

Fuck, I sure am.

"Eat 'em up," Buchko says as soon as the anthem singer walks off the ice.

"Every time," I reply, though this will be the last time.

I don't know what's going to happen here tonight, but I know that when it's all over, I'm walking out of here with a prize I already lost once.

I'll never make that mistake again.

I line up at center ice for the face-off and crouch low, ready.

"Kick his ass, baby!" Grace's voice rises above the crowd, my ear tuned to the pitch of it.

I love her so goddamn much.

———

## GRACE

The Bearcats draw first blood early in the second period, but the Grinders answer them within minutes. The rest of the game, they stay tied 1–1. With two and a half minutes left in the third, I've chewed my fingernails down to nubs. Decker has taken two shots in the last six minutes, both of them gloved by the Bearcats' goalie. When he hits a third that pings off the post, I can't hold in my scream of frustration. And when a Bearcats defenseman tries to goad him into a fight with a shove to the chest, I nearly climb over the glass and tackle him myself.

"What does that man think he's doing?" Decker's mother cries, her eyes narrowed with fury. I see instantly where Decker got his killer instinct.

As thanks for encouraging me to talk to my own family, I've been helping Decker thaw relations with his. It's slow going, because the Brooks family isn't particularly effusive. I finally gave up on their family dinners and just invited Dr. and Mr. Brooks to Dad's house for ours. The first time, they looked like they'd been given front-row seats at the circus, but they've learned to loosen up. The jerseys they're wearing were their idea, even if the finer points of hockey culture still elude them.

"Don't worry, Kay. Decker's focused," Mr. Brooks says. He's lining up for yet another face-off in Bearcats territory.

For just over two minutes, it looks like the game will head into overtime. My stomach is in knots. I don't know how Decker stays so calm out there, but several players have tried to lure him into fights, and every time, he's shrugged them off, skated away. Lined up again.

And then, with four seconds left on the clock, as a Bearcats defenseman gets ready to whip the puck into the neutral zone, Decker strips it right off him. He pivots, pulls back his stick, and then…he pauses. And in that pause, the Bearcats goalie commits to the fake-out. He dives, leaving the top shelf wide open for Decker to land an impressive slap shot so lethal, his stick snaps on impact.

I suck in a breath, and then the entire arena erupts. The last seconds tick off the clock, and the Grinders have done it. Decker has done it. Three Stanley Cup championships.

My phone is exploding with texts and photos from the watch party at the Half Pint. Dad sends a photo of himself and Corianne in Grinders sweaters, their faces painted, screaming at the camera. Archer is beside them, roaring with tears in his eyes. Dan's in the background in a Grinders T-shirt, his usually stony face smiling.

Carson sends an absolutely unintelligible string of emojis that I think must include some typos, or maybe I just don't get what she's referencing with the maracas? And Wyatt sends a photo of herself behind the bar, holding Owen in a headlock. He's grimacing, but there's a hint of a grin there, too.

*Wyatt: Decker better bend you over that cup and fuck you senseless.*

"Oh my god," I mutter, quickly swiping the text away before Decker's parents can glimpse it.

The cup presentation takes about half an hour, and I sob as Decker accepts the trophy from the NHL commissioner and hoists it, skating a lap. I'm just so proud of him.

When they finally let us out onto the ice, I make a very careful beeline toward him. He's about three inches taller that usual in his skates, and I launch myself at his chest, my feet instantly lifting off the ground.

"You did it!" I cry, not even a little bit bothered by the fact that he smells like a frozen sweat sock. Being in his arms right now feels too good. When he finally sets me down, he keeps grasping my arms, like he needs to make sure I'm actually here, that it's not all a dream. "How's it feel, big guy?"

He smiles, a real Decker Brooks smile, the one he reserves only for me. He takes my chin between his thumb and forefinger, tilting my lips up to meet his. What starts as a gentle brush quickly deepens, his arms going around my waist, his mouth slanting over mine. Soon I'm off my feet again and we're spinning on the ice, my hair flying out behind me.

He drags a skate and slows us to a stop. "I love you, Grace McBride," he says, that smile so warm that I don't feel the cold of the arena.

"I love you too," I reply. When he sets me down, I glance over at the cup, now being passed between the backup goalies. "But are you sure you're ready to give it up? You could go another season. I mean, this jersey was expensive. I could get some more wear out of it."

He looks at the cup, then back at me.

"I'll wait for you," I tell him, "if that's what you want."

He lowers his forehead until it presses against mine, that grin never dimming.

"The only thing better than winning that cup," he says, his voice gravelly, "will be loading up the Bronco tomorrow and driving home with you."

# ACKNOWLEDGMENTS

First and foremost, I need to thank Tiffany Schmidt. Your keen editing eye and fierce encouragement is the only reason this book exists. Every writer deserves a Tiffany Schmidt in their life, and I am so so grateful that you're mine, dear friend.

Thank you also to my agent, Stephen Barbara, who's been a great support through this indie publishing journey, and to Alison Cherry, copyeditor extraordinaire. All errors in this book are mine.

Thank you to Sarah Hansen at Okay Creations for this incredible cover (and the covers for the upcoming books in the series!). I appreciate your patience throughout our search for the perfect smiling blond man. It wasn't easy, but we persevered.

Thank you to Highlights, the most magical retreat center where people don't usually write books like this, but apparently the muse isn't picky. I wrote the bulk of the middle of this book there, and I don't know if I would have been able to muddle through without your cozy cabins and glorious meals.

Thank you to Hannah Slaughter for all the breakfasts, all the book reviews, the fabulous design eye, and just generally being an amazing friend.

Thank you to my book club! We don't really have a name, but who cares, because we have an epic group chat. Your support and enthusiasm for my books makes writing so much more fun.

Thank you to my local indies, Bear Den Books and Union Ave Books, for being so supportive of me and my work. I look forward to spending all my royalties in your stores.

And finally, thank you to Adam, who did plenty of solo

parenting while I cranked out this book over many late nights. I wouldn't want to do this life with anyone but you. These books only exist because of the space you make for me.

Thanks to my boys, who I hope never read this, and also Poptart the Pup, who did lots of snoring on my feet while I wrote.

# ABOUT THE AUTHOR

Lauren Morrill is the author of sweet YA and spicy adult romance. She lives in Knoxville, TN with her husband Adam, their two boys, and Poptart the Pup.

# ALSO BY LAUREN MORRILL

## SPICY ADULT

<u>Standalones</u>

Sister of the Bride

<u>Cardinal Springs</u>

More Than A Feeling

Caught Up In You (fall 2024)

Just What I Needed (Spring 2025)

## SWEET YA

Meant to Be

Being Sloane Jacobs

The Trouble With Destiny

My Unscripted Life

Better Than the Best Plan

It's Kind of a Cheesy Love Story

www.ingramcontent.com/pod-product-compliance
Lightning Source LLC
Chambersburg PA
CBHW031203010826
48971CB00013B/1310